# Searching for Cunégonde

## *A Novel*

## Scott R. Larson

www.ScottLarsonBooks.com

*To*

*Teresa and Maggie*
*who have given me so many moments*
*to seize, keep, and cherish*

*My Mother*
*who always knew that*
*I would be a writer*

*My Father*
*the best possible example a man*
*could be for another man*

Many thanks to

Dayle Moss
for going beyond the call of friendship to devote
so much time, thought, care, expertise, judgment,
support, and involvement in my quest to tell
my odd stories, and yes, for being a godsend
as well as a great friend

Michael Morrow
for being there through Dallas's journey
from the beginning to the (probably) final moment,
for understanding what I was trying do to better
than I understood it myself, and for that knack
of having just the right specialized knowledge,
including era-appropriate gunrunning tips

Marcella Peralta Simon
for support, encouragement, and for giving a real
test to my ability to (sometimes) pull off a twist
not signaled ten miles in advance

Claes Johansen
for helping to improve my writing through your example,
through your feedback, through your intimate knowledge
of great writers who went before, and by challenging me
to look at my ideas through a different lens

# Contents

# 1
# Connemara

THE SUDDEN RAIN shower did not bother Fiachra. He was, in fact, well used to it, and the shower passed. He now had to contend only with the brisk wind.

He glanced at the sky. Because he could read the weather in the same way a Dublin man could read a bus schedule, he knew another shower would come shortly. This would not be the first St. John's Eve where clouds and rain obscured the late-evening sun.

He picked up one stone and then another. He studied each one long enough to take in every facet of its surface before placing it in the one spot where it would nest the most comfortably among the other stones. He was satisfied only when the stone lay in its place as if it had always been there. Then he would turn his attention to the next bit of rock that would become part of his wall.

The young stranger stood behind him. Water dripped from his blue plastic raincoat. The way Fiachra assembled the structure like a jigsaw puzzle fascinated him. Wary of distracting him, the man remained still, feeling awkwardly invisible. He was, however, anything but. Fiachra had spotted him minutes earlier. The old man was practiced at studying people without looking in their direction. He usually had them well sized up before they were aware he had seen them.

This stranger was unusual, definitely a foreigner. After the shower, he had uncovered his head to reveal long, thick, black hair. His face was brown, not unlike a strong cup of tea with only a drop of milk. His eyes were exotic. Perhaps Asian, Fiachra thought, but he was not certain. The stranger had walked up the road as if he

1

knew where he was going. Fiachra wondered if he was a tourist or perhaps one of those Spanish students in Galway he had heard about. Fiachra ignored him.

"Pardon me, sir."

He sounded English. Fiachra pretended not to hear.

"Hello? Sorry to bother you."

Fiachra said nothing until he had finished situating one more stone in its place. He turned his head slowly. The lad's flowing hair was longer than it had first appeared, almost down to his shoulders. His face was smooth. He had definitely not grown up outdoors with wind, rain, and hard work.

"I am looking for someone meant to live in the vicinity. He's an American."

Fiachra shrugged and looked at him blankly. Sometimes he had been able to discourage tourists by pretending not to have English. Sometimes a few words of Irish would make them give up. He had a feeling, though, this one would be persistent.

"His name is Green. Dallas Green. Would you happen to know him by any chance?"

It was not in Fiachra's nature to give information to people he did not know. He respected the privacy of his neighbors—even those he himself did not know much about.

"Yeh might try the priest," he grunted.

"Of course, thank you. And where might I find the priest, please?"

With a slight motion of his head, Fiachra directed the young man's eyes toward the church spire farther down the road.

"Very good. Thank you. You have been quite helpful."

As the stranger walked away, Fiachra took note of his backpack. It looked expensive. Definitely a tourist. The old man was curious in spite of himself. That Yank had been around for several months. This was the first time, as far as Fiachra knew anyway, that someone had come looking for him.

Fiachra looked skyward again. He had a few more hours for wall building before it would be time to go home and light the bonfire.

The stranger neared the village. He was struck by the barren and battered beauty of the Connemara landscape. Trees were permanently bent by the wind. Rock covered much of the land. It was cold for June.

The church was small, homely, and deserted. He explored the interior, imagining what the stained-glass windows might look like on a sunny afternoon. He admired the craftsmanship of the wood-carved stations of the cross.

Close to the church was a humble cottage, which he thought might be the priest's. He knocked on the door, but there was no response.

Farther down in the village was a pub. The interior was dark and thick with the smell of smoke—a mixture of peat burning in the fireplace and men smoking cigarettes at the bar. All sound died when he opened the door, but not one man looked in his direction.

He took a stool at the end of the bar, dropping his backpack to the floor. After a few moments, murmured conversations resumed. Voices were so low that he discerned no specific words. He wondered whether they were speaking in English or the Irish language. The publican added occasional grunted comments to a conversation at the other end of the bar. He made no immediate move to attend to the newcomer.

As he waited, the young man studied the shelves behind the bar. Bottles of whiskeys and other spirits lined the main one. Faded photographs were tacked to the wall. One was of a Gaelic football team holding a trophy. A couple were of fishermen with their catches. In the middle of the counter was a choice of four beer taps.

After several minutes, the publican made his approach with an impressive display of indifference.

"Are yeh all right there?"

"Yes, thank you. Guinness, please."

"Pint?"

"Yes, a pint, thank you."

The publican began the methodical process of filling the glass halfway, then setting it down. While the foam settled, he returned to his regular customers. In time he went back to the tap and finished filling the glass. He placed it on the counter, where it continued to settle, while he went back to his default spot.

When the liquid underneath the foamy, white top layer was solid black, the publican made his leisurely way back. He picked it up and set it down in front of the stranger.

"Punt seventy." He timed his pause precisely. "When you're ready."

Understanding the word "poont" to be an Irish pound, the customer counted out the money.

"Would you happen to know a man living locally named Dallas Green?"

The men at the other end of the counter went dead silent while pretending not to listen.

"Green? That wouldn't really be name from around here now. Are you sure it's here he's living?"

"That's what I've been told. Can you tell me where I might find the priest?"

The door flew opened as if blown by a gale. A stout man with wild, white hair appeared. He unbuttoned his heavy coat, revealing the black garb underneath and clerical collar. The local men all nodded in his direction, each murmuring, "Father…"

The priest's gaze landed on the newcomer.

"Are you the fella I heard was looking for me?"

The fact he spoke at a normal volume made him sound, in comparison to the others, as though he were shouting.

The stranger stood and said, "Yes, Father. I was hoping you might help me find someone."

The priest hung his coat on a rack, almost as if he had not heard the question.

The young man added, "May I buy you a drink, Father?"

"At this hour of the day? Well, I suppose there's no harm just this once. That's very kind of you."

He turned to the publican.

"A hot whiskey, Padraig."

The publican nodded.

4

"Come sit by the fire with me," said the priest. "I'm chilled to the bone. I cannot believe how cold it is for June."

As they took their seats at a small table, the priest shook his hand.

"I am Father McGinley. And who might you be?"

"My name is Alex, Father. Alex Malaka."

"Well, sure and that's not an Irish name," said the priest with a twinkle in his eye. "Not one I've ever heard of anyway."

"I'm looking for an American who, I understand, is living here. His name is Dallas Green."

The priest nodded. "Yes, I believe I know the man you're speaking of. Mind you, I have not met him properly, but I see him at Mass sometimes. He always stands well in the back. Never takes a seat in the pews."

"Funny, nobody else here seems to know him."

"Oh, you can be sure and certain they all know him—if only to see. Believe me, he was well spotted from the day he first arrived. You can be assured he has been studied and well discussed."

"Can you tell me where he lives?"

"Do you mind me asking what your business with him is?"

"It's rather complicated. You see, I have never actually met him. It's my friend who knows him—in a way. When we learned that he was living in Ireland, it came as a happy coincidence. We both have favors to ask of him."

"Ah, favors. Will he be happy to see ye at all, I wonder. And where is this friend of yours?"

"He's in Galway. I left him there this morning. I was in more of a hurry than he was. You see, we are traveling around by thumb, and you cannot always be sure to get a lift—especially in the less populated areas. He stayed back to spend more time with someone. With any luck he will be along shortly."

"So your friend knew Mr. Green in America…?"

"No. As I say, it's rather a complicated story."

The publican set down a short glass steaming with the scent of cloves.

"There you go, Father. Just as you like it."

"Good man, Padraig. *Go raibh maith agat.*"

The priest smiled, as he eagerly warmed his fingers by tracing the contours of the glass. He glanced at the clock behind the bar.

"It's late enough. Are you sure your friend will come at all?"

"Oh, he'll be here. You can count on that. So can you tell me where Mr. Green lives?"

"Although I know Mr. Green by sight, I cannot claim to know him personally. I would very much like to, though. What I do know about him is that he clearly likes his privacy. I hesitate to share his whereabouts without knowing that he would want me to."

"When he knows who is coming to see him, I don't think he'll mind one bit," said Alex. "In fact, I am sure he would be grateful to you."

The priest savored his drink, then set it down.

"People here are quite mindful of privacy—their own and that of their neighbors. I suspect that is why Mr. Green is here in the first place. As a blow-in myself, I feel I should respect that."

"You're not from here?"

"Certainly not. Can you not hear it in my speech? I was born in Buncrana, though I am sure I do not sound much like a Donegal man these days. I was too long away. I was a good many years in Australia and am not that long home. I don't know how I found myself here of all places. I think it might be someone's idea of easing me into retirement."

"Will you have another hot whiskey, Father?" asked Alex, noticing the priest's empty glass.

"Now I don't think that would be wise at all. What kind of example am I setting by drinking at this time of day? On the other hand, what harm? After all, it's not every day we get a visitor from... where did you say you were from, Alex?"

The young man signaled the publican to bring another drink. Padraig nodded, giving no sign it might be unusual for the priest to have a second one.

"We traveled here from Switzerland."

"Ah, so you are Swiss?"

"No," Alex smiled. "A bit farther away than that. Is there no way I can convince you to tell me his location? I assure you, he will not mind in the least."

"Come here to me. You seem a sound lad. Perhaps there is a compromise. I am after all the parish priest here, and by virtue of residing here, Mr. Green is one of my parishioners. In the course of my duty as shepherd, I make a point of calling to each home in the parish at least once during the year. As I have yet to call on our Mr. Green, I suppose today is as good as any other day to fulfill my priestly task. And if you happened to come along on that errand, well, where's the harm in that?"

"Splendid," grinned Alex, as Padraig brought the second hot whiskey.

Observing how much the priest enjoyed his drink, the young man said, "You are wise to have a hot drink. I cannot believe how cold it is. I am actually accustomed to winter in June, but not in the northern hemisphere."

"You should have been here a few months ago for the right winter. Then you would have seen the difference."

Alex finished his pint and saw the priest had drained his glass as well.

"Shall we go now?" the young man asked.

"My, you are hopping to go. This wouldn't be a case of Mr. Green owing you money, would it?"

"No, no, it's nothing like that."

Alex went to the bar to pay for the priest's drinks.

"Thank you," he said to the publican. "Will you do me a favor? A friend of mine will be arriving, and I expect he will come here looking for me. He'll be the same age as myself but fair-haired. Father McGinley and I are leaving now to pay a visit to Dallas Green. Would you be so kind as to direct him in that direction?"

Padraig looked over at the priest, who gave him a nod. The publican in turn nodded at Alex.

The air outside felt all the colder for the two of them having sat by the turf fire. Father McGinley led the younger man up a steep, narrow, twisty road. The higher they climbed, the harder and colder the wind blew.

"The Meteorological Service did not lie about today's weather. That's a particularly fierce wind, even for here. By the way, Alex, where were you planning to stay tonight?"

"To be honest, we were hoping to be able to stay with Mr. Green."

The priest shook his head with a bit of a laugh.

"Well, I hope our Mr. Green is ready for visitors."

About a half-mile up the road they came to a dirty white cottage nestled in the fold of a hillside. A few of the roof slates were missing. The gusts shook two bare trees. Nailed on the wall next to the front door was a splintered block of wood. The words Tig Bronagh were carved into it. A long-haired man in jeans and a black woolly jumper was preoccupied with gathering a few small logs from the stack next to the house.

Father McGinley tried calling to him over the noise of the wind, but he did not hear. The priest shouted more loudly, and the man turned with a start, dropping the logs.

# 2
# Tig Bronagh

THE VISITORS WERE completely unexpected. I can only imagine the look I had on my face. It would have been a look of sheer panic. There was absolutely no doubt in my mind that I was about to die.

The best thing about the cottage's location had been the lack of visitors. It had been months since anyone besides Bernie Conneely had shown up there.

This was exactly what I had wanted. My goal had been to vanish completely from the face of the earth. I had never before been in a place that felt as remote as that wind-battered corner on the farthest edge of Europe.

"Well and truly the back of beyond," someone on the bus had said.

During my time there, I had found myself hiking a few times the several miles to the bluff where I could look out at the sea. From that vantage, all that could be seen between myself and the horizon was endlessly churning water. That spot truly felt like the edge of the world.

I had been delighted to find that people paid no attention to me. I sensed they were curious all right, but few asked me any questions. Well, the woman in the post office, which was also the local shop, asked quite a few at first, but she soon got the message I wasn't the chatty type. Bernie, who rented me the cottage didn't ask a lot of questions. She was just glad to get the cash. I couldn't believe how cheap the rent was. On the other hand, it wasn't as though the place was in great shape or in demand.

I had never felt so alone and isolated in my life. It was perfect. The longer my solitude persisted, though, the more apprehensive I became about the day it would inevitably end. I knew it was only a matter of time before someone would come looking for me.

At night I would lie in bed, listening for sounds until sleep finally overtook me. In my twenties, my sleep had been plagued by panic attacks with no discernible cause. With time they had gone away, but now I was kept awake at night by fears that were all too concrete. Each morning my first waking thought was whether this would finally be the day.

I had known they would come for me. I had imagined all the possible ways it might happen, how it could play out. I have to confess, though, that it never once occurred to me it would end with the arrival of the local parish priest and a young brown-skinned man carrying a backpack.

"Sorry to have startled you, Mr. Green," shouted the priest over the wind's roar.

The look on my face concerned him.

"Is this a bad time?"

No words came from my gaping mouth. Thinking I had not heard him, Father McGinley repeated his question more loudly. Seeing them stare at me helped bring me to my senses. Whatever was going to happen, there was no point standing there like a fool.

"Sorry, Father. You took me by surprise."

"I have come to offer an apology."

"Apology? To me? Why?"

"For neglecting you. I have been meaning to call to you for a very long time. It took the arrival of this young man to finally provide the pretext."

The younger man extended his hand, and I shook it. His handshake was surprisingly confident and firm, given how slight he was.

"Alex Malaka. So glad to meet you at last, Mr. Green. You are a difficult man to track down."

"Not nearly difficult enough," I muttered.

"Sorry? I did not catch that. It's very windy."

"Sorry," I said more loudly. "Have we met?"

"No, but you have met my friend. You are going to get quite a surprise in just a little while."

His smile was disarming. It made me shudder.

"Not the best day for weather," said the priest, pulling his coat tighter in the most obvious manner possible.

"I'm sorry. Please come in. I'm not very well-equipped for visitors, but I'll put the kettle on. I can at least make us some tea."

"That would be lovely," said the priest.

The place was a mess. You can get into some bad habits when you live completely alone. I put a log in the stove. Then I filled the kettle and set it on the stovetop.

"Would you mind watching the kettle? Uh, Alex, is it? There are teabags in that cupboard over there and cups in that one. I think there should still be some milk in the fridge. Excuse me, I have a quick chore to do outside. Father, would you mind coming with me?"

"I can help you," said Alex with an eager smile.

"Thanks, but I need to have a quick word with Father McGinley."

The priest was loath to be dragged back out into the cold, but he went grudgingly.

"Sorry to land on you like this," he said apologetically. "I have wanted to meet you for quite some time. I see you at Mass sometimes, but you are always gone before I have a chance to speak with you afterwards."

After a pause, he added, "I notice you never take communion."

"I'm not a Catholic, Father."

"Were you never baptized?"

"Oh, I was baptized all right, but it was in a different church."

"I see. Well, you know there is a Protestant church in Clifden."

"I don't really belong to any church anymore, Father, but I do like going to a Mass sometimes. I've always liked the Catholic services. I made some friends a long time ago who were Catholic, and I have always found something comforting about the way Catholics do things. I hope you don't mind me crashing your Mass."

"Oh, not at all. You are more than welcome anytime. Would you have any interest in perhaps joining us, I mean formally?"

"I don't think so, Father. You see, I've kind of worked out my own relationship with God. I know you probably don't really like to hear that, being in the line of work you're in, but I feel like I can get closer to Him if there isn't too much organized religion in the way."

"You should not underestimate the importance of fellowship and community when it comes to being closer to God."

"Yeah, yeah, I know. Anyway, that's not what I wanted to talk to you about. I need to know who this guy is you brought here."

"I'm afraid I know nothing about him. He just appeared in the village this afternoon. I did not get a lot of information out of him, except that he has come from Switzerland."

"Switzerland?"

"He says that his friend, who will be coming later, knows you."

"Knows me? Knows me how?"

"He didn't explain. He is very mysterious, I have to say, but he assured me that you would be glad to see them. Are you all right? You seem to be trembling."

"You see, Father, there is a reason I came here and have been keeping to myself the way I do. It's kind of hard to talk about, but, well, you see, I've done some pretty stupid things. I got mixed up in something that I shouldn't have. I took some photographs that were a bad idea. And now there are some very dangerous people out there who are not happy with me. I know it is only a matter of time until they send someone after me."

"I'm sure it cannot be as bad as all that. Do you owe them money?"

"It's worse than that. You see, someone close to me was killed, and when they get their chance, there is no doubt they will do the same to me."

"Hold on. Surely, you don't think that Alex could be an assassin?"

"No, he doesn't really seem to be the type, but he could be the advance guy—the one who locates me and smooths the way for the other guys. That would be the sort of person they might use, you know, someone who does not look threatening. In order to put me off my guard."

"I think you are worrying about nothing. As far as I can see, this is nothing more than a well-intended visit."

"But how did he know where to look for me? Nobody knows I'm here. I mean, absolutely nobody. I haven't told anyone. Not even my parents. Not my brother. Not..."

I looked down at the ring on my finger.

"Not... not any of my friends. None of them. There is no way he—or anyone else—could have known where to look for me."

The priest stroked his chin.

"Yes, well, that does seem odd all right. You must have let somebody know and simply forgotten about it. What other explanation could there be?"

"There is no explanation, Father. The only way he could have found me is through spies or informers or something. I was stupid to think that I could stay in Ireland and not be found, but I didn't know where else to go. I'm kind of at the end of my rope."

"I'm sure it's not as bad as all that," he said, putting his hand on my arm. "Sometimes we make things worse in our heads than they really are."

He glanced at the band on my ring finger.

"I take it you're a married man, Mr. Green?"

"Yes, I suppose. I mean, I was. I am. It's kind of complicated."

"Everyone I have met today has a complicated story. You are clearly going through quite a difficult time, Mr. Green."

"You can call me Dallas, Father."

"I firmly believe, Dallas, that things are not as dire as you fear. Trust me. It will turn out all right in the end. Shall we go back inside? Ask Alex your questions. I am certain there is a perfectly benign explanation."

We went back to the warmth of the cottage. Alex had filled three cups.

"I was afraid the tea would get too strong, so I went ahead and poured. Do we all take milk?"

I went to the cupboard.

"I think I might have some cookies, I mean, biscuits."

I emptied the packet of biscuits onto a plate on the table and then took a seat.

"Sorry I don't have more to offer. Like I was saying, I'm not used to getting many visitors."

Father McGinley said, "Dallas is very curious as to how you managed to find him."

"My friend had his address."

"What address?" I asked. "They don't even use addresses here."

"Well, your location then."

"And who is your friend?" I asked.

Alex smiled.

"He's really keen on surprising you. We were supposed to arrive together, but he can be stubborn sometimes. You see, last night he, well, we were in a pub on Dominick Street, and he met a girl."

"And why does he want to see me?"

"He wants to thank you for something—in person. Also, to be honest, when we learned where you were living, it seemed like more than coincidence. You see, you might be able to do an important favor for me."

"A favor?"

"Yes, but I'm afraid that's another long story, and there's plenty of time for that. I do not want you thinking we only came to ask for a favor."

"Father McGinley says you're Swiss?"

"Swiss? Oh no. I have been living in Switzerland, but I'm not Swiss."

"Where are you from?"

"Buenos Aires."

I felt as if my heart had stopped. My earlier panic returned with more intensity than ever.

"*¿Usted es argentino?*"

If he was at all surprised or impressed that I spoke to him in Spanish, he didn't show it.

"Yes. Well, half anyway. My father is Indonesian."

His being Argentine seemed too much of a coincidence.

"*¿Y cuál es su nombre completo?*"

"*Me llamo Alejandro. Alejandro Malaka Navarro.*"

When he said his name, his voice changed, completely embracing the South American vowels and the double-letter R. It was the first evidence that English was not his mother tongue.

"I was in Argentina years ago. I went there looking for a friend."

"Where did you go?"

"Mendoza first, then the capital."

"And did you find your friend?"

We were interrupted by a sudden roar. For a terrifying moment, I thought a bomb had gone off, and I nearly passed out from fright. It was followed by a battering noise like boulders landing on the roof.

"A thunderstorm," said Father McGinley. "There's nothing quite like an Irish summer."

Looking concerned, Alex stood and went to the window.

"I hope he is okay. I wish he had come with me instead of delaying."

"He will be drowned," said the priest, "if he tries to make his way up the road in this. If he is wise, he will wait it out at the pub."

The heavy rain made it dark in the house, even though we were still hours away from sunset. I stood and flipped the wall switch for the overhead light, but it did not illuminate.

"The electricity's gone," I said. "That happens a lot here. I'll light a couple of candles so at least it isn't so gloomy."

"Well, I'll hardly head back in this," said the priest. "I hope you don't mind if I wait it out, Dallas. With any luck, it will pass quickly. I'm sorry now I didn't bring a gift to thank you for your hospitality."

"I have a bottle," I said, going to the cupboard and retrieving a bottle of Powers. "I don't have any ice, but I don't suppose you want ice anyway."

"Just a drop of water will do me," said the priest.

"Same for me, please," said Alex.

I had no sooner filled the glasses than the priest raised his.

"To weathering the storm. *Sláinte*."

I had long since formed a good impression of Father McGinley from the way he said the Mass and from his homilies. Seeing how much he liked whiskey made me like him even more. I put another log in the stove.

"At least we're not relying on electricity for the heat."

"Weather like this always makes me think of ghost stories," said Alex. "I almost expect a phantom to appear suddenly."

"If it would put you at ease," said the priest, "rest assured that, if necessary, I can perform an exorcism."

Alex and I looked at him quizzically. It seemed an odd joke for a priest to make. He smiled mischievously.

"It would not be my first one, you know. I have performed one before."

Alex's jaw had dropped.

"You have?"

"Yes," he smiled. "I mean, it was not exactly by the book. You are really supposed to clear it with Rome first. This was done in a more, uh, unofficial capacity. You see, in Australia I was working among some of the native people, the aborigines, and they had their own traditional beliefs. Sometimes it was easier to work with what they were comfortable with than to be too concerned with the Vatican's rules. It was really more for the man's psychological benefit than a true spiritual remedy."

"That's good to know, Padre," I said. "I mean, in case we have a need for it."

"It's not something I would do here, of course," he said. "I mean, unless it were under very unusual circumstances. Is there anything more in that bottle?"

"There sure is, Padre," I said, as I refilled the glasses. "And when that runs out, I have another one."

"Oh, my. Mind you, I would not normally have more than the one glass, but…"

There was a loud pounding on the door. We all looked at one another to be certain we had all heard it. It was hard to distinguish it from the noise of rain pounding the roof. We heard it again. Alex smiled at me eagerly, encouraging me to waste no time.

The whiskey and the conversation had relaxed me, but now the fear gripped me again. I did not hesitate, though. Usually, just the one glass of whiskey was sufficient to bring out my fatalistic streak.

I opened the door. The water was falling in buckets. Two drenched figures stood before me with hoods over their heads. Would they have guns, I wondered, or knives? Or would they simply use their bare hands? I stood motionless, waiting to see what would happen.

"Are you going to ask us in?" pleaded a young male voice, impatiently.

"Yes, yes," I said, coming back to life. "Sorry. Please come in."

They shook themselves like dogs, as they removed their coats. One was a woman with short-cropped hair. The other was a man, slightly taller than me. He had long, flowing, blond hair and hazel eyes. There was an ecstatic grin on his face. As impossible as it seemed, it was a grin I knew well. In the very moment when I had expected to become a ghost, I had instead met one. How could he be here in front of me now? And looking so much the way I always remembered him? The way he looked that summer when we went to Mexico together?

"*Onkel* Dallas!" he cried, as he wrapped his arms around me and hugged me until there was no more air in my lungs.

# 3
# Cubans

IT TOOK A WHILE before my brain was able to work in any kind of rational way. I could not stop staring at him. The resemblance was uncanny. I choked up.

"Lukas? Lukas Wolf? You're so tall. How can you possibly be this tall?"

"Well, I am eighteen years old now. You should know that. After all, you never missed any of my birthdays."

Of course, I knew he was eighteen. In my mind, though, he had always continued to be the shy, little boy I had met a single time in an apartment in Fulda. Now fully grown, not only did he look amazingly like Lonnie, but he had Lonnie's posture. He had Lonnie's facial expressions.

"How did you know where to find me?"

"How do you think? As long as I can remember, your birthday gifts arrived almost exactly on time, including the last one. I did not have that one in my hands, however, until I went home for Christmas. The parcel had your return address on it with the name of this village."

Like Alex, he spoke English perfectly, although there were hints of German in his accent.

"Even with that," said Alex, "it was still a bit of work to find you. Irish postal addresses, at least in the country, do not seem very precise."

Father McGinley smiled.

"You see there, Dallas? You did let someone know where you were after all."

"I always wondered if you got the gifts I sent you."

"I'm sorry," said Lukas, a bit sheepishly. "We were not very good writing back to thank you, but I always looked forward to the annual parcel from America. I was the envy of all my friends—especially when the first one came with the *Star Wars* toys. No one else had them. Every year Mama warned me that the gifts might stop coming, that I should not be too eager for them. She would say, 'Enjoy the gifts you have received, but we cannot expect him to go on sending gifts year after year.' But somehow I knew you wouldn't forget me. Every year I knew you would send another one, and you always did."

"They weren't really from me, you know. At least that's how I thought about it. They were from your dad. I was just sending them because he couldn't. God, Lukas, he would have loved you. He really would have. It's so unfair that he never got to know you."

"Perhaps you can tell me some stories?"

"I sure can. We got up to a lot of stuff back when... well, back when the two of us were the same age as you and Alex."

"I would like that very much. Oh, I am afraid I have forgotten my manners. Everybody, this is Annika."

She shook my hand. "Very pleased to meet you."

Her accent sounded German but more pronounced than Lukas's.

"Nice to meet you too. I'm Dallas, but I guess you know that. This is Father McGinley, the parish priest here. Can I offer you some whiskey? Are you hungry? Let me see what there is around here to eat."

"Don't worry about us," said Annika. "We have brought our own food."

She and Lukas opened their backpacks and pulled out some soda bread, cheese, fruit, and a bottle of Paddy's. That reminded Alex that he too had come with a few provisions. He produced a loaf of white bread and a paper bag full of cold, cooked sausages. He also pulled out a box of cigars.

"They are Cuban," he said with a grin. "I can't wait to try one."

"Really? I've only smoked a Cuban cigar once in my life," I said, wistfully remembering a night on Russian Hill thirteen years earlier.

"I never have," said Alex.

"Neither have I," said Lukas.

"Oh my," said Father McGinley, "I would rarely touch a cigar, although I might make an exception, given the evening that's in it."

Alex handed cigars out to the men. Annika glared at him expectantly.

"Uh, would you like one as well, Annika?"

"Yes, please."

Lukas was already balancing his between his teeth.

"Who has a match?"

I reached for my box of sturdy wooden Irish matches.

"You know you need to cut the tip off first, right?" I asked.

Father McGinley had already pulled out a pocket knife. He handed it to Lukas.

"Shall we show these wee lads how it's done, Dallas?"

"Cut off the tip? Like this?"

"I wouldn't cut off so much," I said.

"Yes," agreed the priest. "Most people cut off too much. A wee bit will do."

I struck the match and held it just below the end of Lukas's cigar.

"Turn it while I hold the flame underneath it. Don't let the flame touch it. Okay, now put it in your mouth and start puffing, but don't puff too hard."

He exhaled softly a couple of times and coughed. Meanwhile, Alex had taken the knife from him and offered it to Annika who, in turn, produced her own much larger knife. She cut off her cigar's tip smoothly and lit it herself. After a few puffs, she blew smoke rings. She must have done this before, I thought. The smoke did not bother her at all.

Alex offered the priest's knife to me. Soon I was puffing away, thinking about San Francisco and expensive scotch whiskey. I handed the knife back to Alex, who studiously imitated the rest of us. Like Lukas, he needed a few minutes to become accustomed to the smoke.

Finally, it was the priest's turn. Clearly, in his time he had smoked more cigars than the rest of us. He leaned back in his chair, stared into space, and enjoyed the sensation.

For several minutes we all remained silent, savoring the experience.

"I'm so happy you're here," I said to Lukas. "I always wondered if I would ever see you again. Do you remember the time we met?"

He shook his head.

"No, but Mama has told me about it many times. So many, in fact, that I can remember it through her."

"And how is Renate?"

"She is good. I think she is quite happy. Six years ago, she was married. He is quite a wealthy man. It made things comfortable for her. As for me, I don't think he liked having me around so much, and to be honest, I did not care for him either."

I smiled.

"Just like your dad. He had a stepfather too. Two of them in fact. He hated both of them. With his second stepdad, I was always afraid one of them was going to kill the other."

"Yes, well, my stepfather's solution was to send me to boarding school in Montreux."

When he said the name of the place, he sounded just like a Frenchman. Who would have thought Lonnie McKay's son would grow up speaking so many languages?

"In the end, it was for the best, but in the beginning I was lonely. I do not think I would have gotten through it if not for Alex. We were roommates all four years."

"Yeah, Lonnie and I were like that. We were outsiders in our town. We didn't have anybody but each other all through high school. It's great to have a good friend at that age."

Lukas smiled at me indulgently.

"You know, not everything about me has to be some reflection of my father's life."

"I'm sorry. It's just that you look so much like him. I still can't get over it."

"Really? Do you honestly think so? We only had one photograph of him, so it was difficult for me to tell."

"Yeah, you are definitely your father's son. Was it lonely growing up alone? I mean, without any brothers or sisters?"

"Actually, I have a sister. Well, a half-sister, but she is only five years old. I don't know her all that well. She was born while I was away at school."

"There is something I am tempted to tell you, but I'm not sure I should."

"You cannot say something like that and then not tell me."

"I don't know if it's really my information to share. Unfortunately, whiskey has a way of loosening my tongue."

"What is it?"

"You have a brother. Well, a half-brother."

"I do?"

"Yeah, and he's just a couple of years older than you."

"Was my father married when he…?"

"No, Lonnie was never married, but I think he would have married your mother if it had worked out."

"Wow. A brother. That is a surprise. I did not expect that."

Annika tugged on his shoulder and said something to him in German. As they chatted quietly, the priest stood.

"I have to say, I have enjoyed meeting all of ye very much, but as the rain has finally stopped, I should be heading home."

"Will you be all right, Father? It's getting dark out there."

"Not a bother. I'll be grand."

He wobbled a bit as he put on his coat.

"I'll walk you part of the way back, Father."

"I assure you it's not necessary, but I won't mind the company if you insist."

"I do," I said, putting on my own coat. "I'll be back in a bit, everyone."

Lukas and Annika were too engrossed in their conversation to pay much attention. Alex sat quietly, appearing to ignore them even while listening. I guessed German was another of his languages.

The road was wet, but the clouds were gone. The sky was a dark shade of blue. It was about nine-thirty, and the sun was still well above the horizon. The light would linger until after midnight. In the distance we could see flames.

"Not a bad night for the bonfires after all," said the priest. "It's been quite a day."

"It certainly has. When I woke up this morning, I had no idea it would turn out like this."

"Did I not tell you there was no cause for worry? I knew that young man could not mean anyone harm. He was secretive all right, but I suppose he was right not to ruin his friend's surprise. I didn't quite get the entire story of your connection to Lukas, but perhaps you can relate the tale another time."

"Yeah, you'll have to come again. It's been good to have people around for a change. I've definitely been spending way too much time on my own."

"About the things you were telling me… about the people you think are after you…"

"Yeah, I shouldn't have bothered you with any of that, Father. Please forget about it."

"Well, it is not the sort of thing that is easy to forget. Have you thought about going to the Gardaí?"

"The police? I… I don't think that would be a good idea."

"Come here, if you are in some sort of trouble, I'm sure they would be understanding enough. I would happily put in a word for you. Having a priest backing you up still counts for something in this country."

"I can't really do that, Father. You see, for years I have been doing some, um, freelance work, and I was told that if the local police in any country where I was working got wind of it, it would mean big trouble—for me and for the people I was working for. Going to the cops isn't an option for me. And there's another thing."

"Yes?"

"There were Argentine guys involved. When I found out Alex was from Argentina, it just seemed like too much of a coincidence."

"Yes, that is interesting all right."

I was now eager to change the subject.

"Alex mentioned you're from Donegal. I've always meant to go up there to see what it's like."

"Ah, yes, my native Tyrconnell."

"Is that the name of your home town?"

"No, Tyrconnell is an old name for Donegal. It means the land of Conall—after an old king."

"And what does Donegal mean?"

"Let's see, the original Irish would be *Dún na nGall*. It means the fort of the foreigners."

"Why is it called that?"

"Where Donegal Town is now there was once a settlement of Vikings. They were the foreigners. Just one of many waves of foreigners that have invaded this island over the centuries."

"I guess that's me as well. Just one more foreigner invading your country."

He laughed.

"Well, you're very welcome. I'm glad to have finally met you properly, Dallas, and now that I have, you can expect me to call on you again."

"You're always welcome, Padre. I'll be sure to keep a bottle in the press for you."

"I hope you haven't gotten the wrong idea there, Dallas," he said with a little embarrassment. "It's not really like me to take a drink. Tonight was, as you say, the exception that proves the rule. Well, you've walked me far enough. Go back to your visitors."

"Okay, Father, and thanks again."

"I'll look for you at Mass," he called as he rounded the bend.

I made my way back up the road. Despite what he had said about the exception proving the rule, I had a feeling that I now had a new drinking buddy. That was something I had been missing.

When I got back to the house, I found Alex sitting alone in the armchair, still savoring his cigar and looking reflective.

"Where are the others?"

With his head he motioned toward my bedroom door.

"They went in there. They said they were 'tired.' I hope you don't mind."

"Well, I suppose they have to sleep somewhere. There's a bed in that other room, but it's not made up. I think there are some blankets around here somewhere. You are welcome to it."

"I'm not tired yet. Anyway I don't mind sleeping on the sofa or on the floor if you want the other bed."

"I'm not tired either. I was hoping to talk to Lukas some more, but I guess there'll be time for that tomorrow. Can I get you anything?"

"I wouldn't say no to another glass of whiskey."

"A man after my own heart. I'll join you."

We clinked glasses.

"*Salud*," I said.

"Cheers," he said.

"*Estoy contento que usted esté acá,*" I said. "*Me gustaría aprovechar de la occasion de hablar castellano.*"

He laughed.

"Is my Spanish that bad?"

"No, no, your Spanish is quite good. It's just that you sound like a *chileno*. It is strange to hear that accent coming from a North American. Now why are *you* laughing?"

"Because when I was in Chile, I was told I sounded like a Mexican. Well, I guess that's progress."

"You know, Mr. Green..."

"Call me Dallas. 'Mr. Green' sounds like you're talking to my father."

"Very well... Dallas. Tell me, is that your real name or is it some sort of nickname?"

"It's my real name."

"*Bueno. Si yo puedo llamarte por tu nombre, pues nosotros nos podemos tutear, ¿no?*"

"*Claro que sí.* Now what were you going to say?"

"Before I met you, Dallas, I had a hypothesis."

"And what was your hypothesis?"

"I always thought Lukas's mother made up the story about his father being dead. I thought that perhaps *der Onkel* Dallas in America was his real father, that it was simply easier to tell Lukas his father was dead rather than tell him his father had abandoned him. After all, why would you keep sending birthday gifts year after year unless he was your son?"

I removed a cigar from his box and offered it to him. He took it and with his eyes invited me to take one for myself. I was glad for the chance to speak Spanish again, although he clearly preferred communicating with me in English. I also liked that he felt friendly enough toward me to use the informal *tú.* That was unusual, given the age difference between us.

As I lit my cigar I said, "And now that you've met me, do you still think that?"

As he lit his he said, "I think my hypothesis was wrong. I have seen the photograph of Lukas's parents, and there was never any question the man in the photo was his father. My mistake was thinking that you would turn out to be the man in the photograph. I still do not understand why you sent him all those gifts."

"When I met Lukas, it broke my heart. It was so unfair he and Lonnie would never know each other. The gifts were just my way of trying to make up for the unfairness. Lonnie would have definitely been in his life if he hadn't died."

"What about the other son whom you mentioned? Was your friend in his life?"

"No. He never knew that son either."

"It sounds as though your friend was busy in his short life."

As we spoke and relaxed under the influence of the whiskey and cigars, my impression of Alex changed. For one thing, he was much older than his years. Physically, he was definitely a teenager, but his manner was assured and mature, nearly haughty. That he had gone to a private Swiss boarding school was a tip-off he came from wealth. He would have been accustomed to a home with servants, although he clearly had no problem roughing it while off on an adventure.

"You must know Lukas pretty well," I said, "after sharing a room with him for four years."

He puffed his cigar.

"That is true. There is nothing like sharing a room with someone to learn everything about him. I know every dark and dirty secret about him, and he knows every dark and dirty secret about me. I always know what he is thinking, and he always knows what I am thinking."

I laughed.

"I can't imagine either of you have many dark and dirty secrets at your age."

"I suppose," he said contemplatively, "it is relative. I only know they can seem dark to me. In any event, no one knows me as he does. I shall miss him very much."

"So this is your big post-graduation summer adventure? My friend and I had one of those at your age. Where will the two of you be next year?"

"I shall be at Oxford in the autumn. Lukas has been accepted at Brown University in the U.S., pending approval of his student visa."

"Yeah, I bet you will miss him. Well, you can always write to each other and maybe get together in the summer."

"It was hard for me to leave Argentina and live in a country where I did not know anybody. I do not look forward to doing it again."

The sound of panting could be heard through the bedroom door.

"Do they think we can't hear them?" said Alex with annoyance. "These are our last few weeks together. Is this how he wants to spend them? Could he not wait just a couple of months longer? Then he could go ahead and screw every woman at Brown if he wants."

I knew exactly how he felt. I wished I had some profound wisdom to offer, but in that moment I was preoccupied with bittersweet memories and an overwhelming sense of being older but not wiser. I took another sip of whiskey.

"Yes," I said quietly, "he is definitely his father's son."

# 4
# Alejandro

ALEX AND I HAD fallen asleep in our chairs. That is where Annika spotted us as she slipped quietly out of the bedroom and headed to the bathroom. It was early in the morning, but because of the time of year, the sun was already low above the horizon.

She stepped gingerly through the shadows in her bare feet. She did her best to make no noise, but she stubbed her toe on the leg of a small table. She stifled her reaction to the pain, but it was enough to wake me. I kept still until she had been to the toilet and then made her way back to the bedroom.

I looked at Alex to see if he had also wakened. He was motionless with his head tilted at an odd angle. He was so still that I actually feared he wasn't breathing. I stood and brushed his cheek ever so lightly with the back of my hand—just to assure myself he was alive. Despite a chill in the room, his face was surprisingly warm. I went to the wardrobe and retrieved two blankets. I laid one over him carefully, and then pulled the other one around me as I sat back down.

In the faint light streaming through the window, I studied him. Asleep, he looked younger than before. There was no sign of a beard, and his black eyelashes were unusually long. I indulged in a brief moment of envy, wishing I was that age again, able to look in a mirror and see a creaseless face and hair without strands of gray. To have so little of my life behind me and almost everything ahead.

The envy was quickly supplanted by a surprising emotion. I felt strangely protective, nearly paternal. Because he was in my home, I was responsible for him. As hard as it was to get my head around it, he was the same age as Lonnie's son, and I was the same age as Lonnie. I was old enough to be this grown man's father.

How had my own life turned out so differently from my father's? When did I stop assuming that, by the time I was this age, I would be married with children? When Dad was the age I was now, he had already been married twelve years. He had one kid in sixth grade and another in fourth.

If I had it to do over, would I do it any differently? But how? After all, when it came down to it, there was only one person I ever truly wanted to marry. I did marry her, and look how it turned out.

I made my own visit to the bathroom and settled back into my chair to watch Alex some more. Private Swiss school. Oxford. I wondered who his family was. Would I have heard of them? I thought about how different his and Lukas's lives were from the lives Lonnie and I had led. Yet when it came down to the truly important things, were they really any different?

I fell asleep to be wakened a couple of hours later. All three of my guests were rummaging through the kitchen in search of breakfast.

"There should be some cereal in the cupboard," I mumbled, "and milk in the fridge, and I think there's still some bread in the bread tin."

It was much harder to wake up this time.

"Is there any coffee?" asked Lukas, opening and closing cupboards.

"There's a jar of Nescafé somewhere. I'm afraid that's all I have. That's all I can get in the local shop. It's actually been enough to turn me into a tea drinker."

Annika, the most efficient of the three, had already revived the fire in the stove and put on the kettle.

We sat around the table, making the most of what food I had. I regretted not having any bacon or sausages, so I could show them what an Irish breakfast was like.

"So what is it you do here?" asked Lukas.

"Well, funny enough, I have sort of gone back to my roots. I've been farming."

"Farming?"

"Definitely not the kind of farming they do in California. The farms here are a lot smaller, and it is mainly livestock—not crops. Cattle and sheep. At first I was just renting this place from the woman who owns it. She inherited it from an old maiden aunt of hers. It was in pretty bad shape, so I worked out a deal with her to fix it up in exchange for part of the rent. Then she asked if I could help out her husband with the farm. They're both getting on in years and don't have any children, so I have been helping with the animals, making the silage, cutting turf, stuff like that. Otherwise, I spend a lot of time taking photographs. That's my main line of work—photography. I've also been trying my hand at writing, but I'm not much good at it."

"Why did you come to Ireland?" asked Annika.

"That's a story too long and uninteresting to bore you with now. Lukas, tell me what was it like going to school in Switzerland. It must have been pretty interesting to go to high school in a whole different country."

"Yes, it was a crazy time to be away from home. I was in Montreux only a few weeks when the wall in Berlin came down."

"Yeah, that was definitely an incredible time," I said. "You know, I was actually in Berlin myself when the wall fell."

I fought not to be distracted by a flood of memories.

"I'll never forget those days—for a whole lot of reasons."

"Really? That's amazing. It was so strange to be hearing about everything going on in Germany and not being there. When I went home the next summer, everything had changed so much. All my life I had lived on the border with the DDR, never crossing to the other side. Now people were going back and forth all the time. After I went back to Montreux for my second year, the country was reunified officially. It was such an important time, and I felt that I had missed most of it."

"And next year you're going to college in the States?"

"Yes. That reminds me of the favor I wanted to ask. You see, I had to apply for a student visa to be able to go, but since my father was American, I should be a United States citizen, right?"

"Yeah, as far as I know, if one of your parents is American, then you're American."

"Mama took me to the U.S. Embassy to see if I could get a U.S. passport, but they said I could not inherit citizenship from my father because they were never married."

"That doesn't seem right."

"What I was wondering is whether you would be willing to sign a statement that you knew my father and that he was a U.S. citizen. Mama thinks it might help."

"Sure, I'll do whatever I can. Anything."

"Do you have a piece of paper?"

I found a scrap of paper and a pen and gave them to him. He scribbled something down.

"This is Mama's address and her telephone number. If you talk to her, she can tell you what you need to do."

"Okay, sure. I hope it helps. I have had some experience with immigration bureaucrats myself, and they're not always the easiest people to deal with, but I'll do whatever I can."

"Thank you, *Onkel* Dallas."

"Are you German too?" I asked Annika.

"No, I am Austrian."

"Annika is traveling around the entire world," said Lukas enthusiastically. "Not just around Europe like Alex and me, and she's doing it completely by herself. I think that is so cool."

"I have seen nearly all of Europe," she said. "I go to America next."

"I wish I was going to America with you," said Lukas. "That is where everything is happening. All I am hearing about is this fantastic new movie by Steven Spielberg where the dinosaurs all look completely real. It is already playing in America, but it won't be in Europe until next month. We have to wait longer for everything here."

"Do you like traveling by yourself?" I asked her. "Wouldn't you feel safer traveling with friends?"

"I feel quite safe with this," she said.

She pulled out her knife and displayed it with an air of total confidence.

"And she knows how to use it," said Lukas admiringly.

Turning to his friend, Lukas said, "I thought she might travel with us for a while, Alex."

"You mean, go to France with us?"

"No, no, she has already been to France. I thought we might change our plan and go with her to Iceland."

"Iceland?"

"Yes, she is flying to Reykjavik. After that, she is going to Greenland. I thought we could go with her and then fly back to France afterwards."

"But that leaves barely any time for France and Spain. You know I have to go home by the middle of July."

"Well, Iceland or France, what does it matter?"

I felt awkward listening to them. Alex was doing his best not to appear upset.

"You know I have a particular reason for wanting to go to Paris. It's important."

"Hey, no problem. You go to Paris, and I go to Iceland. We can meet in Paris in a few weeks."

"If that's what you want."

"Yes, that is what I want. It is no big deal. You don't mind do you?"

"No, of course I don't mind. Have a good time in Iceland. When do you go?"

"The flight from Dublin is tomorrow," said Annika.

"Tomorrow? Then you probably want to leave here today."

"Yes, that's true."

"But I thought you wanted to spend more time with your *Onkel* Dallas."

"Yes, I do," said Lukas, turning to me. "And I will. Maybe when we are both in America. Sorry not to be staying longer this time, but there will be lots of times in the future, no?"

"Sure," I said. "How are you getting to Dublin?"

Annika held up her thumb. "We'll get a lift from somebody to Galway and then get the train from there."

"There's a guy named Tommy Flaherty in the next village who drives a hackney. I could get him to take you to Galway."

"No, thanks," she smiled. "We will be fine. I thumb everywhere all the time. It's no problem."

Soon Lukas and Annika had gathered up their backpacks and were ready to leave. Their departure felt sudden.

"I wish you could have stayed longer, Lukas."

"Yes, me too, but I will see you again soon, *Onkel* Dallas. I promise."

He turned to Alex. "I'll see you in a few weeks in Paris, okay?"

"Sure, okay."

"You're sure you don't mind?"

"No problem."

As the two of them started down the hill, Alex called out, "Watch your back, Lukas!"

Lukas turned his head with a perplexed look. Alex shrugged.

"She has a knife, and she knows how to use it."

Still looking confused, Lukas followed Annika toward the village. I felt bad for Alex. I knew exactly how he felt.

"Well, I suppose I should be going too."

"Look, you're welcome to stay as long as you want. It's no problem."

"You are very kind, Dallas, but I do not want to impose. You barely know me. The friend of your friend's son is hardly a connection that obliges you to open your home to me."

"Hey, that doesn't sound like a South American to me, Alex. *Tú tienes tu casa aquí.* That's what people always said to me when I was there. I think you and I have become friends in our own right. I'd like you to stay. You're good company."

I tried to read his face as I spoke. Given our age difference, I was no doubt pretty boring to him, perhaps even more boring than traveling by himself. I found myself hoping, however, he would decide to stay. I had meant it when I said he was good company.

"Well, maybe I could stay another night if it is not an imposition. If you are certain you don't mind."

"Don't worry about that. Besides, didn't you say you had a favor to ask me?"

"You are being so good to me that perhaps I should call you *Tío* Dallas. Maybe you are becoming my uncle as well."

"Or you could just call me Dallas. To be honest, the uncle thing makes me feel kind of old. Tell you what, I can go down to the post office and ring Tommy Flaherty and hire him to drive us around this afternoon. I could show you the sights of the area. There are some interesting things to see, lots of great scenery."

"Thank you, but that is not necessary. I think I might go for a walk by myself. If your village has a butcher, I might get us some nice cuts of meat and show you how Argentine steaks are prepared."

"That sounds great. The best steak I ever had in my life was in Mendoza. I think you will be impressed by the meat in the local butcher's. I even know some of the cattle quite personally."

True to his word, Alex came back from the village with two prime cuts of beef. He had instructed the butcher exactly how he wanted them cut. He had also shopped for onions, garlic, and other vegetables. He fried the meat on my stove as best he could, although I think a barbecue like the one we had in California would have suited him better.

He served the meal as if we were in a restaurant. It was the best meal I had had in ages. To top it off, he had picked up two bottles of Bordeaux from the off-license.

As we dug into the meal, I turned on the radio to 2FM. Through the scratchy reception we dined with songs like "Living on My Own" by Freddie Mercury and "Go West" by Pet Shop Boys. Inevitably, we also heard "In Your Eyes," the song by Niamh Kavanagh that had become unavoidable since winning the Eurovision Song Contest a month earlier.

"I'm glad you decided to stay," I said as I sipped the Bordeaux. "Not a bad wine."

"It certainly justifies its reputation, although being Argentine, I prefer Malbec. Do you know it?"

"I sure do. You know, you're a great cook, Alex. You could definitely make a career as a chef."

"Not very likely," said Alex wistfully. "My grandfather has always been clear I will become part of the family business."

"And what is the family business?"

"They are bankers, although they have some holdings in the energy sector."

"I see. And is that what you want to do?"

He shrugged.

"It is what I am expected to do. My mother is an only child, and I am her only son. I have two younger sisters, but I do not think either of them will have a head for business. Pardon me for asking, Dallas, but are you religious?"

"I'm not sure how to answer that. Religion was a big part of my life growing up, but when I got older, I started having doubts. Lonnie decided early on it was all a big scam, and I guess he had lot of influence on me, but I've never stopped believing in God. I think it's just churches I've lost faith in. Why did you ask me that?"

"I've been going through something, and I'm trying to figure things out. I have been doing my best to expose myself to new ideas. I would like to hear more about your friend Lonnie."

"Really? How much time have you got? Does this have something to do with the favor you said I might be able to do for you? Maybe you should tell me what that is."

"All right, but it hardly seems right to bring that up now. I mean, you have been so good to me even though Lukas has gone. I do not want to impose."

"Like I told you already, you and I are friends now. This has nothing to do with Lukas. If there is something I can do for you, tell me."

"I have made a mess of your kitchen. I should wash the dishes."

I stood and refilled our glasses.

"Forget the dishes. Let's move to the more comfortable chairs, and tell me what that favor is."

"I think I may have two cigars left."

Upon seeing my smile, he retrieved them. Once they were lit, we settled into our chairs and continued to sip the wine.

"I am afraid that I will bore you with my story."

"What story?"

"There is a story that has been told and retold in my family for my entire life. By now I know it by heart."

"And this has something to do with the favor you want to ask me."

"Yes."

"Then tell me. I like a good story."

# 5
# Communion

"MY FATHER WAS born on Java during the Second World War. His family were *Indische Nederlanders,* which is to say they had a mixture of Dutch and Indonesian ancestry. Because of their Indo heritage, they had avoided the concentration camps during the Japanese occupation, but at the end of the war they were persecuted by the Indonesian nationalists. When independence was finalized in 1949, they became entitled to repatriation to the Netherlands with full citizenship. My grandparents, however, chose to remain and become part of the new Indonesian nation, but as my father, Agus, grew up, he found himself restless. He did not feel at home in Indonesia as his parents had.

"As the year 1967—and the expiry for availing of Dutch citizenship—approached, he resolved to emigrate. He landed in Amsterdam at the age of 23, eager to begin a new life. Fortunately for him, at that moment the Dutch economy was booming. He talked his way into a job with Royal Dutch Shell and was trained as a computer programmer in The Hague. Thanks to a gift for that sort of work, he flourished within the company.

"In 1973 he attended a petroleum conference in Paris where he became acquainted with an executive from an Argentine energy company. During a dinner he was introduced to the executive's daughter Ana, who was a student at the Sorbonne. The two of them fell instantly in love.

"There was resistance at first. My grandparents would have preferred that my mother marry someone from a family whom they knew, but it was soon clear there was no separating the two of them. He journeyed to Paris to see her whenever he could. He was frequently on the A1 autoroute between Holland and the French capital in his red Alpine A110 convertible.

"That was the journey he was making in April 1974."

The mention of the month and year distracted me from Alex's story. The following month my best friend Lonnie would die on the Autobahn in West Germany.

"That time he had made a diversion in Antwerp, where he spent a considerable portion of his savings—more than 40,000 Belgian francs—on a diamond ring. He was planning to propose marriage. He was heedless of the speed limit because time was not on his side. Ana had told him her grandmother, to whom she was very close, lay on her deathbed in Buenos Aires and she was to take a flight home that evening.

"Stopping for petrol in Arras, my father noticed a young hitchhiker on the side of the road. Feeling in the mood for a chat, he decided impulsively to give him a lift, hoping a bit of conversation would calm his nerves and provide a distraction. He got more than he bargained for. The young Irishman was full of information, opinions, and general commentary on any subject that arose. He was on his way to Andalusia for the Feria de Abril de Sevilla.

"Upon reaching the capital, they were mired in traffic unusual even by Parisian standards. My father switched on the radio to find out what was going on. He had been extremely occupied at work the previous several days and had not followed the news. France's president Georges Pompidou had died suddenly a few days earlier, and a massive state funeral was in progress at Notre-Dame Cathedral. Heads of state from all over the world, including Heath from the U.K. and Nixon from the U.S., had converged on the capital.

"My father despaired of reaching Ana's apartment in time. It was on the Left Bank, not far from Notre-Dame. He could not believe his bad luck. He was desperate to deliver his proposal before she left France. She had lately spoken of being disillusioned with her studies, and he feared that, once home, she might well decide not to return. His best course would have been to go directly to the airport and surprise her, but he did not know for certain from which of Paris's three airports she would be departing. His only option was to make his way to the Latin Quarter in whatever way was possible.

"Somewhere in the Tenth Arrondissement, he made his apologies to the hitchhiker, as he could carry him no farther and would abandon the car in the first available parking space. The two said their farewells, never to see one another again. As quickly as possible, my father made his way on foot to the nearest Metro station in hopes that the trains would be running more or less normally.

"The platforms and the trains were packed. Each train he rode was excruciatingly slow. He could imagine being trapped underground well into the night.

"Finally—shoulder to shoulder on the steps with his fellow travelers—he emerged from the Odéon station. Above ground the streets were no less thick with humanity. Arriving at her building, he glanced at his watch and was relieved that he should still be in time. He rang her apartment and thanked God when he heard her voice through the small speaker.

"She was startled by his appearance, particularly the anxiety in his eyes. She asked him what was wrong. Catching his breath, he reached into his pocket. The big moment was at last at hand. Then his heart sank. The ring box was not in the pocket where it should have been. It was not in any pocket. He checked them all again in disbelief. He was dead certain of having placed it in the inside pocket of his coat. Bitterly disappointed that the most important moment of his life would not go according to his plan, he fell to his knees, professed his love, asked for her hand, and apologized abjectly for having no ring. He should have known it would not matter. It was the gesture and his efforts which sealed the engagement."

My mind wandered again. So that's how it's done, I thought. Maybe things would have turned out better for me if I had known how to be as romantic as Alex's father.

"Once she had finished her last-minute packing, he accompanied her on the train to Roissy-en-France and Charles de

Gaulle Airport. After an emotional farewell at the gate, he made his way back to his car in the Tenth Arrondissement. To his relief, the car was as he had left it. He was unnerved to think that his expensive ring had been left in an unattended car on a Paris street. His anxiety grew, as he searched every corner of the car. No ring was to be found in any compartment, under either of the seats, or under the mats.

"He thought of the hitchhiker. The bearded young man had seemed honest enough. My father had told him of his plans to propose, but he had not mentioned the ring. Could the ring have fallen out of my father's pocket? Could his passenger have spotted it and, giving in to temptation, pocketed it? Or was the stranger actually a skilled thief who had picked his pocket without detection?

"The loss was devastating, financially and emotionally. After their marriage, my parents settled in Buenos Aires, and I was born about a year after. My father joined my grandfather's company, which gave him more than ample opportunity to make back what he had lost from the engagement ring's unfortunate disappearance. The tale of the lost diamond became something of a family legend. The story was repeated time and again. In truth my father has never gotten over it. The worst of it was not knowing what had happened. He went so far as attempting to track down the hitchhiker. He has wondered to this day what he would learn upon locating him. Would he deny the theft or might he confess? Perhaps he would have been tortured by guilt all those years and would welcome the opportunity to repent. In any event, he had too little information to go on. It would remain an unsolved mystery eating away at Papá."

"That's quite a story," I said, draining my glass, "but I'm not sure what favor you think *I* can do."

"Perhaps none at all," said Alex, "but when Lukas told me that you were living in this part of Ireland, I convinced him that we needed to visit you. He had been uncertain whether it was a good idea, but I persuaded him for my own selfish reasons. You see, my father gathered precious little information from the hitchhiker, but he did remember him mentioning he was from Galway."

"Really? Well, Galway is a much smaller area to search than all of Ireland, but it is still a pretty large place to cover. You're hardly going to knock on every door in the county. What else do you know about him?"

"As I say, just a few details. For one thing he attended Trinity College in Dublin."

Something clicked.

"Go on."

"He said he had spent a few years in Latin America. He had been in Mexico for a while. Also Argentina."

"I can't believe this."

"What?"

"What was his name? Do you have any name at all?"

"It was an Irish name. Something like Shamus."

"Séamus."

"Yes, something like that."

I laughed, as I reached into the press and pulled out the bottle of Powers. I poured us each a glass.

"What is so funny? Do you know something that might help find him?"

"Alex, *mi amigo,* I think you just hit the jackpot. Against all reasonable odds, I think I just might actually know the guy you're looking for."

"Really? That seems too good to be true."

"Yeah, it does, doesn't it?"

"Does he live here now?"

"I have no idea. I haven't seen him in, let's see, twelve years. In fact, I have only met him three times in my whole life, and as it happens, I need to talk to him myself."

"How do you know him?"

"I met him the first time in Mexico City. He and another guy got me mixed up in some political stuff that almost got me thrown into a Guatemalan prison. The next time I ran into him in France. And the third time... well, we don't need to get into that right now."

"Do you know where to find him?"

"No idea. The trouble is you can't trust what he tells you. For example, the first time I met him he called himself Séamus, but the second time he was using the name Declan. I do know some details that may be enough to track him down—or at least his relatives. He told me once that both of his parents were teachers and that they also owned a pub. Most importantly, I know his last name. It's Costello. That should be enough information to narrow down our search. We need someone who can ask around and see who might match what we have to people in this county. I think we have just the man right here in the village."

"The priest!"

"Bingo, amigo."

The next morning we walked down to the priest's house. We found him under a bit of pressure.

"I'm up to my eyes, lads. I have a Month's Mind in an hour, and I have absolutely nothing prepared. I'll call up to you in the evening and hear what you have to say then. Sound?"

I sensed an angle. Coming to the house in the evening would allow him to draw out the visit, but I didn't mind. I would make sure to have an extra bottle of whiskey.

He arrived around eight o'clock carrying a leather duffel bag. In a business-like manner, he set it down on the table and pulled out a box and a bottle.

"What's going on, Father?"

"It has occurred to me, Dallas, that you have made your home here in this cottage and that you have done a fine job of fixing it up."

"Not really. I just cleaned it up a bit and repaired a few things. I still need to paint it, and there's a lot of other work to do. I'm pretty bad about procrastinating. I just never seem to get around to it."

"Well, my point is that this is now your home and, as far as I can tell, it has never been properly blessed—at least certainly not by me."

"Blessed? Why? What does that involve?"

"It's simple really. I will say Mass, and then I will declare the house blessed, and that will be that."

"I don't know, Father…"

"Don't worry. I'll look after all the details. All you need do is sit."

I still wasn't quite sure whether this was the right thing to do, but it was easier just to go along with him. The three of us sat around the table.

"Alex," he said, "would I be right in guessing you might have been an altar server at some point in your life?"

"Yes, I was, Father, although I cannot say I am a good Catholic anymore. To be honest with you, I find myself drawn to many aspects of Buddhism lately."

"Yes, well," he said, pulling on his priest's vestment, "we shall leave that to one side for a later discussion. The important thing is that you know what is required. Indeed, on this occasion I am giving you a promotion. This evening you are hereby an honorary Minister of Holy Communion."

He pulled out a well-worn typed sheet and placed it in front of Alex, who was only slightly less confused than I was.

"If you say so, Father."

Wasting no time, the priest made the sign of the cross and declared, "In the name of the Father, and of the Son, and of the Holy Spirit."

Alex made the same sign with his hand and said, "Amen." Feeling awkward about the whole thing, I imitated him.

"Peace be with this house and all who live here," said the priest.

"*Y con su espíritu,*" said Alex, not bothering to consult the paper in front of him.

The priest continued with the ceremony, every so often directing Alex to read something from his sheet.

"In you every dwelling grows into a holy temple," he recited haltingly. "Grant that those who live in this house may be built up together into the dwelling place of God in the Holy Spirit."

This went on for a long time, and my mind wandered. It snapped back to attention when Father McGinley held up a white wafer and said, "Blessed are you, Lord God of all creation, for through your goodness we have received the bread we offer you…"

*Jesus,* I thought as he continued the liturgy, *he's actually going to give Communion!* I had the distinctly uncomfortable feeling that I should not be there.

He produced a chalice and poured a small amount of his wine into it.

"By the mystery of this water and wine may we come to share in the divinity of Christ who humbled himself to share in our humanity."

He raised the chalice, and as he continued, I felt as if my mind were leaving my body.

"The Lord be with you."

"And with your spirit," said Alex and I together.

Before I knew it, he was reciting the Lord's Prayer.

"Our Father, who art in heaven…"

Holding the wafer above the chalice, he said, "May the Body of Christ keep me safe for eternal life," and then he ate it.

Lifting the chalice, he said, "May the Blood of Christ keep me safe for eternal life," and he drank the wine.

He offered a wafer to Alex and said, "The Body of Christ."

Alex quietly said, "Amen," before consuming the wafer.

Then he passed the chalice to Alex and said, "Blood of Christ."

Alex said, "Amen" and drank.

The priest handed Alex another wafer and motioned toward me. Alex looked at him questioningly, and the priest gave him a reassuring nod.

"The Body of Christ," said Alex, offering me the wafer.

I was overcome with panic. I knew enough about Catholicism to understand they believed that the bread and wine were literally the body and blood of Christ. I felt I was crossing some sort of line.

"Father, you know I'm not a Catholic. I wasn't baptized in your church."

He smiled.

"Normally, you would not be given Communion, but there is an exception in this case. In the blessing of a home, the head of the house always receives Communion. I'm certain that's written somewhere."

I looked at him skeptically.

"Are you sure about that? That... that doesn't quite sound right. Is that a real thing?"

"For this night at least, it's the rule," he said confidently.

Alex again offered me the wafer and this time said, "*El cuerpo de Cristo.*"

I chewed the wafer nervously, expecting lightning to strike me.

Reverently, Alex offered me the chalice.

"*La sangre de Cristo.*"

As I took it from him, our fingers touched, just for a moment. As before, I was surprised by how warm his skin was. At the same time our eyes locked. It was only a split-second, but it seemed to last an age. I got lost in his deep, dark, brown irises. Something was eerily familiar about them, as if this was not the first time I had gazed into them. They were like tunnels to his soul. I was certain I knew what he was feeling and that he knew what I was feeling. It was a scary, fleeting, and exhilarating sensation. It was the kind of spiritual experience I had longed for and expected but didn't have that night when, as a child, I was made to stand up in a revival meeting and declare I had accepted Jesus.

*I understand now why it's called Communion.*

I drank from the chalice. For some reason I had thought the wine would taste better than it did. I immediately felt guilty for that thought.

My head floated until I heard Father McGinley reciting, "Be their shelter when they are at home, their companion when they are away, and their welcome guest when they return. And at last receive them into the dwelling place you have prepared for them in your Father's house, where you live for ever and ever."

"Amen," we said.

The experience left me in a stupor. I could not say how exactly, but the experience had changed me. I was somehow different. In some strange and mysterious way I was now bonded in my soul to Alejandro Makala Navarro forever. Stranger still, I felt as if the bond was not new but had been established years earlier.

I slowly gathered my wits.

"Are you sure that was kosher, Padre? I mean, giving me Communion like that?"

"I have absolutely no doubt it was what I was meant to do," he replied as he put his things back into his bag.

"That wasn't just your way of ambushing me into joining your church, was it?"

"I assure you, my only interest was in having this house blessed. Now what was it ye two lads needed to discuss with me this evening?"

I got out the glasses and poured the whiskey. Alex told Father McGinley the story about his father and the mysteriously vanishing diamond ring. I added my own stories about meeting Séamus Costello in Mexico and France. The priest looked at me with great interest.

"It seems to me, Dallas, you have a good many tales to tell. Perhaps you could relate to us more of your own story? For example, I still do not understand exactly how you wound up in this far-flung corner of Connacht. Or about your friendship with young Lukas's father. Fortunately, this evening I am in no hurry."

"It's not all that interesting, Padre. There isn't that much to tell."

"Father McGinley is right," said Alex. "I want to know more about your time in Argentina and about that friend you were looking for? Did you ever find him?"

"Well, maybe after I've had a few more glasses of whiskey. If I start telling my life story, there's going to be a few things I'm kind of ashamed to talk about. I'd rather hear about exorcisms in Australia and whatever else goes on in the Outback. And I'm sure Alex can tell us some interesting things about life in Buenos Aires."

"Okay," said Father McGinley, taking a sip, "I'll tell you a few tales about the wilds of Down Under, but then you have to promise to tell us your story, Dallas."

I was glad someone besides me would be doing the talking for a while. I took my own sip and smiled with relief.

"We'll see."

# 6
# Reports of a Murder

ON THE DAY AFTER my twenty-eighth birthday, I did something completely unplanned and irresponsible. I got on a plane in San Francisco with my friend Miguel Ángel Contreras Vargas. We flew first to Los Angeles and then, after a layover, to Santiago.

By doing this I had actually managed to waste two great opportunities. Not only had I walked away from the great job I had just restarted in San Francisco, but I had also blown off a pretty good offer in Seattle. So dropping everything and taking off for South America was pretty much the most immature thing I had done in a life punctuated by lots of immature decisions.

On the plane I felt wretched mainly because of having trashed myself badly the previous night at my sad, one-man birthday party. When I informed Ángel I was definitely going to stop drinking forever, he just laughed and told the stewardess we each wanted *two* cans of beer with lunch. That was on the L.A. flight. It got worse on the LAN Chile flight because Ángel was even more comfortable with those air hostesses. He flirted with them shamelessly in Spanish and persuaded them to give us extra drinks. By the time we landed in Santiago, I had completely given up trying to save my health.

The silver lining was that the drinks and Ángel's antics took my mind off the fact I hated flying. Sitting next to him, I kept trying to get my head around the fact that I was there. Until a few hours earlier, I had never expected to see him again in my life. Somehow I had managed to break the cardinal rule of male friendship. I had fallen in love with his girlfriend. On top of that, I had lied to him about who I was and the real reason our paths had crossed. I had upset him with comments about politics that I didn't really understand myself. Despite all that, he had made a huge detour on his way home from France to find me in San Francisco.

I never understood what he saw in me as a friend beyond the fact that I reminded him of a good friend he had made in high school in Virginia. For my part it just felt good to be around him. He had the sort of outgoing, good-natured personality that people were drawn to. Though he was shorter than me by a couple of inches, I was in his shadow. I didn't mind. After all that had been my role with Lonnie. Maybe that was it. Maybe in his charming, seductive, Latin American way, he was essentially another Lonnie. He was certainly the one who had succeeded in filling the hole in my life that Lonnie had left.

When we landed, I was tired, dehydrated, and more than ready to escape.

"God, I'm jet-lagged," I said. "What time is it here?"

"Jet lag? It is only four hours difference. Wait, no, it is five hours difference because of *la hora de verano.*"

"Hour of summer? You mean daylight savings? Anyway, I'm pretty sure I'm jet-lagged."

I hadn't thought about the fact that the seasons were backwards in the Southern Hemisphere. Stepping down the stairs from the plane, it was confirmed by that first blast of dry, warm air. From one day to the next we had gone from San Francisco's cold December damp to South American summer. It may not have been quite as hot as Kern County in June, but it was close enough— especially considering it was only about eight in the morning.

Ángel was annoyed as we walked through the terminal to find that they had changed the name of the airport since he had last been home.

"It's Pudahuel. Just Pudahuel. No one is going to call it Arturo Merino Benítez International Airport."

As we left baggage claim, Ángel's two brothers were waiting for us. I got a firm handshake from each of them, but Ángel got enthusiastic hugs. I wondered how long I would need to be away from home to get a hug like that from my brother.

The older one pointed at me and said to Ángel, *"¿Habla éste algo de castellano?"*

*"No, Mati, tú tienes que hablerle siempre en inglés. ¿Te conviene?"*

He shook my hand and said awkwardly, "How are you? I am Matías."

*"Él está bromeando con usted,"* I said. *"Yo puedo hablar un poco de español."*

*"Menos mal,"* he said, relieved to know Ángel had been joking about me not knowing any Spanish. *"Mi inglés es pésimo. Y tú me puedes tutear, eh? Éste es Sebastián, la guagua de la familia."*

I shook hands with Sebastián, who was seventeen and the youngest of the family. I would learn that *guagua* was the Chilean word for baby, apparently because it sounded like a baby crying "wah-wah."

My immersion in Spanish had begun. My Spanish was going to get a real test, and I would need to get a whole lot better. As we walked to the parking lot, I tried to think of all the words I might need to use.

In Spanish, I asked Matías, «Why do you not know English as well as Ángel? Did you not learn it in Virginia like him?»

«I did not go to Virginia with my family. Only the three youngest children went to the United States. I was at university here in Santiago, and Verónica was working.»

We piled into a brown Chevette. Matías took us on a race down a highway that circled the city outskirts. The car radio played Spanish-language pop songs through its tinny speakers. The passing landscape was strangely familiar. The land was brown and dry. The trees and bushes were dark green. The Andes towered in the distance. We could have been in Southern California. Names like San Pablo and Los Olivos on the road signs only reinforced the illusion of being in my home state.

"What is it like in California?" asked Sebastián enthusiastically and in quite good English. "We never got to go there when we lived in the United States. *Tiene que ser el descueve!* I would love to go there."

«Don't annoy the visitor with a lot of questions, Bati,» said Matías. «Remind me again how you got out of going to school today? Careful, Gringo, he will drive you crazy with questions if you let him.»

Apparently, everyone in Chile had to have a nickname. By default, mine was to be Gringo.

"Batty?" I said. «Is that what they call you? In English, 'batty' means you are *loco*.»

«You definitely have that right,» chuckled Matías.

The teasing did not discourage Bati in the least.

"Yes, I'm Bati, and he's Mati. *¡Bati y Mati!*"

While I tried and failed to come up with the Spanish word for 'rhyme,' Bati was already coming up with more questions.

"I believe the music in the United States is very good. What kind of music do you listen to?"

"I like 'heavy metal' and 'hard rock,'" I said, hoping those terms would be understood without translation.

"*¡Choro!* Me too!"

«He doesn't know what he's talking about,» laughed Mati.

Apparently, Mati's English wasn't so *pésimo* that he couldn't follow our conversation.

"Yes, I do. Do you know Álvaro Peña? He is so good."

"Uh, no. I wouldn't really know any Chilean bands or singers."

"You should know him. He played with Joe Strummer before Joe Strummer was in The Clash."

"Really? You're right, I should know him."

"When we get home, I will play some of my records for you."

The music on the radio stopped abruptly, and a news bulletin was read out in a deep, male voice. I paid only half-attention since it was hard for me to follow. Then I heard the name John Lennon. Everyone in the car went silent. They looked stricken.

"*¡Qué chucha!*" said Bati soberly.

"What is it?" I asked. "What did he say?"

Bati looked at me in shock.

"John Lennon is dead."

"What? No, he isn't."

"He is," said Ángel. "Somebody shot him last night in New York."

"That can't be right. It's some kind of joke, right? It doesn't make any sense."

To receive news like this in a foreign country and in a foreign language made it feel as though it was not real, yet I had no choice but to accept it.

"This is it," I said glumly. "The Beatles will never get back together. I can still remember the Sunday night Lonnie came over to our house and we saw them for the first time on *Ed Sullivan.*"

Bati looked at me in awe.

"You actually remember when the Beatles were together?"

I suddenly felt old.

We were quiet the rest of the way to Las Condes.

Their house was in a neighborhood of expensive homes, each with a well-maintained garden. It was not that different from a Southern California suburb.

I was nervous going into the house, knowing I would meet Ángel's father. He worked for the government, and given the reputation of the Pinochet regime, that was intimidating. His sons were nice, normal people, I reassured myself, so how bad could he be?

I was introduced to Ángel's mother Lucía and his younger sister Camila, a timid teenager with bangs hanging down to her eyebrows. Lucía, on the other hand, was elegant with perfectly coiffed hair and carefully applied makeup. Her dress looked expensive, as did her extravagant earrings. I wondered if she might not be attending some formal occasion later, or had she dressed up because her long-absent son's homecoming was a special occasion? She was courteous but formal with me, extending her hand with a reserved smile.

«You are very welcome to our home, um, do I have your name correct? Dallas? Is that not a city in North America?»

«Yes it is, *señora,* and it is also the name of me.»

I did my best to be friendly, but my mood had been blackened by the news about John Lennon. We had a few minutes of polite conversation before Ángel's father Lautaro made his entrance.

Like his wife, he was dressed immaculately. His dark suit looked as though it had never been worn before. His moustache was perfectly trimmed, and every hair slicked back from his receding hairline was waxed perfectly into place. Unlike his wife, who had a constant air of being on edge, he was relaxed and friendly. He shook my hand vigorously.

"You are very welcome, young man," he said genially in English. "*Tú estás en tu casa.* Please, you are at home here. I think my son Miguel Ángel has told you that we were two years in Virginia. We like the United States very much. You have a great country."

"*Uh, gracias.*"

«You must find it hot here,» said Lucía somewhat apologetically, as she fanned herself lightly with her hand.

«Well, it's definitely warmer than I'm used to for December, but it's not a problem. Hot weather is something I'm definitely used to.»

«Your *castellano* is very good!» she said.

Shy and earnest, Camila chose this moment to speak up and use her English.

"I absolutely love being in heat."

My effort at stifling a laugh was so painfully obvious that everyone looked at me with concern.

"*La frase* 'in heat' *quiere decir, uh, otra cosa en inglés,*" I tried to explain diplomatically.

«*Bueno,*» said Lucía, «you must be tired after your journey. Perhaps you would like to bathe or shower? Please make yourself at home. We can talk more later. You will be sharing Ángel's room if that is all right.»

«That's great,» I said. «He and I are accustomed to sharing a room.»

On walking into Ángel's room, I had a flashback to my childhood, and it made me laugh. Suddenly, I was ten years old again.

"Bunk beds? Really? Who usually sleeps here with you?"

"At one time I shared this room with Bati. He got his own room when Verónica moved out, but we never bothered changing the beds."

"I don't think I brought enough clothes—and definitely not the right clothes," I said, thinking how well-dressed Ángel's parents were.

"Don't worry about it. We can go shopping and buy you a few things if you want."

"I wish I had had time to go to the bank before I left."

"I told you not to worry about that. I will lend you whatever you need."

"I hate borrowing money from you. If I write you a check, would you be able to cash it at a bank here?"

"I think so, but please don't worry about it."

"Your sister is really cute."

"She's nineteen years old," he said gravely.

"Hey, I didn't mean I wanted to date her. I just thought she was pretty. She's kind of shy, though. Does she have a *pololo*?"

"She's nineteen years old."

"That's old enough to have a boyfriend."

"It's too young for you to be asking so many questions about her."

After we had both shaved and showered, Ángel took me for a walk around the neighborhood. I couldn't get over how familiar it felt. The streets were wide, the houses were big, and the lots were large. Many houses were Spanish-style, complete with the red-tile roofs. Others were quite modern and sprawling. All had green lawns. More than a few had swimming pools. Though I should have known better, I found myself expecting Chile to be like Mexico. It was nothing like Mexico.

When we returned home, the smell of dinner filled the house. I looked at the clock on the wall and saw that it was a little past one o'clock.

"Has your mother started dinner already?"

"*Almuerzo* is at half past one," said Ángel. "That is the main meal of the day."

I used the time before *almuerzo* to consult my well-worn English-Spanish dictionary—the same one that Antonio had made me buy in Guaymas—so that I would have a few words ready to throw into the conversation during the meal.

The seven of us sat around a dining table with a linen tablecloth. The dishes were china and the cutlery real silverware.

Wanting to make a good impression, I said to Lucía, «The food smells delicious. You must have been working in the kitchen all morning.»

She smiled indulgently at the compliment, and everyone else chuckled. A tired, middle-aged woman with gray hair appeared through a doorway carrying a large pot.

«It is Esperanza who made the *almuerzo*!» laughed Bati. «Does your mother cook all the meals in your house?» asked Lucía.

«Yes, she does, *señora.*»

«And does she not have any help?»

«Not with cooking. She does it all herself, but our family was smaller than yours. I have just one brother. Now that he and I do not live at home, she just cooks for herself and my father.»

«Well, I have to admire her.»

The pot was full of delicious stew containing chicken pieces and vegetables.

«This is *cazuela de ave,* a typical dish in Chile. Here. Put these in it,» said Lautaro, pushing two small serving bowls toward me.

One of them I recognized.

"Chile!"

«Yes, we are in Chile.»

«No, I mean, chiles, like we have at home for Mexican food.»

«We call that *ají.*»

«I suppose it would be too confusing if it had the same name as the country. What is this one?»

«That is cilantro. It is good with the *cazuela.*»

Lautaro took the cork out of a previously opened bottle of wine and poured a small glass for everyone, including Bati, though he got only half as much as the others and with added water.

«*Vino tinto.* You cannot have *cazuela de ave* without *vino tinto.*»

He raised his glass.

"*¡Salud! ¡Y bienvenido a nuestro estimado visitante de Estados Unidos!*"

"*Gracias. Ustedes son muy amables.*"

In English I quietly said to Ángel, "You'd never get wine with dinner in *my* parents' house—especially in the middle of the day."

When we had finished the stew, Lucía rang a little bell she kept close to her on the table. Esperanza came promptly to take the dishes away. For dessert she brought a rich sponge cake called *torta tres leches* and coffee. The food was all good, but I was disappointed in the coffee. A tin of Nescafé instant coffee was placed on the table for mixing with hot water from a pot.

In a low voice I said to Ángel, "I thought in South America the coffee would be really good. I mean, isn't this where most coffee comes from?"

He laughed, "We don't grow any coffee in Chile. You're thinking of Brazil or Colombia."

The conversation continued around the table long after the dishes had been cleared. This was typical. They even had a name for it—*la sobremesa.* Not being used to it, I found myself wanting to get up.

«May I help wash the dishes?»

Once again, I was the subject of indulgent laughter.

«We do not make guests wash dishes.»

I was not the only one who was eager to leave the table. Bati tugged at my shirt sleeve.

"I will show you my records now. Come to my room."

«You are going to annoy Dallas,» said Mati.

«He doesn't mind. Do you?»

«No, I don't mind. I'd be interested to see what music he listens to.»

Bati's room could well have belonged to any number of teenage boys in the States. Posters of The Clash and Def Leppard were displayed proudly on the walls. Also adorning them were several of soccer players. Each one caught an athlete in glorious mid-action with a look of exhilaration on his face. The players invariably had shaggy black hair, white shirts, and short black pants. As far as I could tell, they all belonged to a team called Colo-Colo.

He pulled an LP out of its sleeve and put it on his turntable. He smiled wide at me, as Joe Strummer's inimitably rich voice sang about London calling to the faraway towns.

"*Es bien bueno, ¿no?*" he grinned enthusiastically.

"*Sí, muy bueno.*"

"That was terrible news about John Lennon, no?"

"Yeah, pretty terrible."

If he was upset by it, he wasn't going to let it dampen his enthusiasm. He pulled out another album.

"Here is my newest one. I just bought it a few days ago at a record shop in the city center. It is so good. Do you know them?"

He showed me the album cover. It was familiar in a completely unexpected way. The art consisted simply of a large, vaguely militaristic logo that I knew well.

"I think someone has ripped off some friends of mine," I said. "Or else my friends were the ones who ripped off someone else. That looks just like the logo of a band I know in San Francisco. What album is this?"

He handed it to me and said, "Oober-ben-hay."

"What?"

I turned it over, and the name ÜberVenge was printed on the back. There was also a photo. It was a bit blurry in a deliberate, misguidedly artsy sort of way, but the faces were distinct enough. Johnny was in front with a microphone, flanked by Terry and Rick with guitars. Behind them on the drums, shirtless and flailing as if in a spasm, was Justin, his hair whipping in several directions at once.

"When did they record this?" I asked no one in particular. "They must have actually splurged on a recording studio before they split up."

"So you do know them?"

I showed him the back cover and tapped it with my finger.

"See that crummy photo there?"

He looked at it closely, trying to figure out why I was pointing it out to him. His eyes settled on the tiny vertical line of type along the photo's edge.

*Photograph by Dallas Green.* His jaw dropped, and his wide eyes stared at me in awe.

"*¡Bacán! ¡Hombre!* You're famous!"

# 7
# Las Condes

AT SIX O'CLOCK in the evening, we again gathered around the table. This time it was set with small plates as well as cups and saucers. In the center was an assortment of small cakes and pastries—and that can of instant coffee. The day was still bright, and the windows were open so that we could feel the light breeze.

«This is the *once,*« said Lucía. «I believe you call it 'teatime'?»

«That's more of a British thing than an American thing. Did you say it is called 'own say'? Like the number eleven?»

«Yes, exactly.»

«And why is it called eleven if you have it at six o'clock? Why isn't it called *seis*?»

«Everybody has a different explanation for that,» said Lautaro with a wink. «Some people say it is for the eleven letters in *aguardiente,* which some people prefer to drink instead of tea or coffee.»

Though he appeared to be dressed for work, Ángel's father had been home all day. I wondered if he had stayed home specially because of Ángel's and my arrival.

«Would you prefer tea?» asked Lucía.

«No, thank you. Coffee is fine.»

«Speaking of *aguardiente,*» said Lautaro with a conspiratorial smile, «perhaps, instead of coffee, you would prefer to join me in something a little stronger than coffee?»

He went to a cabinet and took out a wide-bottom bottle that looked as though it should have been a flower vase. It contained a rich, reddish-orange liquid. He poured a tiny bit in a small glass and offered it to me. I looked at Ángel, wondering if this were some sort of trick—or perhaps a test.

Seeing Ángel's encouraging smile, I said, «*Sí, por favor.*»

Lautaro offered to pour glasses for the others, but Ángel was the only other one to accept. Lautaro lifted his glass and said, «*¡Salud!*»

It had a taste of cherry and was as strong as hell.

«This is called *enguindado*. It is very *chileno.*»

I answered Ángel's parents' polite questions about my family and my now-former job in San Francisco. Bati informed them that I was a famous photographer in North America, and they were curious to know more. I told them about the photos I had taken of the reclusive filmmaker Logan MacCaul and of the spy in East Berlin, both of which had wound up becoming kind of a big deal.

«And he took the photo of ÜberVenge on their album!» added Bati.

After the *once* Lautaro, Ángel, and I remained at the table. Lautaro poured another round of *enguindado.*

"Ángel tells me you have come to Chile in the hope of finding a friend of yours."

Now that this moment had come, I was nervous. The fact that Ángel's father worked for the governing junta made me uneasy. I had read terrible things about the military coup seven years earlier, and I didn't know what sort of skeletons I might be digging up.

"Yes, sir. Shall I tell you the story?"

He nodded. His expression had become serious, in fact grave.

"You see, I made a good friend about nine years ago while I was traveling in Mexico, but then he went to Chile and I lost touch with him. I have been trying to find out what happened to him ever since. This is what I know. Sometime in late 1971, he and two friends traveled from Mexico to Santiago. I know they were here because, a few months later, he sent me a postcard. That was the last time I ever heard from him. I became worried about him when… well… you know…"

"Did you try communicating with his family?"

"He didn't have any family. His mother abandoned him as a kid, and he was all alone in the world. I tried writing to the family of the two friends he was traveling with, but I never got an answer."

"It seems to me your best course of action would be to ask again for information from his friends' family. Perhaps the three of them returned to Mexico."

"Maybe. It's just that… I think he would have written to me if he had gone back to Mexico. I got a bad feeling when…"

"After the *golpe de estado*."

"Yes, after that. Is it possible to find out if there is any record here of him being arrested?"

"Why do you think he might have been arrested?"

My pulse quickened.

"He and his friends came here because they were interested in what the government at that time was doing."

"I see. Are you saying they were involved in leftist politics?"

"I… I suppose they were. He was young, and his friends were students. So yeah, I think they were attracted to some of the ideas of that government, but I don't think they would have been involved in anything illegal or violent. They were good, decent guys."

He thought it over for a few moments and then said, "What you are asking is not particularly easy. You see, it was a time of chaos. The previous regime would have done everything it could to confuse the record-keeping systems. The transition to new functionaries after the change of government would have been, let us say, extremely challenging. What I am saying is that any records from that time would not necessarily be complete, accurate, or uncompromised."

"I understand, but could you check anyway? Just to see if his name shows up anywhere at all?"

He laid a notepad and a pencil on the table.

"Write down his name and the year of his birth, as well as those of his friends. I cannot promise you anything, but I will see if anything turns up. Please do not get your hopes up."

"Thank you, sir," I said, as I scribbled on the paper. "I appreciate this a lot. His name is Antonio. Antonio Vega, I think, but I believe he was traveling under the name Miguel Pérez Rivera."

"He used a false name?"

"He changed his name to get a passport. He had no birth certificate of his own, so he used one that belonged to the dead brother of one of his friends. It was just so he could travel. It wasn't to deceive anybody."

"I see."

That was all he said, but his face was full of doubts about Antonio and maybe also about me. I looked at Ángel, who did his best to look encouraging. The silence was awkward.

Then Lautaro said, "I hope you will have a good time in Chile. Please enjoy yourself. I am sure that Ángel will look after you well. You will find our country peaceful and quite safe. I must advise you, however, elements are still present that want to undo the progress of the past few years. You must be cautious about people who try to befriend you. They may not always have your best interest at heart."

He took another sip.

"Our two countries have been good friends for a long time. To be honest, though, we have not cared much for your President Carter. He is not a man who appreciates the difference between one's friends and one's enemies. We are much more encouraged by his successor. President Reagan has a much more realistic view of the world. Well, I am sure I have bored you enough by now with all my talking. You young people must be eager to go out and enjoy yourselves."

I was dead tired and had been looking forward to going to bed. Ángel, on the other hand, was full of energy. He was eager to show me some of the bars and clubs in Las Condes. It would soon be explained to me that Chileans "*somos como los gatos.*" Like cats, they were prone to stay up all hours of the night.

We went to one bar after another. Despite being a Tuesday night, they were all packed. As he had promised, Ángel introduced me to the country's most popular liquor, pisco, a high-proof, fermented-grape product that was served in a variety of mixed drinks. I settled on one called piscola, which combined pisco and

Coca-Cola. Reminiscent of rum and Coke, it was not really my sort of drink, but at least it had the benefit of containing some caffeine.

Everywhere we went, Ángel ran into someone he knew, and they all peppered him with questions. How was his time in France? Who was the gringo with him? Was he still in school? Did he have a job yet? As I did my best to follow the various conversations, it dawned on me why he may have gone to the trouble and expense of seeking me out in San Francisco and inviting me to go home with him. I'm sure he was sincere about wanting to repair the great friendship we had started in France and also about helping me track down Antonio, but there was something else. Now that he was twenty-three years old and had finished his university education, he would undoubtedly come under pressure from his parents to settle down and start a career. As long as I was his houseguest, he had a convenient pretext for delaying all that under the guise of being a considerate host.

It was well past midnight before the last club we visited began to clear out. Ángel looked at the clock above the bar, and said, "Ay! Look at the time! We need to get home."

"So now you're in a hurry? You haven't been in any hurry all night until now."

"We have to be back before the *toque de queda.*"

"The what?"

"*Toque de queda.* It is illegal to be out between two and five in the morning."

"Really? What'll they do if they catch us? Shoot us?"

He didn't laugh.

"Come on. We have to hurry and hope we can get a taxi."

On the ride home, he told me about the overnight curfew that had been in effect since martial law had been declared in 1973. Over time its duration had shrunk gradually—it was now in force only three hours each night—but it was still a serious matter to violate it.

With the streets mostly deserted, we made it back in record time. Trying not to laugh too loudly, he fumbled with the key to the garden gate and then with the one for the front door. We thought we had managed to slip into the house undetected, but as we crept carefully through the dark hallway, we heard his mother's voice.

*"Miguel Ángel, mi amor. ¿Eres tú?"*

*"Sí, Mami."*

«Come say goodnight.»

I intended to continue to our room, but he dragged me into his parents' bedroom. In the light of twin table lamps, his parents greeted us. Propped up on a mountain of pillows, open books lying in front of them, they were wide awake.

«Come give me a kiss, my boy,» cooed Lucía, as she removed her glasses. «No matter how old you are, as long as you are under our roof, your mother will not rest until she knows you are home safe.»

I felt awkward standing in their bedroom, but they behaved as though it was the most natural thing in the world to receive visitors in bed at that hour of night.

«What about all the time I was in France, Mami? Did you worry about me every night then, too?»

«Of course, I did. I always worry about you.»

He kissed her on both cheeks. Then she looked at me expectantly. The motion of Ángel's head told me I was meant to do the same. She smelled of rose-scented perfume.

«Good night, Dallas. Sleep well.»

I could not get used to the way she pronounced my name. It sounded like she was calling me Doll Ass.

Ángel kissed his father on both cheeks, but I settled for a handshake.

«It is good to be young, no?» he said, returning to his book.

When we got to our bedroom, Ángel wasted no time stripping down to his underwear and scrambling into the upper bunk.

"Hey, how come *you* get the top bunk?"

"Because it is my room, and I was here first."

I settled into the lower bed and looked up at the wood slats, surprised I was still awake after such a long day. It was warm enough that I didn't need the blanket over me.

"Well, I guess we finally don't have to share a bed anymore," I said.

"Are you lonely down there?" he teased. "Do you miss me?"

The entire time I had stayed with him in Bordeaux, there had been only one bed for the two of us.

"Yeah, in a strange way I do. I think sharing a bed reminded me of being a little kid and crawling into my brother's bed when I got scared."

While we had been out and talking to his friends in Spanish, it had felt like I was a different person. Now I was me again. Well, I guess a different me.

"You're kind of old to get scared at night, aren't you?" he yawned.

"Do you remember what I was telling you in San Francisco…? When was it? Was it only last night? Man, it seems so much longer ago."

"No. What did you tell me?"

"Really? You don't remember? I told you my deepest, darkest secret, and you don't remember?"

"You do too much talking when you should be asleep. How can you be awake? I'm falling asleep."

"All evening I was fighting to stay awake, and I couldn't understand how you kept going. Now that I've finally got my second wind, you want to go to sleep."

"Are you lonely? Is that it? Do you want me to come down and give you a hug?"

"Why? Do you want to?"

"No way, *huevón.* I'm going to sleep."

"It's weird hearing you but not seeing you. It's like you're a disembodied voice from on high, like…"

"Like an angel?"

"Very funny. I was telling you about the overwhelming fear I get sometimes at night. That was a hard thing for me to tell you. I never talked to anyone about it before."

"Oh, yeah. That. I remember now. That's your deepest, darkest secret?"

"Yeah. It might not sound like much to you, but when I was dealing with it by myself, it was huge. It got really bad right before I went to France, mainly because of other stuff going on. It got better when I was in France. I think getting away from San Francisco and everything that was going on helped. What made the most difference was…"

"What?"

"You won't want to hear it."

"Then don't tell me."

"But I want to tell you."

"Then tell me."

"I don't want to make things uncomfortable between us."

"*¡Chuta!* Either tell me or don't tell me. I want to sleep."

"I think Valérie cured me. She changed everything. With her my soul was at peace."

He said nothing.

"And I think *you* cured me, too."

"Me?"

"Yeah. Being around you, I've learned something about myself. I realize now I'm not meant to be alone."

"*Huevón.* You only figured that out now? That is obvious. No one is meant to be alone."

"Yeah, well, I always thought I would be alone—my whole life. Now I know I can't be alone. I know that now because of all the shit I went through, and also because of you and Valérie. My problem now is that I can't think of one of you without thinking of the other."

"It should not be that difficult. We are two different people."

"Do you miss her?"

"Of course, I do. I always think about her."

"You were doing a lot of flirting tonight. I thought maybe you had moved on."

"That is just the way I am. *Me gusta coquetear.* It amuses me. You know what you said about not separating Valérie and me in your mind?"

"Yes?"

"This might be the time to tell you about my grand theory."

"Theory? What theory?"

"Do not laugh. I have reflected on this for a long time, and it explains a lot. The more you think about it, the more it will make sense to you. You see, when it comes to falling in love, I believe in a particular phenomenon in the universe which I call *gemelos eróticos.*"

"Erotic twins?"

"Yes. You may think I am crazy, but listen with an open mind. Do you remember the moment we met?"

"Extremely well."

"You called to me. You called me Miguel, and for a brief moment I was certain you were my friend Jeff from Virginia. You thought I was your friend Antonio, and I thought you were Jeff."

"Yeah, I remember."

"Jeff and I were best friends in high school. We did everything together. Then I met Janet, and I fell in love with her. I went out with her, and I noticed something strange. In various little ways she reminded me of Jeff. She and I became close. The hardest part about moving back to Chile was that I would never see her again. When I think back on it, I am convinced that Jeff was put on earth to lead me to Janet. Does that sound crazy to you?"

"Frankly, yes."

"There is more. While I was in Bordeaux, I was good friends with a guy on the football team named Christian. We hung out together all the time. Then one day I walked into a shop on the Rue Sainte-Catherine in Bordeaux and saw Valérie for the first time. I did not see a woman who was older than me. I saw only a beautiful woman, and I did that thing you noticed this evening. I flirted with her. Something about the way she laughed reminded me of Christian. That made me like her immediately. I was then convinced that Christian had been put on earth to lead me to Valérie. This phenomenon has happened to me other times as well. I eventually gave it a name. Has it not happened to you?"

"That sounds nuts to me."

"Go beyond your skepticism and think about it. If you are honest, I think you will see this pattern in your own life."

His words prompted me to go on a mental tour of my entire romantic history, and I was surprised to realize there was something to what he was saying. Did being best friends with Lonnie in high school not lead directly to my mad crush on Linda? Did being friends with Antonio not pave the way for my infatuation with Marisol in Mexico? I certainly would not have become involved with Lana if not for having first been friends with Keith. The more I thought about it, the more I saw Ángel's *gemelos eróticos* pattern everywhere.

"So are you saying that, for me, you and Valérie are *gemelos eróticos*?"

"Now that I think about it, no. That doesn't work. According to the rule, you have the male friend *before* you meet the corresponding woman. You did not meet me until *after* you already knew Valérie."

"So what was the point of telling me about your theory?"

"Only that it was something interesting to talk about. If my theory is correct, it could be good news for you."

"Why?"

"Because if Valérie and I are not *gemelos eróticos* for you, that means my *gemela erótica* for you is still out there somewhere, probably here in Chile. You will soon be meeting the woman of your dreams thanks to me."

"You come up with some crazy stuff sometimes, you know that? It's times like this I miss Lonnie. He would have laughed his ass off at your theory."

"Yes, I miss Lonnie too."

"You? How can you miss him? You never met him."

"Yes, I have. You forget. When I met you, Lonnie was *your* name. A person's name is important. You are not quite the same person anymore since you changed your name back to Dallas."

"Of course, I'm the same person. I wasn't different just because I was calling myself by a different name."

"Yes, you were. In calling yourself by a different name, you were an entirely different person. Now that person is gone."

"There you go again, coming up with more crazy stuff."

There was no response.

"Damn shame about John Lennon," I muttered sadly.

As I drifted off, all I heard from the angel on high was light snoring.

# 8
# Santiago

BY THE TIME WE woke the next morning, the sun was already shining brightly. Ángel and I dragged ourselves to the dining room—the kitchen was apparently off-limits to us—and Esperanza brought us bread, jam, and Nescafé for the *desayuno.*

"I suppose everyone else has had breakfast already," I said.

"Papi and Mati are at work. Camila is at university, and Bati is at his *colegio,* his high school."

"And your mother?"

"She is in bed."

"Is she sick?"

"No. Lots of women here have their breakfast in bed. In fact it is not unusual to spend the entire morning in bed."

I wondered what my mother would think about that. She was up by seven every morning—even when she didn't need to be.

"So what does your mother do?"

"Do?"

"You know. Does she work?"

"No, she doesn't have a job. She is in charge of the house."

"Doesn't she get bored?"

"She has friends, and she has her family. She visits them often. She goes out to lunch frequently. Also, she has her charities."

"Charities?"

"Yes, she belongs to several women's organizations that do charity work. They organize events to raise money for the poor."

"Really?"

"Why do you sound surprised?"

"I don't know. I guess I always thought of helping the poor as more of a leftist thing. Your family is pretty conservative."

"Socialists and Communists talk a lot about the poor, but their interest is strictly political. The concern my mother and her friends have is humanitarian. Poverty is a huge problem in this country."

Surprised by Ángel's defensiveness, I made a note to myself to avoid too much political talk. Yes, he had made it clear to me that he was uncomfortable with his country's suspension of democracy, but he was still a lot more conservative than anyone I knew in San Francisco. Maybe that was one of the reasons he and I got along so well. I was from a pretty conservative place myself. I wondered if any of my San Francisco friends would be impressed by Lucía's charitable work.

For the next couple of weeks, Ángel was my personal tour guide around Santiago and central Chile. Thanks to him I had opportunities to shoot photographs someplace new every day.

The sunny, hot weather made me forget it was December. There were, however, occasional reminders of the time of year, such as Christmas displays in store windows. I stopped in front of one to admire the elaborate decorations, including a white-bearded mannequin in the familiar white-fur-lined, red coat.

"Looks like Santa comes here," I said, "just like he does back home."

"Of course. Only here he is called *el Viejito Pascuero.*"

"Don't people here think it's strange that he's dressed that warm when the weather's so hot?"

"Of course not. Everyone knows that it's freezing where he lives, you know, at the South Pole."

We walked down the wide boulevard that cut such a huge swathe through the city center, Avenida Bernardo O'Higgins.

"It is named for the first president. He liberated Chile from the Spanish."

"Seems kind of funny that he has an Irish name."

"Why? Don't lots of people have Irish names in the U.S.?"

"Yeah, but I just thought everyone in Chile had Spanish names."

"Spanish, Mapuche, English, German. We are a melting pot too. Maybe not as much as the U.S., but people here have ancestors from everywhere."

He showed me La Moneda Palace. It was an impressive, wide, gray building set well back from the street. Armed soldiers were strategically positioned all around it.

"Is that where Pinochet lives?"

"No. Nobody lives or works there at the moment. It is still being repaired since being bombed by the Air Force in 1973. It should be finished soon. That is where Salvador Allende died."

In spite of the heat, thinking of the violence that had occurred in this spot gave me a chill.

"Is it okay for you to be saying his name out loud?"

"Of course. Why wouldn't it be?"

"Just wondering. I don't know the rules. I don't have any experience with life under a dictatorship—except maybe for those few hours I spent in East Berlin."

"Does this feel like a dictatorship to you?"

"Well, no, not unless I start thinking about it. I mean, people are going about their business just like anyplace else, but I have to admit those soldiers make me nervous. Don't people have to be careful not to say the wrong thing?"

"If people don't break the law, then they don't have anything to worry about. Just like in your country."

"But it's not exactly like my country, is it? We don't have a *toque de queda* every night. Am I okay taking any photos I want, anywhere I want? Even ones of La Moneda?"

"Yes, of course," he laughed. "You may want to step farther back, though, and not point your camera in the direction of those soldiers."

"Are you joking?"

"No. Look, you have to use good judgment when taking photographs. Don't tell me it's not the same in your country. When we lived there, my father sometimes took us to military bases where he was working. Photographs were not allowed there."

"That's different than a building in the middle of a city."

He shrugged.

"Of course, things are stricter than they used to be. I don't mean to pretend that they aren't."

I had to admit it did not feel the way I had always expected a dictatorship to feel. Nothing frightened me the way Checkpoint Charlie had. Still, I could not help being nervous whenever we passed a soldier with a sub-machine gun.

During one of our long walks through the capital, he took me to the entrance of a park. It was an ornate structure with columns, arches, and steps, like a small castle. The sight of a fancy fountain with a statue of Neptune made my heart skip. It was an image long since burned into my memory.

"I've seen this."

"You mean in a picture?"

"Yeah. It was on a postcard. Antonio sent it to me. It was the last time I ever heard from him."

"Yes, I remember you mentioning it to me once."

I was frozen in place.

"He was actually here. He actually stood here and looked at this, just like I'm standing here now. It's so strange to think about. I remember what he wrote on the card. He said this was a beautiful country and that I would like it because it was a lot like California."

Ángel waited patiently until I was finally ready to continue.

One day we took a bus to Viña del Mar, a city about 75 miles away. We joined the crowds sunbathing on the narrow strip of beach between the city and the ocean. As usual, Ángel was striking up conversations with any female close to his own age. He was a shameless flirt. I lay soaking in the sun and wishing I had richly dark skin like him. I knew all too well I was going to get a sunburn.

Ángel loved going out at night. He dragged me out at least two or three nights a week. After he had become bored with all the places in Las Condes, we began taking taxis or buses to the center of Santiago. One night he met a woman he really got on with. They were having such a great chat that I felt like a complete fifth wheel, sitting at the bar getting lost in my thoughts. By this time I had given up on pisco drinks. No more piscolas or pisco sours for me. I was sticking to Escudo, though I didn't like it as much as my favorite U.S. or Mexican beers. When he finally came back over to me, I figured it was time to leave.

"Do you have money for the taxi home?" he asked.

"Yeah, I think so."

"If you don't have enough, tell me and I will give you some. You know the address to tell the driver, right?"

"Why do I have the feeling I'm going home alone?"

He grinned mischievously.

"I'm going to stay in *el centro*. Here are my keys for the gate and the house. You will want to go soon so you are back before the *toque de queda*. Do not let the driver overcharge you. He will probably try because you're a gringo. Try not to act like a tourist."

"Where are you going to stay tonight?"

"I will get a room." He winked. "There are places that rent rooms for a night without asking questions as long as you have cash."

"So you're just going to abandon me?"

"No, I'm giving you permission to abandon me. Do not look so sad. You're a big boy, *huevón*. Some night you will want to do the same."

I had become so accustomed to Ángel organizing everything and taking me places that I had become like a child. It was strange being responsible for getting myself back to the house.

On the ride back, I tried to chat with the driver, but it was hard to understand him. I don't think I did a very good job of convincing him I wasn't a tourist. When he dropped me off and saw what a nice neighborhood it was, he asked for way more than we usually paid. I gave him the usual amount plus a bit more—just so he wouldn't be too disappointed. He frowned but did not make a fuss.

I crept quietly into the house, dreading what was going to happen. Sure enough, as always, I heard Lucía's voice.

"*¿Miguel Ángel?*"

I actually toyed with the idea of trying to imitate his voice but wisely thought better of it. Instead, I said, "*Buenas noches, señora,*" and hurried toward our bedroom.

«Miguel Ángel,» she said firmly. «Come give your mother a goodnight kiss.»

«Uh, he isn't here, *señora.*»

«What? He is not with you?»

«Uh, no. Don't worry. He's staying somewhere else tonight.»

She sounded concerned.

«He should be at home. I do not like this at all.»

Then I heard Lautaro's voice.

«Dallas, please come in. We will say goodnight to you.»

Reluctantly, I went in to their bedroom. As usual, they were sitting up with their pillows against the headboard. Lucía's book was open on her lap. Lautaro was holding a newspaper called *El Mercurio.*

«Did Ángel stay over at a friend's?» asked Ángel's father leadingly.

He used the word *amigo* for friend, and that gave me my cover.

«Yes, that's it. He met a friend of his, and he decided to spend the night over at his house.»

Technically, I was lying since I was using the masculine version of the word friend, but I could tell by the twinkle in Lautaro's eye that he knew exactly what was up. He did not seem the least bit bothered.

«You see, my love, he's with a friend. There's nothing at all to worry about. Remember, he was abroad for a long time. He is still catching up with his friends. Young people can go all night long. They do not need as much sleep as old ones like us.»

«I'm sorry,» she said, «but it is a mother's job to worry about her children. The world is such a dangerous place. How could I not be concerned?»

"By the way, Dallas," said Lautaro, "I have heard back from all the departments that I queried. I am afraid the news is not what you hoped for."

I braced myself for whatever he had to tell me.

"Yes?"

"They did find a mention in the records of a Daniel Pérez Rivera and a Gustavo Pérez Rodríguez of Mexican nationality.

They arrived in the country in 1971 in the company of a minor. According to the information we have, the two of them departed the country in the early days of September 1973, shortly before the *golpe*."

"But what about Antonio? I mean, Miguel Pérez Rivera. Did he leave with them?"

"As far as we can tell, no. There is no official record of anyone with that name leaving Chile."

"So, he could still be living here," I said hopefully.

"Perhaps," he said carefully, "but there is no record of him at all—anywhere. If he had been living in this country for the past nine years, he should have turned up somewhere."

"Is... is it possible that...?"

"Go on. What do you want to ask?"

"I have read about the people they call *los desaparecidos*. The people who have vanished since the *golpe*. Is there any way to find out if he is one of them?"

He considered his words, as he spoke.

"During and after the *golpe,* many people were arrested for opposing the change of government. Those people have gone through the judicial system and, by now, are either still in prison or have been released. Some have chosen to live abroad. If your friend were one of those, there would be a record."

"But what about the people who disappeared. The ones who were not officially arrested."

I did not know what kind of trouble I could get into by saying this to him, but I had come too far to give up now.

"There is something you need to understand. When the previous illegal government fell, many people chose to leave the country. Many crossed the border to Argentina. In some cases their families have chosen to pretend they do not know where they are, to say they are the so-called disappeared to slander the government. You do not want to fall prey to propaganda."

"Do you really believe all those people who have been written about and whose families have begged for information about them are doing it just to harass the government?"

His face tightened.

"In many cases, yes, but... Look, this country went through a civil war. In a war, not everybody can or will follow the rules. You understand me? We did not start the war. We were not the ones who ignored the Constitution and the Supreme Court. We were not the ones who stockpiled weapons sent by Fidel Castro from Cuba and who built a private army. We were not the ones who wrecked what had been a strong economy with discredited Marxist ideas. If some of our soldiers, in the middle of the chaos, went over the line here and there, well, I for one will not blame them. I am sorry I could not be of more help in learning what happened to your friend, but I assure you, I have done my best."

I had nothing more to say to him except, "Thank you, sir. At least I know more than I did."

I turned to leave when Lucía cleared her throat and tapped her cheek. Every night since I had been in their house, I had kissed her goodnight along with Ángel. It felt strange to do it without him there, but I leaned down obediently and kissed her two cheeks.

"*Buenas noches,* Dallas," she said warmly.

"*Buenas noches, señora.*"

Lautaro summoned me to his bedside. Every night I had shaken his hand. This time he reached out and gave me a hug.

«*Un abrazo, joven.* I know it has not been easy for you, missing your friend. I have friends I miss too.»

"*Buenas noches,* señor."

When I got to the bedroom, I encountered Bati in his pajamas.

"I woke and heard you and my parents talking. Is something going on?"

"No, everything's okay. It's just that your father had some news—actually non-news—about my friend who I've been trying to find out about."

"Antonio."

"Yes, Antonio. He would have been just a few years younger than you the last time I saw him."

"You miss him a lot, don't you?"

"Yeah. It's crazy. I only knew him for a few weeks, but I've never been able to forget him. It drives me crazy not knowing what happened to him."

"What was he like? Tell me about him."

"Look, it's late. You should be in bed. Don't you have school in a few hours?"

"That's okay. I don't mind. I'd like to hear about him. Where is Ángel? Did he not come home?"

"No. He's spending the night somewhere else."

"If you want, I can sleep in his bed, and you can tell me about Antonio until we fall asleep."

"Wouldn't you rather be in your own bed?"

"I don't mind. This used to be my room, you know, and that used to be my bed. I made Ángel sleep on the bottom."

So we went to bed, and Bati asked a million questions. I told him all about Antonio. How he came along with Lonnie and me from Benedict Canyon to San Diego and across the Mexican border and all the way to Mexico City in a '66 Chevy. How Lonnie and I got him drunk and he got sick because he was way too young for that kind of crap. How he fetched my clothes from a hotel room where I had been assaulted by a beautiful girl's extremely angry father. How he taught me Spanish during long days of driving while Lonnie was sleeping off a hangover in the backseat. How he could tell cool and scary ghost stories around a campfire. How he was the bravest person I ever knew and managed to get us out of a Mexican jail. How he stayed by me and took care of me when I thought I was dying from Montezuma's Revenge. How I said goodbye to him because he and his new friends wanted to see for themselves the new socialist paradise that Salvador Allende was building in Chile.

I wondered if I should be mentioning that last part to him. After all, it probably would not have made his father happy. In the end, it did not matter. By that time Sebastián had fallen asleep.

# 9
# Vero

CHRISTMAS CAME AND WENT. Growing up in Central California, I had never experienced a Christmas with snow, but at least I had always experienced it in winter. It was strange to see all the signs of the holiday—decorations, gifts, the tree—in such hot weather and under a sun that did not set until nine o'clock at night.

Ángel's family graciously included me in all of their holiday activities, as if I had always been one of them. I relied on Ángel to help me find gifts for all of them because I didn't have a clue what to buy. At least I could buy them with my own money. Well, sort of. I had gotten my dad to wire some down, and he knew I was good for it, once I got back home.

"Why does everyone keep wishing me a happy Easter?" I asked him.

Whenever I said *Feliz Navidad* to somebody, they said *Feliz Pascua* back to me. I had been taught that *Pascua* meant Easter.

"Easter is *la Pascua de Resurrección*," explained Ángel. "Christmas is *la Pascua de Navidad.* At least that's how it is in Chile."

There was a big turkey dinner on Christmas Eve, which was not served until around sundown. Afterwards, the family invited me to go to Mass. To his mother's annoyance, Ángel had a habit of avoiding Mass, but he went willingly that night. Going to Mass was a big deal in the house. Lucía went as often as three times a week, usually taking one or more of her children with her.

The church was decorated with bright colors for the holiday. The candles' light made the decorations glow magically in the dark interior. As I listened to the beautiful voices of singing children, I was struck by how much better this was than the austere holiday services of my childhood.

I observed Ángel closely as he sat, knelt, and stood with everyone else during the service. It was the only way I could be sure what to do from one moment to the next. As we recited the Lord's Prayer, I admired his fresh haircut and brand-new clothes. He was so comfortable with the ritual that I wondered why he resisted attending church. I envied that he had no need to ponder his religious identity. Though he attended Mass only a few times a year, he was unquestionably Catholic. I, on the other hand, had no idea what I was. I could not imagine going back to the church in which I grew up, and I did not belong to any other church. For whatever reason I always wound up with the Catholics, but I was not one of them. Amid all that beauty and fellowship, loneliness overcame me. I had not stopped believing in God, but I had stopped believing in other people's ability to connect me to God. I had stopped believing in churches even while envying those who had not.

I wished I could be Ángel. Not to belong to his family or to have lived his entire life, but to inhabit his body and to have his personality instead of mine. Of course, that made absolutely no sense, so I was left simply with gratitude for being his close friend. I wondered if it would always be like that.

At midnight we exchanged gifts. Every single member of the family had gotten me something. We ate a fruitcake called *pan de Pascua* and drank *cola de mono,* a sweet, cold, milky drink containing coffee and *aguardiente*.

On Christmas Day everyone slept late. In the afternoon we enjoyed an outdoor barbecue under trees that shaded us from the hot sunshine. It was the best Christmas I had had in years.

A few days after New Year's, a letter from California arrived for me. The envelope was thick, and I knew from the handwriting it was from my mother.

The envelope contained a Christmas card from my parents, a note from my mother, and another envelope. Her few lines included a bit of news about the health and ailments of various relatives, a few words about my brother, his wife, and their kids, and also an assessment of the local weather.

She ended by writing, "I hope you are safe where you are and that you are with people who will look after you. I don't know one of those countries down there from the other, but it sounds like it could be one of those places where a lot of bad stuff goes on. Anyway, this letter came for you a few weeks ago and I thought it might be important, so I'm glad you sent us your address. We love you and miss you. Love, love, Mom."

I studied the envelope. The handwriting was a woman's. The stamp and postmark said Mexico. It was addressed to me at my parents'. There was no return address. My heart raced as I considered whether it might be from Marisol.

I opened it nervously and began to read. It was in Spanish and much easier to understand than it would have been just a few weeks earlier. My Spanish had improved a lot. I turned the paper over to see the signature. The name was Catalina Pérez Rivera.

I turned it back over and continued reading.

«Very dear and very remembered Dallas,

«I hope this letter finds you well and happy. It is no doubt a great surprise to receive a letter from me. I have the sad duty to inform you that my mother, Marta González de Pérez, died one month ago. May she rest in peace. She had been ill for a long time. She often spoke of you and the visit that you made with your friends Lonnie and Antonio, which she remembered fondly. Indeed, we all remember your visit with much affection.

«As you can imagine, we miss our mother very much, and the house is not the same without her. My father mourns her day and night. One of our most difficult duties has been going through her things and disposing of those items we cannot keep. In doing this, I came across three letters you had written to her. This came as a complete surprise, as she had never mentioned these letters to anyone, and I do not understand why she did not share them with us. You must have thought us badly educated not to have answered them. I now belatedly thank you for them and for your thoughtfulness. I can only think that my mother, not having been well for so long, always meant to respond herself but was never able to manage it. You see, my mother was not one for reading or writing.

«In each of your letters, you ask about Antonio. I wish I had news to share with you about him, but I am afraid that we are as ignorant as you about where he is or what has happened to him. I can, however, tell you this much at least. In September of 1973 Daniel and Gustavo returned to us, much to our relief. They had had two interesting years in Chile and had made many friends. They and Antonio, or Miguel as they called him, had become involved in various projects to help the poor and to support the government by organizing in various communities. Sadly, the political situation turned dangerous. They no longer felt safe and were advised to return to their own country. Thanks to God that they did not delay their departure. If they had, it could have ended badly.

«While they were in Chile, Miguel became friends with a family called Muñoz, who had children close to his own age. They more or less made him one of their own. When Daniel told him that he and Gustavo were returning to Mexico, they begged him to go with them. He responded, however, that he preferred to remain with his new family.

«That is the last we know of Antonio. After the *golpe,* Daniel wrote to the Muñoz family, but the letter came back.

«I wish I had happier news to share with you and that I could tell you more about your dear friend Antonio. Please know that we are all well and think of you often. Daniel is now a school teacher. He is married and has two children. Graciela is also married and lives thirty miles away from us. Our father still works in his garage, although I fear his heart is no longer in it.

«Please write us again if you have the time. I am sure that you are busy. I imagine you are married by now and have your own family. We would love to know about your life now. Again, many warm regards to you and your family, which I send to you in the name of my family and in my own,

«Catalina Pérez Rivera ('Cati')»

A wave of emotion had come over me. In my mind I saw Cati as I had known her, a bright and precocious girl of about ten. I thought of Pancho and how he had been so good to us, repairing our broken-down Chevy and inviting us into his home. I thought of Marta and what a warm-hearted woman she was. How sad the house must now be without her. I sat down at a desk and immediately wrote my own letter back to Cati, thanking her with all my heart and expressing my deepest condolences. I told her I was now in Chile and looking for Antonio. I asked her to please send me the address, if Daniel still had it, of where he had tried writing to the Muñoz family.

My quest for Antonio was not quite finished after all. I now had a bit more information to follow up on. It was still like looking for a needle in a haystack, but at least now the haystack felt slightly smaller. I had the name of a family.

The next time I saw Lautaro, I shared my new information with him, but he was not encouraging.

"Muñoz is a very common name in this country," he said. "If you can get a former address for them, that may help. I can ask around, but frankly, I would not be optimistic. You understand, they would not have been in the same social circles as ourselves and our friends."

With the holiday celebrations over, Ángel went back to his previous routine. He insisted on going out two or three nights a week, usually to the city center. At least once a week, he left me to take a taxi back by myself while he spent the night downtown. As far as I could tell, it was with a different woman each time.

"May I take this as confirmation that you are officially over Valérie?" I asked him one night, as we sat in one of his favorite Santiago bars.

He smiled.

"I will never be 'over' *la belle* Valérie. She is not the sort of woman a man gets over—as you know as well as I do. Still, I am not going to live the life of a monk simply because she is 11,000 kilometers away. Do you know what I miss most about her?"

"I don't think I want to hear it."

"Her feet."

"Her feet?"

"Yes, she has the most exquisite feet. No other woman has feet like hers. I become excited just thinking about them. The mere memory of the shape of her sole now threatens to make me lose my balance and fall off this stool."

"Really? Her feet?"

"Yes. The feet are the most erotic thing about a woman. Do you not find that?"

"But are you ever planning on seeing her again? Do you think you'll go back to France?"

"I cannot say. My life at the moment is all possibilities and no commitments. I like being in a position where every direction is, for the moment, open to me."

"But you know that can't last, don't you? Sooner or later, you will have to make some decisions. Won't your father expect you to go to work at some point?"

"Of course. That is why I am enjoying this moment as much as I can."

"I'm thinking that maybe it's time for me to go back to California."

"You can't. Aren't we having fun, just like I promised you when I found you in that little apartment in San Francisco? Why would you want to leave? My family loves having you around."

"I came to find Antonio, and I feel like I've just about exhausted all the possibilities. The search for the Muñoz family has turned out to be a wild goose chase. I'm waiting for more information from my friend in Mexico, but she hasn't written back yet, and I don't know if she will."

"And what will you do if you go back to California?"

"I'll get a job and save as much money as I can. Then, when I have enough, I will go to France and find Valérie."

I waited for his reaction, but he only smiled.

"So you have chosen her over me?"

"It's not like it's a competition. I'm in love with her, and while you may still have feelings for her, I think it's pretty clear you have moved on."

He laughed.

"You and I are different, *huevón*. If I spend the night with a woman, do you think I have chosen her over Valérie? They are different things."

"Yeah, you are definitely right about that, *huevón*. You and I are very different."

He was surprised but impressed. It was the first time I had thrown his favorite epithet back at him.

"You may think we are different, but we really aren't. In any event, it is not for us to choose which one gets Valérie. That is for her to decide, and I have no doubt that, in the end, she will choose you."

"Me? Why? She knows you a lot better. You and she were together. I know for a fact that she cares about you. Why would she choose me over you?"

"Why does a woman do anything? Who can know? In any event, my soul has already told me that you have replaced me in her heart, even if you do not know it, even if she herself does not know it. So, yes, I think I will have little choice but to, as you say, move on."

"I hope you're right. God, I hope you're right. Now I need to ask you for something."

"My permission? You do not need my permission to go to her."

"No, it's not that. I need to ask you for her address. I have to write her as soon as possible, but I don't have her address in Bordeaux. I forgot to get it from her before we separated in Deauville."

He laughed.

"So I hold your romantic future in my hands? You need me to get back to her. I like having this power over you."

"Please don't be a jerk."

"Don't worry. I am only teasing. Ask me again tomorrow, and I will give it to you."

Ángel went to another part of the bar, leaving me to drink my Escudo alone. He had found another young woman to chat up. After a while, the two of them left. As he walked out of the place, he subtly made the hand signal informing me I was on my own for the rest of the night.

I glanced at the clock above the bar. He had left a bit earlier than usual. I ordered another beer.

As I pondered our conversation and what it meant, I noticed a woman with short-cropped, coal-black hair at the other end of the bar. She seemed to want to draw my attention. She was about my age and quite attractive. Actually, I had found women in Chile generally quite attractive. With a finger she indicated that I should go over to her. She had not done it in a flirtatious way. It was more the way you would get a waiter's attention. Surely, it was intended for someone else, but her impatient look made clear I was the one she was waiting for.

Curious, I wandered over and sat on the stool next to her. She immediately interrogated me in Spanish.

«Gringo, how do you know Miguel Ángel Contreras?»

«We're friends.»

«Really? Since when?»

«Since last September. I'm sorry, but if you were hoping he would ask you out, he's already left.»

She laughed.

«If I was looking for a man, I could do much better than him. I think a gringo might be more my type.»

«I'm sure you're right. If only you knew where to find one.»

My words seemed to come from a stranger. I was a different person when speaking Spanish. I recalled what Antonio had said when I asked him what it was like to be bilingual. It was like having two different people living in your head, he said. I finally understood now what he meant. We continued our banter for a good long time.

«So you are the *norteamericano* who is staying with the Contreras family?»

«Yes, that would be me.»

«Do you know who Ángel's father is?»

«Yes, of course. I'm staying in his house.»

«I mean, do you really know who he is—what he does?»

She was aggressive with her questions. I wasn't sure how much I should say to someone I had only just met.

«I know generally. I'm not an expert on him.»

«Do you know he has blood on his hands?»

«All I know is that he is the father of one of my best friends and that he and his family have been extremely hospitable to me.»

«So you don't care that he is a murderer?»

«Are you saying that he himself has personally killed people?»

«He is morally responsible for their deaths. Every bit as much as if he had tortured them and shot them himself.»

The passion in her voice was arresting. Her eyes flashed with emotion. They were also extremely beautiful.

«Look,» I said, «I've been hearing different versions of what happened in this country for years. As an outsider, it is hard for me to know what is true and what isn't—especially when one person's story contradicts someone else's—but I'm willing to listen to you and to hear your version so that I'm better informed.»

She was disgusted.

«I do not have a 'version.' I am telling you what is true.»

«Okay, then tell me the truth. I want to hear it. Since I have been here, I've only been hearing one side. I'd like to hear yours.»

I extended my hand.

«I'm Dallas, by the way.»

«Vero.»

«Vero?»

«Yes. Vero, as in *verdad*,» she said, using the Spanish word for truth.

«Well, Vero, tell me the truth. I have as much time as you want to tell it to me.»

«You do?»

She looked up at the clock archly.

"Jesus!" I said. «I lost track of the time. *¡El toque de queda!* I need to get a taxi right away.»

«You won't get a taxi now. They have all stopped for the night.»

«But I have to get back. What am I supposed to do?»

«I don't know, Gringo. What *are* you going to do?»

I panicked.

«I don't know. Listen. I hear it's possible to rent a room for the night around here. Do you know of such a place?»

«Yes, of course. Do you want to take me to such a place?»

I thought I had misunderstood her.

«Please. If you could show me where such a place is, you would save my life. I've heard a person can get shot for being out too late.»

«No problem. I will save your life. Follow me.»

She calmly finished her drink, picked up her purse, and headed for the door. I chugged what was left of my beer and followed her. She led me down one dark, narrow street and then another. We came to the entrance of an apartment building. She pushed one of the buttons next to the door. After several seconds, a voice answered through the tinny speaker.

"*¿Sí?*"

"*Habitación,*" said Vero. "*Por favor.*"

Several minutes passed before a short, squat, old woman appeared at the door and let us in.

"*Catorce mil,*" said the woman, holding out her hand. "*Por favor.*"

Vero gave me a look. I reached into my pocket and counted out the money. I still had not gotten completely accustomed to the large amounts of pesos involved in every transaction. It took hundreds of pesos to make the equivalent of a few dollars.

The woman led us up a couple of flights of stairs. The elevator must not have been working. To my surprise, Vero came with us. The woman stopped in front of a door in the corridor and handed me the key.

With the slightest trace of a smile, she said, "*Pásenlo bien,*" and then left us.

I looked at my watch and said to Vero, «Thanks, but it's gone past two. What are *you* going to do?»

«What do you think, Gringo?»

«You're staying here too?»

«Of course. Didn't you invite me?»

I opened the door. It was a tiny, gloomy room with nothing in it but a small double bed, a nightstand with an ashtray and a small radio, and a sink. Behind a door was a toilet.

As I watched Vero surveying the accommodation, it dawned on me what should have been obvious from the beginning. She was a prostitute, albeit a politically engaged one.

«So how much are you going to cost?» I asked her.

«What do you mean?»

«If you are going to stay the night here with me, you probably expect to be paid something.»

She slapped me hard across my face.

"*¡Idiota! Yo no soy ninguna puta!*"

«Excuse me,» I said, rubbing the soreness on my cheek. «It's just that I'm confused. The culture is different here than what I'm used to.»

«Culture has nothing to do with it,» she said sternly. «There is well-educated and not well-educated.»

«So did you think I wanted to sleep with you?»

«I will tell you what I think.»

«Please.»

As she spoke, she became increasingly agitated.

«I think you are a bourgeois pig. I think you are a part of a system that exploits the Third World. I think you are a passive supporter of a capitalist system that presses its heel on the throat of the people.»

Her anger unnerved me.

«Okay, okay. You don't have to get so upset. I get your point.»

«Do you? Do you?»

She slapped me again across the face, harder than before.

«What are you going to do about it, you running dog capitalist?»

She had now made me angry.

«Hey, there's no reason to be hitting me!» I yelled at her. «We can talk like civilized people.»

She struck me again.

«Civilized? Do you want to know what your imperialism has done to the civilized world?»

«Stop it, will you? You're acting crazy!»

She pushed her face up against mine.

«You are an exploiter of the masses, you and your cursed Uncle Sam!»

She raised her hand to strike me again, but this time I grabbed her wrist and held it. As she struggled to free it, we toppled onto the bed. The more she tried to loosen my grip, the more my fingers clenched. As the fingernails of her other hand came at me, I grabbed that wrist too.

"What the hell is wrong with you?" I asked.

In a suddenly quieter voice, she said, «Call me a Marxist.»

«What?»

«I said, call me a Marxist.»

«Why?»

«Just do it.»

«Okay. You're a Marxist.»

«Say it like you mean it.»

She struggled to free one of her hands and managed to scratch my face.

«Say it like you really mean it!»

I completely lost my temper.

"You're a goddamn, fucking Marxist!" I yelled at her in English.

«Good. Now call me a Communist.»

«You're a goddamn, fucking Communist!»

«Regressive!»

«Radical!»

«Colonizer!»

«Terrorist!»

«Right-winger!»

We screamed at each other while continuing to wrestle around on the bed. She ripped my shirt. I tore her blouse. Before I knew it, we had completely pulled the clothes off each other. She had the muscles of an athlete. I tried to pin her between my naked legs, but in no time she had rolled over and squeezed the breath out of me with her knees against my ribcage.

«Fascist!»

«Revolutionary!»

«Exploiter of the masses!»

Her breath against my face was like a blast from a furnace. I thrust my mouth against hers and kissed her so hard on the lips that mine felt bruised. She drew blood by biting my lip.

«Running dog capitalist!»

"Fucking leftie!"

«Imperialist!»

"Goddamn pinko commie!"

She pulled my hair, and I pulled hers. She arched her back and slipped out of my grasp. The room was stuffy and warm. We were both now so sweaty that it was impossible for either of us to maintain a grip on the other. She rolled on top of me and glared at me with a stare that proclaimed her dominance. I thrust up at her. She clutched my shoulders. I grabbed her buttocks. Her panting overwhelmed my ears. The smell of her filled my nose. The feel of her skin was like touching an electric fence. My exhaustion gave way to exhilaration. The intensity of it overcame my brain. In one cataclysmic, giddy moment in which the entire universe seemed to pause in wonder, my entire life drained from my body and flooded my pelvis.

I lost consciousness.

# 10
# Toque de Queda

WHEN I FINALLY came to, I needed several moments to work out where I was and how I got there. Already awake, Vero sat with her shoulders against the headboard. The sight of her unnerved me because her posture reminded me uncannily of Ángel's mother.

The thought of Lucía caused me to worry about what might be going on in the Contreras house this morning. Not only had Ángel not come home the night before but neither had I. What had gone through Lucía and Lautaro's minds as they waited up for us in bed?

Vero retrieved a cigarette from a pack on the nightstand. She lit it and then saw my eyes were open. She took the cigarette from her mouth and handed it to me. I shook my head, but she stubbornly insisted. I took the coffin nail and had a long drag while she lit another for herself.

«So...» It was a struggle to form words, especially in Spanish. «What was that?»

«What was what?»

«You know. What were we doing? Was that some sort of game we were playing? Were we playing roles in some drama of yours?»

She took a deep drag and exhaled luxuriously.

«I think these occasions are generally better if one does not talk about them too much.»

«I guess I just want to know if we are friends, enemies or... I don't know. ¿Pololos?»

She laughed at my use of the Chilean word for boyfriend and girlfriend.

«You are surprisingly amusing, Gringo.»

«Listen. About what happened. You know, I did not expect or plan that.»

«Yes, that was obvious. North Americans do too much planning. I prefer to live in the moment. That was a good moment.»

She reached over and turned on the little radio that was on the nightstand. The voice of a man reading the news came out of its small speaker.

«I was serious about listening to you. About hearing a point of view that I do not get in the house where I am living. I would like to see you again, but because I want to talk to you, to listen to you.»

«Only talk?»

«Look, this happened at kind of a confusing time for me. I'm not sure what I am feeling, but even though you make me crazy, I like you. There's something about you.»

On the radio, the man had finished reading the news. Now a song was playing. It sounded terrible on such a cheap radio, but the melody was unmistakable.

«Something wrong? You look strange.»

«I know that song.»

«Everybody knows that song. It is a stupid, old Mexican song that everyone laughs at. Perhaps my grandmother might have liked it way back when she was young, but everyone my age thinks it is *fome*,» she said, using a Chilean slang word for something that was a real drag.

She looked at me with surprise.

«You like it, don't you? You like that old Mexican song.»

«It's just that I haven't heard it in a long time. The first time I heard it…»

«What? Were you with a Mexican girl? That makes sense. You know, when you speak Spanish, you sound like a Mexican.»

«Yeah? So? Until I came here, the only people I ever spoke Spanish with were Mexicans.»

«What was her name?»

«I'm not going to talk about it,» I said as I reached over and turned off the radio.

«You're quite romantic, aren't you? That's funny. If you want to see me again, I will be in the same place at the same time on

93

Friday night. I advise you, however, that you not tell Miguel Ángel that you are seeing me. He and his family would not approve.»

She crushed the butt of her cigarette in the ashtray and got out of the bed.

«And now I have somewhere I should be. *Hasta la próxima.*»

There was no bath or shower with the room, so she dressed and went out with a torn blouse and smelling like she'd just had sex.

My head fell back on the pillow. I could not make the words *bésame mucho* stop repeating in my brain. I was overcome with a profound sense of loss and regret that was as strong as it was unexpected. Soon I was asleep again.

When I woke, I got dressed and went out into the street. It was clogged with cars and the pungent odor of bus exhaust. People rushed on their way to work. I grabbed a taxi and went back to Las Condes.

Ángel had gotten back ahead of me. He was amazed at my behavior.

"*Huevón,* my mother freaked out last night. I had to make up a story about both of us staying over at my imaginary friend's house. Then I had to invent a story to explain why you did not arrive home with me this morning. *¿Qué pasó, hombre?*"

I smiled and said nothing. That drove him crazy.

"*Hombre, dime. ¿Qué pasó?* And what happened to your shirt?"

"I think I met your *gemela erótica.*"

His jaw dropped.

"*No lo creo.* So now it is you who has 'gotten over' Valérie."

"I don't know what's going on. It's confusing. I'm still trying to figure out what happened, and what it means."

"So tell me. What's her name? Who is she? I probably know her."

"I don't think so," I lied. "She's from out of town."

"From where?"

"Uh, I think she said Antofagasta."

I just pulled out a name I had seen on a map. Someplace as far as possible from Santiago.

"Antofagasta? Really? Antofagasta? Are you seeing her again?"

"I'm not sure. Maybe not."

Another lie. I had no reason to doubt Vero when she had said Ángel and his family would not approve.

I wondered how I would manage to meet her on Friday without Ángel seeing her. As it happened, Friday unexpectedly turned out to be a rare evening when Ángel did not want to go out. Lucía and Lautaro had invited some friends over for the evening, including their daughter who had been in school with Ángel. Curious, he decided to stay home so that he could see her. Nobody minded when I made my excuses and called a taxi to go out.

I hung around the bar for a good hour, waiting for her to show up. I had just about decided I had been stood up when she walked in the door.

«I thought you weren't going to come.»

We kissed on both cheeks.

«You gringos are too punctual. It's so boring.»

«What would you like to drink?»

«Pisco sour, please.»

I ordered two. I was getting to like them better, although I still wished I could get a frosty, cold margarita.

She said, «I did not think *you* would come.»

«Why?»

«I did not think you would have the courage. I thought perhaps you would have told Ángel you met me, and he would have convinced you it was a bad idea.»

«I choose my own friends.»

«So is that what you have decided we are? Friends?»

«I don't know what we are. You confuse me.»

As we talked, I could not take my eyes off her. I had found her attractive from the first moment I saw her. Looking at her now, knowing exactly how her skin felt, how her sweat smelled, I found her absolutely magnetic. Her deep, brown eyes were like a constant invitation. I was already familiar and comfortable with her various facial expressions.

«So, shall I continue your political education?»

«Is it safe to be talking about such things in such a public place?»

«This is the safest place. There is so much noise, nobody can hear anybody else.»

We sat for a couple of hours. Over two more rounds of pisco sours, she recounted her experiences as a member of the Socialist Party and the various projects on which she had worked for the Popular Unity government.

«And how are you able to live here now under this government when so many other people disappeared or had to leave the country?»

«Not every member of the Socialist or Communist parties was arrested or had to flee. Just the ones they saw most as threats. The prisons would not have had space for all of us. Besides, I may have had some connections that were in my favor.»

«What connections?»

She glanced at the clock.

«See the time? What are you going to do? If you were to leave now, you would have just enough time to get to Las Condes.»

«Or I could stay over again here in the city center.»

«Well, at least you know now where to get a room.»

«What about you?»

«What about me?»

«Do you want to…?»

«*Hombre.* Just say what you want. Maybe *gringas* think a man always asking for permission is attractive, but it isn't.»

«Can we spend the night together again?»

«Yes, of course. Let's go.»

We went to the same apartment building. It was a different room but identical to the other one.

«Can we do it my way this time?» I asked.

«What way is that?»

«Without the fighting and the name calling.»

«Gringo, this is going to be so boring.»

«I'll try not to make it boring.»

I caressed the back of her neck and kissed her softly on the cheek.

«Boring.»

Stung by her feedback, I became more aggressive. I kissed her on the mouth, exploring every recess with my tongue.

«Better,» she said when I had moved my tongue to her shoulder.

I removed her blouse carefully, mindful of the damage I had done to the other one, and began to explore her body with my fingers and tongue. I was encouraged by a soft gasp suggesting pleasure.

«Call me...»

"I'm not going to call you any of those political names."

«No, call me...»

"I said I'm not going to call you names this time. We're doing it my way."

My mouth traveled the length of her abdomen, my nose finally reaching the distinctive aroma below. In my excitement, I twirled her hair with my tongue.

She moaned with satisfaction and cooed, «Call me Miguel Ángel.»

My head jerked.

«What?»

«Call me Miguel Ángel.»

«Why?»

«Because that is who you really want.»

«What the hell are you talking about?»

«He is the one you want. I have seen the way you look at him.»

«You're crazy. Would I be here with you... like this... if I was interested in him? You don't know anything about the two of us.»

«You want me because I remind you of him.»

I studied her face, and it was true. There was in fact something about her that reminded me of Ángel. I had not been conscious of it before.

«Why do you have to keep playing mind games? Can't we just make love without you making everything weird?»

«I am not one of those people who does everything the way you are supposed to. I do not feel an obligation to be what other people think is normal. Is that too hard for you to accept?»

«Yeah, maybe it is.»

She stared into my eyes with a look that was unnervingly hypnotic.

«Kiss me.»

I pressed my mouth as hard as I could against hers. I ran my hands up and down her body, luxuriating in the radiating heat. My mind emptied, as she became my sole focus. The excitement grew until it consumed me.

She said it again. «Call me Miguel Ángel.»

I had no resistance, no identity of my own. The words coming from my mouth were hers, not mine.

"*¡Miguel Ángel!*" I shouted, as the pleasure coursed through my body. "*¡Miguel Ángel, yo te quiero!*"

"*Qué bueno,*" she murmured. "*Qué muy bueno.*"

"*¡Ángel, yo te adoro tanto! ¡Yo te deseo completamente!*"

In my body's subsequent collapse, I lay waiting for life to return to me. I could not comprehend what had just happened.

"Are we ever going to be able to do this," I panted in English, "without you totally messing with my mind?"

"*¿Cómo?*"

"*¿Por qué tienes esta obsesión con Ángel? ¿Estás tú enamorada de él? ¿Qué haces tú conmigo? Yo no te entiendo. No entiendo nada.*"

«It's just that I think that you are in love with him and that sleeping with me is the only way you can have him,» she said, as she laughed tauntingly.

Anger welled within my exhausted body.

«That makes no sense. Yes, he is my friend. Yes, I can even say I love him, but I love him like a brother. I would do anything for him. And yes, in some strange, weird way you do remind me of him, but it's you I am here with, not him. Why do you have to keep bringing him into it?»

She caressed my cheek.

«So I do remind you of him,» she said triumphantly. «Of course, I do. Everybody has always said that he and I are very much alike.»

«Who says that? Why would they say that?»

She laughed.

"*Idiota. ¿Aún no has cachado? Es mi hermano.*"

# 11
# Breakthrough

«YOUR BROTHER? He can't be. I've met the whole family. I've met all his...»

It dawned on me. I had never met Verónica, the older sister. The one who had already moved out on her own before the family went to Virginia. On *la Noche Buena*—Christmas Eve—I had briefly wondered why she had not come home to celebrate with the family and then promptly forgot about her.

«They never talk about you.»

«They don't? Well, that's not a surprise, is it? My father disowned me when I said I was going to join the Socialist Party. Unlike myself, he and my mother are quite happy to see other people oppressed.»

«Your mother does charity work for the poor.»

Vero laughed.

«You mean those society events where all the women have their hair styled and put on their most expensive clothes and sit around drinking tea and coffee and congratulating themselves for the good works they are doing? Don't make me laugh. Yes, they are happy to throw a few crumbs here and there, but they don't want to change the system in any meaningful way.»

«So, that's what this is about? You picked me up in a bar because it's your own weird way of getting back at your family?»

«Maybe, but not entirely. I liked the look of you, and you turned out to be more interesting than I thought you would be.»

She reached for her purse and pulled out two cigarettes.

I said, «I don't think I can see you again. This has gotten too complicated. Every time I think I've met someone, it turns out I'm just being used.»

«Hey, you got laid, didn't you?» she said, as she handed me my cigarette. «How are you being used?»

«Now that I think about it, I've always been used. It's my own fault, but it's true. My first time was with a girl in Mexico. I thought we were in love, but looking back on it now, I think I was just a convenient way for her to lose her virginity. Then I slept with the girl I was in love with all through high school, though I knew she was just getting back at her jerk husband. Then I was with a woman in San Francisco, but she just wanted someone because her husband was a closet case who never paid her any attention. Now you're just using me in some game with your family.»

«Poor boy. Well, at least it sounds like you had a good time all those times you were being used.»

«The only one who didn't use me was Valérie. She actually liked me for myself. I know she did. It was different with her than with anybody else. She actually did her best to not get involved because she didn't want to hurt me—or to hurt Ángel. I really loved her. I spent a whole night sleeping in the same bed with her, holding her, but we never made love—though I wanted to. She's the one. She's definitely the one. I should be on my way back to her right now instead of getting distracted by you. What the hell is wrong with me?»

«You and Ángel shared a woman? You are only proving my theory.»

«Look. It's been nice knowing you, and I've mostly had a good time with you, but in the morning I'm going to leave here and start making arrangements to go home to California. Then, once I have saved enough money, I'm heading to France.»

«I'm actually kind of sorry. The more I know you, the more I like you. Tell me something. How did you and Ángel meet? How did you wind up sharing a woman?»

«It's kind of a complicated story.»

«We cannot leave here for several more hours.»

«I met Valérie in Deauville. She told me she had a boyfriend in Bordeaux. When she mentioned he was from Chile and what his age was, and that his name was Miguel, I got the crazy idea that he might actually be my friend Antonio. In fact, I got so obsessed with the idea that I went to Bordeaux to meet him, and of course, he wasn't Antonio, but we wound up becoming friends—in spite of everything. I know, it's kind of a crazy story.»

«I'm confused. Was your friend's name Miguel or Antonio?»

«Antonio, but he used the name Miguel to get a passport. He went to Chile from Mexico with two other guys. That was during the Popular Unity government. They wanted to experience the 'socialist paradise.'»

«He was Ángel's age?»

«Yeah.»

«Three Mexicans? One of them the same age as Ángel?»

«That's right.»

«Was his older brother called Daniel?»

I sat up with a start.

«Yes, he was.»

«And the other one, a cousin, I think, Gustavo?»

«Yeah, yeah, that's them. You knew them?»

«Not well, but I do remember them. Yes, Miguelito was quite cute. Very bright. I liked him. He smiled all the time, and he was always telling jokes. His teeth would stick out like a donkey's when he laughed. The other two were kind of boring.»

«Do you know what happened to Miguel?»

«Let me think. I believe I heard the other two left the country shortly before the *golpe.*»

«That's right. What about Miguel?»

«It seems to me that, by that time, Miguelito had been living with Vicente and Maite Muñoz in Barrio Brasil.»

I kissed her enthusiastically on the lips.

«You're amazing. Thank you so much. Do you know if those people still live there?»

«Oh no, the DINA would definitely have been looking for them. I think I heard someone say they had been arrested, but then I think I also heard that they had gone to Argentina.»

«Can you find out? Is there someone you can ask?»

«Yes, I can ask around.»

«Tell me something.»

«Yes.»

«Something just occurred to me. A few months ago in East Berlin, I met a Chilean woman whose name was Muñoz. Could this be connected to her?»

«What woman?»

«Her name was Paulina Muñoz Rojas. I don't know if I'm supposed to tell you this, but as a favor to Ángel I delivered a letter to her from your mother.»

«Paulina? You saw dear Paulina? My God, how was she?»

I had actually found her quite sad and bitter, but I did not want to say that.

«She is well. She was very hospitable to me. She gave me coffee and cookies.»

«I miss Paulina so much. I wish I could see her. You surprise me, Gringo. You are not what you seemed at first. To answer your question, however, Paulina would not be related to Vicente and Maite. In this country, Muñoz...»

«Yes, I know, it is a very common name.»

«I am glad because this means that you and I will see each other again after all. Am I correct? Does this mean you will not leave Chile immediately?»

«If there's any chance at all that I might find Antonio, I am going to have to stay. I can't tell you how happy I am to get this information. How can I thank you?»

«You could make love to me again.»

«Really? I'd feel like I was cheating on Valérie.»

«Did you feel like you were cheating on her the other times?»

«I wasn't thinking clearly.»

She began rubbing my thigh.

«Then don't think clearly now.»

«If we do it again...»

«Yes?»

She entwined her legs around mine.

«Can we do it without playing any of your weird games?»

«No.»

She massaged my left nipple with her finger.

«And what weird game would you make me play this time?»

«When you are giving it to me…»

«Yes?»

«When you are giving it to me with all your strength and your passion…»

«Yes?»

«I want you to call me Antonio.»

«That's not going to happen.»

Her hand was finding its way into places where my preferences were largely irrelevant.

«Tell me something, Vero.»

«Yes, Gringo?»

«Did you actually find me attractive?»

«Yes, of course. That is a stupid question.»

«Not just because I was your brother's friend?»

«Not only that.»

«What else?»

«As I said, I liked the look of you.»

«Really?»

«Yes. In a funny way, you remind me of my husband.»

«Your what?»

«You both have an adorable look. The look of an innocent lost in frightening world.»

«You're married?»

«Only technically.»

«You can't be married.»

«It's not a big deal.»

«No, you don't understand. You can't be married.»

«There it is. That is the look I was talking about. Like an animal frozen in the headlights of a car.»

«Listen to me. I swore to myself and to God that I would never again get involved with a married woman. I have had too many bad experiences. This can't be happening.»

«Calm down. It's not a real marriage. I mean, it is legal and everything, but it was what you would call a marriage of convenience. It did not mean anything.»

«So you and he weren't lovers?»

«Oh, we were lovers all right. Definitely lovers. In fact, incredible lovers. But the marriage wasn't real. It was only to help him. To help his situation.»

«That's all I need. Another jealous husband out looking for me.»

«I promise you, he will not be jealous, and he is not in the country.»

«Where is he?»

«He is in Cuba. He is working on projects for the government there. He had to leave Chile after the *golpe*. He can't come back. He would be arrested immediately if he tried to enter the country.»

«I think I am going to be sick.»

«You are definitely not a *chileno*.»

«When do you think you will have some information for me about the Muñozes?»

«I should know something within a couple of days. When and where do you want to meet?»

«Maybe we should meet in the daytime. In a public place.»

«You are no longer fun,» she pouted, as she fingered my belly button.

A few hours later, when I arrived back in Las Condes, Ángel, Mati, Camila, and Bati were having their *desayuno.* Ángel greeted me with a wide grin.

"How was your night out?" he asked suggestively. "At least this time your shirt is intact. I think Esperanza has finished mending your other one."

I wondered if, when we were alone, I should tell him that I had been sleeping with his sister. I decided against it—but only for the time being. I still regretted having deceived him when we first met, and I wanted to be nothing but honest with him.

Later in the day, Ángel received a postcard in the mail. As he read it, a strange look came over his face.

"Who is it from?" I asked.

He looked at me with wide eyes.

"It's from Janet. Do you remember me telling you about Janet?"

"Yeah, your girlfriend in Virginia. What's she say?"

"She sent this from Cuzco in Peru. She finished college last year, and now she's traveling around South America."

A smile came over his face.

"She will be in Santiago next week."

"So she hasn't forgotten you."

The giddiness in his smile was unusual for him.

"I cannot wait to see her."

From that point on, it was hard to talk to him about anything other than his anticipation at seeing Janet again.

On the day of my appointed rendezvous with Vero, I tried to make an excuse to go to the city center on my own, but Ángel insisted on going along. Rather than try to hide my secret from him any longer, I figured this was probably the time to be honest with him.

"There is something I need to tell you," I said, as we rode in the taxi.

"Yes?"

"I have met your sister Verónica."

"You have? Where? How?"

"It's a long story."

He looked at his watch.

"We have time."

"The thing is, she knew Antonio."

"She did? Really?"

"Yeah, she remembered him and the two guys he came to Chile with. She knew the family he was living with when the *golpe* happened."

"That's amazing news. How did you say you met my sister?"

"I am going to meet her now to get the details about the Muñoz family. Isn't that great? I'm finally getting close to discovering what happened to Antonio."

"Yes, it's like a miracle. So you became acquainted with Vero how…?"

"She must have seen me talking to you somewhere. She approached me and introduced herself."

He was suspicious.

"And that's it?"

"More or less."

"Somehow I think, less."

When we walked into the café, she was seated at a table. The expression on her face was controlled, but I saw a flicker of surprise and annoyance. Forewarned, Ángel simply bore into her with his eyes, as we took our seats.

"*Tanto tiempo, hermano,*" she said curtly.

"*Sí. Todos te extrañamos mucho por la Pascua.*"

«The gringo said none of you even mentioned me.»

I felt invisible, watching them converse. I studied one and then the other, cataloguing their similarities and differences. Something was almost identical in the way their lips moved.

«Are you surprised? You broke our parents' hearts.»

«They broke mine.»

«What did you think was going to happen? It was a war. What choice did Papi have? Everyone was divided into two sides. What was he supposed to do?»

«It was a legally and constitutionally elected government.»

«A government that ignored decrees from the Supreme Court and raised its own private army.»

«It was finally going to do something for the poor.»

«It was turning the country over to its masters in Moscow and Havana.»

They began to raise their voices.

«Now we have a Fascist dictatorship!»

«Instead of a Communist one!»

People sitting near us looked uncomfortable. As for me, I was becoming, strangely and unexpectedly, aroused.

Ángel calmed himself and laid his hand on top of his sister's.

«Look. Let's not talk about politics. I was not meant to be here. It is the gringo who came to see you.»

«I'm glad you came, Ángel. I've missed you.»

«Yes, I've missed you too. Did the gringo tell you he saw Paulina?»

*You know, the gringo has a name,* I thought.

«Yes, he did. Isn't that amazing?»

Ángel looked at me warily.

«Yes, it is. It seems you two have gotten to know each other quite well.»

«He said he carried a letter that you had brought from Mami for Paulina. That was kind of you, *hermano.*»

He shrugged.

«Mami and Paulina were friends. It had nothing to do with politics.»

She put her hand on top of his.

«You and I should have nothing to do with politics either. We're brother and sister after all.»

«I don't think you are capable of leaving politics to one side.»

«You are right. It is difficult for me, but I will try.»

«Me too. I don't think Papi will talk to you, though, or Mati or Camila.»

«Let's just start with the two of us, and see how that goes. *¿De acuerdo?*»

*"De acuerdo."*

«It's great that the two of you are talking,» I said, «but I was wondering, Vero, what information you have for me?»

«Yes, I had forgotten why we were here.»

She handed me a piece of paper.

«I spoke with someone, and he assures me that Vicente and Maite and their children—presumably including Miguelito—did indeed go to Argentina. I have no more information beyond that, but I can give you the name and address of a woman in Mendoza, who helped many Chileans after they left the country by way of the Uspallata Pass. If you can find her, perhaps she will remember them and be able to tell you something about what their plans were or where they went after that.»

I stared at the paper and the lines scrawled on it. To my surprise, my eyes began to tear up. At last I had something concrete that suggested Antonio was still alive. For years I had feared that he was dead, that his body lay somewhere anonymously in some unmarked mass grave. Now I had a realistic hope he was somewhere out in the world.

«Verónica, I cannot tell you how much this means to me.»

She moved her hand from Ángel's to mine and looked at me with a kindness I had not seen in her before.

«Yes, I can see that it does.»

For most of the taxi ride back to Las Condes, Ángel remained silent. Then he spoke.

"I told you to stay away from my sister."

"You were talking about the other one. The nineteen-year-old."

"You should have understood I meant both of my sisters."

"Vero hardly needs your protection. She's older than you. She's my age."

"I don't like thinking about you and her together."

If he only knew the half of it.

"You don't need to worry. I probably won't be seeing her again. Anyway, I've made a firm decision."

"What's that?"

"As soon as I find Antonio—or else hit a dead end—I am going to leave. I'm going back to France to see Valérie. She's the one I'm meant to be with. I'm sure of it."

"For what it is worth, you have my blessing."

"I do?"

"Yes. I think I told you I expect the two of you to be together in the end."

"And you're okay with that?"

"Yes. Right now I am only looking forward to once again being with Janet."

# 12
# Janet

AS SOON AS WE got back to the house, I sat down and wrote a long letter to Valérie. I wished I could write it in French. Too bad she didn't speak Spanish instead of French because I could have managed a decent enough letter in Spanish. I did throw in a few French words when I knew them to at least show I had made an effort.

I told her I was in Chile to look for Antonio, but I was deliberately vague about the details. I didn't want to spend a lot of time writing about Ángel and his family—especially Vero. I told her how much I missed her and thought about her. I told her I was definitely going back to France to see her. I wrote that I hoped her visit to Brittany with Logan had gone well. I said I hoped that her father was doing better and that she was okay.

As much as I wanted to ask her to write me back, I didn't. Since I didn't know exactly where I would be for the foreseeable future, I just told her that she needn't worry about answering and that I would be writing her again soon. The silver lining was that I wouldn't be disappointed when I didn't hear back from her.

Finally, the day of Janet's expected arrival came. All we knew from her postcard was that she would be traveling by bus from Antofagasta. Ángel insisted on spending most of the day at the central bus station, watching the arrival of every single bus from the north. Four buses were scheduled to arrive from Antofagasta that day.

"It is a long journey," he said. "She will have been on the bus all night. She will be exhausted when she arrives."

"You know," I said, "she has your address. She was no doubt planning to get a bus or a taxi to your house. Why didn't you just wait for her at home?"

"I want to surprise her. I want the first thing she sees when she descends from the bus to be me."

"Man, you've got it bad. If you were this hung up on her, why didn't you do something about it a long time ago? Why wait all these years for her to just show up?"

The question annoyed him.

"And why are you not in France?"

I shut up.

Throughout the day, we drank many cups of coffee, lunched on greasy empanadas, and solved all the problems of the world with our continuous, meandering conversations. I suspected that the entire day might turn out to be a waste of time. After all, people's plans can change for all kinds of reasons.

Finally, in the middle of the afternoon, another bus from Antofagasta arrived. As the passengers filed off, I knew immediately which one was her. She was tall and solidly built with a mass of orange-colored curls on her head. Her eyes were a striking shade of green, her face was sprinkled with faint freckles. Her shirt was tied in a knot in front of her waist, and her khaki shorts covered little of her thighs. Wearing a large backpack, she had the unmistakable confidence of a young North American tourist as she stepped to the ground.

Ángel's face lit up. So did hers.

"Mike!" she screamed. "Is that you?"

"Mike?" I wondered aloud.

"It's an old joke. She just said that because everyone in high school called me that. Except her. She always called me Miguel."

By the time he finished explaining, she had rushed over and thrown her arms around him. They both beamed.

"Miguel, I can't believe I'm actually here."

Her voice had the faintest trace of a Southern drawl. The sound of it made me strangely homesick.

"I've been having the best time traveling all over South America. I've been to Ecuador and Peru and Bolivia and now here. This is such a beautiful country. The Atacama Desert was so impressive. I've never seen anyplace so dry in my life. How are you? You look great. It's so good to see you."

"Janet, this is my good friend, Dallas Green. Another North American."

She shook my hand energetically.

"You're from the States? Nice to meet you." Turning back to Ángel she said, "You know what the first thing I did was when I touched the ground in the Southern Hemisphere? I found a restroom and went in and flushed the toilet."

"Why did you do that?" asked Ángel.

"To see if it was true that water drains in a different direction in the Southern Hemisphere."

"And does it?"

"I don't know," she laughed. "I couldn't remember which way it drains in the Northern Hemisphere!"

A young man standing behind her quietly cleared his throat.

"Oh my God. Where are my manners? Miguel, Dallas, this is Donal."

I had paid no attention to him. He was a tall, unassuming guy wearing small, round glasses. He had long, wispy, light-brown hair and a droopy mustache. He politely shook my hand and said, "Pleasure." He sounded English.

"Nice to meet you, Donald."

"Donal," he corrected matter-of-factly. "No D on the end."

Only someone who knew Ángel as well as I did would have caught the trace of disappointment crossing his face for a scant moment.

"Welcome to Chile, Donal," he said graciously. "You are very welcome. You have arrived in time for *once,* for tea. I'll get us a taxi."

"Is it far?" asked Janet.

"It's about half an hour by auto," he said.

"Donal and I have booked a room at a hotel here in the city. We should probably check in first."

"Definitely not," said Ángel. "You are staying with us. It is all arranged. My family is expecting you."

"Very kind of you," said Donal, "but I doubt you bargained for the pair of us. We'd hate to impose."

"*No seas tonto,*" said Ángel. "*Ustedes tienen su casa acá. Yo insisto.*"

"Sorry, mate, I'm still working on picking up the lingo."

"He's insisting we stay with them," said Janet. "Did I tell you, Miguel, that I got my bachelor's degree in Spanish? I've really improved my fluency since I've been on this trip."

Inevitably, the two of them gave in to Ángel's insistent offer of hospitality. Because he had the longest legs, Donal sat next to the taxi driver, which meant the rest of us were crammed in the back seat. Ángel positioned himself in the middle, so he could lean over Janet as he pointed out various landmarks during the drive. Occasionally, I caught him staring bitterly at the back of Donal's head. Though Ángel behaved like a perfect host, because we were pushed against each other, I could feel the tension in his body. He clearly wished Donal would disappear.

"I can't wait to see your family again," said Janet enthusiastically. "Little Camila and Sebastián must be all grown up now, and I can't wait to meet your other brother and sister. This is so cool!"

When we got to Las Condes, I experienced something like *déjà vu.* It had not been long since I was the one receiving the warm and polite greeting from Lucía. Now the new gringos were the objects of Mati, Camila, and Bati's fascination. In fact, their interest in Janet and Donal was greater since they already knew her and wanted to catch up with news of her family and her life since high school.

Sitting at the table for the *once,* we learned through Lucía and Lautaro's polite but methodical questioning that Donal was from Liverpool, England, specifically a district called Vauxhall. That made sense because the sing-song quality of his speech reminded me of the way the Beatles spoke.

Everyone was confused by his name.

"Is it not Donald? Like McDonald's?" asked Bati.

"No," said the soft-spoken visitor. "It is Donal without the second D. It is actually an anglicization of the Irish name Domhnall."

"Oh, so you are Irish," said Mati.

"I'm from England," said Donal. "My grandparents were Irish."

"Cool," I said. "I'm part Irish. My mother always talks about her great-grandmother from County Cork. I'd like to go to Ireland someday."

Ángel glared at me. Apparently, I was being too friendly.

"How did you and Janet meet?" asked Camila abruptly, unable to hide her curiosity.

Ángel rolled his eyes.

"Well, where to begin?" said Donal. "Actually quite funny, as it happens."

Before he could get any further, Bati changed the subject to the Beatles, wondering if Donal had ever heard them play live. He replied that he never had, as he was only twelve years old when they broke up. He had, however, been a number of times to the Cavern Club on Mathew Street where they had played. The Beatles questions kept coming until he eventually made it clear that he was not an expert on the Fab Four.

"I don't listen to their music all that much," he confessed. "It's not really my style of music. I'm actually keener on Led Zeppelin. If I'm being honest, I was much more affected by John Bonham's death than by John Lennon's. Quite a coincidence the two of them died only four days apart. I grant you, Bonham's demise wasn't the tragedy that Lennon's murder was, but it meant the immediate end of Zeppelin—just as they were about to begin an American tour."

His insights into British music were fascinating, but out of loyalty to Ángel, I was careful not to appear too interested in what he had to say or to be too friendly to him. As I deliberately stayed quiet, my mind wandered.

I thought about how long I had been living with the Contreras family, how gracious they had been to me, how they had made me feel as if I were one of them. They were sincere in not wanting me to leave. As much as I was enjoying this extremely hospitable aspect of Chilean culture, I knew my parents would be mortified that I had let these people lodge and feed me for so long. My father would not understand how, at my age, I could go so long without having a job.

As I reflected on it, I couldn't understand it either. I needed to get on with my own life. I needed to figure out what I wanted to do for a living, where I wanted to live, and all the other things that normal adults do. Living off Ángel and his family was too damn easy, but it was not sustainable. It was time to grow up.

Did I want a family of my own? I had always assumed I would have one someday, just as my father had. But with whom? When I asked myself that question, the only face I could see belonged to a woman in France, and that was crazy. For one thing, I did not know her that well. For another, there was a language barrier between us. Why could I not get her out of my mind? I traveled back in time mentally, searching for clues in my memories. I revisited the last time I had seen her.

Ever since that day in Deauville, those moments had played over and over in my head.

"We will not say *adieu*. We will say *au revoir*."

She had made a point of not saying farewell but of saying until the next time. She called me "*Dallas, mon amour*" and said something in French. I wished with all my heart I could remember exactly what those words had been, and what they had meant. My sense was that she had said she truly loved me though she did not know what the future held.

I recalled the last time I had looked into her eyes. Maybe I had seen only what I had wanted to see, but I had had absolutely no doubt she felt exactly the same as I did.

In my own private world, while the others conversed, I finalized my plan for getting my life back on track. I would go back to my own country. I would get a job. I would save money until I could afford to go to France. Once there, I would convince Valérie we should make a life together. It could be in France. It could be in California. It didn't matter to me. All that mattered was that she and I would be together.

Ángel's glaring stare pulled me out of my thoughts. Clearly, he needed me to actively share his less-than-impressed attitude toward the Englishman. The music discussion had advanced to the point where Janet was now saying how much she liked Sheena Easton.

"I think she has a great voice. She's English, isn't she?"

"Scottish," said Donal.

The *sobremesa* continued a good long while and ended only when Lucía made the practical suggestion that the visitors might want to get settled in their rooms. Some reshuffling had been required to accommodate the newcomers. It was hard to miss the satisfaction on Ángel's face when his mother told Janet she would be sharing Camila's room, and that Donal would share Mati's. A good Catholic family like the Contrerases would never consider letting an unmarried couple share a bed under their roof.

Ángel dragged me into our room. He closed the door and lowered his voice.

"What do you think of the English guy?"

I shrugged.

"He seems okay. It's cool he knows so much about what's going on with British music."

Wrong answer.

"Do you think they are together?"

"Well, they are traveling all over South America together. That seems pretty together to me."

"I think maybe they are just friends."

"Well, they must be pretty good friends to be spending all these weeks together in such close quarters."

"You need to find out more about that *ahueonao*."

"Me? Why?"

"Because you will understand him. You and he speak the same language. I will tell Mati you are trading beds with him. You will get to know this Donal by sharing a room. You can talk to him late into the night, you know, like you do with me."

"I have to sleep in Mati's room?"

"Yes. Only for a few nights."

"And what am I supposed to be finding out exactly?"

"Just learn everything you can about him. Find out how long he has known Janet. Find out if there is something serious between them. You need to be James Bond for me."

"You don't ask much."

"*Mira,* you owe me a favor. I gave you my blessing with Valérie, and I did not murder you for sleeping with my sister. You owe me a lot."

"Okay, okay. I guess it's finally time for me to start paying my rent."

It was already late in the evening, but the visiting continued for a few more hours. Lautaro had arrived home late, and always the good host, he offered drinks to everyone, introducing the visitors to the wonders of pisco and aguardiente. Janet was obliged to repeat her update of her family for him, and she also recounted again her four years in the Romance Languages department of Ohio State University. When she asked Ángel some questions about his time in Bordeaux, Donal found it impossible to stifle a yawn.

"I must apologize," he said. "I'm absolutely knackered. I think it's time for me to kip down for the night."

Ángel shot me a look. As Donal stood, I did as well.

"Yeah, I think I'll hit the hay too."

We said our good night to everyone, and Donal looked at me curiously as I followed him to Mati's room.

"Sorry, are you sleeping in here as well?"

"Yeah, Mati and I swapped. I guess he thought you might want to share with a fellow English-speaker."

"To be honest, I haven't picked up the language as quick as I thought I might. I regret now not going for Spanish instead of French when I sat my A Levels."

"So you know French?"

"Better than I know Spanish at any rate," he said, wasting no time slipping out of his jeans and putting his glasses on the night table. "I also took a French course at uni. I have to say, your Spanish seems quite good."

"Yeah, I took it in high school, but I didn't learn much then. I picked up a bit when I went to Mexico for a summer, and then I took it in college. Most of what I know, though, I've learned since living here with Ángel and his family."

He was already in bed. I quickly followed suit.

"Perhaps I should have you tutor me," he said.

"You know, that's not a half-bad idea. Especially if, in exchange, you could teach me French. I picked up a few words when I was in France, but I need to learn it a lot better."

"Any particular reason?"

"Well, you see, there's this woman…"

"Ah, yes," he smiled. "*Cherchez la femme.*"

"Look for the woman, right?"

"Spot on. Sounds like you've got a solid start there, mate."

"I suppose things would be simpler if I just found an American girlfriend or, for that matter, any woman who speaks English. At least you and Janet speak the same language."

"Yes, in theory, though we do misunderstand one another badly at times. I believe it was George Bernard Shaw who said the U.S. and Great Britain are two countries separated by a common language."

"That's a good one. So, how long have you and Janet been together anyway?"

"Sorry, mate, don't mean to be rude." His voice trailed off. "Afraid I'm losing the battle to keep my eyes open."

"That's cool, but I'm going to hold you to those French lessons."

There was no further response.

Ángel would be disappointed by his initial intelligence report from James Bond.

# 13
# Over the Andes

ÁNGEL WAS INDEED unhappy the next morning about getting no additional information about Donal—other than learning he had studied some French.

"I'm going to help him with his Spanish, and he's going to help with my French," I said, probably a bit too enthusiastically, as we had our bread and coffee.

Exhausted from their journey, Janet and Donal were still asleep.

"If you want French lessons," he grumbled, "you could ask me. After all, didn't I study at a French university?"

"Yeah, but that would be weird."

"Because the only reason for your interest in the French tongue is to seduce my French *polola*?"

"*Expolola,* but yes, that is why it would be weird. And also because you are calling it the French *tongue*. So what's the plan for today?"

"When they finally wake up, I suppose we will give them the customary tour of Santiago, you know, as I did for you when you first arrived. I don't suppose we could get away with you giving a separate tour to Donald."

"Donal. And no, that would be strange and rude. Look, I know it's a big deal for you that Janet is here, and that's all you can think about, but I need to do something important, and I don't think I can do it without your help."

"What is that?"

"When you and I saw Vero, she gave me a piece of paper with the name and address of a woman in Mendoza. She may be able to tell me something about what happened to Antonio. I need to see her. How far is it to Mendoza?"

"It's on the other side of the mountains. The journey takes an entire day by bus. Sometimes the queue is long at the border, although maybe the new tunnel has improved things. In any event, it would be better to wait until the situation with Janet becomes clearer."

"When will that be?"

"How should I know? Perhaps if James Bond were providing me with better intelligence, I could plan better."

"Do you know how long the two of them are planning to stay?"

"She did not say, but I will do anything I can to make it a long visit."

"Yeah, I know how Chilean visits go. Frankly, I don't think I can afford to wait for your love life to get 'clearer.' I need to go as soon as possible. I'll go by myself if I have to."

"What's your hurry? You've waited years to find him. What's a few more days or weeks now?"

"What about your promise to help me find him? This was going to be your way of helping make up for all the awful things that happened in your country, the things your father was a part of. Remember?"

His eyes flashed with anger.

"My father was only doing his job. Whatever happened, he was not involved in the dirty part of it. He couldn't be. You know him now. Do you think he is capable of that? Hasn't he been helping you with your search? You can't blame an entire country for what only some of its people did. You sound like Vero when you talk like that."

"He must have known what was going on. He could have said something. He could have protested."

"It is so easy to judge when it's not your country."

We were getting perilously close to repeating the argument we had had in Berlin the previous year and which almost ended our friendship forever.

"Look, I don't mean to keep going over the past. All I care about is finding Antonio. It's important to me, and I don't want to wait any longer. If you can't go with me, then I'll just go to Mendoza by myself."

"That is your choice."

The two of us, each disappointed in the other, sulked in silence while finishing our *desayuno*. After a few minutes, Ángel's face broke out in a devilish grin.

"*Espera.* This is perfect. Of course."

"What?"

"You don't need me to go to Mendoza with you."

"It would be a heck of a lot easier if you did."

"Your Spanish is fine. You'd manage okay. You just need someone with you for moral support, to be with you in case you get into any trouble."

"Trouble? What kind of trouble?"

"You know. Trouble. We are talking about Argentina after all."

"So what's your point?"

"You are going to ask your new best friend Donal to go with you to Mendoza."

"Why would I do that?"

"Because he is your new best friend."

"And why would he want to do that? Do you think he'd just happily leave his girlfriend here with you while I drag him off across the Andes with me?"

"She's not his girlfriend."

"*Estás loco, hombre.*"

"*Huevón,* you owe this to me."

"Look, I'll ask him. He's going to think it's damn weird, but I'll ask him. Just don't be too surprised when he looks at me like I'm crazy and says no."

"Just make it sound as though it will be a lot of fun. Make him think you really want him to go with you."

It was after dinner before we finally got around to the tour of Santiago. Janet had done her research thoroughly beforehand and knew exactly what she wanted to see. Top of her list was the Museo Nacional de Bellas Artes in the Parque Forestal. After a couple of hours lingering over the large collection of paintings, we had coffee in the museum café. Ángel wasted no time in pushing his agenda.

"Dallas," he said nonchalantly, "tell us about your upcoming visit to Mendoza."

My cheeks burned.

"The main reason I came to Chile," I explained to the visitors, "was to find a friend of mine, who was living here in 1973."

"He was here during the coup?" gasped Janet.

"Yeah. I never heard anything from him again after that, and I've been worried about him ever since. Thanks to new information I got from…"

I felt Ángel's hard stare.

"…someone I met, I now know he left with a family for Mendoza, just over the Argentine border. I have the name and address of someone who might have known him, so I'm going to check it out."

"I hear Mendoza is beautiful this time of year," smiled Ángel. "The sky is the most dramatic shade of blue, and they produce a lot of wine—some say almost as good as Chilean wine. The vineyards are supposed to be lovely, and I believe the annual wine festival will be held soon."

"Yeah," I said, "well, I'm not going for sightseeing. I'm just trying to find my friend."

"Still, the vineyards are worth touring, and the eastern face of the Andes makes quite a dramatic backdrop. Definitely worth seeing."

"Are you going as well?" Donal asked Ángel.

"No, unfortunately, I can't" he replied, gazing a bit too obviously at Janet.

His stare told me I was not finished talking.

"Uh."

I struggled not to sound totally awkward.

"So, uh, Donal, would you be interested in going? It would just be for a couple of days. Then we'd come right back."

He said to Janet, "What do you think? Sounds as though it could be a rather good time."

"That sounds like a great idea!" she said. "You and Dallas should go."

"I say, you mean the three of us, eh?" said Donal, looking a bit confused.

"No, you should go to keep Dallas company, and that will give Miguel and me a chance to catch up with each other. We have a lot of time to make up for."

Donal was crestfallen, and I felt sorry for him. I had honestly not expected it to work out like this. I tried to cheer him up.

"Like I said, it should only take a couple of days, maybe three. One day to get there, one day to do what I need to, and then another day to come home. We'd be back in Santiago before you know it."

"Of course," said Ángel slyly, "once there, you may find that one day in the city is not enough. You might want to stay longer, you know, to explore the rest of the province. No reason to hurry back."

"Are you certain?" Donal asked Janet in a plaintive voice.

"Yes, it sounds like a wonderful idea. You can tell me all about it when you get back."

I was astounded that Ángel's ploy had worked so easily. He sipped his coffee like the cat that got the cream.

"We can go to the bus station now, so you can buy your tickets," he said. "You could go as soon as tomorrow."

"Right. So. Very well then," said Donal with more politeness than enthusiasm.

When I got a chance to talk to Ángel alone, I made one last plea.

"I wish *you* would come with me. I'd feel a lot better having you with me instead of him. I totally rely on you for everything."

"Did you see how quick she was to send the *inglés* away with you? I think she wants to be rid of him almost as much as I do. This is looking very good."

"Did you even hear what I said?"

"Yes, yes, you are going to miss me. Like you said, you won't be gone long. You will be back before you know it. Maybe you will bring this Antonio with you, and I will finally get to meet him."

Donal and I got tickets for a bus departing early the next morning. We decided to defy the Chilean habit of staying up all hours and go to bed early.

Before I went to bed, Lautaro invited me for a chat in his den. He poured two glasses of aguardiente and handed one to me.

«I understand you are going to Mendoza tomorrow.»

«That's right. Is there anything I should know before I go?»

«Just have your passport ready when you get to the border. Be polite to the guards and answer all their questions. Above all, be patient. You will be fine.»

«I have the name and address of someone who might know something about my friend Antonio.»

«Did you get that from my daughter Verónica?»

I wondered how he knew. I was pretty sure Ángel had not told him, so I also wondered how much he knew about me and Vero.

«Yes, sir.»

He paused a few moments before asking, «How is she?»

«She seems to be fine. I don't know that much about what she is up to. We… I… you see…»

«This is a small country. I do not need you to report her activities. I just wondered if she is… happy.»

«I think so. As far as I could tell anyway.»

He smiled a bit ruefully.

«It is difficult for parents sometimes to accept that their children have their own lives—and not always the lives we would have chosen for them. Did she try to turn you against her family?»

«I can make up my own mind about what I think of people. You and señora Contreras have been hospitable to me.»

He waved his hand and shook his head, embarrassed to be thanked.

«I think it is normal, when we are young, to be idealistic. People who are the age of you and Ángel like to see the world in black and white.»

Did he not realize I was four years older than Ángel? People always assumed the two of us were the same age.

He continued, «Groups with political motives often take advantage of idealistic young people and their good intentions. These political operatives can be quite... seductive.»

Seductive. That was a good word for it all right.

«Well,» I said, «sometimes there *are* things that are clearly good and other things that are clearly bad.»

He smiled.

«You are no doubt right, *joven,* and yet sometimes life is a paradox. Sometimes you have to tolerate a bad thing to prevent an even worse thing. *¿Me entiendes?*»

«Yeah, I think so. It's just that...»

«Yes?»

«Well, I'm just doing my best to live my life so I don't have to make choices like that. I know I haven't always done the right thing, but I keep trying not to let that stop me from doing the right thing now and in the future.»

«And I hope that you succeed. I hope you never have to make an impossible choice between a lesser evil and a greater evil. I promise you, however, that when the survival and wellbeing of your own family is at stake, you will always choose them over anything else. That is right and wrong at their most elemental.»

We sat in silence a few minutes. I did not know what else to say, so I waited for him to speak again.

«Have a safe journey tomorrow. Good luck in your search. Come back to us afterwards. This is your home, you know.»

In the morning, Ángel and Janet came with us in the taxi to the bus station.

"*Huevón,* I am going to miss you."

Ángel was surprisingly sentimental.

"I'll just be gone a couple of days, and then I'll be back. It will be like I was never gone."

"What if you discover where your Antonio is? You may find that Mendoza is only the start of your journey."

"It will probably just be another dead end. I don't think you'll miss me that much," I said, winking as I glanced at Janet.

"Take care of yourself, *huevón.*"

He wrapped his arms around me in the now-familiar Chilean *abrazo fuerte*. In the morning's dry heat, we felt each other's warmth through the thinness of our tee-shirts. It was an indescribable joy to feel such a close connection to another person and not feel embarrassed about it. I don't know why neither of us wanted the hug to end. There was no way to know at the moment it would be years before we saw each other again.

Donal and Janet also had a hug, but theirs was more awkward. He and I then climbed aboard the bus, threw our backpacks onto the overhead rack, and settled into our seats. Because I felt sorry for him, I insisted that he take the window seat.

The bus was impressive. It was large, modern, and German-manufactured. I had been expecting something like the buses in Mexico, but this one was comfortable and spotless. Best of all, it had air-conditioning. That made a huge difference in the summer heat.

After traveling out of the sprawl of Santiago, the bus headed north up the main highway to the town of Los Andes. It turned onto a two-lane road and up into the mountains. From this point, the road was steep and winding, especially when we got to the section known as Veintenueve Curvas, a series of switchbacks that had to be seen to be believed. I took it on faith there were twenty-nine of them since I was too busy to count them. I angled every which way—to the point of almost crawling into Donal's lap—in an effort to snap some decent photos.

"Damn," I said. "I wish the bus would stop so I could get a decent shot of this scenery. It's pointless trying to shoot anything worthwhile through the window of a moving bus."

The vehicle lumbered in one direction and then the other as it climbed the face of the mountain. At times I worried the bends in the road were too tight for the size of the bus and it wouldn't be able to negotiate the turn. Looking back at the downward view threatened to give me vertigo.

Finally we neared the summit. A Swiss-style hotel stood near a beautiful alpine lake.

"I wonder," said Donal, "if we're anywhere nearby to where the rugby team plane crashed. As I recall, it was flying from Mendoza to Santiago."

"When was that?"

"It must be nearly ten years ago now. You remember it, don't you?"

"Was that the one where the survivors had to eat the passengers that died?"

"Yes. It was a rugby club from Montevideo. They were to play an English club in Santiago. The poor devils were trapped on a glacier for more than two months before a pair of them succeeded in walking out and alerting the outside world."

"Boy," I said nervously, looking out the window, "I hope this bus manages to stay on the road."

A few minutes later we entered a tunnel. The darkness seemed to last forever. It was a relief to finally see the light at the end. The view was spectacular, the landscape being very different from the west side of the Andes. It was not unlike crossing the Sierra Nevada and descending into the strikingly dry landscape of the California-Nevada border area.

Ten miles farther, we stopped for the border control, the actual border having been in the middle of the two-mile Túnel Cristo Redentor. We were all required to get off the bus and to line up for the Argentine border agents. They were in absolutely no hurry. The guy looking at my passport took time to study every single page, including the blank ones and the front and the back. I was pretty sure he had no idea what any of it said or meant.

A different guy went through our backpacks. Fortunately, neither of us had that much to search through. He did spend an awful long time looking over my camera, making me nervous that he would try to open it and expose the film. I had thought things were strict in Chile, but the Argentine guys were much scarier than the Chilean ones.

It took two hours for something that should have taken thirty minutes. We finally climbed back into the bus and enjoyed the vista before us. The narrow road wended down a narrow valley flanked by spectacular brown slopes on either side.

"This is bloody amazing," exclaimed Donal. "I wouldn't have missed this for the world."

"I'm glad. I wasn't too sure how interested you were in coming along."

"I wasn't all that certain you were keen to have me come. It honestly seemed to be Miguel's idea more than yours."

"Was it that obvious?"

"I'm not exactly blind, you know. It was evident from the outset he only wanted to have Janet on her own."

"Are you and Janet...?"

"A couple? In my dreams, mate. No, we only met a week ago. We crossed paths at Machu Picchu. I fancied her straight away, and we got on famously. All she could talk about, though, was her friend Miguel whom she hadn't seen for years and how much she was looking forward to seeing him again. I was hoping it wouldn't work out, that he would be married or engaged or something, but it looks as though he was as eager to see her as she him."

"I'm afraid you're right there, Donal. He was awfully excited when he got her postcard."

"That's it then. I expect I'll be finishing my South American tour the same way I began it—solo. You see, this holiday was planned for months, ever since my final year at uni. I was meant to go with my girlfriend. Just a few weeks before we were to leave, she broke it off with me. I was gutted, but in the end I decided to go ahead on my own. When I met Janet, I was certain the story was going to have a happy ending after all."

"Man, that's a tough one. For what it's worth, there are an awful lot of attractive women in South America, especially in Chile. You might meet someone else."

"What's your own story? Is someone waiting for you back in the U.S. of A?"

"Now that's a very long and complicated story. Probably one that would require a bottle or two of Malbec wine."

"Sounds bloody good to me, mate."

It was a couple more hours—after the sun had set—before the bus emerged from the mountains and headed into the city of Mendoza.

# 14
# Mendoza

WE FOUND A cheap hotel and got a room for the night. Despite our talk about Malbec wine, we were both exhausted and happy just to go to bed.

In the morning after the *desayuno,* I showed the address to the guy at reception and asked him if he could point me in the right direction. I had hoped he would show me a map—or better yet give me one—but instead he went into a long, detailed description, complete with waving arms and fingers pointing in the air, that I could only half-follow. I glanced at Donal, who looked as clueless as I felt. After asking him several times to speak more slowly, I finally gave up and hoped I would figure it out as I went along.

We easily found the thoroughfare called Beltrán Sur and followed it toward the city center. The sun was brighter and hotter than it had been in Santiago.

We walked about a mile before coming to the second street he had mentioned. After that, I just wasn't sure, so I stopped people on the street and showed them the address. People were helpful enough, but more than a few just scratched their heads and walked away. Some tried to talk to us in English, and that was nearly worse.

"Damn," I said. "I wish Ángel would have come with me."

"Sorry, I'm not much help to you."

"It's not your fault. I'm glad you're here. It's just that people here are harder for me to understand than the people I know in Santiago."

By trial and error we eventually found the street in the address. Finding the house itself was another challenge. A lot of the homes did not have numbers on them—or at least any numbers we could see. We finally worked out which one it must be. It was a modest, one-story dwelling with a small garden. That the garden had long since dried up did not seem encouraging.

An iron fence stood between us and the house, and the gate was locked. I rang the bell on the gate. After a couple of minutes, I rang it again. A tired-looking woman in a light robe emerged from the house. She looked at the two of us with curiosity. I read from my scrap of paper.

"Patricia García Blanco. *Por favor.*"

She snatched the paper from my hand and studied it.

"*Patricia García Blanco,*" she repeated, as if correcting my own unintelligible pronunciation. "*A ver.*"

She pondered a few moments, turned on her heel, and went back into the house. I was afraid she would not come back. After a few minutes, she returned with a man who looked as tired as she did. She had given him the paper.

"*Patricia García,*" he said slowly, so as to be understood, "*ella ya no reside acá.*"

«Do you know where I might find her?» I asked, taking care to pronounce each Spanish word as clearly as possible.

He shrugged and looked at the woman. She shrugged. My heart sank. Then a thought occurred to him.

"*Usted puede preguntar al inmobiliario. Al agente quien nos alquila la casa.*"

«Can you give me the address of the agent?»

"*¿Tiene lápiz?*"

I handed him my pen, and he scribbled the rental agent's address on the paper.

"*¿Por dónde...?*"

He pointed down the street and then indicated a right turn, as he described the route to the office.

"*Gracias. Muchas gracias. Yo estoy muy agradecido.*"

He nodded. Relieved to be done with us, the pair did not delay in returning to the house.

"Well done," said Donal. "I might not have done as well in French."

We pounded the sidewalks again, but this time it was easier to find what we were looking for. It was only about a half-hour's walk to get to the real estate office, but it was closed. We looked at our watches.

"They must be closed for lunch," I said.

"I wonder how long we'll have to wait for them to finish their siesta."

"You want to grab a bite while we're waiting?"

We walked in the direction of the city center until we found a small restaurant that looked okay. We went in and took a table. A balding, bored-looking man brought us yellowed menus.

"I'm famished," said Donal. "We barely ate anything yesterday."

"Me too. I could eat a horse."

"I wonder if they eat horse here. They do in France."

"I know they definitely eat beef. I keep hearing how great the steak is in Argentina. I think I'm going to try this *churrasco a la parrilla.*"

"Sounds scrummy. I'll join you."

"And it's definitely time to try that Malbec wine."

"I like the way you think, mate."

After the waiter had poured the wine, we clinked the small round glasses.

"To finding your long-lost chum," toasted Donal.

"To meeting South American women," I responded.

The Argentine steak lived up to its reputation. I had never had such a thoroughly delicious cut of sirloin, and it was grilled to perfection.

"Back home," I said, "I would willingly drive an hour or more to a fancy restaurant to get a steak like this, and here we're getting it in an ordinary restaurant that doesn't look like anything special."

"Definitely the best I've ever had," agreed Donal, "and I must say, the wine's not at all bad either."

His pronunciation of "eye-ther" stuck in my ear. Because Donal spoke the same language I did, it was easy to forget he wasn't American—at least until he said something that sounded strange.

How unexpected, I thought, to be eating steak in Argentina with an Englishman whom I had met only a couple of days earlier.

My mind wandered. It occurred to me that I no longer thought about Lonnie as much as I used to. As recently as a year earlier, I would not have been able to have a meal like this without imagining Lonnie sharing it with me, anticipating his reaction to everything. I would hear his voice. One thing Lonnie loved was a good steak, and it broke my heart he wasn't there to experience it with me.

It also broke my heart not to think of him more often. The less I remembered him, the more it felt as though he were slipping away from me for good.

"Thinking about your friend?" asked Donal, breaking the silence as he refilled my glass.

"Yeah, I am."

We stepped out the door into the late afternoon. Between the heat and the wine, I felt a bit woozy in spite of having had coffee after the meal.

"That meal was absolutely the dog's bollocks," enthused Donal.

He was more giddy than I was, and as we walked down the street he sang, "Don't cry for me Argentina…"

"Did you just make that up?"

"Don't you know that song? From *Evita*?"

I shook my head.

"Who's Evita?"

"You have to know it. The record has been out for years now— in the U.K. at any rate. Last year I went to London with friends to see the stage version in the West End. It was brilliant. It's by the same blokes who made *Jesus Christ Superstar*."

"Oh yeah, I know that movie. That was pretty cool. Sing it again."

Pretty soon he had me singing "Don't Cry for Me Argentina" as well. People gave us strange looks as we proceeded down the street, singing more loudly as we went.

As we neared the real estate office, we tried to stop singing, but the music had taken on a life of its own—to the increasing annoyance of passers-by. Only when I saw that the office was open did I gain control of myself. I hurried through the door to find a bored-looking, heavyset man shuffling papers on his desk. He looked up at us with an expression suggesting he did not think we were real.

"*Caballeros*," he said tentatively.

"*Por favor*," I said awkwardly, "*yo estoy buscando a alguien.*"

"Yes?" he said in heavily accented English. "You are looking for someone?"

I referred to my paper.

«*Sí*,» I said, determined to stick to Spanish. Maybe because of the wine, I was in a mood for mastering the language. «Patricia García Blanco. She rented a house from you. At this address.»

I handed him the paper.

«Can you tell me where I can find her? I need to ask her something important.»

He shrugged.

«She does not live in Mendoza anymore.»

My heart sank.

«Can you tell me where she lives now?»

«No,» he said, handing the paper back to me.

«Do you mean no, as in you won't tell me, or do you mean no, as in you don't know?»

He shrugged.

«There is nothing I can tell you. I am sorry.»

«Is there anybody who might be able to tell me?»

He weighed what words would get me out of his office soonest.

«She has a cousin here in Mendoza.»

«She does? Can you tell me where to find him?»

He hesitated. After an internal debate, he laid a telephone book on his desk and thumbed through it until getting to a particular page. He scanned a column until he found what he was looking for. He set the book down in front of me with his finger next to a name.

«That's him?» I asked.

His slight nod was barely perceptible. I hurriedly jotted down the name, address, and phone number before he put the directory away.

«Thank you. Thank you very much,»

He returned the book to its drawer and shut it.

«Good day, *señores*,» he said with a tone of regret for getting involved.

Back on the street, we settled into the now-familiar routine of stopping friendly-looking passers-by and asking for help finding the address. We avoided anyone who looked as though they remembered us as the two annoying foreigners singing loudly. We were fortunate the address turned out to be only about a half-mile away.

It was a house similar to the one we had previously visited. It had a similar iron gate. I rang the bell. A balding man with thick, horn-rimmed eyeglasses came out. His ample belly was covered by an over-sized sports jersey with vertical white and baby-blue stripes and a yellow insignia over his heart.

"*¿Sí?*"

"Alberto Romero Blanco?"

He looked at us curiously.

"*¿Quién pregunta?*"

"*Yo me llamo Dallas. Por favor, yo estoy buscando a Patricia García Blanco.*"

He studied me and then Donal and then me again.

"*¿Y ustedes son...?*"

"*Yo soy de Estados Unidos. Yo busco a un amigo, y yo creo que su prima puede ayudarme.*"

"I do not think I should talk to you," he replied nervously in English that was surprisingly good.

Given that his cousin had been helping people to escape from the Pinochet regime, it was understandable why he might be apprehensive about talking to a stranger from North America.

"Look," I said. "You don't have to worry. I'm not CIA or anything."

"And I'm definitely not MI6," Donal chimed in.

"I have nothing to say to you," said Alberto, as he turned to go back into the house.

"Please, I'm desperate to find my friend. You might be my last hope. Can't you just tell me where to find your cousin?"

"I am sorry."

"Please."

To my surprise Donal called out after him, "Just for the record, mate, you lot most definitely stole the World Cup."

He stopped in his tracks and turned to face us.

"The cast on van de Kerkhof's wrist was completely illegal," he said with annoyance.

"Bollocks. You were stalling for time. You were doing anything you could to throw the Dutch off. You had your own referees, and they were so one-sided it was a bloody joke."

"What the hell are you two talking about?" I asked.

"The 1978 World Cup. It was here in Argentina, and they bloody well stole it."

"That is a lie," said Alberto. "And who are you to talk? The English did not even qualify."

"Maybe not, but Dalglish and Souness are two of Liverpool's best players, and they played for Scotland. They defeated the Dutch fair and square, which is more than I can say for you. If they had only gotten the points, it would have been them in the final."

"Wasn't a Scottish player expelled for using drugs in the match with Peru?"

"It doesn't matter. Scotland lost that one."

Alberto had come back to the gate so he could look Donal directly in the eye.

"Tell me something, Gringo. What the hell happened to George Best?"

"Blimey, I wish I knew. He was Man United's best ever. He was bloody brilliant. I don't know what happened. Last I heard he was in the States playing for rubbish clubs over there. No offense, Dallas."

"None taken. I didn't know we had soccer teams."

I was mesmerized by the way the two of them could go on and on about soccer teams and players I'd never heard of.

"Just wait until next year," continued Donal. "England will definitely be back in the World Cup. We had no trouble making it to the European finals last year."

"Ha! You are still living in 1966."

"Not a chance, mate. The team England has now is class. We've got the likes of Bryan Robson, Kenny Samson…"

"There is a young Argentine player you need to watch out for," said Alberto. "He is only twenty years old, but he is already better than George Best ever was. Listen to my words. Remember the name Maradona."

The argument had enthused Alberto. He turned to me and said, "Why is United States not serious about football?"

"You mean soccer? I don't know. I guess it's because we have our own kind of football. Soccer is boring. It takes too long to score."

"Tell me about your friend."

"Antonio? What can I say? He and my friend Lonnie and I traveled around Mexico together. We got close. He made me want to learn Spanish. Then he went to Chile because he wanted to see what socialism was all about. After the military took over, I never heard from him again, but I've never forgotten about him. I found out recently that he and the people he lived with came here to Mendoza, and I think your cousin might have helped them."

Alberto turned serious.

"Do you know what is going on in this country? Do you understand how things are here?"

"Not really, to be honest. I know you have a military government—the same as Chile."

"No, it is not the same as Chile. This country is at war. It began when Perón came back from his exile eight years ago. He expelled the Montoneros from his party and they went underground. Perón was president for only a few months when he died and his wife became president."

Donal perked up.

"Evita?"

Alberto rolled his eyes.

"Eva Duarte de Perón died many years ago. She was never president. It was Perón's third wife who became president after him. She was a disaster. She unleashed the military against the Montoneros and the ERP. Then the military removed her, and they have been in power ever since. Even after wiping out most of the Montoneros and the ERP, the junta persists with the war. It is not safe for anybody under the merest suspicion of supporting either of those groups."

"Is your cousin in hiding?"

"Not exactly, but let us say that, in her own self-interest, she has been avoiding some of her former friends."

"Can you tell me where she is?"

"She is in Buenos Aires. She and her daughter live with her nephew."

"And do you think it would be all right if I talked to her? Just to ask her about my friend, to find out what she remembers about him and where he might be now? I swear that's all I want. I don't want to get her or anyone else in trouble."

Alberto said nothing for a while. He took a good look at the two of us, as if he were deciding once and for all whether he could trust us.

"*Mira.* Come into the house. I will ring Patricia, and if she agrees, you may speak with her."

"*Gracias.* I can't tell you how much I appreciate this."

He opened the gate and led us into the house. He took us to a room with a desk and a phone.

"*Momentito,*" he said as he disappeared for a few minutes.

"You're a genius," I said to Donal. "That was a great idea getting him to talk about soccer. It made all the difference. You managed to get his confidence."

"It wasn't intentional," shrugged Donal. "I've never been able to get over that World Cup final."

Alberto reappeared.

"I will call her now."

"How is her English?" I asked.

He held out his hand and wobbled it palm-down to indicate, so-so.

"Would you talk to her for me? You know, translate?"

He nodded, and then dialed the number. He spoke to someone I presumed to be the nephew or the daughter. After a bit of conversation, he paused and then began to speak with someone else.

*"Patricia, hablas con tu primo Alberto. ¿Cómo estás?"*

They exchanged a few pleasantries before he explained a North American had a few questions for her. He listened to her reaction and then told her that we seemed to be all right. When she agreed to hear the questions, he looked at me.

"There was a family from Santiago that came to Mendoza after the *golpe* in Chile in 1973," I said. "There was a couple, Vicente and Maite Muñoz. They had a sixteen-year-old boy with them named Miguel. He was from Mexico."

Alberto dutifully related it all to her. Then he listened.

"She says many people came to Mendoza from Chile during that time."

I tried to think of something distinctive about Antonio, something that might have stuck in her memory. I thought back to what Vero had said about him. I called up my own memories of what it had been like to be with him.

"Tell her that he smiled a lot, that he liked to tell jokes. Tell her he had teeth like a donkey when he laughed."

Alberto translated my words. He listened. He nodded.

"She thinks she remembers him. Miguelito. She remembers that, the way he spoke, different from the others, she did not think he was Chilean."

"Does she know where he is now?"

After a bit more conversation on the phone, Alberto said, "By coincidence, she met him about a year ago. It was in the city center of Buenos Aires."

He listened some more and then added, "She almost did not recognize him. He was a grown man."

# 15
# B.A.

I WAS STRUCK DUMB.

For years I had thought often about Antonio, and when I did, I always saw him as the fourteen-year-old boy I had known in 1971. It took this long to dawn on me he would now be a twenty-four-year-old man.

Alberto looked at me expectantly. I focused my thoughts.

"Does she know where he lives? Does she have an address or a phone number?"

He talked with her some more.

"She knows nothing else about him. They just happened to meet by chance that one time. Wait, what's that? She says he said something to her about working in a cinema. As a…"

He made a spinning motion with his hand. Antonio was working as a projectionist.

"Anything else? Can she remember anything else?"

After some more conversation: "That is all. She knows nothing else."

"Does she know the name of the movie theater?"

After the usual delay: "No, she did not think to ask him."

"Please thank her for me. I am very appreciative. Would it be all right for me to visit her in Buenos Aires? Just in case she remembers something else in the meantime?"

He said his goodbyes to her and then said to me, "Yes, you may visit her when you go to Buenos Aires."

Alberto wrote down her address and phone number for me.

"I can't thank you enough for your help. You don't know what this means to me."

"On the contrary, I think I do. I have had to undertake my own searches for old friends. I know how important it can be. I wish you good luck in your quest."

I continued thanking him as he walked us back to the street. Locking the gate after us, he said to Donal, "Remember my words, Gringo! Watch out for Maradona!"

"What do you think, Donal old buddy?" I asked, as we headed toward the hotel. "Are you up for a trip to Buenos Aires?"

He smiled.

"I certainly can't say I have anywhere else to be. I must admit I've become rather intrigued by this quest of yours. I'll happily tag along if you want me. I look forward to meeting this Antonio or Miguel or whatever his name is."

"Excellent. I think this calls for another bottle of Malbec."

Neither of us was all that hungry after our meal, but we were both definitely thirsty. On the way to the hotel, we came across a bar that looked suitable. Once seated inside, we ordered a bottle of red.

"It's all coming together, Donal. I've as good as found him, haven't I? I know he's in Buenos Aires. I know he works in a movie theater. It's just a matter of time now. After all these years of wondering about him, I'm finally going to see him again."

"Cheers, mate," said Donal, raising his glass, "and well done. He must mean quite a lot to you."

"It's weird. I mean, we just spent those few weeks together, but there was just something about that time in my life. Everything changed for me in Mexico. It's hard to explain how it got so important for me to find him again. Probably because I never had that many friends, and I've lost some of the good ones. The toughest one was my best friend Lonnie. He was only twenty-one when he died. Another good friend, Keith, died last year."

"You and Miguel—I mean Janet's Miguel—seem to be quite close friends."

"Yeah, Ángel's been a good friend. The funny thing is we would never have met if I hadn't gone looking for Antonio and found Ángel instead. It's a miracle we are still friends—I mean with me falling in love with his girlfriend and all."

"You're joking, right?"

"Nope. True story."

"Come to think of it, I suppose that's not unlike how I met him myself. I doubt he and I will become friends, though."

"Yeah, probably not. I'm sorry the thing with Janet didn't work out for you, but it's good news for me. Since Janet showed up, Ángel seems to have forgotten about Valérie."

"Who?"

"Valérie. The woman Ángel and I were both in love with."

"It's all quite complicated, isn't it?" said Donal, looking a bit drowsy. "If I were in your place, frankly, I would be on a quest to find my lady love. I'd be looking for Valérie instead of that Antonio bloke."

"You make an excellent point. After I've found Antonio, the very next thing I'll do is take off for France and find my lady love, as you call her. Lady love. I like the sound of that. You limeys definitely have a way with the language."

"Did you actually just call me a limey? Do you yanks really use that word? I thought it was just in old films."

I was feeling a bit drunk, but pleasantly so. I thought ahead to my quest in France. Money was going to be a problem. I had some savings in the bank in San Francisco, but I now owed most of that to my dad. I wondered how much a plane ticket to France would cost. I definitely needed to replenish my bank account somehow, but that was a problem I would leave for *mañana*. Right now I was just going to enjoy the Malbec.

Donal and I sat and talked for hours. I told him all my stories about Mexico, San Francisco, the Deauville film festival, Bordeaux, and taking the train from Paris to Berlin. He told me about studying Business Economics at the University of Liverpool, about playing bass guitar in a band called Dais, and about the time he and his friends Niall and Paul went to Morocco. By the time we were on the day's third bottle of wine, I had told him every detail I could remember about Marisol, Lana, and Valérie. He waxed eloquent about Imogen, Vanessa, and Jill.

It was late when we got back to the hotel. I asked the guy at the desk the best way to get to Buenos Aires. He said we should go to the bus station first thing in the morning to make sure we got tickets for the next evening's departure. It would take us all night, he said, to get to the capital. Donal and I didn't relish the idea of getting up early, but the guy insisted we should not delay getting tickets. He said he would give us a wake-up call.

It seemed as though our heads had only hit our pillows before he knocked on our door. I wondered if he ever slept. We went down for *desayuno,* but he insisted we go to the bus station before breakfast.

"I will keep the *desayuno* for you," he said.

There was a surprisingly long line for tickets, so we were glad we had listened to him. With that task accomplished, we had most of the day to wander around the city with our packs on our backs. We spent a lot of time hanging around the Plaza Independencia. The shady trees and breeze flowing over the large, ornate fountain made it an oasis. Street performers, caps and boxes awaiting coins, provided entertainment. I easily used up a roll of film, as I wandered among the many people enjoying the day.

Later I went to a stationer's shop to buy paper and an envelope. I sat in the plaza and wrote another letter to Valérie. I told her about my new friend from Liverpool and how we had crossed the Andes together. I said we would soon be in Buenos Aires and that I was optimistic about finding Antonio. I asked Donal for some French phrases to add.

*Tu me manques beaucoup,* he suggested. *J'espère te voir bientôt. Je pense à toi souvent.*

"You're truly besotted by this woman, aren't you?"

"Yeah, I am."

"Does she reciprocate your feelings?"

"I think so. I mean, I hope so. It's been so long since I've seen her, I guess I'm not sure."

"Tell me again why are you here instead of in France sorting this out?"

"Because I'm an idiot. As soon as I find Antonio and catch up with him, my next priority is France."

The rest of the day dragged until it was time to board the bus. The bus journey to Buenos Aires in the dark was interminable. It took more than four hours just to get to Córdoba. It was eight hours more to get to B.A. Donal had no trouble sleeping, but I could not get comfortable in my seat. I spent hours looking out the window at the darkness, wondering what scenery I was missing.

B.A. was massive compared to Mendoza. Relieved to be off the bus, we wandered around the city center in the relative cool of the early morning. I popped a new roll of film in the camera and began to make like a tourist. The place reminded me of Paris. La Avenida 9 de Julio was a lot like the Champs-Élysées. The Plaza de la República and its obelisk brought back memories of Place de la Concorde. It was no surprise to learn that B.A. is called *la París de Sudamérica*.

I stared at every face I passed. Could I at any moment randomly run into Antonio? I was happy knowing it was at least a possibility.

Now experts at finding addresses in strange cities, we arrived at Patricia's apartment building before lunchtime. I pressed the button next to the name "P. García B." I heard her voice through the tinny intercom, and my mind flashed back to visiting Paulina Muñoz in Germany. Despite a strong presence of armed, uniformed men everywhere, B.A. still did not have the same feel of repression as East Berlin.

We were invited up to the apartment. We climbed three flights of stairs and knocked on the door. A woman with a pale, round face and short-cropped, black hair opened it.

«Good day,» I said in Spanish. «I am Dallas Green, and this is Donal Ryan. Your cousin Alberto told you about us by telephone.»

«You are welcome. Please come in and sit down. My mother is preparing the *mate*.»

«Your mother?»

«Yes.»

«So you are not Patricia?»

She laughed.

«This is Patricia,» she said as an older woman emerged from the kitchen.

Patricia carried a kettle on a tray. There was also a cup with a metal straw. The cup was actually a gourd embraced by shiny metal ribbons rising from an ornate base resting on small, round feet. She invited us to sit.

«And this is Mónica, my daughter,» she said.

With no further ado, Patricia made tea but in a way I had never seen before. In an unhurried ritual, the tea leaves were steeped in the gourd cup with water from the kettle. When it was ready, Patricia drank it all, using the straw. She then refilled the cup with hot water. When the second serving was ready, she offered it to me. I wondered why I should have to use the same cup, but I said nothing.

Following her example, I drank through the straw. To be honest, I didn't care for it. It didn't just taste like grass. It tasted like bitter grass. To be polite, I forced myself to drink it all and then handed it back to her. She filled it again and offered the third serving to Donal.

«Do you speak English, Mónica?» I asked.

She shook her head.

«Just a little. I studied French in school.»

Donal beamed. He had been dying to find a way into the conversation.

"*Moi aussi! J'ai étudié le français á l'école en Angleterre.*"

"*Vous êtes donc Anglais?*"

"*Mais oui. Vous parlez très bien.*"

"*Pas de tout.*"

The goofy look on his face suggested he had wasted little time getting over Janet.

As Donal courteously choked down the *mate,* I asked Patricia all the questions I could think of about Antonio. Did she really have no idea in which movie theater he was working? Mónica said something to Donal in French.

"Monique says she would be happy to make a list of the most likely cinemas. In fact, she would be willing to take us to each one and help us enquire about your friend."

"Monique is it now? *Merci beaucoup, Monique. Yo estoy muy agradecido.*"

She was as good as her word. Armed with a newspaper's movie listings, she accompanied us on an excursion covering much of central Buenos Aires. We took a few buses, but most of it was on foot. Our task at each movie theater began with a conversation with the person sitting in the box office, followed by a talk with a manager who was summoned to deal with us. At the fifth theater, we hit paydirt.

At first, the squat, bald man with a moustache was annoyed by the distraction, but Mónica charmed him. She explained we were looking for a cinema employee by the name of Miguel Pérez who was about twenty-four years old. As she spoke, he nodded.

«Yes, Miguel Pérez worked here for about a year,» he told her.

«Is he here now?» I asked.

He shook his head.

«He quit. About six months ago. He left me in quite a bind too.»

«Is he working at another cinema?»

«Not in this city. He said he was emigrating.»

«Emigrating?»

«Yes, he said he was going to France.»

«France?»

«Yes, at least that is what I think he said. France.»

«Do you have any way of communicating with him? Do you have an address for him or a phone number?»

«No. Why would I?»

«Do you have his address or phone number in Buenos Aires, so that we might talk to his family?»

«This was his address. He lived here. In a room upstairs.»

«By himself?»

«Yes.»

146

«Do you have a way of contacting any of his relatives or friends?»

«I am afraid not.»

«And are you certain he emigrated? He definitely left the country?»

«I have no reason to think otherwise.»

My heart sank. I could not help but laugh at the irony. The previous year I had seized on the idea he might be in France and went looking for him there. It turned out I had been too early.

*Well*, I thought, *I guess I now have two reasons to go back to France.*

Mónica and I thanked the man for his time.

«Perhaps he changed his mind,» she said. «Maybe his plans did not work out. He might still be here in Buenos Aires.»

«Maybe, but even if that were true, how would we find him in a city this size? No, I have a feeling he went to France. He was always definite in his strategy. I think I've hit another dead end.»

I brought Donal up to speed on what we had learned.

"*C'est dommage. Allons boire un verre pour noyer nos chagrins.*"

Donal had adopted the distracting habit of always speaking in French. It was his way of holding Mónica's attention.

"You guys go ahead," I said. "I'm kind of bummed out. I think I'll just go for a walk by myself."

Donal set his eye on a bar across the street.

"Suit yourself, mate. Mónica and I will be over there, waiting for you. *Si cela vous convient, Mónica.*"

"*Oui, ça me convient,*" she said, apparently happy to hang out with Donal in the bar.

It was getting dark. I wandered up and down streets of a city I did not know. I kicked myself for having gotten my hopes up. I had been so sure I would be having a happy reunion with Antonio, reliving our old adventures together. Instead, I had traveled all this way across South America for nothing. What an idiot. I wondered if Antonio even remembered me anymore.

I recalled Mónica's words. Could he have changed his mind? Could he still be in Buenos Aires? Once again I took notice of each passer-by, searching for some sign of familiarity. That's when my mind played a trick on me—or so I thought. I spotted someone familiar. He was walking away from me, but one brief glance was enough to convince me I knew him. I followed. The gap between us grew, so I had to step up my pace. Was I crazy? It was so unlikely.

He walked quickly, almost as if he was worried someone would follow him. The faster he went, the more determined I was to catch up to him. The chase went on for three blocks until he stopped at the door of a large brick building. He pressed a button on the wall and was buzzed in.

There was no time to think about the wisdom of what I did next. I rushed after him and caught the door before it could close. I followed him up the stairs. He climbed two flights before he noticed the sound of my footsteps coming after him. He stopped dead in his tracks and turned around.

We stared at each other in disbelief.

"What? Aw fer feck sake. You? How?"

# 16
# The Meeting

"THIS CANNOT BE happening, sure it can't."

I needed a moment to process the face. Actually, I needed a hell of a lot more than a moment, but a moment was all I had.

"Séamus? Or is it Declan now? I have trouble keeping up."

"What do you want? How the feck did you find me?"

"Find you? I wasn't even looking for you. What the hell are you doing here? In Buenos Aires of all the fucking places?"

"Look, we can sort all this out if you like, but this is not the time or the place. Do you hear me? You have to disappear. *Now!*"

"Why are you so anxious to get rid of me? What's up? Does this have something to do with Antonio?"

"Who?"

"Antonio. The guy I was with that time you spotted me in the Águila in Mexico City. He's been living here. Is that why you're here?"

"Aw Jayzus. Would you ever use yer head, Austin. Why would you think I remember or care about this feckin' Antonio? Why would I have anything to do with him? Can you not get it through your thick skull this has nothing the feck to do with you?"

We heard the sound of footsteps on the stairs below.

"You need to vanish," he hissed. "You most definitely do not want to meet these men. Trust me."

"Who are they?" I asked. "Montoneros or something?"

"Shut the fuck up!" he whispered between clenched teeth.

"Which way should I go?"

"Jayzus. It's too late. There's no leaving now. Whatever you do, do not open your mouth. Do not speak. If they cop on you're a yank, we're both dead. Got that?"

Two stocky men of medium height and flowing black hair emerged from the shadows below. One had an ugly scar on his cheek, the other an unyielding stare.

"*¿Quién es?*" said the scarred one, eying me intensely, while the other took Séamus's rucksack from him and inspected it.

"*Un colega,*" said Séamus. "*No se preocupe. Se puede confiar en él.*"

Séamus's Spanish was quite good. I shouldn't have been surprised, given that I first met him in Mexico. He seemed like a completely different person when he spoke it.

"*¿Usted es también irlandés pues?*" the man demanded to know.

Mindful of Séamus's warning not to talk, I nodded ever so slightly.

«You know,» he continued, «one of this country's greatest independence heroes was an Irishman. Admiral William Brown. Do you know him?»

I fought the panic. There was no way I could get away with not responding, but I had no idea if they would be able to tell the difference between the Spanish of an Irishman and that of an American. I glanced at Séamus, but he refused to give me any kind of signal. I swallowed and gave it my best shot.

«And the first president of Chile was an Irishman too,» I said, striving to make my Spanish sound like Ángel's. «Bernardo O'Higgins.»

He continued to study me.

«Why have you brought a camera?»

My heart beat so hard I couldn't imagine they all didn't hear it.

«It has nothing to do with this. It is for something I am doing later.»

The camera bothered him, but he said no more about it.

«So why are you standing here in the corridor? Let us go into the room.»

I wondered if I might get away with excusing myself at this point, but I was afraid it might seem suspicious, so I followed. The room was bare except for a table and chairs. We sat.

«What do your people say, Irishman?»

Only one of them did any talking. I gave him the name Número Uno.

«I have been authorized to offer you a dozen M–16s and a half-dozen AK–47s,» said Séamus smoothly. «We can also provide you with a quantity of explosives.»

«Quantity? What does that mean precisely?»

«It will depend on what can be spared.»

«Can you not be more precise?»

«Not at the present time, but we should also be able to provide quite a few CZ 75 pistols and a good number of cartridges, thanks to our friends in Moscow.»

Número Uno raised an eyebrow.

«Do you get many supplies from the Soviets?»

«Quite a few. They disguise their ships as fishing vessels and anchor them offshore. They are easy enough for us to get to.»

«Interesting. I have been told to emphasize it is extremely important the weapons cannot be traced.»

«Do not worry. Do your people agree with our view of the coming situation?»

«About the English, you mean?»

«Yes.»

«We are not as certain as you are,» said the Argentine. «We see it as likely that the government will be at war with the English within a year or two. The generals will need a distraction, and the Malvinas issue has been festering for quite some time.»

«Thatcher's popularity has plummeted since her election,» said Séamus. «We do not think she will have the nerve for a major foreign adventure this early in her government.»

«If it results that she does, however, then you and we shall have a common enemy, no? That could work to our advantage.»

«Perhaps. Are you still considering the Algeciras operation?»

«Yes.»

«I see. There is something I do not fully understand. In doing this, will you not effectively be supporting the military government?»

«Yes, but you must remember, in the beginning we were all *peronistas*—up until the Ezeiza massacre. The split has been to our disadvantage. Our hope now lies in some sort of reconciliation.»

«Well, that is your concern. Personally, I do not see the English launching a military operation 12,000 miles from London, but if they do, then you will have your weapons.»

«Very good. There is one other matter, no?»

«You have some cash to dispose of.»

«We cannot make use of it in this country. If you could take it off our hands…»

Número Uno produced a cloth sack.

Séamus took a medium-sized wooden box from his rucksack and placed it on the table.

«That should be the equivalent value.»

The Argentine opened the box and studied its contents carefully. From where I sat I could not get a good look at it, but I had a feeling it was jewelry.

«Very well,» he said, closing the lid. «We shall meet again at the appointed time and place.»

He looked toward me icily and added, «Next time please do not surprise us with people we do not know.»

«Understood. I will definitely come on my own next time.»

The Argentines stood and left. Séamus and I remained frozen in our chairs. Long after the sound of their footsteps had died away, I got the nerve to speak.

"Shit. That was intense. I can't believe we got away with that."

"You think *we* got away with something, do you, Austin?"

"You know damn well my name's Dallas. Why do you do that?"

"This isn't funny, and it doesn't matter one fuck what your name is. You know I have to kill you now, right?"

I studied his face for a sign. There was no trace of a smile on his lips or glint in his eye.

"You're joking, right? You wouldn't actually kill me, would you, Séamus?"

"Tell me again about that lad in San Francisco who was asking all those questions about me. The one who knew so much about me."

"Him? I never saw him again. He vanished off the face of the earth. I don't expect I'll ever see him again."

"You can see this has gotten feckin' awkward, can't you?"

"Look, I didn't understand anything you guys were talking about. In fact I've forgotten about it all already. There's no way I'd be talking to anyone else about it."

"You mentioned the Montoneros."

"Some guy I was talking to in Mendoza mentioned them. I don't know anything about them. Look, I came here to see a woman who used to help people escape from Chile after the Pinochet *golpe*. I'm on your side. Didn't I help you get your package into Guatemala that time? Didn't I almost get thrown into a prison because of it? You owe me."

He buried his head in his hands.

"Jayzus, Austin. You're like a bad penny. How do you manage to appear at the strangest times and in the strangest places? It's too much to believe it's a coincidence."

"I thought you gave up all this political stuff, Séamus. When we had that drink in Deauville, it sounded like you had given up on Karl Marx. You said Marxism wasn't paying well."

"That's true, but some things you get involved in are hard to get out of again. Besides, I have never gone off the idea of getting the bloody Brits out of my country. Also, it turns out there actually are ways of making liberation politics profitable if you know what you're doing."

"Just tell me you were joking about killing me. I met a woman that time in Deauville, and it would be a terrible tragedy if I never got to see her again. I have to go back and find her."

"Feck. You're always searching for someone or other, aren't you, Austin? It was some Mexican girl in D.F. Now it's this Antonio one here and then some woman in Deauville. You should just pick one person to look for. Then find them and feckin' stay with them."

"You're right. From this moment on, I'm completely focused on getting back to France. If I'm not dead, I mean."

"C'mere to me and listen. Go home. Go tomorrow. Not the day after. Tomorrow. Do not delay. Get the feck out of South America. You don't have to worry about me ending your wretched life, but I can't guarantee your safety. I have no idea what those lads made of you or if they have ways of checking up on you. If they figure out you're not who I said you were, it won't be good for either of us. Get the hell out of Dresden before the firebombing starts. That's what I'm going to do."

"Yeah, me too. It's definitely time to go home. Where are you headed next?"

"Why do you want to know? So you can surprise me there?"

"No, so I can make sure I never go anywhere near it."

He stood to leave.

"I checked out this building beforehand. There's a side entrance into a laneway. I'm going out that way. I suggest you do the same, but wait until I'm well gone. *Slán abhaile,* Austin."

"Thanks, Séamus. And one other thing."

"Eh?"

"*Póg mo thóin!*"

"Never gets old," he said, walking out the door. "*Imeacht gan teacht ort! Smuigín!*"

I sat alone in a daze for quite a few minutes, then stood up and walked down the stairs. I didn't bother looking for the side door. My state of mind was such that I figured I either had a guardian angel looking out for me or I didn't. I left the building the way I had entered it and headed back toward the cinema. As I walked, I felt a slight relief to have gotten out of the building in one piece. My mind raced ahead to finding Donal and Mónica and how I would explain to them that I would be getting a flight home the next day.

Lost in my thoughts, I never noticed the two men coming up behind me. One grabbed my arms and held them. The other roughly grabbed the strap around my neck and pulled it over my head, nearly taking half of my jaw with it in the process.

"Hey!" I yelled.

I grabbed helplessly for my camera, but they shoved me to the pavement and gave me a few kicks in the side. As suddenly as they had appeared, they were gone. I lifted my head and felt something warm dribbling from my gums. I looked around, but there was no sign of them—or my camera. Was it the two guys from the meeting? Was it just a random mugging? There was no way to know, and it didn't really matter. I had a sickening sense of loss. That Nikon F2 had been with me since Cal State Bakersfield.

I stood and wiped my mouth with the back of my hand. My knee ached from having hit the ground. My hand was streaked with blood. I felt my teeth with my tongue. Luckily, none of them were broken, but my chin hurt like hell. Several people were on the street, but none of them came near me. They all meticulously avoided looking in my direction.

I stumbled slowly toward the cinema. People streamed out of its doors. I looked up at the marquee to see what was playing. It was a movie called *El rey y el pájaro.* It must have been a children's movie because I now found myself surrounded by parents with their children. Distracted, I tripped and tumbled to the ground again.

Awkward and embarrassed on my hands and knees, I looked up. In front of me was an elegantly dressed couple with a small boy between them. Of all the people surrounding me, he alone made eye contact with me. He stared intently with large brown eyes. They bored straight through my brain. I looked up at the parents. The father was an unusual-looking man. The mother averted her eyes, as if offended. She yanked the boy away, and the three of them hurried down the street.

I stood and steadied myself. I spotted the bar and warily crossed the street to it. I went in and wandered the dark interior until I found Donal and Mónica sitting at a small table. They were having a great chat in French.

"We had nearly given up on you, mate," he said. Getting a good look at me, he exclaimed, "Bloody hell! What happened to you?"

"I'll tell you in a minute. I need to find a restroom first. Where is it?"

"The gents? It's back that way."

I washed my face and hands and did my best to rinse the blood out of my sleeve. I went back out to Donal and Mónica.

"Are you all right?" asked Donal. "What happened?"

"I'll tell you what the hell happened. I got mugged. They took my camera."

There was no way I could tell them about Séamus or the Montoneros.

"Blimey, man, you need to go to the coppers and report it straight away."

I glanced at Mónica. Her expression was doubtful.

"Frankly, I don't think there's any hope of getting it back," I said. "I'm just lucky they didn't take my wallet as well. I hate losing that camera. It had sentimental value, and it won't be cheap to replace."

"*¿Has perdido muchas fotos con el aparato?*" asked Mónica.

"I guess that's lucky too. I only started a new roll once I got here in B.A. so I didn't lose too many photos. The rest are safe in my backpack."

"You should go to the police anyway, mate. It can't hurt to report it."

"Honestly, I don't want to take the time. Things have changed, and I need to talk to you about it. What are we drinking?"

"Mónica has persuaded me to try a fernet *con Coca.* It's rather, um, interesting. Shall I order you one?"

A waiter in a white jacket had appeared.

I looked at their drinks with Coca-Cola mixer and said, "I don't think so. *Una cerveza por favor.*"

"Well, here's some good news," said Donal. "Mónica has been telling me she and her mother share their apartment with Mónica's cousin. He is away for a few days, and she knows he wouldn't mind if we used his room while he's gone."

«That is very kind of you,» I said to her in Spanish. «In my case, it will be for one night only. I need to get a flight back to the United States tomorrow.»

"Did you say tomorrow?" asked Donal in English.

"Yeah. I've got an open return ticket from Santiago to Los Angeles with LAN Chile. I need to get it changed so I can fly home from here."

"Why the sudden hurry?"

The waiter had returned with a bottle of Quilmes Imperial. We fell silent while he poured it ceremoniously into my glass.

"I just need to get back. I've clearly hit a dead end in my search for Antonio. It's time I went back to work and began saving up for my trip to France. I've spent too much time hanging out in South America."

"Is this because you were robbed? I know it was a shite thing to happen, but you shouldn't let it put you off your plans. You might still come across more information about your friend."

"Sorry, but my mind's made up. Sorry to bail on you, but this shouldn't affect your plans. What will you do now?"

He glanced at Mónica.

"I might hang about B.A. a bit and see how things go. Get to know the place a bit better, you know?"

A bit of color appeared in Mónica's cheeks.

«Please do not be rash,» she said in Spanish. «You are welcome to stay with us as long as you want. It is not a problem.»

"I really hate to see you go, mate," said Donal.

"Gracias, but it's a done deal. Anyway, without me tagging along, the two of you can get away from this Tower of Babel thing we've got going on with *français, español,* and English."

When we got back to the apartment, Donal and I negotiated how we would sleep in one room with a single bed. In the end, he offered to sleep on the floor since I was only going to be there for one night.

"Weren't your friends in Santiago expecting you to go back to them?" he asked. "I seem to recall you telling Miguel you would see him in a couple of days."

"Yeah, I'll have to write to them and explain. I feel bad that we didn't have a proper goodbye."

The next day, after I had said my goodbyes and thanks to Patricia, Donal and Mónica went with me to the airport. When I saw the first sign for it, its name was strangely familiar: Ezeiza. After a few minutes, it came to me. Número Uno had referred to something he called *la masacre de Ezeiza,* something that had split the *peronistas* in two bitter factions. Had it happened at this airport where I was now planning to make my escape?

To arrange my flight, I had to talk to many people. Every paper-pusher I met tried to send me to see someone else. Luckily, my Spanish was good enough to argue with all of them. More luckily, Mónica was even better at arguing. In the end, we got Aerolíneas Argentinas to accept my LAN Chile ticket for a flight to Lima and a connecting flight to Los Angeles, and there was an available seat on that evening's flight. My friends spent their day hanging out with me until it was time to board.

At the gate Mónica and I hugged.

«Thank you for your help. You turned out to be a really good friend, considering I only met you yesterday.»

«I wish you would have stayed longer,» she said. «Please come back someday.»

"*Bon voyage,* mate," said Donal, also giving me a hug. "Good luck finding your French lady love."

"Good meeting you, man. If you ever get to San Francisco or Bordeaux or—hell, I don't know where I'll be, but I hope we meet again someday. Both of you," I added with a wink and a glance at Mónica.

I settled in for a five-hour flight to Lima, where I had to kill several boring hours at Jorge Chávez Airport. I boarded another plane for a nine-hour flight to Los Angeles. Despite having nothing better to do than sleep on the plane, I arrived at LAX exhausted as well as grimy and dehydrated. I wandered out to the bus stop and waited for the bus to Bakersfield. Fortunately, I was able to find enough American money at the bottom of my backpack to cover the fare.

I'm not sure what ungodly hour it was when I got to Bakersfield. I had to bum change off a stranger at the bus station for the pay phone.

"Hello?" said a worried voice on the other end of the line.

In my family, calls at that time of night were a cause for concern since they almost always meant bad news.

"Dad? Is that you? Dad, it's me. Dallas. I've come home."

Ever one handy for a *New Testament* reference, he said simply, "The prodigal son."

# 17
# The Funeral

"SO YOU NEVER did find your friend Antonio?" asked Father McGinley, as he took another sip of Powers.

"No, I never did."

"'Tis a pity, so it is."

"Yeah, well, I kind of got distracted after I left Buenos Aires."

"Let me understand. Are you saying that you have made yourself a recluse here in Connemara simply because of your encounter with that pair of Argentine lads a dozen years ago? That seems an excessive reaction to me. I'm sure those Montoneros, or whatever you call them, have long since forgotten about you."

"No, no. It wasn't that meeting that has me worried. I only told you about that because you asked about the time I spent in South America and because that was the last time I saw Séamus Costello."

The three of us had sat for hours at my table, putting a serious dent in the whiskey bottle. I had told them more than I intended about my time in Chile and Argentina, although I did abridge it somewhat. There was no reason, for example, to bother them with too many details about Vero.

"It is interesting," said Alex, "that you were in Buenos Aires. To think that our paths might have crossed. It would not have been likely, I suppose. After all I would have been only six years old."

"Six?"

A strange feeling came over me.

"Alex, did your parents ever take you to the movies?"

"Yes, sometimes."

"Did you ever see one called *El rey y el pájaro*?"

He searched his memory for a moment.

"Yes, I remember that. It was about a chimney sweep and a shepherdess, and there was an evil king who was after them. I had forgotten all about it. Why do you ask?"

"I'm probably crazy, but I think I might have seen you coming out of the movie theater. Do you remember seeing someone trip and fall when you came out of the cinema?"

"No, I don't, but I would have been very young."

"You're making me feel old, kid."

"Let us not talk about feeling old," said the priest glumly. "So tell me, Dallas, have you ever seen your friend Angel since that time?"

It amused me that he pronounced the name as the English word angel instead of attempting the Spanish pronunciation. Yet it seemed appropriate, given that he was after all a priest.

"No. I mean, we write each other letters off and on, and we've talked on the phone a few times. The funny thing is that I wouldn't have to go all the way to Chile to see him. He's lived in Virginia for years. After Janet finished her tour of South America, he missed her so much that he went to see her in the States, and he ended up staying. They've been married for, let's see, eight years now. Man, time flies, doesn't it? He and Janet have three kids—at least the last time I heard."

"Yes, I find the older I get, the faster time passes. It has been fierce flying by for me, I can certainly tell you. And on that topic, this night has flown by, and I should be off for home. It's the scratcher for me. I have my orders. I will make enquiries around the county and see if I can identify a home place for your Séamus Costello. Leave it with me, lads. I will report back when I know something."

"Thank you very much, Father," said Alex.

"Yeah, thanks, Padre. It will certainly be interesting to see him one more time after all these years. He definitely better not call me Austin again."

We had no idea how long it would take Father McGinley to come up with information, so I went back to my usual routine of spending part of each day helping Paddy with the farm chores and then spending some time fixing up the cottage. Alex was a great help. For a privileged, rich kid, he was a darn good worker. Despite having no previous experience on a farm, he was game to try anything. I had a good laugh the first time he tried to milk a cow, just as Paddy had laughed at my first attempt. Paddy and Bernie were fascinated by Alex. When we had finished for the day, she would invite us in for a cup of tea so she could pester him with questions. Silly questions like what people ate and drank where he came from, as if he were from another planet instead of another country. She also spoke to him carefully and slowly, as if his English wasn't pretty much perfect.

In the evenings we got into the habit of going down to the pub. I had previously avoided it since it felt awkward being the only one who didn't know everyone else. Having Alex with me made all the difference. Not only did we have each other to talk to, but some of the regulars began to talk to us as well. Like Bernie, they were curious about Alex and wanted to ask him their odd questions.

On a sunny and halfway warm day, I took advantage to put a fresh coat of paint on the cottage. While it may have been a warm July day by Irish standards, it was nothing like the July days I knew as a kid in California. Because of the sun, the two of us took off our shirts, though I found it a bit cool. I had never been one to tan easily, but I was surprised to see how pale I had become. Alex didn't have to worry about that. He had his own permanent tan that looked great on his wiry upper body. I wished I had an eighteen-year-old body instead of my stupid forty-year-old one.

We heard back from the priest sooner than we had hoped. A full week had not passed when he showed up at the cottage late one morning in a state of excitement.

"Quick, lads," he said. "Turn on the radio."

"The radio? Why?"

"Never mind. Just tune it in to the local station, not RTÉ."

I fiddled with the dial until I found the frequency. An announcer was reading a news bulletin.

"What are we listening for?"

"The deaths."

"The deaths?"

Confused, Alex looked at me as if to ask whether I knew what he was talking about. I shrugged.

"Yes. I heard it this morning. They will repeat it now in a few minutes."

I was familiar with the radio death notices all right, but I had no idea why it was so important to listen to them at this particular moment. Among the many strange things I had discovered about living in rural Ireland was the reading of death notices on the radio. Three times a day, the names of people who had recently died, as well as the times and places of their funerals, were read out.

"Quiet," said Father McGinley eagerly. "It's starting."

The usual vaguely sentimental music played, and then a man's voice announced in a somber monotone, "The death and funeral notices for Saturday, the third of July."

"Man," I said. "Tomorrow's the Fourth of July! I forgot all about it."

"Shhh!" said the priest sternly.

A few names with the details of their funerals were read out. Then the priest alerted us by his expression and gestures that we had arrived at the important one.

"The death has occurred of Proinsias Costello, An Fheirm and formerly of Costello's Pub, Coillte Coileáin. Deeply regretted by his wife Bríd; his sons Francis, Martin, Séamus, and Declan; his daughters Nuala and Kathleen. Reposing at home Monday evening from five o'clock until seven. Removal from his residence on Tuesday morning to the Church of Immaculate Conception for Funeral Mass at eleven o'clock with burial afterwards."

The announcer continued on to the next name, but Father McGinley turned the radio off and clapped his hands together.

"That's it, lads," he said. "The timing is absolutely providential. I rang the priest over there, and not only were Proinsias and his wife owners of the local pub, but Bríd is the former principal of the national school and Proinsias was retired from teaching in the secondary school. This is your man, Dallas. There can be no doubt."

"Great work, Padre. I suppose we shouldn't bother them until the funeral is over with."

"Bother them? No, we must go to the funeral."

"But we don't know these people. It doesn't seem right to intrude on them at a time like this."

"I don't know what funerals are like where you are from, but in this country this is precisely the time you want to intrude on them, as you put it. It is the one day that we can be certain that this Séamus will be there. No matter what far-flung place in the world he was, if he's an Irishman, he will be home for this funeral. That's the beauty of it. It is the one day you can be sure to find him at home."

"It just seems disrespectful to show up out of the blue at the funeral of someone we don't know."

"Lad, that funeral will be attended by every friend, relative, neighbor, and acquaintance that man ever had. Anyone who ever met the man—even once—or merely heard about him or knows someone who knows him will be there. In this country it is disrespectful *not* to go to a funeral, no matter how tenuous the connection. No, the three of us most definitely need to go and sympathize with Séamus Costello and his family."

"And where is that place exactly?"

"Coillte Coileáin. That would be about forty miles from here. Not far in the grand scheme of things. I'll drive us in the parish auto."

"I cannot thank you enough for your help, Father," said Alex. "I scarcely believe I will soon meet the man who has been an obsession of my family for so many years."

"We should celebrate," I said. "Shall we have a drink to toast the padre's great work?"

"In the middle of the day?" said the priest. "Not on your life. I have people to call on this afternoon, and it wouldn't do to have whiskey on my breath. Well, maybe just the one. I mean, given the day that's in it, but just the one."

After downing three glasses of Paddy's each, we said our goodbyes to Father McGinley, who ambled happily down the road back to the village.

"This would not be happening but for you, Dallas. Thank you so much. Do you look forward to seeing him again?"

I had mixed feelings. After I met him that time in Buenos Aires, I definitely never wanted to see him again. Now after all that had happened since then, it definitely felt like tempting fate.

On Monday the three of us piled into Father McGinley's old Ford Escort and set off down the winding roads of Connemara. I had no clothes I considered suitable for a funeral, but the priest assured me I would be fine. Alex produced a nice pair of slacks and a pullover sweater from his backpack and looked quite presentable.

As we neared the village, I asked, "So the funeral is in their house?"

"That's right," said the priest. "That's how it's done here."

"Why wouldn't they have it in a church?"

"Oh, the church is part of it too. Mass will be said in the church tomorrow. This evening there will be prayers, you know, praying the rosary, but this time now is for callers to sympathize with the family. We will stand in a long queue to shake hands with all of them and, of course, view the remains."

"You mean, the body will be in the house? Where will they have it?"

"Why, in the sitting room, of course. Where else would you expect to see him?"

This was definitely going to be different from any funeral I had attended before.

"And how will we know which house it is?"

"Don't you worry about that."

He was correct. Finding the Costello home was not a challenge. We came upon a traffic jam of cars as well as people on foot and on bicycles. There were also a couple of tractors. The nearest we could park to the house was about a half-mile away. We joined a stream of people walking in one direction. As we trod the narrow road, we continually met people coming back from the house.

After several minutes, we reached the house, a white dormer bungalow. It had been painted recently, and the garden had been tended lovingly. We waited forty minutes to get to the front door. In a strange way, it reminded me of being in line for a ride at Disneyland.

As we gradually shuffled forward, Alex and I got more than a few stares. I was used to it by now. Strangers stood out like sore thumbs. While I had become known in my own local area and did not get the looks so much anymore, whenever I ventured outside the locality, I was again an object of curiosity. I could just about hear the whispers of people conjecturing what possible connection I—and especially Alex—could have to the Costello family.

We made our way slowly inside the house. A somber man greeted us and invited us to sign a guest book on a small table. As we continued into the sitting room, I got my first view of the main event. An open coffin was in the center of the room. I glimpsed the man lying inside. His shiny, bald head looked as if it were made of wax. Men, women, and children sat along the walls of the room, all dressed in their best suits or dresses, their hair combed or styled perfectly. It was now clear why the line moved so slowly. Every guest took time to shake hands and say a few words to each and every family member. Some paused for in-depth conversations, holding up everyone behind them. Deeper into the room's interior, I could hear most people repeating the same four words to each person.

"Sorry for your trouble."

It was a funny thing to say. For me, trouble was a problem or inconvenience, not a description of bereavement. Yet each person who heard the words was visibly grateful. Father McGinley went ahead of us. He had his own particular words of comfort. He spoke to each one as if he knew them well, though I was sure he had not met any of them before. Alex followed the example we had seen and repeated, "Sorry for your trouble." Once or twice, he slipped and whispered, "*Lo siento mucho.*"

I shook the limp hand of a young boy, whose eyes were still wide from looking at Alex. He looked up and quietly said, "*Go *raibh maith agat.*" I had long since learned the Irish words for thanking someone. From the corner of my eye, I spotted a dignified, white-haired woman. Dressed in black and sitting in the last chair, she was the main object of everyone's attention. A woman I took to be her daughter sat supportively at her side. The older woman—the lady, for there was no other word to describe her—greeted guest after guest, speaking a few carefully chosen words to each one. She was not only a grieving widow but also a dutiful and gracious hostess.

As we neared her, I mumbled, "Sorry for your trouble," so many times the words lost their meaning. I had ceased noticing the questioning looks every person gave me. I glanced at Father McGinley and was shaken out of my robotic pattern. He was shaking hands with someone I recognized. His curly, black hair now had streaks of gray, his face was rougher with a few creases, and he had put on a few pounds since Buenos Aires. It was him. It was Séamus.

He took little notice of Father McGinley, and he eyed Alex with curiosity. As he turned toward me, I anticipated the inevitable look of shock. Our eyes met. His face did not change as he shook my hand.

"It's been a long time, Séamus," I said.

His expression still did not change.

"I'm Declan," he said patiently.

"So it's Declan again now," I said, continuing to shake his hand. "Anyway, I'm sorry about your dad, but you and I need to talk."

"Sorry? Talk? Talk about what? Do I know you?"

"Come on," I said, lowering my voice and ignoring the stare of the impatient, elderly man behind me. "I know it's your dad's funeral, but this is important. You can't get out of this by pretending you don't know me."

"It's Séamus you want. He had to step out for a bit. He'll be back soon."

"What kind of game are you playing? Wait, are you serious? Are you really not Séamus?"

"I told you. I'm Declan."

"You mean you guys are twins?"

"Thank you so much for coming," he said, extricating his hand from my grip while he turned to the next man.

"Wait," I said, refusing to move. "I'm confused now. I've got to know. Was it you or him I met that time in Deauville?"

By now just about everyone in the room was focused on my conversation with Declan. I could feel every stare. Ignoring me, Declan proceeded to thank the elderly man. I glanced ahead and saw no one in the queue ahead of me. The widow and her daughter looked at me curiously. Father McGinley and Alex waited at the far end of the room.

I gave up and continued down the line, repeating, "Sorry for your trouble," to the remaining, dumbfounded family members. A couple of them thanked me, but most of them just stared.

When I came to the end of the line, I bent down slightly and told the widow, "My sincere condolences, ma'am."

Despite it being her husband's funeral, she was pleasant and calm. She was also sharp and alert. She had missed nothing, including my awkward encounter with Declan, yet she put me totally at ease.

"A friend of our Séamuseen's, are you?"

"Séamuseen? I mean, yes, I am, ma'am. Séamuseen and I are friends going way back."

"Séamuseen has met a good many interesting people on his travels, but we are rarely fortunate enough to welcome any of them here in Coillte Coileáin. You are very welcome. He should be back soon. Please stay and have a drink while you wait."

She pointed me toward the door to the kitchen. Through it I saw a gaggle of older men around a table with an assortment of bottles. They raised their glasses, laughed, and talked loudly. They enjoyed themselves in a way I had never seen people enjoy themselves at a funeral.

"Thank you very much, ma'am. Again, my condolences."

Father McGinley and Alex eyed me curiously.

"I thought that was him," I said quietly. "I was sure it was. Apparently, he has a twin brother. Our guy has taken a breather, but he's supposed to be back soon. His mother invited us to have a drink while we wait."

"I guess we'll just have to make the best of it," said the priest with a smile, already halfway to the table.

In no time he had joined the ongoing conversation, and a smiling fellow cheerfully poured him a glass of Jameson.

"Fancy a drink?" I asked Alex.

"I have heard about Irish funerals," he said. "Apparently, what I heard was true. This is quite different from an Argentine funeral."

I helped myself to two glasses and filled one for me and one for Alex. A particularly jolly man raised his glass to us and said, "*Sláinte!*"

"*Sláinte!*" we said back to him.

"And very different from a North American one. I like it. This isn't a bad way to send someone off."

The friendly fellow came nearer and began to ask questions. He wanted to know where we were from and how we knew the Costellos. As I dealt with the impromptu interview, I spotted someone in a black suit slipping into the kitchen through a back door. The curly-headed man paid me no heed as he worked his way through the crowd toward the living room—until I pressed my hand on his shoulder.

"*Dia dhuit,* Séamuseen."

He turned toward me, and his eyes grew wide. At last I saw the look on his face that I had been expecting since arriving at the funeral.

# 18
# The Photograph

"JESUS, MARY, AND Joseph!" he hissed. "What the feck are you doing here, Austin? And don't waste your time trying to speak *as Gaeilge.* Your Irish is shite."

"Sorry for your trouble, Séamus, and sorry to barge into your father's funeral, but we need to talk."

"I can't feckin' believe this. It's my first time home in eleven years, and you feckin' show up. How did you even find my home place?"

"Look, I know this isn't the best time and place to talk. Can I trust you to hang around until after the funeral so we can ask our questions?"

"Who is 'we'?"

"These are my friends, Alex Malaka and Father McGinley."

He stared, his jaw hanging.

"Yeh, I'll be happy to talk with ye tomorrow night, but it will be late enough. Come to the Mass, if ye like, and the cemetery after. There'll be a meal and a lot of hanging about all night. It'll be the wee hours before ye get yer chat. I'm fierce curious now, though I suspect I'll regret it."

"Okay, we'll leave you alone until tomorrow night, but there's something I have to know right now. Was that you I ran into that time in Deauville?"

"Yeh, it was me. Who did you think it was?"

"You were using the name Declan."

"I see. You met my brother, did you? Yeh, sometimes when things get a bit dicey, I've been known to use his name. You know, for convenience. That's the handy thing about having an identical twin. Jayzus, I hope you didn't say anything to him. He doesn't know the half of what I've been up to. None of them do."

"I don't know the half of it either, and up to now that's how I've liked it. Anyway, I'm sorry about your dad. Your mom is an impressive woman. She had no idea who we were, but she was extremely gracious to us."

"Yeh," he said, walking away, "that's Mam. Every stranger and blow–in gets the welcome of the world."

He resumed his place in the receiving line.

"So, that's him," said Alex. "The legendary hitchhiker."

"The trouble with Séamus," I said, "is you can't always be sure he's telling the truth. He's always got some angle, but we'll do our best to get the story out of him. I'm just worried he'll take off before we get to talk to him."

"He wouldn't abandon his own father's funeral," said the priest confidently.

"Frankly, I wouldn't put it past him."

"He certainly won't miss the burial. We'll come back tomorrow for the Mass and the rest of it. You'll be able to keep an eye on him."

"This funeral sure seems to go on for a long time."

"We haven't been here for most of it," said Father McGinley. "When the body was brought home, there would have been friends, neighbors, and family in the house overnight, waking the deceased. He will not have been left alone from the moment he died until he is laid into the ground."

As Father McGinley drove us home, I worried about his ability to navigate the narrow, twisty roads after his several glasses of Jameson, but to his credit he got us home safely. It was no time at all until we headed back to Coillte Coileáin the next day.

On the chance there might be time to wander about and take photos, I brought my camera. This one I had had for about a dozen years—ever since I got back from South America. Instead of getting another Nikon, I had gotten a Canon F–1, a brand-new one with electro-magnetic shutter speed control.

When we got to the church, every pew had been claimed, so we waited outside until the hearse arrived.

A stout, gray-haired priest, resplendent in his white vestment, walked ahead of the coffin. He said a few words at the nave entrance, then led the pallbearers inside, as a hymn was sung. The three of us stood in the vestibule with a group of men who were shuffling their feet and casting their eyes downward.

Family members placed a Bible, a cross, and rosary beads on the coffin. Others went to the altar for readings. I thought Séamus was one of them until I realized it was Declan. I saw Séamus later when he read a prayer of the faithful from the altar. In his homily, the priest spoke of Proinsias, or P, as everyone called him, paying tribute to his life, his family, and his contributions to the community. He recalled that, in his youth, P had been a standout player for the local football club, leading them to two championships. He sympathized with Bríd, P's wife of many years, who had been his constant companion since secondary school. He spoke of P's close relationship with each of his eight children, most of whom had stayed close to home. The exception was Séamus.

"Though not ones to trouble others with their worries," said the priest, "P and Bríd always longed for the day their Séamuseen would come home. P called him the prodigal son. In his last hours, P's prayers were answered. Upon word his father was in his last hours, Séamus returned in time to say his goodbyes, making his father the happiest man in heaven."

As the priest told the story, I was moved by the pervasive sound of sniffling from the nave.

During the Eucharist, one of the priest's assistants came to offer it to the men in the vestibule. I stepped outside to avoid it, as did another man. We stood silent and curious about each other's story. Father McGinley gave me an inscrutable look. Was it sympathy? Disappointment? Despite the basic meaning of the word, Communion made me feel entirely isolated.

One of Séamus's brothers spoke in remembrance of P, praising him as a wonderful father. An invitation to prayer was followed by a period of silence. The signs of farewell were made with holy water and incense sprinkled on the pall over the coffin. After a song of farewell and prayer of commendation, the coffin was carried out of the church in a procession.

We were among the crowd following the coffin to the graveyard. The wind turned brisk. It began, as the locals said, to spit rain. Nobody paid much attention. More prayers were said over the casket in the freshly dug grave.

The prayers over, the priest announced all were welcome for food at the pub. The milling crowd dispersed gradually. We followed the throng to the village.

Inside, turf blazed in the fireplace. Tables were positioned in every available space. Many people were already digging into bowls of stew. A line had formed at the bar, black porter being the preferred drink. Rising chatter and laughter filled our ears.

"Is this a funeral or a party?" I asked.

"At times, it is difficult to tell the difference," smiled Father McGinley.

He insisted we were obliged to have a pint—as a sign of respect.

More than one pint was consumed by the time we found a place to sit and have our stew. Because beer and whiskey now flowed, some of the locals found the courage to approach us and ask, in so many words, who the hell we were. Father McGinley had no trouble fielding the questions. It was more important to him to make the story good rather than strictly accurate. Before long he was telling people Alex and I were old friends of Séamus and that the three of us had had fabulous adventures together in the Americas.

I, on the other hand, soon ran out of patience explaining myself to old codgers. When a man in a black suit, reeking of cigarette smoke, sat next to me, I was on the point of saying something rude until I realized it was Séamus.

"Shall we have our chat, Austin?"

He was tired. I felt sympathy for him and didn't bother protesting his deliberate mistaking of my name.

"It's kind of noisy in here," I said. "Want to go outside?"

"I have a better idea. Follow me."

He led the three of us to a storeroom at the back. At the far end was a smaller door. Behind it was an unsteady set of narrow stairs. We emerged in a musty attic, not quite large enough to stand in. There were wooden crates of varying shapes and sizes, some stacked. Séamus sat on one, and we joined him. He pulled a pack out of his coat pocket and put a cigarette in his mouth.

"Fancy a fag?" he said, offering the pack.

Alex willingly took one, but Father McGinley demurred—for a moment.

"I'm not really meant to smoke anymore," said the priest. "Well, just this once. For the day that's in it."

Séamus took a long drag and said, "I always came up here to hide. It was a good place to disappear when there was work for doing. It looks no different now than it ever did. Funny how time stands still in some places. In other places, there's no stopping it."

We waited, as he took another puff and gazed into space for a moment.

"So, tell me, what is so important you had to track me down to my own home place on the day of my da's funeral in the back of beyond?"

His face turned deadly serious. His eyes bore into me.

"I hope to God this isn't about what happened in Newtownbreda. Jayzus, Austin, please don't tell me you were the yank with the camera that night."

It was as though the room's air pressure had increased by several pounds per inch and my head was about to be crushed.

"Shit, Séamus, did you have something to do with the explosion?"

"You mean it *was* you? Well, isn't this just feckin' lovely. Feckin' lovely. You're in some serious shite, my friend. Jayzus, Austin."

There was something desperate about the way he sucked on his cigarette. He glanced at Alex and Father McGinley.

"Why have you brought these two into it? What do they have to do with it?"

174

"Look," I said, "can we pretend that neither of us said what we just said? I didn't come here because of that. I'm here for a completely different reason."

He buried his face in his hands, ash falling from the butt between his fingers.

"A completely different reason? It never ends. So why *are* you here?"

"It's the last thing you were expecting," I said. "Did you happen to be hitchhiking in France in the year... when was it, Alex?"

"Nineteen-seventy-four. April."

It was oddly comical to see memories and questions play out on his face. He stared hard at Alex, as if trying to recognize him.

"That's a fair few years ago now. Why would you be asking me that?"

"If you were there," said Alex, "you will have no trouble remembering it. It was an unusually busy day in Paris. It was the day of Georges Pompidou's funeral."

Séamus's eyes continued to lock on Alex.

"What does this have to do with you? You were hardly alive yourself on the day. How old are you anyways?"

"Eighteen."

"Well, I'm definitely not your father if that's what you're thinking."

"I know who my father is. I think you met my father."

I could see the pieces of the puzzle falling into place by the look on the Irishman's face. He turned to me.

"How are you mixed up in this, Austin?"

"It's complicated. It's not important."

"Indulge me. I'm curious."

"Alex is the best friend of my best friend's son. You know, Lonnie, the guy I got separated from that time I met you in Mexico City. The time you said you'd help me, but instead you drove me to the Guatemala border and nearly got me thrown into a prison. That's how I'm involved."

He shook his head.

"You know what's dangerous about you, Austin? You're a magnet for coincidences. You show up at times and in places that make absolutely no sense. I go years without seeing you or even thinking about you—and then suddenly there you are in a place where it doesn't make any sense for you to be. Even here among my own people, I'm not feckin' safe from you."

He turned to Alex.

"So what is it you want to know, lad?"

"Did you take my mother's engagement ring?"

Séamus leaned back. I thought he was about to burst out laughing. He turned to Father McGinley.

"You know, Father, I went to confession about that. I poured my guilty heart out to one of your colleagues. Back when I still went to Mass sometimes. You know what the fecker—sorry, Father—the priest said to me? He said God had mysterious ways of bringing these things back on you. He said, if I didn't make amends and atone, it would come back to haunt me when and how I least expected. I thought he was crazy. So you're the son of the Chinese guy…"

"He is Dutch-Indonesian and now an Argentine citizen."

"Yeh, whatever. How would he have ever been able to track me down? It was the perfect crime. Yet nearly twenty years later, here you are. You tracked me down. Feckin' amazing."

He leaned closer to Alex.

"So now that you found me, what is it you're expecting?"

"Do you still have it?"

"Have it? You mean, the ring? Did you think I would still have it after all these years? That I wouldn't have sold it for whatever I could get for it? Did you really come here expecting to get the ring back?"

"The important thing was to find you, to meet you, to find out what became of the ring."

Séamus leaned back again, running his hand from one side of his jaw to the other. An odd smile came over his face.

"You've won the lotto, Alex. I can show you what you're looking for. If you want it back, you can just take it. Bet you didn't expect to get so lucky."

Alex was astounded.

"Really?"

"Not a bother. Follow me so."

We went back downstairs. The pub was more packed than before, the atmosphere more festive. We navigated our way through the crowd. Séamus led us to the far end of the room where his mother sat, a daughter on either side of her. They minded her, as she held court to the never-ending arrival of more sympathizers and friends.

Séamus pushed his way past them all. Her eyes went immediately to him.

"How's it goin', Mam?"

"Oh, Séamuseen, I was looking for you."

"Mam, did you meet my friends? They came a long way. That's Austin. He's from Texas, and this here is Alex. He's from Indonesia."

"Argentina," said Alex quietly, as Bríd took his hand in hers.

"You are so very good to have come all that way. Are you long home?"

The question confused Alex, but I had learned that here "home" always meant Ireland—even though it wasn't your home. Alex's eyes narrowed. I followed his gaze to the pendant she wore over her black dress. It hung on a gold chain necklace and was in the shape of a heart. In its center was a sparkling diamond.

"My," said Alex. "That is a lovely pendant."

She touched it lovingly.

"Our Séamuseen brought it to me. Years ago. All the way from France. Can you imagine? I don't know how he ever afforded it, especially in those days. None of us had two coins to rub together, I can tell you. You know, I am lucky to have always had most of my children around me, but Séamuseen has always been such a worry to me. This necklace has always been a comfort to me in his absence. It is like having part of him home safe with me."

"It is beautiful. May I ask a favor?"

"Yes?"

"May my friend Dallas take a photograph of the two of us? I would like to send it to my own mother in Buenos Aires. I know she misses me as you have missed your own son."

Flustered, Bríd fussed with her dress and her hair.

"I don't know what kind of state I'm in. It's been such a long day. I'm sure I don't look right at all."

"Believe me, Mrs. Costello, you are absolutely beautiful. I can't tell you how much it would mean to my mother and me to have this memento."

"Well, I suppose, but Séamuseen will have to be in it as well."

Her son, who had been smiling at the encounter, was now uncomfortable.

"You know I don't like having my picture taken, Mam."

"If I can have mine taken, then so can you."

Once back from the car with the camera, I knelt down before them and adjusted the F–stop and shutter speed. They were easy subjects. Despite her reticence, Bríd smiled radiantly. Séamus turned his head downward, attempting to hide his face. Alex grinned broadly in satisfaction, knowing I would be sure to focus on the diamond on the widow's breast. As unlikely as it would have seemed, his quest had been an unmitigated success.

Over the crowd's din, I heard a bow drawn against a fiddle's strings, then the tapping of a drumstick on a bodhrán. The music had begun. The chatter gradually ceased, as everyone's attention was drawn to the skeletal figure barely filling his black suit. Eyes closed, the old man sang in a raspy timbre. His voice went up and down the musical scale. The Irish words were only sounds to me, but the power of grief he evoked was overwhelming. All eyes were fastened on him. The emotion was understood collectively. As moved as I was, I knew the experience was deeper for the others because of their long, common history. As with Communion, this powerful, shared experience made me feel separate.

Afterwards, Séamus and I walked through the village. The breeze was cold. Despite the hour, the last rays of the sun could still be perceived on the horizon.

"What the hell were you doing in Belfast, Austin?"

"If I tell you, will you have to kill me?"

"I heard the story. I immediately thought of you, but I told myself it was a mad notion. They said some yank with a camera was standing on the road when they drove away. It was bad enough it was the South Armagh Brigade lads, but the Argentines were there too."

"It was Número Uno."

"Who?"

"That was my own personal name for him. The guy you and I met that time in Buenos Aires. I couldn't believe it was him after all that time. He looked straight at me through the car window. I knew by the look on his face he recognized me—even though he hadn't seen me since 1982."

"You mean, 1981."

"What?"

"It was 1981 when we met him."

"Right, but I ran into him again. A year later."

"What? You're joking me. How? Where?"

"It's a long story. It doesn't matter now."

"What the hell were you doing in Belfast that night anyways?"

"I was on an assignment."

"An assignment? An assignment for who?"

"I was working as a photojournalist. A colleague and I were there to shoot photos for an article about day-to-day life during the Troubles. I had to meet a guy to give him some news."

"A guy? What guy?"

"It doesn't matter. That's not part of the story, except that I was coming back from meeting him in Belvoir Park. We were walking on the road when I spotted them running away from the truck. I just instinctively started shooting with the camera. They piled into a car as fast as they could."

"Well, you're not the only one who does instinctive shooting, but the lads we're talking about shoot with bullets. How are you still alive? Why are you still in Ireland?"

"I saw how fast they drove away from the truck. They didn't have time to deal with me, and I knew that was bad. That's when I saw him through the car window. Something kicked in. I made a stupid promise a long time ago, and I automatically began shooting. I got a pretty good damn shot of him too, right through the window glass."

"Wait. What? Promise? What promise? To who?"

"You don't want to know. Anyway, I knew he had seen me and that he had recognized me. That's when they stopped and started shooting. With bullets, I mean. I panicked. I ran as fast as I could. If they hadn't been trying to get out of there as fast as they possibly could, I would have been dead. That's how I knew something really bad was going to happen. I ran as hard I could. I ran like a damn coward. When I couldn't run anymore, I dropped to my knees and began dry heaving. That's when the whole world exploded. It fucking blew me into the air. I slid about ten yards down the road. The noise was so loud I was deaf for three days. I read in the papers that the target was some forensic lab. More than a thousand houses were damaged. More than forty destroyed completely."

I took a deep breath.

"And someone died there. Someone who shouldn't have died. And it was my fault."

"It doesn't make sense. They gave a warning before the bombing. People were evacuated. Those lads should have been long gone before that bomb went off. Something unexpected must have happened for them to be there when you saw them. I mean, something unexpected besides you."

He had a dazed look on his face.

"You realize they won't let this go, don't you? The connection between the Ra and the Monteros was always supposed to be secret. No one was ever supposed to know about that, but they know you have photographic evidence. Jayzus, how are you still alive? Why did you not head immediately back to the States?"

"I was in a panic. I just wanted to find the most out-of-the-way place in the whole world. At the time, I thought it was Connemara. I was there once, and it was the most remote place I had ever seen."

Séamus threw his head back in laughter.

"Have you not copped on at all? This is Ireland. On this island every fecker knows every other fecker. And if he doesn't know him personally, he knows his brother or his cousin. You can't hide anywhere in this country. Especially you. You stand out like a sore thumb. I cannot believe you're still alive."

"What am I going to do, Séamus? Can you help me?"

"Jayzus, Austin. I've got my own problems. I'm leaving the country as soon as I can manage. If they got wind of me talking to you, it wouldn't be good for either of us."

"But what am I going to do?"

"For a start, let's go back to the pub for a drink. That's always a good first step to solving any problem."

"Sounds good. Two drinks for the prodigal sons. I'll buy."

"It's my turn. You paid the last time. Besides, they won't charge tonight if they know it's for me."

"How does life get so complicated, Séamus?"

"I'd love to know the answer to that one myself, Austin. Look, we've got a few hours to kill. Maybe you can fill me in on what else you've been up to since all those years ago in Buenos Aires. C'mere to me, did you ever find that woman from Deauville again?"

# 19
# Another Funeral

IT WAS A RELIEF to be home again in California. My parents'
house felt safe, secure, and reassuring—for about half a day.

Mom pampered me the first morning, like a kid too sick for
school. When Dad got home from work, I knew he was still
annoyed about having to drive to Bakersfield in the middle of the
night, but he held his tongue for Mom's sake.

I got the lecture on the second evening.

"So, Dallas, what are your plans?"

"Well, mostly right now I want to catch up on my sleep. Then I
need to see if I have enough money in the bank to buy a new
camera. I told you my Nikon got stolen in Buenos Aires, didn't I?"

"Yes, you did. I was wondering more what your long-term
plans are. I imagine you will be looking for work."

"Yeah, don't worry. I'll pay you back every penny I owe you,
and I need to save up a bunch of money besides. I need to get to
France as soon as I can. I really need to see someone there."

"Yes, well, I'm sure this gallivanting all over the world must
seem like a lot of fun to you, but you realize you're twenty-seven
years old now."

"Twenty-eight, Dad."

"Yes, right. And when I was your age…"

"Yeah, I know, you had a wife and two kids and you'd been
working for years."

"That's right. You might want to think about settling down.
You don't want to find yourself still paying a mortgage when
you're trying to save for your retirement."

"Retirement? Dad, I'm not even thirty yet."

"Time has a way of catching up on you, son. Before you know it, you'll be looking back and wondering where all those years went. You'll wish you had worked harder and saved more."

"Don't worry, I'm definitely going to find work. I have plans."

"Glad to hear it. Walt was saying the other day that he's looking for help. You might want to give him a call."

"I'm not going to go work on a farm, Dad. I'm a photographer. I've won prizes for my work. I'm actually kind of famous in San Francisco for the photos I took in France and Germany."

"That's fine, but I don't know who's going to hire a photographer around here."

"Dad, I'm not staying around here. I need to be someplace where there are major newspapers and magazines."

"So where will you go?"

"I haven't figured that out yet. I need some time."

"You might try the Bakersfield paper."

"I don't think I'm going to be living in Bakersfield."

As he and I talked, Mom was on the phone. She walked into the living room, her face stricken.

"That was Jean Walker."

She hesitated.

"Her nephew Michael died."

I was sick in my stomach.

"You knew him, didn't you, Dallas? Wasn't he a few years older than you?"

"Yeah, he was."

Being home no longer felt safe.

"Lonnie went steady with his sister through most of high school. Lonnie and I stayed at his house in L.A. that time we went to Mexico."

"It's such a tragedy. He was so young and such a good-looking young man. I never understood why some girl didn't snatch him right up. He was sick for such a long time. The doctors were never able to figure out what was wrong."

Michael's death gave me a reprieve from talking about my future. The next day Mom sent me with a casserole to Michael's parents. A familiar face opened the door.

"Linda, I'm so sorry."

She broke into tears. We hugged.

"Dallas, I can't believe he's gone."

"Too many people we grew up with are dying. First Tommy Dowd. Then Lonnie. Now Michael. It's all so crazy."

She took the casserole inside and returned. Stepping outside, she closed the door behind her.

"It's good to see you. Mom's a basket case in there. You don't have a cigarette, do you?"

"No, I keep trying to quit. We can walk down to the gas station, and I'll buy us a pack."

"Sounds good. I need to get out of the house for a while."

As we walked down the street, she held onto my arm.

"How's the real estate going?" I asked.

"Good. It's going really well. The kids are happy in school, and I've been seeing someone. He's a great guy. Things are good. At least they were until... So what are you doing home? Last I heard you were traveling all over the world."

"I was in South America, but I've come back with my tail between my legs."

"Speaking of your tail between your legs, how's Lana?"

"That's been over for a while now. There's a new woman in the picture. She's French."

"I should have known. You were never going to settle for an ordinary San Joaquin Valley girl."

"Hey, you make it sound like I'm some kind of snob. Don't you remember me telling you how I pined over you for ages but couldn't do anything because you were my best friend's girl?"

"Yes, but I never believed a word of it. I think you just always wanted whatever Lonnie had."

I bought the cigarettes, and we lit up. I handed her the pack, but she wouldn't take it.

"Mom won't allow them in the house."

184

"Well, if I keep them, I'll have to hide them somewhere *my* mom can't find them. God, listen to us. You would never know we're almost thirty years old."

"Speak for yourself. I'm never going to be thirty. Next year for me will be the first in a long string of twenty-ninth birthdays."

Back at her house, I said, "Well, I guess I'll see you at the funeral. Tell your parents how sorry I am."

"I will. Tell your mom, thanks for the casserole."

After I got home, I wrote another letter to Valérie. I told her I was back in California and that I would like it if she would write me. This was a scary thing for me to tell her. When I had told her she didn't need to write me because I didn't know where I was going to be, it protected me from disappointment since I wouldn't expect a letter from her. From now on, every day that a letter didn't arrive would mean a day of wondering if she had no interest in writing.

There was a simple church service for Michael. It barely lasted an hour, followed by the burial. As things were ending at the cemetery, I wandered over to Lonnie's grave. I recalled the day of his funeral and the monarch butterfly that appeared like magic in the middle of it. Looking at his plot, that old nagging feeling came back—the one of being convinced Lonnie wasn't really dead. I loved thinking he had played the ultimate fast one on everybody and was out there somewhere, laughing at us.

Linda joined me.

"I still can't believe he's gone either."

"Say, do you know where Lonnie's mom is these days?"

"No. Mom heard she got married again and moved to Oregon."

"Another husband? How many does that make?"

"Four, I guess. I don't think she keeps in contact with anyone here anymore. Were you thinking of getting in touch with her?"

"Yeah. I visited the place where Lonnie was in Germany. I thought she might be interested in hearing about it."

"I bet she would, but gee, I don't know how you'd track her down. When I asked Mom about her, she didn't know what town they were living in or what her last name is now."

I wondered whether I should tell Linda that Lonnie had a son in Germany, but what would have been the point? It did not feel like my secret to share. I wasn't even sure I would tell his mother—if I ever got the chance.

"Did you notice," asked Linda, "that none of Michael's friends from L.A. were here?"

"Yeah, I kind of wondered about that. He lived down there for a long time. I would have thought someone would have come."

"They had their own memorial for him. Mom and Dad didn't make them feel particularly welcome."

"That's too bad."

"Yeah, it is. You knew Michael was gay, right?"

It was the first time I had heard her acknowledge it.

"Yeah, I knew."

"Mom and Dad just couldn't accept it. It's so sad. They'll never get that time back, all the years he was apart from them."

"Yeah, it's a shame. In San Francisco, every other person I knew was gay. It's no big deal up there."

"How much longer are you around?"

"Not much longer, I think. The house is kind of small for the three of us, especially with Dad trying to make me responsible and settled down. I'll be gone pretty soon."

"Well, wherever you go, fly safe, Superboy."

My reprieve came a few days later—like the answer to a prayer. To appease Dad, I was looking over the Help Wanted ads in the Bakersfield paper when the phone rang.

"It's for you," Mom said. "It sounds like long distance."

I couldn't imagine who would call me.

"Hello?"

"Mr. Green?"

"Yes?"

"I'm glad to get hold of you."

I knew the voice well. It was David, my former employer. He was the last person I expected to hear from. It was strange to talk to him while in my parents' house.

"David, how on earth did you know where to call me?"

"This is the emergency number we had on file during your employment. Given the area code, I presume this is your parents' number?"

"That's right, but how did you know I'd be here?"

"I didn't," he said, perplexed at the question.

"Right, sorry. Look, David, I'm sorry about the way I bailed on you in December. It was nice of you to give me my job back, and I was honestly intending to go back to work for you, but something came up, and I had to leave the country. It was a lousy thing to do, and I apologize."

"It's all forgotten, Mr. Green. As it happens, I was wondering if you were available to do some work for us now?"

"Really? After the way I let you down? That's incredibly nice of you."

"You understand, I'm not offering you full-time employment. I'd like to hire you for, say, a six-week contract. We have a new photographer, and frankly, he is not up to the standard you set for us. I was wondering if you could work with him, you know, mentor him to get his skills up to speed. How does that sound to you?"

"That sounds great. I appreciate the chance to make things up to you."

"Not at all. Any chance you could come in tomorrow?"

I saw Mom listening from the kitchen.

"Yeah, I think I could do that. It probably won't be until late afternoon, though."

"Very good. We shall see you then."

As I hung up the phone, Mom said, "It sounds like you'll be leaving again."

"Yeah, I've got a job, and it's perfect. It'll just last long enough for me to save up money for going to France."

"Why on earth do you want to go to France?"

"Mom, there's a woman."

"Aren't there plenty of women here? Why do you have to go all the way to France?"

"Because, Mom, I'm in love."

When Dad got home, he was even less encouraging.

"You're going back to San Francisco for work? Where will you live?"

"I don't know. I'll figure it out when I get there."

"It's very expensive up there."

"I know that."

"That will make it harder to save money."

"Yeah, I know."

"You'll need to buy a car."

"No, I won't. You don't need a car in the city."

"How will you get there?"

"I'll take the bus."

He shook his head.

"I guess you know what you're doing."

That was Dad's way of saying he didn't think I knew what I was doing.

The next morning at the crack of dawn, Dad drove me back to the bus station in Bakersfield. As I got out of the car, he looked at my backpack and shook his head.

"Is that all you're taking with you?"

"Yep."

"Where did you say you'll be staying?"

"I said, I'll figure it out when I get there."

He shook his head again and drove away.

I had several hours to think, as I watched mile after mile of farmland and desert pass by along Interstate 5. In some ways it wasn't that different than riding the bus across Argentina.

The bus station in the city wasn't far from my old apartment. I simply followed my old walking route back to the office. On the edge of Chinatown, I stopped at the camera store where I had bought my Nikon F2. This time the salesman convinced me to buy a Canon F–1. I looked forward to the day I could once more have my own darkroom.

It was strange to walk those streets again. I had not been away long, but it felt different. When I got to my former place of employment, I was happy to see Flaubert's was still across the street. It had not fallen victim to the city's small-business turnover rate.

Dad had been right to wonder where I would stay. I had no idea. Maybe I could ask one of my friends at work if I could crash on a couch for a night or two until I figured it out. As I thought about who I might ask, I hit a blank. Keith, of course, was gone, and James had moved to Seattle to start his own printing business. Would there be anyone left whom I knew?

At least Marla was still at reception. She smiled when I walked up to her.

"Hello, stranger. Long time no see. David told me to let him know as soon as you arrived. Wait just a minute."

After a fifteen-minute wait, she told me I could go in. David was the same as always. If anything he was more mild and reserved than before.

"I want to thank you again, David, for thinking of me. I owe you a lot."

"Not at all, Mr. Green."

"Tell me, how is Amy doing? I was thinking about her a lot while I was away."

"Amy? Why, she's fine. She's quite happy, thank goodness."

It seemed an odd thing to say, given that her husband had died less than four months earlier.

"Now, as I explained on the phone, you will be working with our new photographer. He does not have your experience, but then neither did you when you began here. I want you to teach him everything you can. If it's not too much to ask, I'd like you to turn him into another you. While you work with him, you are welcome to submit your own photos for publication, but I am mainly interested in you mentoring the new man."

"I think I can do that. When can I meet him?"

"How about now? I think I spotted him in the production room just a bit ago. I'll pop over and see if he's still there."

While he was gone, I looked idly around his office. I noticed framed photos of his wife and of Amy on his desk. Amy had a sweet smile, and my heart ached to think about Keith's suicide.

In no time David was back accompanied by a tall man with long, black hair and a thick beard. He was built like an athlete.

"I believe you've met my son-in-law before."

"Son-in-law?"

Had David gone crazy or had I?

"Dallas! You're back! This is going to be so cool!"

"Justin?"

# 20
# Amy

"ARE YOU ALL RIGHT, Mr. Green? You look as if you've had a shock."

"Yeah, I guess I was a little taken by surprise. So, Justin, you and Amy…?"

"Yeah, we're married. Can you believe it? Sorry I didn't let you know, but it all happened so fast, and I didn't know how to get in touch with you. It was all kind of kept quiet. We didn't have a formal wedding, you know, because of it happening so soon after… well, you know."

I tried to read David's face. It had taken me a couple of years working for him to feel I had a sense of what went on in his head. He had one of those faces that never changed. Though he showed little emotion at his son-in-law's funeral, by that point I could tell he was devastated. Now just a few months later, his daughter was re-married, and he was okay with it.

I had mixed feelings. Keith had been my friend. When we moved to San Francisco, he was the only person I knew. No wonder I was jealous when he and Amy got together. It took me a long time to make new friends on my own, and the main one was Justin. Now he too was married to Amy.

Like Lonnie, Keith was someone I wished I could have back for just one day to answer all my questions. With a life as perfect as his, with everything he had going for him, why on earth did he gas himself in his garage? Unfortunately, apart from certain times when I was extremely drunk, the dead never came back for visits.

Amy could not have picked two men more different to marry. Where Keith had been driven, Justin was laid back. You might even say irresponsible. The only thing they had in common was being friends of mine.

"Mr. Green," said David, "Justin has confided in me that he has long harbored a desire to be a photographer. Given that he has no training or experience, I have made him a proposal. He will work with you for a period of six weeks, and we shall see what he can learn and produce in that time. Let us see what you can make of him. Can you be a Pygmalion?"

David's references often went over my head, but I got that one. The only question was whether he saw me as the language professor or the ancient sculptor.

"Hey, you want to get a cup of coffee?" said Justin, as we left David's office.

"Yeah. It looks like we have some catching up to do."

It was strange to drink coffee with Justin at Flaubert's instead of having him make it for me. A former co-worker teased him about "slumming."

"This americano is crap," he shot back at him. "Do you want me to go back there and show you how it's done?"

I was still in mild shock.

"Photography?"

"Yeah, I always admired your talent with the camera. I thought it was so cool that you had a skill like that you were so good at. I've been trying to decide what I want to do for a while now. I thought going back to school would help me figure it out, but that was a mistake. I'm not cut out for studying. I should have known that from high school."

He had changed so much. Except for Keith's funeral, it had been the better part of a year since I had spent time with him. He wasn't the scraggly scarecrow of a rock star I first knew. His hair and beard were well-groomed. He had gained weight, and it was all muscle.

"So I talked it over with Amy, and she asked me who I admired, who I wanted to be like. That's when I thought of you. I told her, you were always kind of a role model for me. You had an interesting job. You were good at it. I've always thought photography was cool. She told me I should give it a try and see how I like it. She said she thought photography was cool too and that she also admired you for being so good at it."

"She said that?"

"Yeah, she did. She spoke to her dad about it, and here we are. I got excited when David told me you were going to come back and teach me."

"It's funny how things work out. So how did the thing with Amy happen? I mean, that was fast."

"Crazy, huh? Like I told you the last time…"

"When Keith died."

"Yeah, then. After he died, I started hanging around the house, doing what I could to help her out with the baby and everything. One thing led to another. I know it's weird. I mean, she had just lost her husband, but we just clicked. She didn't want to be alone, and I wanted to take care of her. We weren't thinking of marriage, but well, one thing led to another, and she kind of got pregnant."

"Kind of got pregnant?"

"Yeah. It just sort of happened."

"What did David say about that?"

"Things were awkward for a while, but when he saw how happy Amy was about it, he came around. He's been really good to me. He's helped us out with money, but neither of us want to be dependent on him. I've got a night job that brings in some money, but it's important to make this photography thing work. After all, I was never going to get rich being a rock musician, was I?"

"That reminds me. I have to show you something."

I dug in my backpack to find a print of a photo I had shot in Santiago.

"Look at this. You have a huge fan in South America."

He peered at Bati proudly holding the ÜberVenge album cover. A grin came over his face.

"Wow, who's that?"

"It's my friend Ángel's little brother in Chile. He found that record in a store down there, and he loves it. When the hell did you guys record an album?"

"When we decided to break up the band, as a last hurrah we put some money together and rented a studio. I didn't think we had sold any copies, but now that I think of it, I remember Johnny saying he found a distributor interested in unloading some of them abroad. That's wild. We actually have fans in Latin America."

"Maybe you guys gave up too soon."

He laughed.

"I don't think so. It was fun while it lasted, but we were never going to be Led Zeppelin. Say, where are you staying?"

"I need to find a place. I came straight here from home."

"Hey, why don't you stay with us? That'd be perfect. It'd be great to have some company, driving in and out to work."

"I don't want to impose."

"It's not imposing. We'll make you earn your keep. With my two jobs, Amy is always stuck at home with the baby. She could use your help in the evenings when I'm gone."

"Maybe you should talk it over with her first."

"We'll talk it over tonight. I'll call and let her know you're coming home with me. She won't mind. She always says how much she thinks of you."

"Really?"

I was surprised because I had never gotten to know Amy. That was my fault. When she and Keith had tried to include me in their plans, I resisted. After he moved in with her, I rarely saw them. By the time they got married, I was so involved with Lana it was like we were on different planets.

"Okay, I'll stay for a night or two if you're sure it's no bother, but after that I should find another place."

"Suit yourself, but I can tell you we're both happy to have you. You'll see."

As we left I said, "You look great. Are you working out or something?"

"Yeah, I joined a gym. It helps with my other job. I didn't think I'd like exercising, but I've gotten into it. You should try it."

Amy

After Justin called Amy from the office, I expected us to head for the bus stop. Instead, he led me to the building's underground parking garage. He unlocked a red Chevy Camaro.

"Is this yours?"

"Yeah, well, ours. Amy couldn't keep her old car since, you know, Keith used it to kill himself. We sold it and used the money to buy this. Hop in."

We emerged above ground to join the cars snaking their way toward the Golden Gate Bridge. Once on the bridge, I gazed out Justin's window at the blue expanse of the Pacific. In the other direction, I saw the bay and the city, dominated by the distinctive shape of the Transamerica Pyramid. I recalled the many times I had walked across the bridge, many times in exhilaration, a few times in despair.

Once in Marin County, we left the freeway and arrived at a familiar suburban house. I had not visited it often, but it had become etched in my memory forever. The garage door opened, and we drove in. I wondered how Justin could handle driving in and out every day and not be overwhelmed by what had happened there.

"So, you guys didn't think about moving?"

He shrugged.

"We haven't seen anything we like better, and it's not the best time for house hunting, you know, with the baby and with me working two jobs."

I didn't know why I was nervous about seeing Amy again. Guilt? Discomfort around someone else's sadness? Maybe because I had never dealt with my own sadness. She was washing dishes when we entered the kitchen. Jennifer played with building blocks on a blanket beneath the kitchen table. Amy turned, smiled, and after wiping her hands with a towel, threw her arms around me. I didn't expect it since it had never happened before.

"Dallas! It's great to see you," she beamed. "Justin has been missing male companionship."

She looked great. I thought grief and a second pregnancy might have taken a toll, but she was happy and healthy. Her pregnancy did not yet show, and she was as slim as ever. I stood awkwardly.

"Amy, I'm sorry…"

"Sorry? About what?"

"About everything. I mean, I wished I could have done more when… I just still feel so bad about…"

I was never the most articulate person, but in that moment my tongue was tied in more knots than ever. She put her arms around me again.

"Hey," she said, "we don't need to dwell on all that, do we? We have to live in the here and now. That's what's so great about this guy. He keeps me living in the moment. We have so much to be thankful for."

"God, Amy, you look great."

She laughed.

"You didn't see me this morning throwing up with morning sickness."

She grabbed the infant and balanced her on a hip so I could get a better look at her.

"Jennifer, do you remember Uncle Dallas? No, of course, you don't. You were just a tiny thing the last time you saw him. She must look a lot different to you now compared to the last time."

"Yeah, she's gotten big. Is she walking yet?"

Amy laughed.

"There's plenty of time for that. I have enough trouble keeping track of her as it is. She crawls all over the house. She's really fast. She tires poor Mommy out, yes she does," she said, snuggling her nose to the baby's.

I was relieved to see how happy she was and pleased that she was so friendly to me. I had always had a nagging feeling Amy didn't like me much, but I must have imagined it. I guess I had never given her a chance to be friends with me. I had fretted that seeing me again now might be difficult because I would remind her of Keith, but I needn't have worried.

Justin was now on the floor playing with Jennifer. He clearly doted on her. It was as if she was his own daughter.

"Is there anything I can do to help with dinner?" I offered.

"Sit down and take it easy, D."

She had given me a new nickname. No one had ever called me D before.

"Tonight you're a guest. Tomorrow you become part of the household. You'll get plenty of chores then."

"Are you sure you don't mind me coming here on top of you?"

"Don't worry," she laughed. "We plan to make you earn your keep."

"Just so you know, I'm going to find my own place in the city as soon as I can."

"Why on earth would you do that? Save your money. You can stay here for free."

"Really?"

"Yes, really. Didn't Big J tell you? We're hoping you'll be able to look after Jennifer sometimes in the evening. You know, to give me a break. You don't mind that, do you?"

"No, I'd be happy to. It's so nice of you. I don't know what to say."

"Just say you don't mind changing a few diapers."

"Well, I guess I can learn. I never had younger brothers or sisters."

"Don't worry," she laughed. "We'll give you plenty of training and practice. You'll be an expert before you're finished."

The three of us soon settled into a routine. I became accustomed to morning and evening commutes. The workday consisted of going on assignments with Justin. It was frustrating not to take the photos myself, but I shot my own photos as well. I did my best to teach Justin how to compose his shots and choose the best camera settings. He wasn't the quickest study, but he was determined and did not get discouraged. I enjoyed spending the time with him.

Most weekday evenings after dinner, he went to his other job in San Rafael. Amy and I washed and dried dishes. Sometimes I did the washing and drying by myself to free her up. When I got time, I wrote letters to Valérie. I sent her Amy and Justin's address and told her I would be there for a few weeks. I crossed my fingers and hoped she would write back.

I liked spending time with Amy, and I became fond of Jennifer. I found myself wishing I had what Justin and Amy had. I wondered if Valérie wanted it too. What would it be like to come home to Valérie every night? It was hard to picture her at home all day.

"Do you ever get tired of being at home? Do you miss having a job?"

When I had first met Amy, she worked in the paper's advertising department. She did not go back after Jennifer was born.

"Sometimes, but not really. I'd like to go back to work someday, but this is okay for now. Sometimes it feels like I'm in hiding. I used to have a busy social life, but I hardly see anybody anymore, and that's okay. Having Little J and Big J—and now you—is enough for me. I do get together with L pretty often. She fills my need for grownup female company."

"L?"

"Yeah, my cousin Lana. She's a few years older than me, but we've always been good friends."

Something rolled over in my stomach.

"So you and, um, L are really close?"

"Yeah. She's just one of those people, you know, we can tell each other anything."

Her smile was enigmatic.

"Um, I met her at your engagement party."

"Yeah, I know."

"She told you that, huh?"

"Yeah, she tells me everything."

"Everything, huh?"

"Yeah, everything."

"So… how is she doing these days?"

"She's good. You know she divorced that jerk Gary. She swore she'd never get married again, but that only lasted a little while. A couple of months ago she fell hard for someone. He's a veterinarian. She loves the way he's so good with animals. They've already moved in together."

"That's nice."

"I'm sorry, D. She made me swear not to tell anyone I knew about you and her. It killed me to be updated on every detail and knowing you had no idea. It wasn't fair to you. I wanted to talk to you about it so much, but I couldn't."

"You knew about us the whole time?"

She nodded guiltily.

"Does David know?"

"No, Dad doesn't have a clue. I kept your secret safe. I never even told Big J about it."

"He never told you he knew?"

"You mean, he knows?"

"Yeah, he does. I finally told him about it after she dumped me. I don't know why I never told him about it before. I guess I was just ashamed. I knew what we were doing was wrong, but I kept thinking it would all somehow work out."

"I did feel bad for you even though it wasn't any of my business."

"I… I don't know what to say… You must think I'm a terrible person. I mean, I was having an affair with a married woman."

"I didn't think about it that way. I know L can be hard to resist when she sets her mind on something—or someone. If it makes you feel any better, she told me you were very sweet with her. She said you were thoughtful and caring. I don't think she appreciated you enough."

"Is there anything she *didn't* tell you?"

"Um, I don't think so."

"You mean, even…"

"Even what?"

"I mean, she must have held back at least some of the details."

"No, I think she shared just about everything."

"Everything, huh? So…"

"For what it's worth, she said you were extremely good in bed."

# 21
# Justin's Other Job

FOR A WHILE AFTER our conversation, I felt awkward around Amy, but I eventually got used to the idea of her knowing so much about me. It made us closer friends and freed us up to talk about lots of other things.

I told her about my trip to France, about meeting Valérie, and about my plan to see her again. To my relief, she did not tell me I was unrealistic. She said she found the whole thing incredibly romantic. She began pestering me on a daily basis to write to Valérie.

"I keep meaning to ask," I said one evening after the dishes were washed, "what exactly is Justin's night job?"

"Didn't he tell you? He's an actor. Can you believe it?"

"An actor? You mean in a play?"

"No, he's in a movie. It's just a low-budget production. They film in a small studio in San Rafael. It's not exactly Hollywood, but at least it pays something. He enjoys it, and we can definitely use the money."

"That's amazing. That's a much better job than being a photographer for a weekly paper."

"It's not as glamorous as it sounds. He comes home most nights exhausted. It's a lot of hard work."

"I can see how he would get cast in a movie. He always had a rock star look. Now with all the working out he's been doing, he definitely looks like a movie star. I've always been kind of jealous of him."

"Hey, D, don't talk like that. You're not so bad yourself. Honestly, I'd say it's Big J who's jealous of you. Being single probably looks pretty good to him about now. I don't think he knew what he was taking on with us two girls, but he never complains. He's so good with Jennifer. I feel so lucky."

"I have to admit, I didn't know what to make of it at first when I heard you and Justin were married. Now it makes perfect sense."

She smiled but said nothing for a minute.

"You know what? I'm going to treat myself to a half glass of wine. I've been good about abstaining because of the baby, but the doctor says a small amount every once in a while won't hurt. Will you join me?"

"Are you sure you should?"

"I wasn't asking for permission," she laughed. "Do you want some or not?"

"Sure. I can't let you drink alone, can I?"

She retrieved a half-full bottle and pulled out the cork. As we sat at the table, she frowned at the label.

"I'm sorry it isn't Bordeaux. That's where you said your girlfriend was from, right?"

The label said Malbec. It was from Mendoza.

"It's okay," I smiled. "I've been where they grow this wine. It's good too."

"Honestly?" she said as she filled two small glasses. "Is there *any* place in the world you haven't been?"

"I haven't been to that many places. I just seem to wind up where they grow wine—starting with the San Joaquin Valley."

We clinked our glasses.

"Cheers," she said.

"*Salud.*"

I liked the way she laughed when she took her first guilty sip. She quickly turned serious, though.

"D, do you have any idea why Keith did what he did?"

The question was unexpected and hit me like a sucker punch. My heart rate quickened.

"Amy, I pretty much lost contact with him after you two got married. I should have made more of an effort to spend time with him, but things in my own life were crazy. He seemed so fulfilled with his life. I didn't think he needed me. Now I lie awake sometimes at night wondering, if I had talked to him more, would it have made a difference? I don't have a clue why he did it. It's never made any sense."

A tear streamed down her cheek.

"I'm sorry. It wasn't fair to ask that. If anyone should have seen a problem, it was me. I was his wife. I'll never forgive myself."

"Hey, don't say that. Things just happen sometimes that don't make any sense, and no one can prevent them. You can't blame yourself."

I wanted to comfort her, but I didn't know how. I laid a hand awkwardly on her shoulder. She wiped away the tear and laughed ruefully.

"Does it seem weird to you that I keep marrying your friends?"

"Yeah, kind of. Keith and Justin definitely don't have much in common. The last thing I would have expected was for you to marry Justin."

"Maybe," she said with a mischievous smile, "you're the one I was always meant to marry, but I just keep missing the target."

"Yeah, that's probably why I got involved with your cousin. I missed the target too."

We laughed, and our eyes met for the briefest of moments. We went quiet. She closed her eyes for five seconds and opened them again.

"You know what? I was so good about staying off wine that it took just that small amount to get me drunk. With any luck Jennifer will stay down for the night, so I think I will go to bed. Send Big J to me when he gets home."

"Sure thing."

"Thanks for putting up with me, D."

She kissed me on the forehead. She smelled of vegetables, dish soap, and baby powder.

"No, thank you for putting up with me. You've been great."

Our eyes locked again briefly, and I felt dizzy. She stood.

"Good night, D," she said quietly.

As she left the kitchen, her slight unsteadiness made a beautiful swaying motion. I poured myself another glass of Malbec and put the stopper in the bottle. After I drained the glass, I uncorked the bottle again and poured another one.

*Shit,* I thought. *I'm starting to fall in love with Amy.*

Lying in bed, I tried to sort out my confused feelings. At my age, I shouldn't be making the same mistakes as before. How could I be in love with Valérie and Amy at the same time? Was it really love or was there something fundamentally wrong with me? Amy was just being nice to me. It would appall her to know what was going through my head. One thing was certain. I needed to find another place to live as soon as possible.

The next day at work, I asked around to see if anybody knew of an apartment for rent in the city that wasn't exorbitantly expensive. By afternoon I hit paydirt. Marla said she had heard Melanie Francis might want to sublet. I quickly tracked her down.

"How's it going, Mel?"

"You know I don't like to be called that."

"Yeah, I remember. I heard you might be subletting your place."

"Yes, that's right. Sheila was invited to teach a summer course at Cambridge, and I'm going with her. We're hoping to sublet for about two months."

"The summer, huh? How soon would it be available?"

"In about two weeks. Why? Are you interested?"

"Depends. How much is the rent?"

"It's not too bad considering it's Pacific Heights. We might be able to cut a little off if you're willing to water the plants and feed the cats."

"Cats, huh? Any chance of moving in sooner than two weeks?"

She barely thought before answering.

"Uh, no. You can have it in two weeks. You can't throw any wild parties or make a lot of noise. It's a quiet building, and we have a good reputation with the neighbors."

"Okay, okay. Let's talk money."

Within a couple of days we had taken care of the paperwork, and I had paid them a month's rent. I would miss Amy and Jennifer—not to mention the free rent—but I knew this was the right thing to do. Justin and Amy were disappointed when I told them.

I looked forward to having my own place again—even if it was for only two months. I had been living in other people's homes seemingly forever.

A few days later while Justin and I were on an assignment, he asked, "Are you interested in earning some extra money?"

"Sure. I could use it to pay my rent."

"You wouldn't have to pay rent if you didn't move out."

"Yeah, yeah, we've been over that already. Tell me about this extra money."

"Stan, the guy at my night job, wants some publicity photos for the movie, and his regular photographer isn't available until next week. I told him I knew a great photographer who might be available immediately."

"Why don't *you* shoot the photos?"

"Because I'm in most of them."

"Right. Sure, I'm game. I've been curious about this movie you're in."

"Great. You can go with me tonight."

That night after dinner Justin drove us up to San Rafael. I had never heard about a movie studio up there, and I was curious to see it.

"I don't know what you're expecting," said Justin, "but it's not a particularly polished operation. I mean, it's kind of rough. You'll see."

Justin drove us to a large metal building in an industrial park consisting mainly of warehouses and workshops. The building's interior was even less impressive than its exterior. Boxes and equipment were strewn along the dimly lit way to where the action was happening. The set was tiny. On a stage under hot, bright lights was an office desk and chair. A guy was barking orders at the small crew.

"Stan, this is Dallas, the guy I told you about."

Stan was middle-aged and wore a tee-shirt too tight for his pot belly. His most notable features were a moustache, his dark glasses, and a bad toupee. Clenching a cigar between his teeth, he looked me up and down like I was a cheap suit on a rack he was thinking about buying.

"I don't know, Justin. He's kind of scrawny."

"Huh?"

I wasn't that scrawny, and what did my physique have to do with shooting photos? There was obviously some kind of misunderstanding, and Stan didn't give Justin much chance to clarify things.

"Wait," said Stan. "Let's try this."

He walked over to a jumbled pile of clothes, grabbed a high school letterman jacket, and handed it to me.

"Here, put this on. You're no spring chicken, but you've got a young face. What are you, thirty?"

"Twenty-eight."

Not knowing why, I obediently donned the jacket.

"Yeah, you're too skinny for an adult part, but with that hair you might get away with playing a teenager. It'd take some makeup, and we'd have to comb your hair over your forehead."

He mussed my hair so it went over my eyes.

"Yeah, that could work. Take off your shirt and show me your upper body."

"Excuse me?"

"Might as well drop the jeans too, while we're at it. Yeah, you know, this might work. It's hard enough to get actors who can play teenagers convincingly. You just might pull it off if we shoot you right. There's a lot of demand for that, you know. Mostly in the gay market, of course."

Was he crazy or was I?

"I don't know why you think I'm here, but…"

"He's not an actor, Stan," said Justin. "He's the photographer I was telling you about. He's really good. His photos have been published all over the world."

"Oh, photographer, huh? Sorry, I thought you were the guy coming in for Justin's next movie."

"Next movie?" I asked. "You mean, you're already lined up to do another one?"

"What do you mean already?" said Stan. "He makes two or three movies a week."

"Uh, what kind of movies are you making, Justin?"

"We make films for the burgeoning adult home market," said Stan, answering for him. "We're filling a much under-served niche in the entertainment industry."

"God, Justin, are you making porn films?"

"We don't like to use that word," said Stan, defensively.

He glanced at his watch.

"Anyway, we're wasting time, and this crew gets paid by the hour. Get into your wardrobe, Justin. Your friend can shoot his photos after we've shot tonight's scenes."

Dazed, I settled on a folding chair and watched things occur.

As we waited for Justin, Stan said to me, "Your pal has a real talent for this, you know. It's a pain in the ass shooting at night, but I agreed to the schedule after he took that job in the city. That's how good he is."

Justin returned and went on the set. He wore a dark business suit and thick, black, horn-rimmed glasses. Someone had combed his hair neatly. He took a seat behind the desk.

"You ready to go, kid?"

Justin nodded.

A woman walked in front of the camera with a clapboard, calling out, "Scene four, take one."

Stan said, "Action."

The lights above Justin burned hot. I couldn't imagine how his suit wasn't drenched with sweat. He shuffled papers on the desk, then pressed a button on the intercom.

"Miss Oliver," he said in a surprisingly deep voice. "Could you come in please? I need you. To take a letter, I mean."

From off-stage, a woman's voice came through a device approximating the sound of a small speaker.

"Right away, Mr. Johnson."

A tall, blonde woman with an hourglass figure walked on set, carrying a notepad and a pen. A short skirt showed off her muscular legs. Her blouse's plunging neckline displayed much of her ample bosom. She gyrated as she walked, then came to a dead stop.

"Where did the chair go?" she asked with exaggerated innocence in an accent that sounded to me like Brooklyn. "Where am I supposed to sit?"

"Oh, sorry, Miss Oliver, they must have borrowed it for a meeting. Perhaps you could sit on the desk for now?"

"No problem, Mr. Johnson," she replied, as she slid onto the edge of the desk and crossed her legs provocatively in front of him.

Justin pretended to be nervous, repeatedly adjusting his glasses while staring at her knees.

"Yes, well, where were we?"

"You're dictating a letter."

"Oh, yes, the letter."

He sat back and folded his hands on his lap, as he stared into space.

"Dear Mr. Peters. This is to acknowledge the receipt of your letter of March 6 regarding the accounts of the Wang Tool Company and the Cox Sausage Factory. Regarding same, we forthwith... uh, sorry, where was I?"

Miss Oliver squirmed back and forth across the table.

"I'm sorry, Mr. Johnson, but this isn't very comfortable. Is there any other place I could sit?"

Justin looked around and said, "Well, perhaps just this once you could sit on my lap. Since there isn't any place else, I mean."

"Yes, that sounds comfortable, Mr. Johnson!"

She hopped straight onto his lap and continued squirming. Justin panted and removed his glasses.

"My, Miss Oliver, I don't know whether this was a good idea after all."

She emitted a small, high-pitched scream and bounced as if poked from underneath.

"Oh, Mr. Johnson, you do seem very excited to be doing your dic... tation."

"Miss Oliver, this won't work. You see, I am a happily married man."

She massaged his lap.

"It feels to me," she cooed, "like your wife must be the happy one."

I watched with my mouth open, as she unbuttoned his shirt and rubbed his chest. He ripped off her blouse. Their arms snaked around each other. They sucked each other's mouths. Justin lifted her, then put her down forcefully on the desk. The papers, telephone, and intercom clattered to the floor. As they writhed on the desk, the remainder of their clothing fell to the ground.

I tried and failed to stop watching. My eyes were frozen. Surely, her breasts couldn't be real. Their size was all out of proportion compared to the rest of her. How did she keep her balance when she walked? Though I couldn't answer that question, I had no doubt what she wore when sunbathing—absolutely nothing. Her tan was uniform over every inch of her body.

The problem with staring at her was that it meant I was also staring at Justin. I had never seen him completely naked before— and certainly not like this. Every muscle, curve, fold, and hair was on full display. The workouts in the gym had definitely paid off. As far as form and shape, he was like one of those statues of Greek gods you see in a museum. As much as I tried not to look, I could not help noticing something else.

He was hung like a stallion.

# 22
# Boys' Night

I MUST HAVE HAD an awestruck look on my face the whole drive home. My brain could not deal with what I had seen. I knew Justin was waiting for me to say something, but we were almost in Greenbrae before I could speak.

"Uh, does Amy know what kind of movies you're making?"

"She doesn't ask me about it. She's just glad I'm making some extra money. The pay is pretty good, and he pays in cash."

"Yeah, for just the few photos I shot tonight, he put a nice, big wad in my pocket."

I thought about what I had just said and flinched.

"Man," I said, "what is there about this business that makes everything come out sounding dirty? Don't you feel weird doing all that stuff with all those people standing around, watching you, and filming it?"

"It was kind of hard to get used to at first. After a while, it just becomes like any other job. You come in and do your work and go home again. I don't even think about it anymore."

"But it's not like any other job. You're spending your evenings having sex—and with someone who's not your wife."

"That's not what it feels like. It actually gets kind of boring. A lot of the sex stuff is fake. It's not as fun as it probably looks."

"Yeah, sounds like a real drag. Every guy in the world is feeling sorry for you."

When we got home, Jennifer woke up and began to cry. Justin told Amy not to bother getting up, that he would get the baby back to sleep. As I drifted off in my own bed, I heard him speaking to her softly, holding her close to him while he carried her around the house. He had a knack for being a dad.

In the morning, Amy made an announcement as Justin and I gulped our breakfast.

"You guys have been so great with all the work you've both been doing, you deserve a reward—especially since Dallas won't be with us much longer."

"That's not necessary," I said. "You work harder than the two of us put together. You shouldn't be doing anything extra for us."

"Relax," she said. "I'm actually doing something nice for myself, and I'm justifying it by pretending it's for you guys. Jennifer and I are going to spend the night at L's in the city. She's alone with the kids for the night, and we're going to keep her company. We have a lot of catching up to do, so we're going to have a girls' night, just like we used to. I can't wait. It's been ages since I've gone out for something fun. Since this isn't a work night for you, Justin, you guys get to have the house to yourselves with no women or babies. You can have a boys' night."

I wondered what she and L would be "catching up" on. It was probably too much to hope my name wouldn't come up.

"Big J, you've been great about abstaining from alcohol, but now you have permission to drink as much as you want tonight—as long as you do it at home."

"Sounds great," said Justin with a smile on his face. "Thanks, babe."

"No problem, Big J. This might be your chance to see one of those trashy movies on TV that I never let you watch when I'm around."

Justin was as happy as a kid who had gotten a candy bar. For me living with a pregnant woman and an infant was temporary, but for him there was no end in sight. No wonder he was excited about a bit of freedom. The funny thing was that, if it were possible, I would have traded places with him.

After work, when we got into the Camaro to go home, Justin proudly handed me a bottle in a paper bag.

"You know when I disappeared after lunch? It was to pick this up at the liquor store down the street."

I slid the bottle out of the bag. It was tequila. The label said Tres Generaciones.

"I don't know this one, but it looks good. Do we have limes?"

"Oh man, I forgot about the limes. We'll have to stop and pick some up. Let's pick up some Chinese takeout while we're at it. Remember when you introduced me to tequila?"

"Yeah, but I'm surprised either of us remember anything about it. We used to get pretty wasted. That was pretty irresponsible of me. You weren't even twenty-one then."

"Those times in the city were the best of my life."

"You mean, besides *these* times with your wife and your family, right?"

"Yeah, right. I mean these times are great, but those times were, you know, more fun. Playing music with my band, getting laid on the weekends, getting drunk with you. Man, I didn't know how good I had it."

We arrived to an empty house. It was eerily quiet and devoid of life without Amy and Jennifer. Soon, however, it was filled with a different kind of energy. We devoured our food with a couple of beers. Justin put the ÜberVenge LP on the turntable, but after a couple of tracks he took it off again.

"We were really crap, weren't we?"

"Hey, my buddy Sebastián in Santiago loves it."

He replaced it with Led Zeppelin's *The Song Remains the Same*. He was happier listening to that. Our meal finished, we dumped the containers in the trash and cleared the table for tequila, lime, and salt.

"I bet you drank a lot of tequila in South America."

"I couldn't find any. Mostly I was drinking pisco—and something called aguardiente."

"I never heard of those. You must have scarfed plenty of tacos and enchiladas, though."

"Nope. Turns out that stuff is just in Mexico—and California. The food in Chile and Argentina was completely different."

"Did you get laid while you were down there?"

"Yeah, and you can't believe how crazy the chick was. She got turned on by all kinds of political shit. It was insane."

So much had changed in such a short span of time, but, soon after we'd downed our shots, it was as though the past year had never happened.

"Hey, man," said Justin, licking more salt from his hand, "before we get too wasted, I have a favor to ask you."

"You might be too late. I already feel pretty wasted. I must be getting old. I think I get wasted faster than I used to. What's your favor?"

"Stan wants me to shave off my beard. He says it makes me look too old. Besides, he says the audience wants to see more of my 'pretty face.'"

"So?"

"I've never shaved off a beard before."

"Well, there's always a first time. For what it's worth, neither have I. I'm twenty-eight, and I still can't grow a decent beard. I give it a try every so often, but it's always embarrassing. Maybe by the time I'm forty I'll be able to grow a decent one. Your beard looks great. You should keep it."

"Yeah, I like it. I don't want to get rid of it, but Stan is pretty insistent. Getting drunk might be the only way I can do it."

"I'm not sure taking a razor to your face while you're drunk is the best idea."

"I know. That's why I want *you* to do it."

"Me? Were you not listening? I have less experience shaving than most women do."

"I'd feel better if you did it."

"Why don't you go to a barber?"

"This beard means a lot to me. A lot of important stuff happened while I had this beard. I want someone who really knows me to shave it off."

"You know you're crazy, right?"

"I don't know how to start. It's too thick to use a razor on."

"No, you can't start with a razor. Even I know that. You need to trim as much as you can with scissors first. Then you finish up with the razor."

"See, I knew you were the right person to ask."

He retrieved a pair of large, rusty scissors from a kitchen drawer.

"Here, you can use these."

"I think we're both going to regret this."

"Where do you want me?"

"Just sit on the chair like you're at a barber shop. Put a towel around your neck and shoulders so you don't get covered in whiskers."

He got a towel from the bathroom and did as I said. I pulled up a chair directly behind him and tried to figure out how it was going to work.

"I think you're still going to get those annoying little hairs on your shirt. Maybe you should take it off."

He obediently pulled off his shirt and then covered himself with the towel again. I tried to concentrate, but the tequila wasn't helping. I clipped as close as I could to his face, taking care not to accidentally cut the skin. His familiar jawline slowly returned. I pondered how our boys' night had turned into a grooming session.

After trimming away as much hair as I could, I said, "I think we're ready for the razor now. Man, there's hair everywhere. I don't think Amy's going to like this."

"We'll have to clean up before she gets home. There are razors in the bathroom."

He looked forlorn, studying himself in the bathroom mirror. He could not stop rubbing his hand over the thick, black stubble.

"Man, I miss it. Why did I let him talk me into getting rid of it?"

"Do you have any shaving soap?"

He found a shaving brush and mug with soap in it. It reminded me of my father's. I put hot water in the mug, made lather with the brush, and gave them to him.

"Where's the razor?"

He got a safety razor from the medicine cabinet.

"You should probably put a new blade in it," I said. "You'll want it good and sharp. There's still a lot of hair on your face, and taking it off is probably going to hurt. A lot."

"Can you do it?"

I thought it was weird he didn't want to do it himself, but I went along with him. He stood trustingly, waiting for me to do everything. I put in a fresh blade and lathered the brush. I dabbed his face until the beard's remnants were covered by soap.

"Let's go back out to the kitchen," I said. "This will be easier if you're sitting in the chair."

He sat and wrapped the towel around his shoulders again. From directly behind him, I worked out the best approach. I still couldn't believe we were doing this.

I dragged the razor along his cheek. Each time the blade caught on a hair, he and I both flinched. Our faces were so close that the mixed scents of his breath and the lather filled my nose. His skin was surprisingly soft and white underneath the stubble.

I dragged the razor across his neck, and I marveled at his trust in me. The tequila had made me light-headed, and I was all too aware I was guiding a sharp blade over vulnerable tendons and arteries. A wrong move could actually prove lethal. It was not an exaggeration to say I had his life in my hands. He was not the least bit nervous. He sat perfectly still, his eyes closed as if in a dream.

I traced the contours of his jaw meticulously, as well as the tricky areas under the ears and the cleft of his chin. I repeated the motions over every inch of his face and neck until his skin was as smooth and slick as possible. I lightly brushed his cheeks with the back of my fingers, searching for any remaining rough bits I might have missed. Glancing at the window over the kitchen sink, I made out a vague reflection of the two of us. I fantasized that his face was my face and that I had been shaving myself.

I took the towel from his shoulders and used it to wipe the remaining bits of lather from his face and neck. His eyes were still closed, as I admired my handiwork. Once again, I wished I were him. Was this what it was like for Pygmalion when he fell in love with the statue he created?

"Not bad, if I do say so myself. You look almost like you did when I first knew you."

He opened his eyes and rubbed his chin hesitantly, as if disturbed by how soft his skin felt. He stood and went to look at himself in the bathroom mirror. He came back, as if in a daze.

"I need more tequila," he said.

As we had another shot, I said, "Well, it's good to know that, if photography work dries up, I can get work as a barber."

"Thanks, man. I appreciate it."

"We made quite a mess," I said, looking at the hair on the kitchen floor. "I wish I could take some of that and make it grow on *my* face."

He put his hand on my cheek.

"Your face isn't as smooth as mine."

"Yeah, but only because I haven't shaved for a week."

He stood behind me and put his hands on my shoulders.

"I owe you a backrub."

"What?"

"Remember that night I crashed in your apartment? When it was really late and I was totally wasted?"

"I think so."

"I got in your bed, and I was almost asleep when you started massaging my back. It was the best backrub I ever had. Do you remember doing that?"

Normally, this was something I would have lied about, but the tequila made lying a challenge.

"Yeah, I remember."

He rubbed my shoulders as he spoke.

"I wasn't sure why you were doing it, but it felt good. I think I said something about, maybe, the two of us should mess around, you know, just for the hell of it. Do you remember that?"

"Maybe. I figured you were drunk. I didn't pay any attention."

"Well, see, that's the thing. I actually thought we were going to do some experimenting. The next thing I knew, you went off to

France. By the time you came back, I'd quit my job at Flaubert's and gone back to school here in Marin. I didn't see you again for ages."

"Yeah, it's like John Lennon said. Life is what happens while you're busy making other plans."

"Would you have done it?"

"You mean…?"

"Yeah."

"Probably not. I mean, no. I'm not into that. I didn't think you were either."

"You know, I could give you a better massage if you were lying down. Let's go in your room, and you can lie on the bed."

"Is that one of your old lines for picking up women? It sounds like you're trying to seduce me."

"I just want to give you a backrub as good as the one you gave me."

I figured, what the hell. I went into the bedroom and threw myself face down on my bed. He sat on the side of the bed, working my back muscles from my neck to my waist.

"It's nice, isn't it?"

"Yeah, feels good."

"You're tense. You need to relax."

I closed my eyes and forced myself to breathe slowly. I imagined I was floating on a cloud. It was a trick I had learned for falling asleep. I became more relaxed, though I still got a twinge whenever he pressed a tight muscle.

"This would work better if you took your shirt off."

Between the tequila and my relaxation technique, I was midway between wakefulness and a dream.

"Okay, now it definitely sounds like you're trying to seduce me. You should know better. How long have we been friends?"

He pulled the shirt over my head, and I didn't bother to stop him. He went back to massaging my shoulder blades. He was right. It was better with his hands pressing my skin directly.

"It's just that there was something about the way you rubbed my back that time. Something... sensual. Like it was more than just a backrub."

"It was all in your head."

"No, something was definitely going on. If I hadn't been so drunk and tired, something would have definitely happened that night."

My body tensed up. I rolled over to look him in the eye.

"Look, something was going on all right, but it's not what you think. It's something that's hard for me to talk about."

One of his hands was still on my shoulder. I gave it back to him.

"Okay, here it is. I was going through some bad shit then. Last year was tough for me. I kept waking up at night and going into a panic. Some nights I didn't think I'd be able to get through it. I thought I was going crazy. In fact, I probably was. I don't know what made me put my hands on your back, but when I did, things suddenly got better. Physical contact was the magic cure. Once I started rubbing you, I couldn't stop because I was afraid the terror would come back. That's what it was about."

"Man, I had no idea. You never acted like anything was wrong. I wish you'd told me. Maybe I could have helped. Does it still happen?"

"Hardly ever. That's the amazing thing. Not long after that, I went to France and met Valérie. Since I met her, I've been better. It's like she was the real cure. Just thinking about her keeps the terror away."

Something dawned on me.

"God, I just realized. You're the *gemelo erótico*!"

"Huh? What's a hay mellow erotico?"

"It's this weird theory that my friend Ángel has. Every woman he falls in love with is paired with one of his male friends. It sounds crazy, but he swears it's true. When I went over my own love life, I came up with *gemelos eróticos* for all the women in my life—except Valérie. I had forgotten about you, but it seems obvious now. It was the lemon smell."

"What lemon smell?"

"That night you had been washing dishes for whatever woman you slept with. The dish soap was lemon-scented. I can still smell it now. Valérie had that same smell because she made lemonade from lemons."

"So do I remind you of your French chick now?"

"No, not really. Actually, not at all. Come to think of it, though, you have long, black hair like she does, but no, you're nothing like her."

He put his hand on my shoulder again. I didn't bother stopping him. My drunken head buzzed with the possible cosmic meanings of Ángel's *gemelo erótico* theory.

"Stan wants me to make a gay movie. I haven't decided if I want to do it, but he said he would pay double. It's not something I'm that comfortable with, but I think I could do it if I had to."

I was still distracted in my own thoughts.

"I couldn't do what you're doing—no matter how much they paid me."

"The thing is, the one thing that would make it easier for me to do it is if I was acting with a guy I knew really well and trusted."

"Do you ever worry about picking up a disease, doing what you do?"

"Huh? No, they're pretty careful about that. We have to get tested every few weeks. What I'm trying to say is, I could do it if *you* would do it with me."

"Me? No way. Not a chance."

I noticed he had been running his hand up and down my upper arm for a while.

"You know, I like you, Dallas. I actually fantasize about you sometimes."

"No, you don't. You're just drunk. Or are you telling me you're gay now?"

"Do you ever think about me that way?"

"Are you crazy?"

He stared at me like an eager puppy, waiting for a better answer.

"Look, I'll be honest. The first time I saw you working at Flaubert's, I couldn't stop looking at you. It kind of scared me. I didn't know what it meant because I usually don't find myself looking at guys. Then you and I ended up getting to know each other and becoming friends. After that you weren't any different from any of my other guy friends. Still…"

"Yeah?"

"Sometimes I remember what it was like the first time I saw you, and I wonder what it was about. I think I know, but I'm never completely sure."

"What do you think it was?"

"I think I was jealous. I've always envied you. I've always wished I had your face and your body. I wish I was you instead of me. I can't believe I'm actually saying that out loud, but I guess that's what happens when you drink too much tequila."

"That's amazing. Don't you understand? That's exactly how I feel about you. I wish I was you."

"No, you don't. No one does."

For a couple of minutes Justin stared at me in a way that scared me. When he finally spoke, he scared me even more.

"God, I want you."

# 23
# The Letter

"STOP IT, JUSTIN. The tequila's made you crazy. You're creeping me out."

"I'm sorry. I'm just being honest. I'm trying to pay you a compliment."

"I don't get it. No guy I have ever known has slept with as many women as you have. You're married. You're getting paid to have sex with women in porn movies. Now you're telling me you're gay?"

"No, I'm not gay. I've never been interested in any other guys. There's just something about you. I don't even think I'm bisexual. I think I'm what they call bi-curious."

"Thanks. It sounds like you think of me more like a woman than a man. Is it because I can't grow a beard?"

"Man, I shouldn't have started this. A lot of it is I'm just horny. I have strange thoughts when I get too horny."

"Horny? How can you be horny? You're married, for Christ's sake. You can have it anytime you want."

He laughed.

"Boy, you sure don't know much about being married, do you? Amy is wrecked most of the time, and who can blame her? She has to deal with being pregnant and taking care of Jennifer plus all of the housework because I'm gone most of the time. When we finally get some time alone, one or the other of us immediately falls asleep."

"What about your night job? Doesn't that provide any, um, relief?"

"Like I told you, a lot of that is fake. There isn't much relief in it, that's for sure."

"Man, I'm sorry about all that. It's not like my life is currently a hotbed of carnal gratification either, but there are limits to what I'm willing to do about it. Even if I wanted to, I wouldn't—because it would be wrong."

"So you think two guys having sex is sinful?"

"That's not what I'm saying. I'm saying it would be wrong because you're married. I'm not going to be involved in you cheating on Amy."

"But it wouldn't be cheating," he said, looking confused.

"Sure, it would."

"If a straight guy has sex with another straight guy just for the hell of it, then it doesn't mean anything. It doesn't count."

"How do you figure that? Of course, it counts. Of course, it means something. Besides, if you're having sex with a guy, then technically I'm not sure you really qualify as being straight."

He was so disappointed that he seemed to pout.

"Look," I said. "If I were to have sex with you, it would definitely mean something. It *always* means something to me. With you it would especially mean something because you're my friend."

He stood.

"I'm going to have another shot. Want one?"

"Sure, why not. This is turning into one hell of a boys' night."

He returned, juggling the bottle, the glasses, the salt shaker, and the by-now-thoroughly-squeezed lime. We swallowed our shots, sitting side-by-side on the bed.

"I might as well finish your backrub," he said.

"There's more?"

"Yeah. Lie down."

Obediently, I fell flat on my face. He went back to working my shoulder blades and my spine. He was more forceful this time, digging deep into the muscles and pressing hard on the bones. I went limp under the force of his fingers. I felt as if my spirit might leave my body. He turned me over, as if flipping over a blanket. I was surprised how easy it was for him. He had a lot of strength in those brawny arms.

"Now for the front rub."

"I've heard of backrubs, but I've never heard of a front rub."

He massaged the tops of my shoulders and then my chest. I didn't like it because it tickled. When his fingers reached my belly, I couldn't take any more.

"Okay, that's it! The massage is over."

He didn't stop. His hands worked their way toward my groin. I grabbed his wrists, but he was too strong.

"Quit it!"

He forced my hands down onto the bed, and then climbed on top. His knees dug into my thighs. I was paralyzed. It had happened so suddenly. He lowered his head so his face was an inch above mine. He stared deep into my eyes. The pain in my legs was severe.

"I think I've figured out what's going on here."

"What do you think is going on?" I said through gritted teeth.

"I think you want this as much as I do, but you can't admit it."

"If I wanted it, I would say so. I don't want it."

The pain caused by his weight burned.

"I think you do want it. I think you are so brainwashed by that church you went to as a kid that you can't get past the idea of it being a sin. You're afraid you'll go to hell."

I was angry.

"*You* can go to hell."

"It's okay. Now that I understand, I know what to do. I'll take the responsibility. You can pretend you don't want it, and I'll do the rest. You explain to God that I forced you."

I was afraid I'd black out from the pain. I had never felt so feeble.

"Get... off... me!"

He leaned down and kissed my cheek. The sweat on his face was fetid. His saliva left a trail like a slug. I shook my head back and forth uselessly. That only pleased him. His lips parted, and his tongue emerged. I knew from his porn film scene that it was huge, but at this proximity it was monstrous. It snaked down my cheek. The moistness couldn't have been more repellent if it had been dripping acid. His tongue circled my mouth, leaving its slime everywhere. I fought the urge to gag and clenched my teeth as it tried to pry its way in. I hated the feeling of helplessness. He had complete control.

I pushed with all my strength and was disgusted by my inadequacy. I kept trying. Justin enjoyed my exertions. He vibrated with excitement.

"I like it when you struggle," he said breathlessly. "Don't stop."

He opened his eyes wide and stared. I tried to look away.

"No, don't stop. It really turns me on."

He moaned, as a shudder went through his entire body. Sensing this was my chance, I whipped my head as far as I could, opened my mouth wide, and sunk my teeth into his ear lobe. I was surprised how warm and salty it was. He cried out, slapping a hand over his ear.

"You asshole! I'm bleeding!"

"Get off me, you prick! This isn't funny."

He snarled viciously like a wounded animal. Justin had always been the most laid-back guy I knew. I never dreamed he could be like this.

"Man," he said, "that church of yours really did a number on you. I mean, I always knew you were kind of hung-up, but I never realized how badly they fucked you up."

I completely lost it.

"Don't you dare blame this on religion or God. This has nothing to do with sin. This is all about evolution. This has more to do with Charles Darwin than Jesus Christ."

"What the hell are you talking about?"

"That wasn't about sex. It was about survival of the fittest. It was about you doing something to me because you could. It was about you being stronger and me being weaker."

"What? You could have pushed me away if you really wanted."

I was humiliated. I was on the verge of tears.

"No, I couldn't. I was helpless. You had me at your mercy, and you're so strong you didn't even realize it. Does that make you happy? You're the hunter and I'm the prey. You're nature's winner. It's like that plane crash in the Andes. The one with the rugby team."

He was cross, as he dabbed gingerly at his ear.

"Now what the hell are you talking about?"

"You remember that plane crash in South America? The one where they were stuck on a glacier for weeks without food. Finally, the ones who survived had to eat the ones who died. If you and I had been on that plane, you would have lived and I would have been dinner. That's just the way it is, isn't it?"

"You're crazy. I was showing how much I like you."

"It's a damn funny way of showing it. It's just as well I'm moving out. Things have gotten too fucked-up. That's the problem with guys—at least straight guys—trying to be close to each other. No matter how much you like each other, want to be around each other, even love each other, it always ends up turning into a competition."

"Look, don't move out. I'm sorry. I got crazy. I'm drunk. I didn't mean to hurt you. We're still friends, aren't we?"

"Look, I'll keep working with you at the paper, but I need to get out of this house as soon as possible. It's more than just what happened tonight."

"Yeah?"

I was consumed with a desire to hurt him. I couldn't do it physically, but I knew another way.

"I think I've fallen in love with Amy."

I had done it. I had used the only poison arrow in my meager quiver. He stared at the floor for a minute, then looked at me.

"What about the French chick?"

"I'm in love with her too. I mean, she's the one I'm really in love with, but the more time I spend around Amy, the more I feel attracted to her. It's just something that happened. It doesn't make any sense."

He was quiet for a few moments before speaking again.

"I could talk to her."

"And say what?"

"I might get her to understand things. She might be okay with it. You know, if I explain it right, she might be up for a three-way."

"Are you kidding me? That's your solution? Man, you need to get your priorities straight. You're married to an amazing woman. You've got a great kid and another one on the way. You can't let idiots like me distract you from that. You're the luckiest guy I know. Don't screw it up. I just hope I can have something like what you have—with Valérie if she'll have me. I have to get to France as soon as I can and tell her. I need to get away from you and Amy before I screw up your lives and my own. Now get the hell out of my room. I'm going to bed."

Justin stood and looked at me with his guilty-puppy face.

"I wouldn't eat you, Dallas. Please believe me. I'd starve before I'd eat you."

"Good night, Justin. You know, I think you've succeeded at something no one else has ever been able to do. You've ruined tequila for me."

"What am I going to tell Amy about this gash on my ear?"

"Tell her you cut yourself shaving."

When Amy came home the next day, she was not at all happy about the mess we had made. We had tried to clean it up, but we'd done a pretty bad job. She went crazy over the hair on the kitchen floor. The only saving grace was that she liked Justin better without the beard. Still, she threatened to never let us have a boys' night again. That was fine by me.

Justin and I continued pretty much as before. I had been afraid he would try to apologize to me, and I was glad when he didn't. An apology would only have added to my humiliation. I didn't want to talk about it ever again, and apparently Justin felt the same.

While dealing with photography and work, things were fine between us. I still enjoyed teaching him and spending time with him. I only felt uncomfortable when sitting next to him during the daily commute. I had no rational reason to feel uneasy. I knew he wasn't going to attack me while driving the car, but I didn't like being close to him in a confined space.

My remaining time living with Justin and Amy was not uncomfortable. Most of the time Justin wasn't around because of his night job. One night—and thankfully it was only one night—my old panic came back. I woke with a start in the early morning blackness. My heart pounded, and my skin shivered in clammy sweat. I had dreamt Justin slipped into my room and crawled on top of me. No matter how much I wanted to move, I was immobilized. I tried calling out but could make no sound. After I woke, I couldn't get back to sleep until I saw the light of dawn peeking under the window shade. Later in the day I remembered another part of the dream. Just before I had woken, I looked at Justin's face, but it wasn't him anymore. It was someone I recognized, but to my frustration, I couldn't remember who.

Though we did not talk about it, things between Justin and me were never the same. I didn't blame him—at least not completely—for what had happened. I understood the kinds of strange, buried thoughts and emotions that can come out unexpectedly when you've had too much to drink, but I could not shake the creepy feeling from having seen such a different side of Justin. I regarded him more or less the same as I would some large, handsome breed of dog: admirable for its strength and beauty—even good, friendly company most of the time—yet still one of nature's creatures to be potentially wary of.

Justin never asked me again to go to his night job with him. In fact, a few days later he told Amy his current film would be his last one. He made it sound as if he had been let go, but I knew better.

A week later Melanie's apartment was finally available. She handed me the keys on the day before her leave of absence began.

"Please don't trash the place, Green. I'm putting a lot of trust in you. I hope you live up to it. Be sure to take good care of our kitties. You have the vet's number if there are any problems. Bruñuel had a bladder infection six weeks ago. It seems to have cleared up, but it could come back. Also, sometimes Dali bullies him. Don't let them get into any serious fights."

"Yeah, yeah, I know. You told me twice already. Just go have a good couple of months in England. If you run into a guy from Liverpool named Donal, tell him I said cheerio."

If I had been better organized, I would have already packed up my things and taken them to work with me that day. Instead I went back to Marin with Justin for one last night. Amy made enchiladas, my favorite dinner. She had Dos Equis for me and Justin and allowed herself a tiny glass of red wine.

"We're going to miss you, D," she said. "It won't be the same without you."

"Sure," I said. "It'll probably be better. Look, I can't tell you how much I appreciate you guys letting me stay here all this time. You saved me a lot of money. That trip to France is getting closer all the time."

That reminded her of something. She hurried to the hallway and came back with an envelope. She teased me by pretending to study it.

"What's this?" she said. "A letter? Hmmm. What interesting stamps. Where could it possibly be from? Let's see what the postmark says. Hmmm. It looks like... let's see. I think it says Bordeaux, France!"

"Give that to me!" I demanded, as I grabbed it.

She had not lied. It was addressed to me in a distinctive, feminine handwriting, and the postmark indeed said Bordeaux. My body wanted to levitate out of my chair.

"Excuse me," I mumbled, as I got up.

Amy giggled, as I rushed to my room and shut the door. I sat on the bed and turned on the table lamp. I was afraid to open it. My long wait was finally over—except for whatever fidgeting and second-guessing I would do for the next several minutes. I carefully unsealed the envelope and slid out the letter. The faint smell of perfume compounded my excitement. The handwriting was simple enough, but the way the letters curved made them hard for me to read. It was different from any handwriting I had seen before. She had written mostly in English. As I made out each word, I spoke it aloud in confirmation.

"Mon cher Dalas,"

How had she managed to misspell my name? I had written her several times, and I had signed every letter. My heart sank. What did it mean that she took so little interest that she had not learned how to spell my name?

"You flatter me with your letters. I was certain you had by now forgotten me. After all, we knew one another seven days only. (I do not include the Thursday evening.)"

She had counted the days. She knew exactly how many days we were together in Deauville—just as I knew and had remembered since the previous September. This was good news. She also remembered the Thursday night. I remembered it as if it were yesterday. She and I had never talked about it. I never knew if she had remembered it too. It was the first time I saw her, the moment our eyes met in a crowded bar the night before the film festival opened. That was all. We did not speak until two days later. She had remembered.

"Your voyage to South America sounds very interesting. I cannot imagine you in Michel's house with his family. I am yet not comfortable with the idea that you and he are friends. It all makes me feel bizarre. I am still annoyed that this has passed.

"The past month has been difficult. My father (the man who I always knew as my father) is deceased. There has been much to do to organise the funerals and his affairs. Also, many discussions with my brother and my sister over all these things. It has not been easy, but it is good that all will be terminated soon. I need to go away from everything.

"If you remain in Californie, perhaps I shall see you some day. My other father (Logan, the biologique one) desires me to visit him. I do not know when this will pass, but I should like very much to go to Californie.

"Enfin, I do not know what you expect exactly. The words in your letters are filled with infatuation though we do not really know one another. Yet they make me smile. Who knows? For me it is difficult to write in English. Please pardon my mediocre writing. The truth is that my life is going in a particular direction, and I am not prepared in this moment to make grand decisions about anything. Yet I do like you very much."

On the first reading everything she wrote went right past me except for the part about her coming to California. It was the best news ever. She wrote the last few lines in French.

"Merci bien de m'avoir écrit. Tant de fois. Je me souviens de toi toujours avec beaucoup de tendresse. Serons-nous un jour ensemble? Dans la vieillesse peut-être? Je ris."

What did she mean by those last words? A French dictionary could tell me the meaning of each individual word, but it was useless for understanding her intent. What did she mean by us maybe being together in our old age? Why did communication have to be so hard?

I trusted that, once we were together again, we would understand each other more easily, just as we had in Deauville. Until then I would cling to the parts of her letter that gave me hope.

# 24
# Luciano

VALÉRIE'S LETTER HAD me floating on air for days. I was more determined than ever to go to France. Thanks to my work for the paper and the rent I saved while living with Justin and Amy, I now had a decent amount of money in the bank. I just needed to decide how much was enough and to make my travel plans.

It would take a bit longer now that I was shelling out for rent in the city, but at least Melanie had given me a good deal. I considered the extra expense worth it because I was a heck of a lot happier living on my own—despite the cats driving me crazy. Dali was particularly annoying. He knew I didn't care for him, and that was his incentive for pestering me as much as he could. Early one morning a tickling sensation on my nose woke me abruptly from a sound sleep and a pleasant dream. Dali had climbed on top of my chest and was rubbing his nose against mine. The message in his judgmental eyes, two inches from mine, was that there was no food in his bowl.

My lifestyle in Pacific Heights was that of a monk. I stayed in at night and on weekends to save money. My personal entertainment consisted of long walks, studying French language books, and writing letters to Valérie.

I was happy back in the city, but living in Melanie and Sheila's apartment made me a nervous wreck. I knew if I broke any of their artistic trinkets—or anything else for that matter—I would never hear the end of it. Of course, that would be nothing compared to the repercussions if, God forbid, anything should happen to either of the cats on my watch. I looked forward to the day when I would no longer have to change—or smell—the litter box.

Despite the stress she sometimes caused me, I liked Melanie. When I had returned to the paper, she had been the only one who didn't treat me differently than before. The others, especially the newer ones, were weird around me, like they thought I was some kind of legend. I was the guy who got the interview and photos of reclusive filmmaker Logan MacCaul when no one else could. People still talked about it and the awards it won for me and the paper. Melanie, on the other hand, continued to regard me as the screw-up she had always thought I was. That was more comfortable for me.

As I approached my target bank balance over the summer, only two things kept me from hopping on a plane. One was finishing my commitment to train Justin. The other was waiting for Melanie and Sheila's return. I wished time would pass faster.

I returned to my old habit of wandering the city during my off hours, shooting photos of anything and everything that looked at all interesting. One evening I negotiated my way through the tourist throng at Fisherman's Wharf, where I met a black-haired couple whose path intersected mine near the hall of arcade games. Seconds after I passed them, something registered in my mind. The woman was someone I knew. A few more seconds were required to work out who. I did an about-face and followed them.

"Yolanda!"

She stopped and turned her head, unsure of where my voice had come from.

"Yolanda! Over here!"

Her eyes found me. She smiled in surprise, then turned serious.

"This is amazing," I said, as I made my way toward her. "How are you? What are the odds we'd run into each other here of all places?"

Her coldness startled me.

"So we meet again," she said.

"How have you been? How did the rest of your time in Europe go?"

"It was good."

Something was definitely wrong. She was not happy to see me. I had no idea why.

"I don't think I'll ever forget that night on the train to Berlin. That was quite a time."

"Ken, this is someone I met last year while traveling in Europe with Annaliese."

He extended his hand.

"Nice to meet you."

"Ken, why don't you go on to the restaurant so we don't lose our reservation? This will only take a few minutes."

Ken was confused but did as he was told. Yolanda remained silent as he walked away. Something was really bugging her.

"He seems nice," I said. "Is he your boyfriend?"

"You know, it took me a while to figure out who you were, but by then, of course, it was too late. We had all split up in Berlin. I never expected to see you again."

"What are you talking about?"

"Didn't you tell me you were from Bakersfield?"

"Yeah. Near enough. What about it?"

"Were you a truck driver about nine years ago?"

"Truck driver? No. What made you think that?"

"So you never drove a truck between Bakersfield and East L.A.?"

The fog in my brain began to lift. In the weeks before going into the army, Lonnie had a job making deliveries to L.A. for a guy in East Bakersfield. I couldn't understand how Yolanda would know about that or how she would connect it to me. Then the remaining fog lifted.

When Ángel and I met Yolanda and Annaliese on that train to Berlin, I had been using Lonnie's name.

"Look," I said, "before we go any further, I need to clear something up. You're going to think it's pretty damn weird."

"You definitely have some clearing up to do all right."

"Does this have something to do with Lonnie?"

"Do you usually refer to yourself in the third person? Or are you going to try pretending you're somebody else now?"

"I'm not pretending. I *am* somebody else. I swear it."

"Why don't you act like a man instead of hiding behind lies?"

"Can we please start over?"

I offered my hand to shake, but she refused it.

"Yolanda, please allow me to introduce myself. My name is Dallas Green. I apologize for not telling you my real name the first time we met."

"This gets better and better," she fumed.

I pulled out my wallet and handed her my driver's license.

"See? There's my ID. I'm really Dallas Green, but I do know Lonnie McKay. He was a friend of mine. In fact, he was my best friend. He's the one who drove a truck to L.A."

She stared at my license, then handed it back.

"Why did you tell us you were Lonnie McKay?"

"It's complicated. I'd be happy to tell you the whole messed-up story sometime, but I know you've got a guy waiting for you at a restaurant, and I don't want to delay you. Just tell me what happened with Lonnie?"

"Your best friend, huh? Well, I'm not impressed by your choice of friends."

"What did he do? Did you meet him?"

"No, I only heard about him later. I didn't want to know anything about him. I only heard his name a couple of times. By the time I met you last year, I had nearly forgotten it, but when you said it and mentioned Bakersfield, it jarred something in my memory."

"So what happened?"

"Your friend used to make deliveries to a warehouse where my cousin Richie worked. In the evenings, his daughter Gabriela always hung out in the office to do her homework. She was really pretty, and Lonnie flirted with her all the time. She was just a teenager."

"Lonnie was only a teenager himself. He would have been eighteen then."

"Yeah, well, Gaby was only sixteen. A couple of times Richie found the two of them in the cab of Lonnie's truck. The second time he blew his top and told Lonnie's boss he better hire another driver. He said if he saw Lonnie's face again, he'd kill him. Weeks later, Gaby came to me in a terrible state. She thought she was pregnant. I took her to a doctor, and he confirmed her fears. Richie was a madman when he found out. It was a terrible time. You have to understand the shame they felt. They are a good family, respected in the community. Richie tried to track your friend down. When the trucking company said that they didn't have his phone number on file anymore, Richie called every McKay in the Bakersfield phone book. No one owned up to knowing him."

"He was never going to find him in a phone book," I explained uselessly. "The listing was under his stepfather's name. By then, he was already gone anyway. He went into the army."

"He changed Gaby's life completely. She was so bright. She could have been anything. Instead, she had to drop out of school. She had to take care of a child when she was still a child herself. It breaks my heart."

"So she had the baby?"

"Of course, she had the baby. I suppose things could have been worse for her. She knew a nice boy who liked her, and he did not mind about the baby. They got married, but they were so young. He's not the world's best provider, but he tries. They've had a tough time because of not finishing school, but they're doing okay now."

Her anger had risen slowly and quietly.

"It's probably better if you don't tell me where to find your friend because, if I knew, nothing could stop me from tracking him down and tying his balls into one hell of a knot."

"Is it a boy or a girl?"

"A boy. Luciano. He's a beautiful child."

"He's about nine years old now?"

"Yes. Will you tell your friend he's a father?"

"I wish I could. Lonnie's dead."

"Dead?"

"He served two years in the army. He was in West Germany and was close to going home. There was an accident with a truck

234

full of soldiers, and he died. Soon after I saw you the last time, I visited the base at Fulda where he had been."

I didn't mention Lonnie's other son. Things were complicated enough as it was.

"Is that true?" she asked me suspiciously. "It's kind of convenient that he's dead."

"It's not convenient for me. I miss him every day. I know he wasn't perfect. Heck, he was irresponsible as hell and sometimes a real pain in the ass, but he was my friend. I'd like to think, if he had known he had a kid in East L.A., he would have tried to do right by him."

"Well, thanks for telling me. At least Gaby won't have to spend her life wondering if he is still out there somewhere. Maybe someday she'll tell Luciano about him."

"Look, I know you're probably about to lose your table at that restaurant, and I don't mean to keep you, but do you think there's any way...?"

"What?"

"Do you think I could meet Luciano?"

"Why?"

"I don't know. I mean, I wouldn't tell him anything about Lonnie. It's just that, well, I think Lonnie would want me to. In case there's anything I could do for him and his mother, I don't know what that would be, but maybe I could do something."

She weighed the pros and cons of what I had said. After hesitating, she opened her purse and handed me a business card.

"Here's my number. The next time you're in L.A., give me a call."

"Thank you, Yolanda."

"Thank *you*. I'm glad we cleared things up. I've spent a lot of time resenting you. It's good to be friends again."

A couple of weeks later on a Friday, I took a day off and hopped a train to L.A. After checking into a motel, I called Yolanda. She said her relatives were getting together for a picnic the following day in Obregon Park and that I would be welcome.

The idea of crashing a family picnic where I knew only one person intimidated me, but I was determined to meet Lonnie's son.

The weather was sunny and hot. The air had the distinctive smell of L.A. smog. Though the park was huge, I had no trouble finding Yolanda's group. There must have been forty of them. I had picked up a few bags of corn chips and a couple of six-packs of beer at a nearby market, which was meager compared to what everyone else had brought. Individual families had brought an array of dishes, including tacos, pasta salads, and spicy rice. Men grilled chicken and corn on the cob on the barbecues. The aromas were wonderful.

I found Yolanda, and this time she introduced me properly to her fiancé Ken. I gathered she had told him the whole story because he smiled at me knowingly.

"Does Gabriela know who I am?" I asked Yolanda. "And why I'm here?"

"Yes, she does. I'll introduce you."

She led me through the crowd. The chatter and laughter made clear how much these people loved being together. She introduced me to various people along the way, mostly in English but sometimes in Spanish, telling them I was someone she met traveling in Europe.

I was surprised to be nervous as we neared the woman laughing with two others. I looked for the pretty teenager Yolanda had described, but I saw a short woman a couple of years younger than me. She was still pretty, but she was also world-weary. She studied me, as if she thought she might find something to remind her of Lonnie. I felt I disappointed her.

"Gabriela? Hi, I'm Dallas. It's nice to meet you."

"It's nice to meet you too. Are you really a friend of Lonnie's?"

"Yes, I am. I was."

"Is it true? Did he really die?"

"I'm afraid so. He's buried in the cemetery in our hometown, about 130 miles north of here."

"I would like to visit his grave sometime."

"If you ever have plans to go there, let me know. I can meet you and show you where he's buried."

"Thank you."

She turned and called, "Luciano! Come here!"

A boy, who had been kicking a soccer ball, ran toward us. A younger brother and sister tagged along.

"Yeah? What is it, Mom?"

His skin was so brown and his hair so black, I wondered if he was Lonnie's at all. I studied his face, the line of his jaw, the cheekbones, the cocky way he held his head. Yes, he was Lonnie all over again, though quite different from blond Lukas Wolf. Gabriela watched me stare.

"*El parecido es asombroso, ¿no?*" she said quietly.

She was right. The resemblance was striking. Yolanda must have told her I knew Spanish, and she apparently chose that language so the boy would pay less notice. It didn't work.

"What similarity is amazing?" he asked.

"His whole life I have tried to get him interested in Spanish," she said, rolling her eyes. "He picks this time to pay attention. Luciano, this is Mr. Green. He's a friend of Yolanda's. He's come a long way to be here."

"Nice to meet you," he said dutifully. "Can I go now?"

"Yes, of course," she said. "I only wanted you to say hello."

"Hello," he said. "Goodbye."

He and the other two ran back to the soccer ball. A man joined them in their game. I presumed he was Gabriela's husband.

"Luciano doesn't know that…"

"He knows Abel is his father."

"Yes, of course. Gabriela, I'd like to do something for Luciano."

"What do you mean?"

I took the envelope from my pocket. She eyed it suspiciously.

"What's that?"

"It's the only thing I could think of to do. Please take it."

"Why? We are fine. We don't need anything."

"It's not charity or anything like that. It's just that I know Lonnie would want me to do something."

"I have three children. I will not have one treated different from the others."

"I understand. Use it for all of them."

"We don't need a hand-out."

"It's not a hand-out. Think of it as… an inheritance."

"Lonnie must have been extremely organized," she said skeptically, "if he arranged to leave something for the child he never knew he had."

"Lonnie and I had… an understanding. An arrangement between us. He was easily distracted, and it was always my job to make sure he finished things he'd started—or else finish them for him. He'd expect me to finish this."

"This will never be finished."

"I understand. Look, Lonnie and I went a lot of places together. Sometimes I had money, and he didn't. Sometimes he had money, and I didn't. If I left a place without paying the check, Lonnie took care of it. If he left without paying, I picked it up. This just is me picking up Lonnie's tab one last time."

"I think meeting you was a mistake."

I put the envelope in her hand. She tried to give it back.

"Yes, there's a check in that envelope, but it's not from me. It's from Lonnie. Cash it and use it however you want. Put it in a savings account for their education. It won't pay for four years of college, but it's a start."

She reluctantly kept the envelope.

"It was not necessary."

"It was for me. It was good to meet you and Luciano. I do have to warn you. If he turns out anything like Lonnie, I'm afraid you're going to have your hands full."

She said nothing. I hadn't thought I wanted any thanks—until I saw her smile. That made it more than worthwhile and kept me in a good mood all the way back to San Francisco.

As I got lost in the ocean's azure beauty on the train journey between Ventura and San Luis Obispo, I knew at least two things for certain. One was that I had absolutely done the right thing. The other was that, thanks to the sudden drop in my savings, the trip to France would be delayed a while longer.

# 25
# Querétaro

IMPULSIVE GENEROSITY OR simply doing my duty? However I thought of it, it led to a few complications in my life.

I now needed to continue working to have enough money for going to France. That meant asking David if he could keep me on a while longer. By this time, I had taught Justin everything I could about my method for shooting photos, so he was now on his own, and my task was complete. Despite this, David was agreeable to keeping me on, making things a bit awkward between Justin and me. The paper didn't need two full-time photographers. To Justin's growing annoyance, I generally got the best assignments because of my experience and, frankly, because I was a better photographer.

Another complication was that summer was now over, and Melanie and Sheila were due back. I would have to find another place to live, and it was unlikely I would find something as cheap as my current arrangement. It would take more time to save up my France money. A couple of weeks before they were scheduled to be back, I began checking the rental listings. It was not encouraging. The city was too damn expensive. By the time they returned, I still hadn't found anything.

I pinned my hopes on the fact the apartment had two bedrooms, and the one where I slept was a combination office and guest room. I knew they liked their privacy and wouldn't be thrilled at the idea of me staying on as a houseguest, but I crossed my fingers and got ready to beg. I would swear to heaven I'd be out of there at the first possible moment.

They arrived home on a Monday in early September. From the window, I saw the taxi pull up in front, and I rushed down to meet them. I grabbed the heaviest suitcases and lugged them up the stairs. I had done my best to have the place immaculate. I also made coffee and also boiled water for tea. They weren't interested in hot beverages, though. They only wanted to talk to the cats as if they were children and to examine them thoroughly for signs of neglect or abuse.

"Looks like you and Dali have bonded," said Melanie, reluctantly impressed, as he rubbed himself against my leg. I resisted my normal impulse to shove him away.

"The place doesn't look too bad," she continued, sounding surprised.

"What have things here been like?" asked Sheila. "Is anybody you know sick?"

"Sick? Not that I know of, but I haven't been talking to many people lately."

"You know what's been going on, don't you?" said Melanie.

"Uh, I'm not sure. What's going on?"

"Don't you read the papers?"

"I *work* for a paper. I don't usually read it though."

"There's an epidemic," said Sheila. "Just among our own friends, we know three who are in the hospital."

"Oh, yeah, we did have an article in last week's paper. They sent Justin down to one of the free clinics to get pictures."

"Everybody knows someone who's sick," said Melanie, "and it's mainly gay men who are getting it."

"That doesn't make any sense. Why would gay men be the only ones to get it?"

"That's what's so scary," said Sheila. "Nobody knows. Everybody is freaked out, and it's not just gay men. Haitians and people using needles have been getting it too."

"Come to think of it, a guy I knew from home died a couple of months ago in Los Angeles. He was gay."

We talked about the epidemic for a while, but there wasn't a whole lot more to say. Nobody had answers to the obvious questions.

At the first opportunity to change the subject, I made my play.

"I've had to put off my trip to France, and I haven't had much luck finding another place to live. Any chance I could stay here just a while longer?"

They clearly weren't thrilled by the idea, but they were happy enough with how they found the apartment that they agreed, reluctantly—as long as I found another place as soon as I could.

"Thanks," I said. "Can I thank you by taking you out to dinner?"

"I'm exhausted," said Sheila. "I don't feel like going out."

"I'm tired too," said Melanie, "but I don't feel like cooking. Where were you thinking about, Green?"

"There's a new Mexican place down the street. I've been wanting to try it since it opened. Did I mention it's my treat?"

Melanie looked at Sheila hopefully.

"It's been months since we've had Mexican," she said.

"Okay," said Sheila, "since he's paying."

After they had unpacked and settled in, the three of us walked the five blocks to Querétaro. As eager as I had been to try it, I had denied myself for the sake of my reunion with Valérie.

As we took our seats, things were not promising. The table was unsteady, one leg being shorter than the others. It was also too small for three people.

The young waiter was an awkward scarecrow with long black, hair. He brought chips, salsa, and menus.

"What would you like to drink?" he asked with a thick accent.

"*¿Habla usted español?*"

His face lit up.

"*Claro que sí. ¿Y usted? ¿De dónde es?*"

"*De aquí.*"

"*¿De veras? Usted habla español muy bien.*"

"*Una cerveza Negra Modelo por favor.*"

"*¿Y para las damas?*"

Melanie and Sheila followed my lead and ordered the same.

"Showoff," said Melanie, unimpressed.

The waiter rushed to the kitchen.

"Well, that's a good sign," I said. "At least the waiter is authentic."

It was a false hope. The sour look on Sheila's face said it all.

"The chips are stale," she said. "I think the salsa is from a jar. Not even a good jar."

"Maybe they put all of their effort in the main dishes," said Melanie optimistically.

"At least we know the beer will be good," I said. "There's no way to mess up a bottle of Negra Modelo."

"Your Spanish is good," said Sheila. "Melanie said you were in Chile. What was that like?"

"Interesting. A good friend of mine lives in Santiago. I stayed with him and his family."

"How did you manage? I mean, with all the oppression?"

"There wasn't really any oppression where I was."

"I've read a lot of articles about Chile. Things are bad there. Everyone is suffering."

"There's definitely poverty, and you see armed soldiers everywhere, but everyday life goes on like it does anywhere else. People just live their lives. Most of the people I saw seemed happy."

"Are you blind or something?"

"Excuse me?"

"How could you not see all the persecution?"

"I'm just telling you what I saw. The streets were full of people going to and coming from work. I know things are tough for a lot of people, but you also see lots of people out having a good time."

"The rich people, you mean."

"Most of the people I saw looked like they were middle-class. Have you been there?"

"I don't need to go there. I know what I've read. I would never support the dictatorship by going there."

The conversation had become uncomfortable, and I quickly changed the subject.

"So, what was England like?" I asked. "Did you have a good time?"

"We loved it," said Melanie. "I wished I lived there. I love the culture, the museums, the theater."

"I wouldn't move until the government changed," said Sheila. "Thatcher is just as bad as Reagan. Maybe worse. She's caused so much misery with her policies. I don't understand how she ever got elected."

"It was exciting to be in the country for the Royal Wedding," said Melanie. "We watched the whole thing on the Beeb."

"The Beeb?" I asked.

"The BBC. *You* watched the whole thing," corrected Sheila. "I couldn't stomach all the money wasted on the monarchy."

"I know," said Melanie, "but I can't help myself. I love the pageantry. I just try not to think about how imperialist it is."

The waiter returned with two beers. A minute later, he came back with a huge margarita and set it in front of me.

"Uh, excuse me," I called after him, as he rushed away. "I didn't order this. *Yo no pedí una margarita.*"

He spun around and said with a broad smile, "*Un obsequio de su amigo.* I will be back to take your food orders."

"What did he say?" asked Melanie.

"I think he said, compliments of a friend."

I looked around, but we were the only customers. I stared at the frosty glass. A wonderful smell of fresh lime, perched on the salty rim, wafted to my nostrils.

"A friend?" said Melanie. "Do you know the owner or something?"

"I think the waiter bought it for you," said Sheila. "You impressed him with your Spanish. I think he has a crush on you."

I lifted the frozen glass and said, "Well, I'm not going to look a gift horse in the mouth. Here's to your homecoming. And thanks again for not kicking me out on the street."

I took a sip and was transported back in time. The taste was exquisite. It had been made with the juice of freshly squeezed limes. Also, I had consumed enough tequila in my time to know that an expensive brand had been used. Even the ice was special. It was not blended but had obviously been crushed by hand. The grains of salt were chunkier than ordinary table salt, and they complemented the taste perfectly. Only once in my entire life had I ever had a margarita so splendid. What were the odds of having the perfect margarita twice in one lifetime?

"It couldn't be…" I mused, savoring the aftertaste.

"What couldn't be?" asked Melanie. "Is that margarita any good?"

"Good? It's perfection. Have a taste."

They each took a sip and were properly impressed.

"Well, at least they know how to make a decent margarita here," said Sheila. "Maybe the food will be okay after all."

The waiter returned to take our main dinner order. Sheila requested *carne asada,* Melanie ordered *chimichangas,* and I went for the *enchiladas suizas.*

"This margarita is amazing," I told him. "Did you make it yourself?"

He laughed.

"No, it was your friend."

"Friend? What friend?"

"He said you would know who."

The tequila had already made me dizzy. Could it possibly be?

"*Y ¿dónde está mi amigo?*"

"*En la cocina. Vaya a saludarle si quiere.*"

I stood.

"Excuse me," I said to the others. "I need to check something out."

As I followed the waiter, I said, "I'm Dallas by the way. What's your name?"

"*Javier. Encantado.*"

"And how do you know my friend?"

"I don't," he shrugged.

He held the swing door to let me enter. Laboring over the stove was a bald, heavy-set man in a greasy tank-top. I looked at him expectantly, but he ignored me.

"He must have gone outside," said Javier, continuing through the kitchen and out the backdoor.

We emerged in a tiny garden behind the restaurant. A man sat casually in a chair, reading a newspaper. A small martini glass containing a brilliant, golden liquid was on his small table next to a cigar box.

"*Allí está,*" said Javier, turning and going back inside.

The man looked up from his paper.

It was him.

"How you doing, kid? Been a while."

I had no words.

"Have a seat. How was the margarita?"

"It... it was great. What are you doing here? How did you know I would be here?"

"I retired from the restaurant business, but I still like to keep my hand in. So the margarita was okay then?"

"You know it was. Is this your place? Is this where you are now?"

He glanced around dismissively.

"This place? Nah. Did you try the food? If you did, you know it isn't my place."

"So you just walked in and asked them if you could make a margarita for someone? And they let you do it? How did you know I was here?"

"Let's just say it was a lucky guess. So, what's new, kid? We have some catching up to do."

"I looked for you when I got back from Europe. I couldn't find you anywhere. You vanished."

"Yeah, sorry about that. Some things came up. I had to do some traveling. I wish now I had stayed. You never told me you met Lautaro Contreras's son."

"Of course, I never told you. When was I supposed to tell you? You disappeared. How do you know about Lautaro?"

"Lautaro and I go way back. So you stayed with him in Santiago."

"How do you know all this? Marty, this is starting to creep me out."

"Sorry I didn't get a chance before to congratulate you on the great job with the photo in Berlin. You went way beyond my expectations. In fact, it went so well I had to wait this much time to see you again. Enough time had to go by, in case anyone was trying to connect the dots."

"Are you going to tell me who you are and who you work for?"

"I'm just a semi-retired restaurant owner. It's better if we leave it at that."

"But you work for the good guys, right? Not the bad guys?"

He sipped his cocktail.

"I don't care for terms like 'good guys' and 'bad guys.' Let's just say that I work for the 'better guys.' I work against the 'worse guys.' You saw for yourself what East Berlin was like. That place was run by the 'worse guys.'"

"You're right, I didn't like East Berlin much. I probably wouldn't have found it any better in Chile, though, if I had been on the wrong political side."

"Yeah, but you weren't. That's the key. Not being on the wrong side. Speaking of Chile, I understand you met Lautaro's daughter."

"How do you know about that? Is there anything you don't know?"

"Did she tell you anything interesting?"

"Yeah, everything she told me was interesting. What are you trying to find out?"

"Nothing specific. I was just curious if she told you anything of *particular* interest to you. For instance, did she say anything about her so-called husband?"

"The most interesting thing she told me was about my friend Antonio. She knew where he went after the *golpe*. That was more than *you* were able to tell me."

"Good for her. Did you find him?"

"No. He had already left for France, and that's where I'm going as soon as I save up enough money."

He opened the box on the table and offered me a cigar.

"Cuban?"

"You know it is. I don't smoke anything else. You ever had an *El Presidente* cocktail? Want to try one?"

"Jesus, my margarita is probably all melted by now, and my friends are probably wondering what happened to me."

He called to the waiter, who came promptly.

"Javier, please bring my friend's margarita cocktail to him. Please tell his friends he has been delayed, and they should have their dinner without him. He'll see them later at home."

"You can't do that," I protested, but Javier was already gone. "They'll think I'm some kind of asshole. How will I explain it to them?"

"You'll live longer, Dallas, if you don't worry about things so much."

He removed two cigars from the box and cut them. He handed one to me, then lit both of them. I puffed. Magically, the rich smoke transported me back to the night I visited his house on Russian Hill. The night he plied me with cigars and insanely expensive scotch.

He sat back and blew a perfectly formed smoke ring. He closed his eyes to savor the sensation. He did not speak for several minutes.

"What if there was a way for you to go to France right now? Without any delay. Tomorrow if you want. And money wasn't a problem."

"It sounds too easy."

"Did I say anything about easy?"

"What are you saying? You want me to take another photograph?"

"Tell me about your meeting in Buenos Aires."

I choked on the smoke in my mouth. I coughed for half a minute.

"How do you know about that? Never mind. I should be used to it by now. Is my personal privacy completely a thing of the past?"

"Do you realize what you are sitting on top of, kid? Many major governments don't know or have confirmation that the IRA and the Montoneros have discussed cooperation. Think about that.

We knew about IRA links to groups like ETA and the PLO, but this Montonero business is new."

"I don't want to think about it. I shouldn't have been there. I didn't want to be there. I have nothing to do with any of it. I've done my best to forget the whole thing."

"Can't say I blame you. You got yourself into kind of a dicey situation. What more can you tell me about what they're up to?"

"You're asking me? I thought you knew everything. I don't know. It seemed to me like kind of a tentative, low-level meeting. They talked about supplying explosives. They talked about some places I wasn't familiar with. One of them was the Malvinas. The other was, what was it now, I think he said Algeciras."

Marty raised an eyebrow. It was the first time I had seen him look surprised.

"You've got a good memory, kid. That's really something. You sure they mentioned those specific places?"

He whistled softly.

"This is big. You have a knack for being in the right place at the right time. I want you to promise me something."

"I don't think I want to hear this."

"I'm being serious here. If you ever come across that Montonero guy again—I don't care where or when—I want you to try to get a photo of him. Will you do that for me?"

"I'm never going to see him again. How would I? Why would I?"

"Just promise me, okay? Promise me that, and I'll have you on a plane to Paris by the end of the week. Deal?"

"Sure, why not? Like I said, I'm never going to see him again."

It was getting late. The sky was darkening. The fence around the small garden was ineffective against the brisk Pacific breeze. I leaned back and puffed.

"So, is that all I need to do for you to send me back to Paris? Just promise to shoot that guy's photo if I ever see him again?"

"Nah, there's something else."

# 26
# Rebirth

"SO WHAT ACTUALLY became of the photo? The one you took of Número Uno, as you call him?"

We were only a third of the way through our second round of Guinness pints. The bartender had already served the third round. Séamus had ordered it. The rich, creamy foam stuck to my upper lip. I wiped it away with the back of my hand. The smell was sweeter than the bitter taste.

"I never developed it. I was too freaked out. I immediately took the film out of the camera. I've got it hidden away in the place where I live."

"So no one has actually seen the photo? Not even you?"

I shook my head and took another sip.

"So you don't know if you actually got the shot. You might not have caught him in your frame."

"Oh, I got him all right. I know that for a fact. I've been doing this too long not to know whether he was in the frame when I clicked the shutter."

"And the only ones who know the photo exists are you and..."

"Número Uno knows. He saw me take it. Now you know too."

"There was definitely a lot of chatter about it. Even I got wind of it. That's not good. Who was this photo supposed to be for?"

"I'm not going to get into that."

"Well, we're not making much headway on solving this," he said, setting down his empty glass and picking up a full one. "You should probably order the next round."

"The next round? I haven't started on the last pint you bought me."

"You haven't copped on to how things work here, have you? You don't want to fall behind with rounds. You don't want to be caught out for the last call."

"What am I going to do, Séamus?"

"Feck all if I know, Austin."

"Are you ever going to call me by the right name?"

"I know your name all right, Dallas. I just like winding you up. Know what I'm going to call you from now on?"

"What?"

"Dallas na nGall. Bet you don't know what that means."

"Dallas of the foreigners?"

He was visibly impressed.

"Well, maybe your Irish isn't so shite after all. How the feck did you know that?"

"Father McGinley told me. That's where the name for Donegal comes from."

"You have a knack for languages all right. Do you know why I'd call you that?"

"Because I'm a foreigner?"

"Because I'm drawing a comparison between you and Diarmait na nGall."

"Who?"

"Diarmait Mac Murchada. He was a king of Leinster a long time ago. He made the mistake of stealing the High King's wife."

"Wait a minute. What's the difference between a king and a high king?"

"It's obvious, isn't it? A high king is higher than a run-of-the-mill king."

"Why would you have both a king and a high king?"

"Let the story take you, and stop asking so many questions. Ireland never had just one king. We had loads of kings. Every other bloke was a king. That's why we were hard to conquer for a long time. When the Normans invaded England, William the Conqueror only had to defeat one king. Anyone who got to Ireland found they had to defeat hundreds of kings."

"That actually explains a few things."

"Your questions have got me off track. As I was saying, Diarmait stole the high king's wife and that got him deposed from his own throne. Do you know what he did then?"

"Is this going to be another history lesson, like the time you told me about Maximilian and Carlotta?"

"He went looking for help from foreigners to get his throne back. That's why they call him Diarmait of the foreigners. He found an Anglo-Norman lad called Richard de Clare. Richard was the Count of Striguil, but the name that stuck for all time was Strongbow. To get his help, Diarmait gave Strongbow his daughter Aoife's hand in marriage. He also made him his heir. When Diarmait died, though, there was a complication. Diarmait's son contested Strongbow's claim to the throne. That's when Strongbow got help from the King of England. Henry II sent in his army, and those English feckers didn't go away for eight-hundred years."

"That's how it all started?"

"Yeh," he said, draining yet another pint. "Because of Diarmait asking foreigners to help him with a local dispute, we were occupied for eight centuries. There's a lesson there, Dallas. When you accept someone's help, there are sometimes serious, unforeseen consequences."

"Believe me, I've already learned that lesson. I've also learned the one about not getting involved with other guys' wives."

He took another long sip of his stout. The more I thought about my situation, the greater the panic I felt.

"Can't you talk to them, Séamus? You could tell the Argentine guy it's all a big misunderstanding. Tell them there's no photo. They might believe you."

"It's not that simple. You see, I have my own problems with the Argentines. Do you happen to remember a jewelry box that I gave them in Buenos Aires?"

"Yeah, I do."

"Well, I pulled a fast one. You know that diamond Mam's wearing? The one your friend came looking for?"

"Yeah?"

"It's valuable. I mean really valuable. I nicked it from your man in Paris to contribute to a republican fund-raiser. A group I was involved with was collecting whatever they could beg, borrow, or steal, so I threw it in, but I could never get that stone out of my mind. In the end, I took it back without anyone knowing. I was going through a guilty phase, and I wanted it for Mam. I had broken her heart so many ways, I thought maybe I could make up for it.

"I swapped a fake diamond for it. Who would know the difference? In time I forgot about it. In the end, the trickster got tricked. Didn't I spot the fake diamond in with the jewelry I was to hand to your man in Buenos Aires. I can tell you, there was hell to pay over that. I played dumb and just about got away with it. Nobody knew I nicked it a second time. Still, people have been looking at me over their shoulders ever since. If anyone found out that diamond was here in Connemara, that'd be me at the bottom of some bog."

"Man," I said, "this just gets better and better. What are we going to do, Séamus?"

"What do you mean 'we,' Yank? I'm on a plane the day after tomorrow. After that, I'll have disappeared off the face of the earth."

He lifted his glass and toasted, "Best of luck to you, Dallas na nGall."

With a sentimental look on his face, he rose and wandered over to where his mother was. I grabbed my pint and went to see what Alex and Father McGinley were up to. I found them squeezed into a corner and deep in chat.

"There you are," said the priest. "Alex has been telling me of his spiritual struggles."

"I guess you're the right man for that, Padre. I wish you could solve *my* problems for me."

"You never know. Perhaps if you told me more about them, I could help you solve them yourself. First, please excuse me. You can have my chair while I head for the gents."

No more than myself, they had had their share of pints. Alex had a faraway look on his face. When he spoke, he slurred his words noticeably.

"I do not think I am a Catholic anymore."

"Join the club, amigo. It's like that song by R.E.M. I lost my religion a long time ago."

"I think I am a Buddhist. I have done much reading about it, and it's what makes sense to me."

"What do Buddhists believe?"

"It is complicated. I don't know if I fully understand it, but I like its message of avoiding self-indulgence and accepting self-denial. It seems right to me. Also, I believe in reincarnation."

"Why? Do you think you've lived before?"

"I do, but probably not in the way you are thinking. Rebirth in Buddhism does not mean you are reborn as another person. That is a misconception, but I think this is not the first time I have existed."

"Can you remember any past lives?"

"Do you remember when I served you Communion in the cottage?"

"Yeah, sure."

"When I handed you the chalice, our fingers touched for a moment. Did you feel something in that moment?"

"Yeah, I did. I don't know how to explain it, but I definitely felt something."

"We connected, didn't we? It was as if we had known each other before, wasn't it?"

"It was strange, but later I remembered the little boy I saw in Buenos Aires. I think it was you."

"Yes, after you said that, I thought I remembered seeing you too, but I cannot be sure. Do I really recall it or is it because you put the idea of it in my mind? In any event, I think it is more than that. I think it goes back farther in time."

"You think we knew each other in a past life?"

"I think I knew you, as you are now, but when I lived in a past existence."

In a trick my mind played, the roar of voices receded to the background. I locked eyes with Alex, and perhaps thanks to the stout, I felt as if I were floating. It was like that moment at Communion and also that moment in B.A.

"Who do you think you were?"

"You will laugh at me."

"The way I'm feeling right now, I'm open to believing anything."

"Lukas and I have been close friends for four years. He has always been the free-spirited one. I have always been the responsible one."

"Sounds familiar."

"Somehow it became my job to watch out for him. In a way, to be his good judgment and perhaps his conscience as well. Over time, he began joking I was the father he never had. We both laughed at the joke, but occasionally I would experience something like déjà vu. It was as if old memories were coming back. Memories that were not from my own life."

"Like what?"

"Odd things. A fragment of being a child in a very hot place. Sometimes of driving a large car on a wide road."

"Nothing more specific?"

"No, not really. When I met you, I thought there was something familiar about you, as if I knew you before."

"Wait. So you think you are Lonnie's reincarnation?"

"I said you would laugh."

"I'm only laughing because you are absolutely nothing like Lonnie. I can't imagine two people more different than you and him."

"Lukas thought it was silly too, but Buddhism teaches that each lifetime consists of personal acts that plant a seed for a karmic result in the next life. One does not become exactly the same person each time."

I took a good long drink. I had heard a lot of strange shit in my life, and this was as strange as anything I'd ever heard before.

"God, Alex, I wish you *were* Lonnie. I'd give anything to have him back, even for just a few minutes, but there's no way I can believe you're him. It's just too crazy."

"You're probably right. Still, there's an interesting coincidence. Lukas's mother told him that his father died in May of 1974. I was born exactly nine months later."

A shiver went up my spine.

"Yeah, that's amazing. I wish to God you were him. I want to tell him so many things. I want to ask him so many things. You want to know my own oddball belief about Lonnie? It's been nineteen years since he died, and I've never been able to shake the nagging feeling he's still out there, that he somehow tricked us. Your idea of being his reincarnation isn't any crazier than that, is it?"

A heavy sadness overwhelmed me. I wanted the impossible to be true. In that brief moment I actually did accept the impossible. The beer helped. I thought, the hell with it, and just went with it.

I set down my glass and put my hands on Alex's shoulders. I stared into his eyes. His body was surprisingly relaxed, and he stared back docilely.

"Lonnie," I said softly. "Are you in there?"

He said nothing. His eyes did not blink. Through my fingers, I felt the slight movement of his body breathing. I swear I felt his temperature rise.

"Lonnie, I miss you, man. You wouldn't believe all the shit that's gone down since you left. Life's gotten more insane since then."

It was probably only the Guinness, but I half-expected to hear Lonnie's voice come out of Alex's mouth.

"Lonnie?"

His eyes widened slightly.

"If you can answer just one question, can you please answer this one? What happened when we were fourteen? What did I miss? What was it you never told me?"

His eyes turned watery. He said nothing. I thought, if I waited just a bit longer, he might answer. It didn't happen. Father McGinley returned and looked at us curiously.

"Am I interrupting something, lads? They're after announcing last call. I'll get the final round."

"Thanks, Padre," I said, still in a daze.

"I don't know how to describe it," said Alex, looking disoriented. "I think you wanted him to speak through me, but that's not how rebirth works. *Bueno, tú debes pensar que yo estoy completamente loco.*"

"I don't know what to think, but I don't think you're crazy. At least not any crazier than me. Maybe the Buddhists are right. Maybe the Christians are right. Maybe in the grand scheme of things, they're both right when it comes to the things that truly matter. I may be losing my religion, but I've never stopped believing in God. I've just stopped believing I'll ever be smart enough to understand God."

"I think you understand more than most people."

He looked so damn young, and I felt so damn old. It amazed me he was content to waste his time talking to me. When I had been his age, the last thing I would have wanted to do is sit in some bar talking to a forty-year-old man. The thing was, I didn't feel like I was forty years old. I felt like I was the same age as Alex—as long as I didn't look in the mirror.

"It's strange," I said, "to think you and Lukas are the same age as Lonnie and me when we had our biggest adventure. All that time flew by in the blink of an eye. I'm jealous of the two of you. It all lies ahead of you. The amazing thing is how much you know compared to Lonnie and me when we were your age."

"I don't know how many adventures Lukas and I will have. I would not be surprised if he didn't come back. I think he might continue traveling with that Annika and maybe go to America with her."

"You don't need to worry about that," I said. "I know his type. He'll wander off with any pretty face he comes across, but he'll always come back to his best friend—sooner or later. You just have to be patient with him."

"May I ask you a question? If I am prying, you do not have to answer, but I am curious. Why did you want to ask your friend about when he was fourteen years old?"

"It's an old mystery. I had forgotten about it until a few years ago. Then something reawakened it, and I've been kind of obsessed about it ever since. These things happen to me. I lose contact with a friend, then I spend years wondering what happened to him and how to find him. Or someone makes me remember something I thought I had forgotten, and I can't stop thinking about it. Does that happen to you?"

"I'm not certain I understand you."

"I know I'm not making sense. It's just that sometimes, years later, you realize much too late that something serious was going on with someone close to you, and you were totally oblivious. By that time, it's too late, but you can't stop thinking about it. That's what's been going on with me. If I think about it too much, it drives me crazy. It's a mystery, and unfortunately, the only person who can solve it for me has been dead for almost twenty years."

Father McGinley returned, balancing three pints in his two hands. He set them down and pulled up a chair.

"This has something to do with Lonnie?" asked Alex.

"Yeah. I happened to have one of those conversations that awakened something I hadn't remembered in ages. Her questions brought out things I hadn't thought about in years."

"She?" wondered the priest. "Who was that?"

"My wife."

# 27
# Vaugirard

STANDING IN FRONT of the door, I wondered if my heart might actually burst out of my chest. It beat so forcefully, I honestly thought I might be having a heart attack. I had waited so long and had come so far. At last the moment had arrived—and I was petrified.

I slipped my arms out of the heavy backpack's straps and let it drop to the floor. At least now it was easier to breathe.

A few minutes before, I had been at the building's entrance, scanning the directory for the apartment number. My shirt had clung to my body. It was drenched from the rain shower that was falling when I had emerged from the Metro.

Before I had managed to push the button, an elegantly dressed woman with white hair and a cane had emerged from the building. She had paused long enough to hold the door for me. She was cross when I had hesitated to take advantage of her kindness.

"*Merci,*" I had mumbled.

She had shaken her head while hobbling down the damp sidewalk.

I had climbed the stairs, looking for the apartment number on each floor. I found it on a door three flights up. I couldn't make my hand knock on the door. Instead of her being surprised by my voice on her intercom, she would unexpectedly find me at her door, looking like something a mangy cat had dragged from the alley.

I tapped tentatively on the door, then again more forcefully. I listened for sound of movement behind the door and heard nothing. A minute later, I knocked again. It was Friday evening, but I hoped she would be home.

I was exhausted. The previous evening I had spent four-and-half hours on a plane to Chicago, then nine hours on a flight to Paris. I knew I stank. For once, I actually needed a shave. If I had been thinking clearly, I would have first found a place to stay for the night and then arrived at her door fresh and clean. Clear thinking, however, was not part of this.

Once Marty had arranged for the transfer of money to my checking account, I had booked the first flight I could get. After landing at Charles de Gaulle Airport, I went straight to the address on Valérie's last letter. It had arrived only a week before, informing me she had moved from Bordeaux to Paris, specifically to a street off Rue de Vaugirard in the 15th Arrondissement.

I heard the soft sound of footsteps. The door opened just enough to show me a cascade of long, straight, black hair. Her head turned sideways, and two dark eyes peered at me.

"*J'y crois pas!* What are you doing here?"

"I told you I would come see you as soon as I could. I'm here."

"I did not expect you. This is not a good time."

"Sorry. I know I should have called first. I couldn't wait to see you. Can I come in?"

"Not now. Maybe I can meet you tomorrow."

"Tomorrow? But I came all this way. I couldn't wait to see you."

"*Tu es complètement fou, tu sais.* Completely crazy."

"I don't disagree. Um, is there a problem? Is someone with you?"

"No, I am alone, but I am not ready for you. This is too sudden. *C'est une intrusion.*"

"What if I come back later? Maybe in an hour or two?"

"*Comme tu es têtu.* Okay, come back in two hours. No, better, meet me in two hours. There is a café on the nearest corner."

"Yeah, I saw it. I know the one you mean. Okay, I'll meet you at the café in two hours. *Au revoir.*"

"*Au revoir!*"

It had not gone as I had imagined. Surprising her on the doorstep had seemed like a stroke of genius—an incredibly romantic gesture. In retrospect, getting a hotel room first would obviously have been the wiser course of action.

I walked to the café and sat at an outside table under an awning. Still dripping from the most recent shower, most of the outside tables and chairs had been shoved to one side. I wanted to be easy to spot when she arrived. It was several minutes before a lanky, young waiter in a white shirt came to take my order. I was tempted to order a double scotch, but I knew that would be a mistake, given how tired I was. I asked for a large, black coffee.

I wished I had picked up a newspaper. I found myself fidgeting. When the waiter brought the coffee, I asked for a pack of cigarettes. He understood me with no problem, despite my not bothering to attempt French. He brought a pack of Gauloises, and one puff sent me back to the previous year in Deauville. That memory was just what I needed. I reassured myself I would eventually quit smoking for good.

Time dragged. I started in alarm upon realizing how much of the pack I had smoked. I ordered another coffee. I would be exhausted and wired at the same time. I checked my watch. It was still on California time, but that didn't matter for calculating how long I had been waiting. It had been two-and-a-half hours. She wasn't going to show, was she?

I rubbed my eyes from tiredness. My eye sockets felt like sandpaper. As I tried blinking the dryness away, I saw her coming down the street. Man, she looked great. Never was the old expression about a sight for sore eyes more apt.

She looked no different from the first time I saw her. She might even have been wearing the same tight pullover sweater. Her black eyes glowed. She had the same tentative smile that had always struck me as a mixture of delight and embarrassment. It was now tinged with nervousness.

I thought she hadn't seen me. She hadn't looked at me directly, but she took the seat next to me.

"*Eh bien.*"

"Hello, you."

She leaned over and gave me a business-like peck on each of my cheeks.

"Did you have a good voyage?"

"It was long, but it was worth it. Definitely worth it. How have you been?"

"The year has been difficult. My father died."

"I was sorry to hear that. I wish I could have met him."

"Your letter about it was nice. Your sentiments were very, um, pretty. This English is difficult. I wish you spoke French."

"I've been trying to learn, and I'll keep trying. I promise. I think your English is getting better."

"I do not think so. So you are here."

"Yes, I am definitely here. You know, I've never stopped thinking about you since I met you."

"That is bizarre. We knew one another seven days only."

"Yes, but they were the only seven days."

"*Comment?*"

"For me, there are no days but those seven days. Sorry, I'm not great at expressing myself, even in my own language—especially in my own language—but I need to make you understand. There were no days before I met you, and there were no days after I last saw you. The only days that exist are the seven I spent with you. Do you understand?"

"*Je ne suis pas sûre.* You do not know me. I do not know you. I think you have a fantasy. A dream. This is not, um, healthy."

"What's the difference between fantasy and reality when it comes to feelings? Either you feel something or you don't. I know what I feel."

"Yes, you know what you feel about the woman in your head. I do not think I am that woman. How can I be?"

"How do you feel about me?"

"The same. I mean, I like the man in my head. The man from the seven days, but are you that man in reality? *Qui peut savoir?* It requires time to know another person. We have not had time."

"Well, let's start having that time. I'm not going anywhere. I'm here for a while. In fact, I'm committed to being here for a long time."

"*Tu es fou.* You think you are amorous, I mean, in love. You have no logic."

"Logic has nothing to do with it. I know I love you. I have chosen to love you."

"*Comment? Tu as choisi d'aimer?* That makes no sense."

"Sure, it does. It's kind of like believing or not believing in God. It's not something you can prove logically. It comes down to faith. In the end, the things you believe—I mean, really believe—are because you choose to believe. Because a feeling in your heart overwhelms you."

She laughed. I loved the sound of it.

"You are not very, um, *romanesque.* These are not words a girl likes to read in a book or hear from a lover. They are like words of a schoolteacher."

"You want me to be more romantic? That's not something I'm good at. I'm not a poet or a fancy-talker, but I do love you. I promise I'll treat you the best I know how. I've done nothing but think of you for a year."

Her eyes turned mischievous.

"There has been no other woman during that year?"

She laughed at the way I struggled to answer.

"I won't lie to you. There were times I got confused. Times I was interested in someone and I thought I might be able to forget you. Every time, I wound up realizing you were the one my heart was trying to find its way back to."

She laughed more.

"*Quelle réponse si maline!* You are like a political."

"What about you? Was there any other man in the past year?"

Her face was enigmatic.

"You know about Michel. He and I had things to finish. Now he is gone, but you know that. You were in his house *là-bas au Chili.* How is he?"

"He is fine. I think he is in love. With an American."

"*Une américaine!* How funny. He once spoke of an American girl. Is her name Janet?"

Her eyes were wistful.

"Yeah, Janet. So there's been no other man?"

Her expression turned defiant.

"That is my affair, but no, I have no time for men. Too much happens in my life. I like my solitude. So you have come to France only for me? You have no other cause to be here?"

"I have a job. I have a contract to shoot photos for a magazine. A guy I know in San Francisco set it up for me. As long as I make my minimum quota for each issue, I get paid. There's some travel involved and some occasional work I have to do for my friend, but I'm based here in Paris for the time being. I only arrived today, and I have a whole lot of government paperwork to deal with so I can work here. I also need to find a place to live. How come you moved here from Bordeaux?"

"I too have a new position. I work at the Cinémathèque Française. It has many film archives and a cinema. This is what I always wanted to do."

"Wow, that sounds perfect for you. That's great. I'm so happy for you."

"So you have no bed for tonight?"

"I can get a hotel."

"It is late. My apartment is a disaster, but if you like you could sleep on my divan."

"I don't want to impose."

"It will not be comfortable."

"Doesn't matter. I'm going to have absolutely no problem sleeping tonight."

"Is that all you have," she said, glancing at my backpack.

"Yeah, I travel light."

She was right about the apartment. It was tiny, and if not exactly a disaster, it was certainly a mess. Clothes were left out everywhere. There did not seem to be a dish or glass in the place not stacked in or around the sink.

"Are you hungry?"

"To be honest, all I'm interested in is getting some sleep."

"You must have something."

From the refrigerator she took a plateful of various cheeses and placed it on the table with half a baguette and a nearly full bottle of red wine.

"*Voilà. Mange.*"

"*Merci.*"

She poured wine into two small glasses while I sliced a bit of cheese. We lifted our glasses.

"*À ta santé,*" she said

"Down the hatch."

She said nothing for several minutes while watching me munch on bread and cheese.

"This is a bad idea, *tu sais.*"

"Eating cheese right before bed? Yeah, sometimes it makes me have strange dreams."

"No, I mean I should have left you to get a hotel. You and me here like this so sudden. It's… *c'est peu commode.*"

"Sorry. I'll find a hotel tomorrow."

"You will not be comfortable on the divan. It is too small."

"I'll manage. Like I said, I'll have no trouble sleeping tonight."

"I would invite you to sleep on part of the bed, but it is not large."

"It wouldn't be the first time we shared a bed."

She laughed.

"I had forgotten."

"How could you forget? I'll never forget it."

"But nothing happened. We slept only."

"It was still the best night of my life."

"You are amusing."

"We could share the bed again, like we did in Deauville. I promise I won't touch you—unless you want me to."

"That was a difficult night. You were very good to me. I can be difficult. Do you understand?"

"I don't find you difficult. I find you wonderful."

"*Flatteur.*"

"So what do you say? We will share a bed again?"

She poured us two more glasses of wine.

"I suppose it is only polite, but I advise you it is a small bed."

It was a small bed. She changed into a nightgown in the bathroom. I had no pajamas, so I did what I always did at bedtime. I stripped down to my underwear and tee-shirt. She slipped under the duvet on her side and stared at the wall next to her. On my side, I lay on top of the duvet.

She turned and said, "You will have cold if you lie like that."

"I'll be all right. It's better this way. Otherwise, I might accidentally rub against you in my sleep."

"That is silly. Put yourself in the bed correct."

"Well, if you insist."

I went in next to her. She lay with her back to me. I could feel warmth radiating from her. I smelled the same perfume I had loved in Deauville.

"Good night, Valérie."

"*Bonne nuit, Monsieur Vert.*"

"Mr. Green. That's a good one. Say, Valérie…"

"*Oui?*"

"Can I kiss you goodnight?"

She turned over and looked into my eyes. The smell of her perfume was stronger. Her face was beautiful.

"*Si tu veux.*"

I put my lips lightly on hers. Their softness soothed me. It was impossible to draw away. My mouth lingered, barely touching hers, brushing her lips sideways, back and forth. She did not draw away either.

I kissed her properly. Her mouth tasted like warm honey, as it had on the beach at Deauville. Our tongues were soon coiled around each other like a nest of snakes.

I shifted my body. The duvet slid to the floor. I ran my hands over every inch of her. Her fingernails dug into my back. Our bodies were so intertwined it was impossible to know where one of us left off and the other began. Was that her elbow or mine? Was that my finger or hers? Our loins were joined so tightly it was impossible to be certain who was penetrating whom. Blood from my arteries flowed in her veins. Her heartbeat quickened, causing my temples to throb. In my excitement I inhaled. In response, she exhaled in exaltation. My delirious brain recalled every moment of her childhood. Her mind foresaw my entire future. For a brief, euphoric moment, we had become one person. She was the half that had been missing my whole life. Never had I felt so firmly I was where I was meant to be. I experienced more happiness than my body could contain, and I felt my spirit leaving my body. I wondered if I might actually be experiencing the Rapture. Was I about to come face-to-face with God? It seemed the logical next step.

"If I died right now," I gasped weakly, "I would be happy. It would be worth it."

"*La petite mort,*" she murmured.

We lay a long time, trying to catch our breaths. It was the second time in a day that I wondered if I might be having a heart attack. I kissed her neck and shoulder.

"What was it you said?"

"*Comment?*"

"Did you say little death?"

"*La petite mort.* Yes, that is what we call, you know…"

"The orgasm?"

"Yes, that."

"You call it the little death?"

"Yes. I think I understand better now why."

"Yeah, me too. I don't think I've ever been more in touch with my mortality than right now. God, I love you."

She said nothing.

"I was nervous about seeing you again. After a year, I didn't know what it would be like. Would you be the same as I remembered? Would I be the same? Would being together again be the same? I didn't need to worry. It is the same. It's actually better. There's no doubt in my mind. You're the one. You're the one I'm meant to be with."

She looked away and was quiet for several minutes. Her silence was so prolonged I wondered if something was wrong. She turned to face me.

"This may be the wrong time, but I need to ask you something."

"A favor? Sure. Anything. Just ask. I'll do anything for you."

"Please do not misunderstand."

"Don't worry about that. Just ask me."

"I want you to marry me."

# 28
# Paperasserie

"SORRY, WHAT DID you just say?"

"I need for you to marry me."

My pulse quickened. It was fear. Despite all my convincing talk, I hadn't thought about marriage. I had focused only on getting to France and seeing Valérie. I hadn't thought further than that. I had expected to have plenty of time to work out the rest. I had been in the hunt. Now I felt as if I had walked into a trap.

I was experienced enough now to know what was happening. It was a reflex action. I had felt this before whenever a relationship shifted out of my control. I focused my thoughts. I had had no doubts getting to this point, and I would have no doubts going forward. Still, I had questions.

"Uh, what happened to me not really knowing you and you not really knowing me?"

She kissed me and looked into my eyes.

"I did not think I could ask you this before, but now I think I can."

"Wow. So I must have been extremely good."

She laughed.

"Yes, it was good. Quite good."

"You're serious about this?"

"Yes, I am serious."

I was no less confused.

"Wait a minute. You're not pregnant, are you?"

She laughed.

*"Enceinte? Non, je t'assure, je ne suis pas enceinte."*

I loved the way she laughed. I loved the sound of her voice when she spoke her own language. I put my arm over her shoulders and kissed her again.

"Yes, I'll marry you. I don't know what the hurry is. Maybe I wish I could have been the one to ask you. None of that matters. Yes, I want to marry you."

"Thank you. Thank you very much for this favor."

"I wouldn't call it a favor. We're doing this for each other. It's something we both want."

"No, I do not explain well. It is a favor."

"What do you mean?"

"I need an American passport. I can have one if you marry me."

"An American passport? Why?"

"Logan wants me to reside with him. He has invited me to California. I worry about his health. He is not young. I have only commenced to know him, and I do not want to lose the time."

"You don't need an American passport for that. You can go on your French passport."

"Yes, but the time for the tourist visa has a limit. I want to reside a long time."

"Let me get this straight. You want to marry me so you can get a U.S. passport and use it to go live in California?"

"Yes. That is it."

I couldn't help but laugh.

"I just committed to being based here for the next couple of years for my work."

"That is good. That is convenient for you. You can have this apartment when I go."

"But if you move to California, I want to go with you. We'll be married."

"Married on the paper. It is not like a true marriage. I would not cause you to go with me if you must stay here."

Her words were like a punch to the gut.

"Don't you see? For me it would be a true marriage. I really want to marry you. I love you."

"We shall have much time together. You will be exhausted of me before I go because of all the time for making the paperwork and the waiting for the government. You can reside here with me if you want. It is the least I can do for my husband. I am happy for you to be here. We shall see what happens. *D'accord?*"

"I like the idea of living with you. This place is small, but that doesn't bother me for now. We might want to look for a bigger place later on. Yeah, I guess we can take it one day at a time and see how things go."

"Yes, that is my manner of thinking. *Il faut le vivre au jour le jour.*"

"And I want you to talk to me mostly in French. I need to speak and understand it better."

She gave me a hug and nuzzled my neck.

"*Je suis heureuse que tu sois ici. C'est vrai.*"

She wasted no time. The next day she took me to the local town hall, the Mairie d'Arrondissement on Rue Péclet, to apply for a marriage license. It was an impressive 19th-century building large enough to have a courtyard. We were told we could not apply until I had been in the country a minimum of thirty days. We needed the time anyway to gather all the required paperwork. I was told to get a medical certificate from a doctor, a *certificat de capacité matrimoniale* from the U.S. Embassy, and a copy of my birth certificate from the Kern County Registrar in California.

As Valérie had anticipated, there was much waiting for all the paperwork to be completed. In the meantime, we got on with our day-to-day lives. Each morning Valérie went to her job at the Cinémathèque Française. It was located in the Palais de Chaillot, across the River Seine from the Eiffel Tower. After making contact with my new employer's Paris office, I began to receive assignments. Every several days I was sent to a different city to shoot photos, usually for an upcoming travel feature. The work was easy but interesting. The main challenge was finding a fresh take on photos of overly familiar tourist landmarks, as well as finding lesser-known but interesting sights.

In the evening, when we were both home, we would take turns making dinner, though my efforts weren't particularly good. Sometimes we would go out for dinner, but the best meals were the ones Valérie cooked. She had a knack for throwing together simple but delicious meals, and she always knew the perfect wine to go with them. We often went out, especially when the Cinémathèque had a good program. Valérie took charge of my education in French cinema.

One night we saw *Jules et Jim*, the Truffaut film I had first heard about from Justin. I was captivated. Jeanne Moreau was more beautiful than I had heard.

As we left the auditorium, I told Valérie, «You know, when Ángel came to find me in San Francisco, he told me that you, he, and I were like the three people in that movie.»

«He did, did he?»

I usually avoided mentioning Ángel, since it annoyed her, but this time I made an exception.

«Do you think I am like her?»

«Like Jeanne Moreau? Only in that both of you are gorgeous.»

While the Cinémathèque was a great way to see classic films, we also went to regular cinemas to see new movies like *La femme d'à côté*, *Coup de torchon*, and *Le chevre*. In subsequent months, we would see *Invitation au voyage*, *La balance*, and *La nuit de Varennes*. Movies in English were no problem for me because they were screened with subtitles instead of being dubbed. Films in French, on the other hand, were a challenge. I relied on Valérie whispering translations, something she did not like to do while she was trying to enjoy the film. Over time, my French improved, and I got better at understanding them.

After a movie, we would often find a cheap local place for a late meal and a discussion of what we had seen. More than once, we were asked to leave because we had chatted until past closing time. Sometimes we were joined by Thierry and Agnès, Valérie's friends since the time they were in school together in Bordeaux. Spending time with them definitely helped to improve my French.

On the weekends I often fell back into my old San Francisco habit of wandering the city on foot with my camera. This suited Valérie since having me around all the time was a major adjustment for her. I would walk for miles, shooting photos like a tourist, awestruck by all the classic architecture and historic monuments and landmarks. Sometimes the two of us would go to a museum. We were spoiled for choice, as it was possible to see a different one every weekend and never see them all. The Louvre alone would have required months of visits to see everything.

Sometimes on Saturday or Sunday, when it was raining, we didn't leave the apartment at all—except to run to the boulangerie for fresh croissants and to the tabac for a newspaper. On those mornings, Valérie would brew thick, black coffee in the stovetop moka pot. We might lie in bed the entire day, reading *Le Monde* or *The Sunday Times* from London—when we weren't making love. Those were the best days. I never got enough of her. When evening came, we would scrape together whatever was left in the cupboard for supper. We'd listen to the radio while making the meal and drinking wine. If we heard a good song by a rock band, like Téléphone, we would dance like silly kids.

Once the thirty-day wait was over, we applied for the marriage license. There was then an additional wait of several weeks before we could get married. Eventually, the day arrived. Thierry and Agnès went to the mairie with us to be our witnesses. For the occasion, I had bought a new suit, which cost a pretty penny. Clothes were expensive in Paris. Valérie wore a simple, blue dress.

«Will you have a wedding in a church as well?» asked Agnès.

The only requirement for a legal marriage in France was to be married in a civil ceremony at the mairie. For most people, however, this was a formality. The real wedding was considered to be a larger ceremony in a church or hotel. That was the one you invited your friends and family to.

"*Non,*" said Valérie emphatically.

«Then do you not want your brother here?» asked Agnès. «What about your family, Dallas?»

I turned to Valérie and said, "We could still have a church wedding if you want. I don't mind if it's in a Catholic church or anywhere else."

"It is not necessary," she said. "I do not need a church's approval for what I do."

The previous night I had called my parents to tell them I was getting married. Mom was emotional, but she did not seem overly disappointed not to be there. My parents' own wedding had been a small affair immediately after the war, and they were never ones for a big fuss. My brother's wife had insisted on a big wedding in Fresno, and that had nearly done them in. I suspected Dad was relieved that I would get married in another country, as it meant he wouldn't have to explain to their friends why I wasn't getting married in the church.

"It might be fun," I said. "We could throw a big party afterwards. It would be a chance for me to meet your relatives. Maybe I could convince my parents and my brother to come."

"It does not interest me," she said.

The ceremony was short, simple, and to-the-point. It was officiated by a mayoral adjunct, an officious, balding, gray-haired man with an exceedingly long, thin nose. Before we began, he took me into a side office and had a chat with me in French. This was to satisfy himself I had a reasonable command of the language, since that was a requirement for the ceremony to be performed. I was relieved and pleased that he judged my French adequate for getting married.

The ceremony itself took less than a half-hour. When he asked if we wanted to exchange rings, Valérie said no. I surprised her by producing a small box with two rings in it.

"I went to a jeweler in Montmartre to surprise you," I whispered.

We put the rings on each other's fingers, and the ceremony continued. When it finished, our two witnesses smiled and clapped. Agnès emptied a bag of rose petals on us, to Valérie's annoyance. As the four of us walked out of the mairie and into the open air, I was surprised to feel suddenly emotional. I could not believe

Valérie and I were married. I stopped, fearing I would embarrass myself by crying. I held it back the best I could, and only Agnès noticed. She put her hand gently on my arm.

"*Ça va?*" she asked.

«*Oui,*» I replied, regaining control. «I guess I'm more sentimental than I realized. You know, we should all go somewhere and celebrate. I mean, at a really good restaurant. This is a special day.»

«Why not?» said Valérie. «Tomorrow we must visit the U.S. Embassy to begin the paperwork for my passport.»

She removed the ring from her finger and examined it in the sunlight.

«How did you get the exact size?» she asked.

«It was just luck. The woman in the jewelry shop had fingers that looked the same as yours, so I took a chance and asked for a ring in her finger size. She said there would be no problem if we needed to exchange it.»

«No, there is no need. It is perfect. Well done.»

She slipped it into her purse, then snapped it shut.

Noting my puzzled look, she said simply, "I don't wear rings."

As for my own ring, I left it on my finger. I never took it off.

We had to walk to three restaurants before we found one that would take us without a reservation. Even then we had to kill time by going to a café for aperitifs until they were ready for us. Given the occasion, I ordered a scotch despite the price being exorbitant compared to the States.

At dinner, by virtue of being the groom, I was handed the wine list, despite knowing the least about wine of our group. Intimidated about making a selection for three people from Bordeaux, I stared at the list for ages. Spotting a Malbec, I ordered it.

«I got a taste for Malbec when I was in Argentina. My friend Donal and I drank a lot of it.»

«It is not truly Malbec if it is not cultivated in Cahors,» said Thierry.

He spoke in the slightly arrogant tone the French sometimes adopt when discussing food and drink.

«It is the same grape surely,» said Agnès. «What does it matter where it grows?»

«They should call it something else,» insisted Thierry.

«Didn't it come from Burgundy originally?» asked Valérie. «Where does the name Malbec come from? It is not the name of a place, like Médoc or Graves.»

That bottle was better than any of the ones I had had in Mendoza. Its taste made me feel as if I were in a dream. It amazed me that Dallas Green from Kern County was sitting in a restaurant in Paris, listening to a conversation about wine in French, and understanding most of it. Still more amazing was that I was married to the beautiful woman next to me. I never dreamed my life could turn out like this.

The next day Valérie and I went to the embassy. We were told that, before she could apply to be naturalized as a U.S. citizen, she would need to apply for a Green Card. This meant another round of paperwork and more waiting. I didn't mind. I was in no particular hurry. Valérie, on the other hand, was frustrated.

"*J'en ai marre de toute cette paperasserie!*" she exclaimed.

«I don't like all the red tape either. We just have to be patient. What's the big hurry?»

«Logan is not getting any younger. I worry about his health. He wants to make one last film, and he wants me to help him. This is important to both of us, to make something that lasts as father and daughter. This is my chance to collaborate with him in a way I was never able to do with the father I grew up with.»

«Okay, I get it. You know, you could go any time you want on a tourist visa. You don't need to be going to all this trouble.»

«No, I want to become an American. Do you remember when I met you? I told you then I wanted to go to California. It has always fascinated me. I have always believed my destiny lay there—even before I learned my biological father was American. When I go, I want to go with no limits.»

«The funny thing is,» I said, «I like it here a lot. I'm not looking forward to going back.»

«Well, we aren't going anywhere for at least a few more months,» she said, «so you still have time to become bored with it.»

Our lives did not change after we were married. Our routine continued as before. When required to travel, I always looked forward to my return to Paris. I hated to be away from Valérie.

One day as I left the magazine office and headed down the street, I noticed a man on a bench. As I passed by him, he called to me. His voice was American.

"Dallas Green?"

"Yes?"

He was five or more years older than me and had curly black hair. His eyebrows were thick and black.

"Got time for a chat?"

"What is it about?"

"We have a mutual friend in San Francisco."

I was curious. He didn't look like a criminal and we were in a public place, so I sat.

"Who's that?"

"The one who got you your job."

"You're a friend of Marty's?"

"Yeah, you could say that. He said you'd be willing on occasion to take pictures for us."

"Yeah, I did tell him that."

"Well, we have an occasion. Are you all right with that?"

"Yeah, I guess so. As long as I don't have to go back to East Berlin."

"No, nothing like that. *Marty me dice que tú hablas bastante bien el español.*"

"*Más o menos,*" I said, making the hand gesture I had often seen in Chile accompanying that expression.

"I'd say a bit better than *más o menos.* That'll come in handy."

"Why? Where am I going?"

"To Spain. I'll fill you in on what we need."

"Okay. Well, you already know my name. What should I call you?"

"Call me Joe."

"Is that like a code name?"

"No, it's my name. Joe Andrade."

"You're actually telling me your name?"

"Of course. Why wouldn't I?"

I had already decided to give him the name Pete since I hadn't expected him to tell me his name. If the government guy I had met in Guatemala looked like Frank Sinatra and the guy had I met in Deauville bore a resemblance to Dean Martin, then this guy was definitely Peter Lawford.

"Can I ask where you learned your Spanish?" I asked him. "Your accent is different than I'm used to."

"*Yo soy cubano.* Born in Havana. I lived in Cuba until I was fourteen. That's when we had to leave. My parents still hope to go back when Castro is gone."

"Where is Marty from? I've never been able to get him to speak Spanish to me."

"You never asked him? He's Cuban too. Goes all the way back to *la Bahía de Cochinos.*"

"The Bay of Pigs? Really?"

"Yeah. He's a real hero, and hardly anybody knows about it. By the way, congratulations."

"For what?"

"For your marriage, of course. She's beautiful. You're a lucky guy."

# 29
# Algeciras

ON ONE OF THOSE rainy Sunday mornings that Valérie and I spent lazily in bed, a random thought came into my head.

«It's strange to think Antonio is here in the same country. He could easily be here in Paris. Maybe in our arrondissement. Who's to know?»

*"Qui?"*

In the beginning, Valérie and I spoke to each other in English. Over time, we found ourselves switching back and forth between languages. By the day of our marriage, we spoke mostly in French. I was pleased with myself for picking up the language quickly. It helped that many French words were similar to Spanish ones.

«You know. Antonio. The friend I lost track of all those years ago. The one who I thought Ángel might be. Remember the reason I went to Bordeaux to meet him?»

«How long has it been since you have seen this Antonio?»

«Let's see, almost eleven years now.»

«And you have not communicated with him in all that time?»

«No.»

*"C'est étrange."*

*"Pourquoi?"*

«Do you think this much about anyone else with whom you have not spoken in eleven years?»

«Not that I can think of. There are usually reasons one does not speak with someone for eleven years.»

«Then why him?»

«I don't know. He and I bonded on that trip in Mexico. I thought he and I would be friends forever. When I heard about what happened in Chile, I worried about him. He's always been on my mind. Though he would be twenty-five now, I still see him as the fourteen-year-old kid I knew. After all these years, I still miss him.»

«Fourteen?»

«Yeah, that was his age when I knew him. Lonnie and I were eighteen.»

«And he has stayed in your memory all these years? *Comme ça?* As a fourteen-year-old?»

«Yeah.»

«What happened when *you* were fourteen?»

«I wasn't fourteen. I told you, I was eighteen.»

«I understand. I want to know what happened to you when *you* were fourteen.»

«Nothing happened when I was fourteen. Nothing unusual or worth mentioning. Why do you ask that?»

«Something happened when you were fourteen.»

In my relatively short time living with Valérie, I had learned things about her. One of those things was her belief she had a gift for analyzing the psychology of those close to her. We may have been in bed at that moment, but metaphorically I was on her couch.

«I don't understand.»

«I think you cannot forget that fourteen-year-old boy because something important happened when *you* were fourteen.»

«What makes you think that?»

«I have an intuition about things. I am certain I am right. If you think about it sufficiently, you will remember something of significance that happened when you were fourteen. Perhaps it is a suppressed memory.»

«I don't think so. I had a pretty boring life as a kid. There's not that much worth remembering.»

«Tell me about you at that age. If you talk, you may recall something.»

«There's nothing to tell. Let's see, when I turned fourteen I was part way through my freshman year of high school. By the time I turned fifteen, I was a sophomore.»

«What happened during your first year of secondary school?»

«Nothing. I just went to school every day. I came home and did homework. I hung out with Lonnie.»

«That's all?»

«Except for…»

«What?»

«Come to think of it, Lonnie kind of disappeared at the end of freshman year.»

«Disappeared?»

«His mother took him out of school for a few weeks. He missed final exams and had to make them up later. I never found out why that happened. Lonnie never wanted to talk about it, and I never pushed him about it. Thinking back on it now, it was kind of strange.»

«What do you think happened?»

«I don't know. It was a crazy time. That summer Lonnie's mother got divorced. She and Lonnie's stepfather had some kind of big blow-out. My parents and their friends talked about it a lot. I didn't want to hear about it. I didn't want to deal with it. There was nothing I could do anyway.»

«Your friend had a stepfather?»

«Yeah, Lonnie's parents got divorced when we were in grade school. Then when we were in junior high, June married Frank. That lasted about a year and a half. Then she got married to Don. That one only lasted a couple of years. After Lonnie died, she met someone else, and they moved to Oregon. I don't know what happened to her after that.»

«Do you think their divorce had something to do with Lonnie?»

«I know Lonnie hated his stepfather. He hated both his stepfathers, but that didn't matter to June. Come to think of it, Lonnie did act kind of strange during the weeks before he was taken out of school. Man, I haven't thought about any of this for years.»

«I told you,» said Valérie, smiling slyly.

«I didn't have a clue at the time, but now I'm starting to wonder…»

«Wonder what?»

«You know, why exactly Lonnie hated Frank so much.»

«What do you think?»

«I don't know, but I'm starting to connect it in my head to the night we met Antonio. It was at a house in Los Angeles. It was where Michael, the brother of Lonnie's girlfriend, lived. We stopped to spend the night before going to Mexico. There was a party that night. We didn't know Michael was gay. The poor guy's dead now. He made a move on Lonnie, and Lonnie totally freaked out. I mean, absolutely freaked out. Lonnie almost killed him. Lonnie always had a problem with gay people. Not that we knew any—or at least we didn't think we knew any—but just the idea of it would drive him crazy. I never thought much about why that was. After all, everybody we knew was the same. Still, Lonnie had more of a problem with it than a lot of guys.

«When we left Michael's, Antonio got in the car with us. He had been living at Michael's, and it dawned on Lonnie why Michael must have been letting him stay there. The idea freaked Lonnie out, especially the fact that Antonio was only fourteen. I was upset, but Lonnie's reaction was over-the-top. It never occurred to me to wonder why.»

«So, you think…»

«I don't know what to think. I knew Lonnie all his life. I thought I knew everything there was to know about him. He knew all my secrets, and I knew all his. At least I thought I did. Now I wonder if I knew him at all. I should have been there for him, but I didn't have a clue.»

«It is all in the past now.»

«Not for me. Not anymore. You have me wondering what exactly happened to Lonnie when he was fourteen, but there's no way to know. No way to find out. It's not as if I can ask him, and there's no one else to ask. I'll wonder about it the rest of my life. Did Frank do something to him? Is that why June threw him out? Am I imagining things? Connecting dots that aren't there? This is starting to drive me crazy.»

A few days later, I found Joe Andrade waiting for me. He caught me as I was headed toward the magazine office.

"They're sending you to Cádiz next week."

"Well, *bonjour* to you too, Joe. Cádiz? That's in Spain, isn't it?"

"Yeah. You'll be doing a tourist piece about the Costa de la Luz and the Costa del Sol. That means you'll be going to Marbella as well."

"Okay. Well, thanks for telling me."

"Wait a minute. I'm not finished. While you're in Cádiz, there's going to be an organized protest through the streets of a port town called Rota. We need you to wander around like some dumb American tourist and snap as many pictures as you can."

"What will they be protesting?"

"There's a major naval base at Rota. It's ostensibly a Spanish base, but it's completely funded by the U.S. and jointly used by both militaries. That's what they're protesting."

"Anything in particular I should be looking for?"

"No, just get as many photos of protesters as you can. Try not to be too obvious about it. Don't act too interested in any one person or group of persons."

"Sounds easy enough."

I asked Valérie to go with me. It had bothered me that we never had a honeymoon. She insisted she didn't want one. It would be a waste of money, she said, since I would be working and the magazine wouldn't pay for her plane ticket. Moreover, she didn't want to take time off from work. I went to Spain by myself.

I flew to Seville and rented a car to drive the seventy-five miles to Cádiz. Having a working knowledge of Spanish definitely made things easier. Still, I became aware of differences between Chilean Spanish and the way it was spoken in Andalusia. When dealing with the airport rental office, the agent repeated back to me what I had just said, but using different words. When I asked for an *auto,* the guy said *coche* back to me. It dawned on me that my *chileno* was different from the Spaniards' *castellano,* in the same way Brits had different words from Americans.

The dry, brown landscape reminded me of home. I could have been driving across the Mojave in California. An hour-and-a-half later, I reached the Atlantic coast.

Cádiz was a picturesque city on a narrow island connected by three bridges to the mainland. Its domed buildings and towers looked like my idea of *The Arabian Nights.* I shot all the tourist-style photos I needed in a single day, concentrating mainly on the Old Town and the waterfront.

On the second day, I drove thirty miles to Rota to shoot photos of the protest. The gathering was huge. The marchers filled the town, particularly clogging the narrow seafront street paralleling the naval base's fence. I saw people of all ages and from all walks of life, chanting and waving their homemade signs. My sense was that most of them were not locals but had come from all parts of Spain. More than a few were from other countries. I had no idea why this particular demonstration was important enough for me to come specially and photograph it.

I did my best to behave like a casual tourist, as I wandered about. As I walked, my mind went back to my conversation with Valérie about Lonnie. Over and over, I searched my memory of that time. I hoped something would trigger a long-forgotten recollection that would make sense of it. All I came up with was more questions.

The following morning, I checked out of my hotel and began the drive from Cádiz to Marbella. According to the map, the fastest route would have been the main highway through Alcornocales Natural Park, but instead I chose to take the coast highway to the Strait of Gibraltar and the Mediterranean. It would take only a half-hour longer, and I hoped for scenic sea views. To my disappointment, the ocean was not visible until nearly the southernmost point of the drive. As the road curved to the northeast, I thought how strange that Africa, specifically Morocco, lay only nine miles away across the water. The road was now a corridor between the Alcornocales and Estrecho natural parks.

A few miles later, the twisty road reached its highest point and a fabulous view. I pulled over at what was clearly a popular stop. A building with a red awning housed a café, bar, and store. The large sign above it proclaimed *El Mirador del Estrecho,* the Viewpoint of the Strait.

The weather was clear, and the African coast appeared amazingly close. To my left, across the large bay, I saw a strangely familiar sight. I had seen an image of the Rock of Gibraltar many times as a kid when Dad watched his Sunday news programs after church. A frequent sponsor had been Prudential Insurance, which used the rock as a logo. I eagerly snapped pictures, the same as the other tourists.

A few miles down the road I came to a town, which a sign informed me was Algeciras. I recognized the name, but with the distraction of driving an unfamiliar road, I did not recall immediately why I should know it. Driving through the town, I chose to turn onto a side street leading down to the sea. I parked the car and strolled down a narrow street, searching for a clear view across the water. As I crossed over to a wider street, I was nearly run down by a blue SEAT Panda speeding toward a hotel a couple of blocks farther away. It was going the same direction I was heading, and I searched my memory for some good swear words I had learned in Chile—just in case I spotted the car again.

When I reached the hotel, the SEAT was parked in front. Three men unloaded luggage from the trunk. They looked pretty tough, and I judged that swearing at them might not be the smartest idea. Not wanting to let them get away with their recklessness entirely, I thought it might unnerve them if I snapped a few photos of them. They might worry I would report them to the police. I stood calmly at a distance, as I clicked the shutter.

One looked over in my direction and scowled. I chuckled with satisfaction to think I had unsettled him. I zoomed in on his face and choked at what I saw in the viewfinder. My shutter finger froze. I lowered the camera and stared with my naked eye. There was no doubt who it was. From the look on his face, I knew he recognized me too. What were the odds I would again cross paths with Número Uno—especially so far from Argentina? It hit me at last why I had recognized the town's name.

He pointed me out to his companions. All three dropped the luggage and headed toward me. I turned and ran. I knew I probably couldn't outrun all of them, but I had no choice but to try. It was not far to the nearest cross street, and when I got to it, I turned. To my relief, luck was with me. I beheld the familiar sight of a green and white car with a red light on top. It was the Guardia Civil. I slowed to a walk, confident that my pursuers would do nothing to me in view of the cops. I looked back to see the trio come round the corner and stop short. Número Uno called out something to the others, and they disappeared in three directions.

I thought momentarily about attracting the Guardia Civil's attention and asking for help, but I wasn't sure that wouldn't put me in a worse situation. Once their car had passed by me, I broke into a sprint. I ran as fast as I could back to my car. Hands trembling, I flailed with the key for what seemed like forever, getting the door open. Once inside, I locked the doors and fumbled with getting the key into the ignition and starting the engine. I headed straight to the main highway and ran a stop sign, as I turned right. I drove out of Algeciras as fast as I could. During the entire drive to Marbella I watched the rearview mirror more than the road ahead. I was sure I would see the blue SEAT coming up behind me.

Once at my hotel, I locked, bolted, and chained my room's door and did not go out. For the first time in my life, I ordered a meal from room service, asking for a bottle of Rioja to go with it. I drank one glass after another, trying to calm down. I wished I had never come to Spain. I wished I was back in Paris. I wished I was with Valérie.

In the morning, my fear had largely dissipated. I figured if they hadn't found me by then, I was probably safe. I gathered the courage to leave the hotel and shoot the assigned photos of the city. Still, I constantly looked over my shoulder. I was never completely at ease until that evening when I had boarded the plane in Málaga.

Back in Paris late that night, I gave Valérie a hug that lasted a good five minutes. She knew something was wrong, but when I said I didn't want to talk about it, she didn't press it.

The next day, I went into the magazine office to use the darkroom. As I made prints of each negative, I separated them into three groups: one for the magazine, one for myself, and one for Joe.

Like clockwork, I found him hanging around, as I left the building. I handed him his envelope.

"How was your trip?" he asked.

"I got lots of shots of that protest you wanted."

"Good. We'll have a look at them."

He studied my face.

"Anything else?"

"There are some other photos as well. I shot them in Algeciras."

He raised an eyebrow.

"Yeah?"

"Yeah. Did Marty happen to tell you about a meeting I was at in Buenos Aires last year?"

"He might have mentioned something about it."

"I ran into one of the guys from that meeting. An Argentine guy. He and two other guys looked like they were getting ready to check into a hotel. I shot a few photos of them—in case you're interested."

"You did?"

"Yeah. They weren't too happy about it either. I don't think they would have let me get away if some cops hadn't come along at just the right time."

"You sure they were Argentines?"

"Well, the guy I recognized definitely was. I don't know about the other two. The weird thing is that I remember that guy actually mentioning Algeciras."

"Really?"

"Really."

"And photos of them are in this envelope?"

"Yeah."

He shook his head in amazement.

"Marty was right about you."

"How do you mean?"

"He said you had a strange knack for being in the right place at the right time."

He pulled the photos from the envelope and glanced through them until he came across the ones I was talking about. He stared at them intently. His jaw tightened, and his face turned serious.

"Which one of them is the guy you know?" he asked, reviewing them a second time.

I took a quick look.

"Uh, none of them. I didn't get him. I had him in my viewfinder, but I was so surprised and scared that my finger froze."

"That's too bad."

"Shit. I blew it. Marty made me swear, if I ever got a chance to get his photo, I would. I never thought it would happen, so I put it out of my mind. Then, I actually got the chance, and I blew it."

"It's all right. You got the other guys. These are damn useful just as they are. Don't worry about it. Still, if you ever got another chance…"

"What's this about, Joe? Why would those Argentine guys be in Algeciras?"

"Is it that hard to figure out? Britain and Argentina are at war. The Brits have a naval dockyard at Gibraltar. The Royal Navy has warships there."

"Oh, right, the Falklands. Wait, so you think those guys were planning to…"

"Look, I shouldn't be discussing this with you. I have to go. I have to make a phone call right away. You've done something amazing here, but your part is done. Your only job now is to go back to your life and forget all this."

"Okay, I guess. It's just that…"

"Just what?"

"I almost shit in my pants when I saw that guy, Joe. I've never been so scared in my life. I was sure I was a dead man."

"But you're not, are you? You're fine."

"Only because those cops came along. I almost got them to stop to tell them what was going on, to tell them how dangerous those guys were."

He turned deadly serious.

"Listen. You can't ever do that. You hear me? What you're doing for us is off the books. Understand? If any local police got involved, it would mean big trouble. This isn't a game. The repercussions would go all the way to the national level. Whatever happens, you have to be invisible, anonymous. Understand?"

"I thought I was just shooting photos. I didn't think it was going to be dangerous."

"It's not dangerous. At least it shouldn't be. That meeting you went to last year wasn't because of us. That was trouble you got yourself into."

"What if I run into that Argentine guy again? He definitely recognized me. Just like I recognized him. What if I run into him again?"

Joe smiled wide and laughed.

"That's a good one, Green. Think about it. You met him once by accident in Argentina. What were the odds you were going to run into him in Spain? I'll tell you. They were a million to one. It shouldn't have happened, but it did. Okay, so you beat the odds on that one, but you know what that makes the odds of you running into him again for a third time? I'll tell you. A billion to one. In other words, it's impossible."

"I hope you're right."

"Trust me," he said, "it can't happen."

# 30
# Bilbao

I DID MY BEST TO follow Joe's advice and forget about my scare in Spain. It took a while to stop looking over my shoulder. I couldn't shake the fear that Número Uno would find a way to track me down.

I had no intention of going back to Spain, but as things worked out, I went back only a couple of months later. My editor asked me to go to Bilbao for a few days. Spain was hosting the World Cup, and he wanted some human-interest shots of the people from all over Europe congregating for the matches. I hesitated, but common sense prevailed. Spain was a large country, and it did seem unlikely Número Uno and I would cross paths again.

The decisive factor was that my editor offered me a pair of tickets to the first-round England-France match. While not a huge soccer fan, I figured Valérie would be interested since her country's national team was playing. I was wrong.

«Have you ever seen me watch a football match,» she asked, «or even talk about football?»

«But France is playing.»

«And…?»

«I've got two tickets. They'd be worth a fortune to scalpers.»

«Don't you have any friends you can invite? Friends who actually care about football?»

«What about Thierry? Do you think he would be interested?»

«When is it?»

«The middle of June.»

«He and Agnès will be in New York in June.»

An inspiration struck me.

"I know someone who would kill for one of these tickets—if I can find him."

The next time I talked to Joe, I asked a favor.

"I need to get a hold of a friend of mine. Problem is, I haven't seen him or heard from him for a year."

"What am I, Green? Your personal secretary?"

"Come on, you owe me since you never found me any information about my friend Antonio. Donal's from Liverpool. I met him in South America. I'm guessing by now he's back in England."

"Okay, give me the full name and any other details you know. I'll see what I can find out."

Two days later, I sat in a booth at our local post office.

"Hullo?"

"Donal?"

"Yes?"

"How the hell are you? It's me, Dallas Green."

"You're joking. Where are you, Dallas? How did you get this telephone number?"

"I'm in Paris. Would you like to see England play France in the World Cup?"

"You're winding me up, right?"

"It's no joke. I swear. Can you get to Spain for the 16th of June?"

"Try and stop me, mate."

A couple of weeks later, the two of us found each other at the appointed meeting place in the crowded streets near San Mamés Stadium in Bilbao. We hugged like long-lost brothers. Donal was beside himself with excitement.

"I'm over the moon," he said. "I can't believe this is actually happening. Have you ever been to a European football match before?"

"European football? No. Well, I did see a college soccer match in Bordeaux once."

We caught up as quickly as we could. He told me about his job, which he hated, with an insurance company in Manchester. I told him about my magazine photographer job in Paris.

It was too noisy for an in-depth conversation. The city buzzed with activity. The crowds pulsed with unbridled enthusiasm. Bars and restaurants were jammed to capacity with fans. Most were from England and France, but plenty of Spaniards and other Europeans crammed into the mix as well. In addition to a range of British accents, the cacophony swelled with shouts in French, Spanish, Czech, and Arabic. Boisterous, drunken supporters competed to belt out the most deafening rendition of their team's chosen fight song. It was a suffocating carnival. From adolescents to the middle-aged, they writhed in the confined spaces like a nest of snakes, each dressed more flamboyantly than the next. Those who merely wore their national teams' jerseys appeared conventional next to the ones sporting elaborate hats, wigs, and masks. English teenagers and a few of their elders had faces covered entirely in white paint with one red horizontal streak running from ear to ear and another from their hair to their chin. This was in imitation of England's flag and its St. George's Cross. Similarly, French faces were slathered with vertical stripes of blue, white, and red in replication of their tricolor.

Inside the stadium we were part of a massive throng. No seat was empty in the whole place. After the national anthems were played and the match began, the roar was deafening. Donal was in his element. He thought he had died and gone to heaven. When the final whistle was blown on England's 3–1 victory, he was ebullient.

"I cannot get over that opening," he screamed in my ear over the crowd's noise. "Less than a minute into the match and Robson scores. Bloody fucking brilliant."

Exiting the stadium took forever. Back on the street, I took charge of finding a place for dinner.

"You have to trust me on this," I said. "I haven't had Basque food in ages, and I'm not going to miss the chance to have it here in the actual Basque Country."

"Where would you have Basque food other than in the Basque Country?"

"I grew up eating Basque food. Bakersfield has some great Basque restaurants. You haven't lived until you've eaten at Wool Growers or the Pyrenees."

"I thought it was Mexican food you fancied."

"Bakersfield has great Mexican restaurants too. It's just hard to find Basque food anywhere else."

We tried three different restaurants before one would take us, and then only after an hour's wait. We squeezed into the bar and ordered our first bottle of red.

It was ten o'clock before we were seated. The place was no quieter or less crowded because of the hour. The food was good, but it was not the Basque food I knew. Apparently, the food I loved in East Bakersfield—and the way it was served family-style with unlimited bottles of red wine—was in its own unique category.

"Good choice on the restaurant," said Donal. "I must say, the food's quite tasty, and the wine's very good."

"It's made me homesick. I had my hopes up it would be the same as the food I knew in California."

Donal was more interested in reliving the game.

"What an experience," he enthused, "to watch the match from the stands instead of on telly at my local. I never dreamed I'd be here. Only a couple of weeks ago, I was worrying England wouldn't be in the tournament at all."

"They barely qualified, huh?"

"No, that wasn't the problem. Certain countries were trying to exclude us because of the Falklands War."

"Speaking of Argentina," I said, pouring more Tempranillo, "whatever happened with you and Mónica?"

"We got on quite well, I have to say. In the end, though, it was time to go home, and that was that. I sometimes wonder if I should have found a pretext to stay."

"It might have gotten awkward. I mean, with your two countries at war now."

"That wouldn't have mattered to me. Personally, I think Thatcher's mad as a hatter. Fighting a war in the South Atlantic is daft. What about you? Did you truly find your French lady love?"

"I sure did. We're married."

"Congratulations, but my invitation must have gotten lost in the post."

"Don't feel bad. Nobody was invited. It was just a basic civil ceremony with us and a couple of witnesses."

"Well, I claim the credit for things working out. Obviously, my French lessons made all the difference. Do you ever hear from your friend in Santiago?"

"Ángel? He's not the best one for writing. Come to think of it, neither am I. Last I heard he had followed Janet back to Virginia."

"She definitely only had eyes for him all right," mused Donal wistfully over another sip. "Did you ever find your other friend. The one we went looking for in Mendoza and Buenos Aires?"

"No. He disappeared off the face of the earth. I just don't have enough information to go on. I don't even know what name he goes under. I wonder sometimes, if he and I met on the street, would we recognize each other."

As Donal told me more than twice, the day of our reunion in Bilbao was the best of his entire life. It was good to relive our memorable journey from Santiago to Buenos Aires. We said our goodbyes the next morning at the airport and promised to keep in touch. We swore we would not wait so long to get together again.

"You'd like Manchester," he said. "It's got quite the interesting music scene."

"Is it mainly punk? I've never been able to get into punk."

"You should at least give the Smiths a try. What do you listen to in France? Are the frogs all still mad over Johnny Hallyday?"

"I'll admit, living there has broadened my musical taste some."

As much as I enjoyed the night in Bilbao, I was more than happy to be back in Paris. I loved my life there. I didn't want anything about it to change.

A few months later, Valérie's Green Card came through. Immediately, she made plans for going to California.

As we lay in bed on a lazy Sunday morning, I said, «What's the hurry in going to the U.S.? I like it here. I don't think I want to go back—at least not yet.»

«Then don't,» she said. «You should stay here.»

«You'd go to California without me? I'd miss you. Wouldn't you miss me? Don't you think you'd be lonely?»

«I will not be lonely. I will be with Logan. We will be working on our film. I shall have much to occupy me.»

«It wouldn't bother you that we would be apart?»

«No. Why?»

I stared into her eyes. I never tired of looking at them. I sometimes felt, if I could look deep enough, I would unlock her soul. By now I knew her well, but I never felt I understood her completely. I was never that good at understanding women, but the fact that she spoke and thought in a different language than mine made her more inscrutable. How had we managed to bridge such a gap? Or had we? Perhaps I needed to believe we had. The only thing I knew with complete certainty was that I did not want to be separated from her.

«Okay, I'll go back with you. I'll talk to my editor about getting out of my contract. Maybe it can be changed to base me in San Francisco.»

«That is not necessary. You must understand I will be extremely busy with the film project. You cannot expect me to have as much time for you as I do now.»

«It doesn't matter. The only reason I'm in Paris is because of you. If you're not here, there's no point in me being here. I'll talk to my editor tomorrow.»

On my way to the office the next morning, Joe was waiting for me. The timing was good. I could let him know about my plans.

"How are you, Green?"

"Fine. Look, I have something I need to tell you. I'm going back to the States."

"Oh?"

"Yeah, my wife wants to spend time with her father in California."

"Don't you have a contract with the magazine?"

"Yeah. I need to see about getting it changed—or just ending it."

He was not happy, but that was his problem, not mine.

"You've done a good job for us, Green. Amazingly good."

"Thanks."

"You've made a difference. It's not an exaggeration to say you've saved lives. You've done a service to your country and its allies."

"That's good to hear. Glad I could help."

"You know that business in Algeciras? You were instrumental in foiling a terrorist attack."

"All I did was take some photos. Lots of people can do that."

"There are some things coming up. Things I can't talk about, but you'd be helping your country a lot if you stuck around."

"I appreciate that, but I'm sure you have other people to help. Right now, the most important thing is my marriage. My wife's going to the States with or without me, and I'm going with her."

He hesitated a moment.

"Your wife just got a Green Card, didn't she?"

"Yeah, it came through the other day."

"You know, that visa could be revoked if it was determined it was based on a sham marriage."

I didn't like the tone of his voice.

"My marriage isn't a sham."

"How long have you been married now?"

"I think you already know."

"It hasn't been very long, has it? How soon after your marriage did she apply for her visa?"

"I think you know that too."

"When things happen that fast, it is often a sign of a marriage for the purpose of immigration fraud."

"Why are you saying that? You know that's not true."

"Do I? Look, I'll cut to the chase. If I have a little talk with people in Immigration, as far as they're concerned, your marriage is whatever I say it is."

"Are you threatening me?"

"Look, Green, I'm not a bad guy. I'm just encouraging you to do the right thing. Things are coming up where we could use the experience you've built up. Experience we've invested in. If you just agree to stick around to the end of your contract, I promise to find a way to make it worth your while."

"What I'm hearing is that, if I don't stay in Paris, my wife won't get to go to California."

"Hey, I haven't seen *my* wife in months. You get used to it. It's not the worst thing."

He smiled at me.

"Absence makes the heart grow fonder," he said with a wink, "if you know what I mean."

I stood there like a fool.

"Think about what I said, okay? That's all I ask. Everybody can win here."

I didn't move, while he walked away. I was so angry I thought I would explode.

The longer I stood there, the more I felt passers-by staring at me. I went for a walk. I followed the Seine up past the Île de la Cité and Notre Dame Cathedral, continuing to the Parc de Bercy. I crossed the river and headed back the other way past the Jardin des Plantes. I walked four miles to the Champ de Mars where the Eiffel Tower was.

How had I gotten into this situation? I wanted to talk to Valérie, but I didn't know what I would say. I had never told her about my freelance work for Joe. That had to remain my secret. She had been ecstatic to get her Green Card. Losing it would be a crushing disappointment. Yes, she could still go to California on a tourist visa, but her heart was set on going with the right to become a U.S. resident. Even if I convinced her to go as a tourist, could I be sure Joe wouldn't have a way to muck that up as well?

As much as I hated it, I saw no way out except to do what Joe had asked. I would have to stay in Paris and let Valérie go to America without me. The thought of it sickened me. I would have to be patient until the end of my contract. That was more than a year away. Given how I felt, though, it might as well have been an eternity.

In the evening, I went home and talked to Valérie.

«Look,» I said, «it turns out my contract is harder to get out of than I thought. I guess you'll be going to California by yourself after all.»

I saw a trace of surprise in her face but no obvious sign of disappointment.

«It is for the best,» she said, kissing me. «I love you very much, but you are a distraction. I will accomplish more without you. After the film is finished, we will be together again.»

It crushed me to see her so nonchalant about the separation, while the mere thought of it was breaking my heart.

«I can't go back to writing letters,» I said. «I'll phone you every night.»

«That will be expensive.»

«I might be able to get someone to pay for it. I think it's owed to me.»

«This will be good,» she smiled. «You will see.»

«Nothing will ever be good again until we're together.»

*"Mon cher,"* she laughed, «*tu es toujours si romanesque.* You know who you are? You are Candide.»

«I never read *Candide.*»

«You must read it. You are like the hero of Voltaire's book. He thinks he is in love with a girl he knew when he was young, and he spends most of his life wandering the world searching for his Cunégonde.»

"Coony Gond?"

«You need to work on your vowels. Cue Nay Goand.»

«Did he ever find her?»

«Yes, but many years later. By then, she was old and ugly. He was disgusted, but he married her anyway.»

«You will never be old or ugly.»

«You are as naïve as Candide.»

The time passed all too quickly. Before I knew it, I saw her off at Charles de Gaulle Airport. At the terminal gate, I stared out the window until the plane disappeared into the clouds.

I took the train and the Metro back to Vaugirard, just as I had the day I had come looking for her. Feeling hopelessly lonely, I climbed the stairs to the apartment. I sat and spent a full hour staring at the four walls.

# 31
# Petra

OUTSIDE, THE ATMOSPHERE was electric. It felt as though anything could happen. Nothing was beyond the realm of possibility. The pervasive mood was that the world was about to change forever.

We were desperate to go outside, to shoot photographs. We wanted to capture as much of it as we could. First, we needed to understand exactly what was happening. We stayed in the room a few minutes longer, our eyes glued to the television.

We watched a blonde woman and three men in gray suits, all grim-faced and sitting behind a wide desk. One of the men—the determined, stocky one with neatly trimmed, brown hair—spoke in German.

"Who's he? What's he saying?"

"Shhh…"

As he droned on, I held my tongue impatiently until Petra could give me an answer.

"He's Günter Schabowski, the Communist Party leader in East Berlin."

After speaking, he took questions from reporters. He was uneasy, nervously referring to a paper in his hand. An increasingly excited murmur could be heard from unseen journalists. After he finished his statement, I was struck by the shell-shocked look on his face as he recited an endless response to someone's question. He and the others stood to leave. You could hear reporters falling over each other in their rush out of the room to file their reports.

"What happened? What did he say?"

"A law has been drafted. It allows any East German to emigrate permanently. They only have to appear at any border crossing."

"You're kidding. When does that take effect?"

"Now. He said it takes effect immediately."

"Are you sure?"

She nodded, looking as stunned as I felt.

"Jesus," I said, grabbing my camera. "We've got to get out there."

Petra was ahead of me. I followed her down the stairs and onto the street. I knew where I wanted to go.

"Where are you headed?" she asked.

"Checkpoint Charlie. It's not too far away. I actually crossed there nine years ago. Man, that sure seems like a long time ago now."

Briefly, I wondered if Paulina Muñoz Rojas still lived in the same flat a few blocks on the other side of the wall. I did not have time to think of her again. A massive crowd had formed around the checkpoint. Young men climbed the wire fence, trying to get a look over the top, to see the other side of the wall. I called out to one of them, a spidery guy with flowing, blond hair.

"Can you see anything?"

"There is a massive crowd over there," he called back in heavily accented English. "It is fantastic!"

We heard a huge cheer from the other side. The throng on our side responded in kind.

"*Die Mauer ist gefallt!*" the crowd chanted over and over. "*Die Mauer ist gefallt!*"

As the numbers grew, the atmosphere became festive with the smell of beer and marijuana permeating the air. People now climbed on the wall itself.

"I'm going up there," said Petra.

"If you go, I'll have to go too."

"Stay here. It's safer," she teased. "I promise to give you some of my reject photos."

"Like hell!"

She scrambled up the wall in no time. Petra knew no fear. Being more cautious, I took longer. When I got to the top, it was worth it. The crowd beyond mirrored the one behind me. At intervals stood the *Volkspolizei.* I recalled how frightened I had been of them during my 1980 crossing. Now, they stood comfortably, chatting with any citizens who wandered up to them.

In no time we had used up the film in our cameras. We wanted to keep watching the amazing scene before us, but without being able to shoot photos, there was no point. We climbed back down to the ground. People now flowed through the checkpoint unimpeded. Many were met by children, handing them flowers. To my surprise, some grownups handed them bottles of champagne.

A sudden, loud noise made the ground tremble. It had all been too easy, I thought. This must be the inevitable government reaction. My instinct was to run from the noise, but Petra's was to run toward it. As was often the case, I had no choice but to follow. The clamor had come from construction workers, using their equipment to batter the wall.

We wandered back toward the checkpoint. An elderly woman stood in the middle of the street weeping. Petra spoke to her in German for several minutes. They both had tears in their eyes.

"What was her story?" I asked, as we resumed our walk.

"She said her son was killed years ago, trying to cross to the West. I told her about escaping with my parents from Hungary in 1956, and how much I wished they were alive to see what is happening. To see the fall of the Iron Curtain."

The night went on, from one amazing scene to another. We reloaded our cameras and continued shooting until we ran out of film altogether. There was no longer any point in us being there, but we continued wandering. We could not get enough of the historic moment. We were high on the collective emotions sweeping over the city.

On the verge of exhaustion, we made our way back to the hotel and climbed the stairs to our room. It had seemingly been the last room available in West Berlin. When the desk clerk had advised us it had but one bed, we had exchanged only the briefest of glances before staking our claim. Now the two of us stood staring at the solitary bed.

"I can sleep on the floor," I said.

"I don't mind sharing a bed," she said. "Do you?"

"I guess not. I just thought you might not be comfortable with it."

"Are you as jazzed as I am?"

"God, yes. What a night. I've never experienced anything like that in my life. I doubt I ever will again. I can't stop thinking about it. I can't stop reliving it. I'm exhausted, yet I don't think I'll be able to sleep."

"I know I won't, despite being on the point of collapse."

I had known Petra Mészáros about four years. By the time my contract was up at the magazine in Paris, I had gotten a job offer from one of the international wire services. Though I suspected Joe Andrade may have had something to do with it, I knew I deserved it on my own merits. By that time, my published work had gotten a lot of recognition. As much as my heart was in California, the offer had been impossible to turn down—not just because of the obscene amount of money involved but also because of the professional challenge. I took a great amount of satisfaction in no longer being a glorified tourism photographer. I was now a bona fide news photojournalist. I had joined an elite group. I was frequently on the ground when worldwide news was made. It was heady stuff.

Petra was my main competitor. Based in London, she was a few years older than me and had a lot more experience. Solidly built, she was a force of nature with short-cropped, brown hair and the longest eyelashes I'd ever seen. When a rush assignment came in, she was invariably on the scene ahead of me. It didn't matter whether it was a scheduled event like the signing of the Single European Act in Luxembourg or an unforeseen disaster like the Pan Am bombing over Scotland. She was always in the key position first and inevitably got the best shot.

It was a point of pride for me to try surpassing her, to get the sensational photo she missed. Our rivalry was never anything but friendly, and over time we became pals. We both knew there was no harm in a certain amount of cooperation if it worked in both our favors.

We sat on the bed, and I calculated how much space our two bodies would require.

"Are you sure you want to share the bed? It's not very big."

"What are you afraid of?"

"I'm afraid you'll roll over and accidentally push me out onto the floor."

"You wouldn't have to worry if you weren't such a lightweight."

She rested her hand on my leg. She had not done that before. I gave her a look, and she looked back.

"Usually," she said, "when it gets to this point and nothing has happened, I get one of two stories. Since I'm fairly certain you're not gay, then it must be the one about the old war wound."

"You know I'm married."

"Do I? Do you?"

"This isn't a good idea."

"Tell me. How long has it been since you last saw your wife?"

I did some quick math and nearly choked on my answer.

"A little more than three years."

"Are you actually certain you're still married?"

"It's not like that. This job keeps me in Europe, and she's busy in California. It was her dream to know her father in America and work on a movie with him. It took them several years, but they did it. Then it turned out to be a trilogy. He's getting old, and he can't work as fast. It's just temporary. She and I will be living together again once everything works out."

"How many years since she went to the States?"

"Seven."

"I trust you've heard of the seven-year itch."

"Very funny."

"Look, Green, surely you know I fancy you. Hell, if I'm being honest, I've wanted to shag you since I first laid eyes on you."

"I don't know why."

"Because you say hopelessly clueless things like that. You're rather sweet in your own naïve kind of way. I'm afraid that's my weakness in a bloke."

My heart had not recovered from the excitement of the night. Now it pounded all the harder from the thrill of an incredibly flattering proposition. Hadn't I already shared so much with her in the past few hours? It had been an experience of literally historic significance. After that, it felt almost wrong to hold anything back. I put my hand on her leg and took a breath.

"Look, Petra, I think too much of you not to be completely honest. If we do this, it's only fair you know I will be pretending the whole time that you are my wife."

"Absolutely not a problem, Green," she replied. "When we do this, I shall be pretending the entire time that you are Rob Lowe."

"The Brat Pack guy? Really?"

"If you don't judge me, I shan't judge you."

Hesitantly, I drew close to her and kissed her on the mouth. My expectations of embarrassed fumbling and guilty probing were instantly forgotten. It was as though I had opened a boa constrictor's cage. Within moments, our clothes were strewn on the floor, and she had managed to press every part of her body against mine. From habit, I tried to roll so that I would be on top, but she had other ideas. I accepted my place underneath and found I was quite happy there.

Her body was nothing like Valérie's. While my wife's skin was soft and white, Petra's body was muscular and every centimeter of it was tanned. In some ways, it was more like a wrestling match than lovemaking. Her strength—just for an instant—reminded me of Justin on our disastrous boys' night. Why had his raw power over me caused terror and resistance, while the force of Petra's body on me now ignited flames of blazing excitement? As she bounced up and down, I was more than happy for her to take the lead—as she always did. I shut my eyes and tried to pretend she was Valérie, but there was no point. This was something completely different. Petra had more than enough energy for the two of us—so much so I nearly felt like a bystander. As exhilarating as the thrill was, I feared I might be superfluous—until it really mattered. When we reached the final, manic frenzy, I knew why I was there. Happily, months of having lived like a monk finally paid off in my climactic contribution. Her scream testified to the vital necessity of my participation. Or was I the one who had screamed?

Her shoulders glistened. Her eyes looked at me as if she were seeing me for the first time. Her smile was one of delighted surprise.

"How old are you again?" she panted.

"Uh, thirty-six," I gasped.

"Are you certain? I mean, I always thought you looked young, but it was positively like having a teenage boy. Rather too quick for my liking. You owe me another go. You owe me another few go's."

"That wasn't as easy for me as it probably looked."

She gave me a few minutes to rest, and then she was off again. I did my best not to disappoint, but I was soon flagging. I clung to my mental image of Valérie. In my twisted state of mind, that was the only way not to be sabotaged by adulterous guilt. The challenge was that no two people could be more unlike than Petra and Valérie. The only way I could make the illusion work was to fantasize that Petra was me and that I was Valérie. Strangely, that got me through the second round. By the end of the third round, I was absolutely hallucinating in an unhinged fashion. By the final climax, I had become Rob Lowe.

She got a fright when I began struggling for breath.

"Are you all right, pet?"

I strained to get the words out.

"Yes, but I'm done for the night. Strange things are happening in my head. I think it's lack of oxygen."

I must have blacked out. The next thing I knew, it was morning, and Petra was getting dressed. The full significance of what we had done hit me at once. Everything had changed. As she put on her shoes, she glanced over and saw I was awake.

"If you ever tell *anyone* about my Rob Lowe fetish," she growled, "you're a dead man, Green."

I searched for words.

"So what is this, Petra? I mean, is this going to be... a relationship?"

She rolled her eyes.

"Don't make this more complicated than it needs to be. Look, we've been good friends for a while. Now we're better friends. That's it really. Isn't it? We don't need to go on about it. I don't want you to leave your wife if that's what you're worried about. I've had relationships. I tried marriage once. It didn't suit."

"Thanks for last night. It made a memorable day even more memorable."

Her patience was at an end.

"Go write a bloody poem if you need to. I really don't need to hear it. Let's get out there and see where this political situation is going."

After picking up more film, we went back to the wall. It was no less amazing than it had been the night before. It continued to be like a huge festival. Crowds had gathered all along the wall, chipping away at it with whatever tools they had—hammers, monkey wrenches, screwdrivers. Some had sledgehammers. A cheer would go up when someone managed to break loose a particularly large chunk.

At midday, we headed to the bureau to use the darkroom. We hated to miss any of the activity, but there was no point shooting photos if they did not get developed and seen. Our chemical trays were side-by-side. We pinned the wet prints on the long string suspended above us and commented on each other's work as the images slowly materialized.

After lunch, we went back to gather up the dried prints. She watched with interest as I segregated my photos in separate envelopes.

"Why do you do that?"

"Do what?"

"Separate your photos like that. It's almost as though you were working for two different employers—with two different agendas."

"I just have my own way of organizing things. That's all."

"It's a funny way of organizing."

Later, as we walked the dark streets back to the hotel, she broke a long silence.

"Are you a spy?"

"What?"

"Are you?"

I tried to laugh naturally, but it must have sounded nervous.

"Why would you ask that?"

"It's certain photos you choose to shoot and how you keep those ones separate. It's the way sometimes, when we're on assignment, you disappear mysteriously for hours at a time. I don't know. It's just a feeling I get. It's as if you have two masters."

"That's crazy. And so what if I were a spy anyway?"

"Seriously? You know as well as I do there are governments that regard us as the enemy. They accuse us of having a political agenda. Scrupulous neutrality is our only defense against being banned or arrested. It just takes one of us to be unmasked as a plant to give them the pretext they need to restrict all of us."

"Look, I'm not saying you're right about me, but just because someone's a journalist, it doesn't mean they can't also do work for themselves and use it any way they want. After all, it's just information. Isn't that our job? To learn things, to document things, then share it? If it can be used against an authoritarian regime, isn't that a good thing?"

"You don't need to lecture me about authoritarian regimes," she said with a hard edge. "Nobody is more anti-communist than I. Don't forget where I was born and what my family went through to escape. When you become a journalist, you need to take a vow of impartiality and leave the political battles to others."

"Don't worry about it. Okay?"

"I guess you know what you're doing."

The words stung.

"Jesus, you sound just like my father. Yes, I know what I'm doing."

"I hope so. I've said my bit. It's your own affair."

I was afraid this would cause a rift between us. Though I'd never admit it to her, I needed and cherished Petra's respect. When we got back to the hotel room, my worries were assuaged somewhat by another night of, as Petra called it, shagging.

She never mentioned my second job again. From that point, I was more careful about how and when I separated my photos.

Her words had intensified the gnawing discomfort I had long had about the inherent conflict between my two jobs. I tried putting it out of my mind, as I always had. That worked for a while.

I tolerated the conflict of divided loyalties for four more years—right up until that night in Belfast when I finally told Joe Andrade that he could go fuck himself once and for all.

# 32
# Rabbit Hunting

I STRUGGLED TO light the cigarette.

"Here, let me do that for you," said Father McGinley.

He took the match before it burned my trembling fingers. After extinguishing the flame with a swift motion, he lit another match, then held it calmly to the tip of my cigarette.

"Is it my imagination or are you smoking more?"

I inhaled as much smoke as my lungs could hold and released it as slowly as possible. I looked around his office. Books and papers were stacked everywhere. How on earth could he find anything in the chaos?

"It relaxes me."

"You've not seemed relaxed since the funeral. Did your friend Séamus say something to upset you?"

"Nothing I didn't already know, Father. Let's just say, my chickens are coming home to roost."

"You must certainly be pleased to have solved Alex's diamond ring mystery. Doesn't that demonstrate things have a way of working themselves out—and in ways you might not expect?"

"Sometimes things turn out all too exactly the way you expect."

"Tell me, how long since you were in your own country?"

"About three years."

"Do you not miss it?"

"Not really. Just some of the people. One in particular. That's the funny thing. She wound up in my country, and I wound up in hers."

"You're a modern-day Laegaire."

"A what?"

"Laegaire He was the son of Crimthan Cass, an old king of Connacht. His story is told in a book by Lady Gregory."

"I'm not much for reading, Padre. Why don't you give me the abridged version?"

"Very well. One day, a golden-haired warrior named Fiachna walked out of a lake and asked Laegaire for help. You see, Fiachna was from the Otherworld, and his wife was a prisoner of Goll in Magh Mell, the Plain of the Two Mists. Without a thought, Laegaire took fifty men with him to join Fiachna in a bloody battle to get his wife back. They succeeded, but Laegaire and his men could not go home again because, if their feet so much as touched the ground, they'd turn to dust. They could only go back for a brief visit and only if they took care not to dismount from their horses. Laegaire's father didn't want his son to leave, so he tried everything to get him to stay. He promised him and his men land, silver, gold, horses, and wives if they would stay."

"I've had conversations like that with *my* father, but he was never that generous."

"In the end, Laegaire and his men lived out their days in Magh Mell. Laegaire married Fiachna's daughter Deorgreine. She was known far and wide as the Tear of the Sun. By all accounts, the prince was quite happy with his life there."

"That's quite a story, Padre. My problem is that I got trapped in the Otherworld, but my Tear of the Sun didn't want to stay with me. You know, the funny thing about living in a different country is that I don't feel at home anywhere anymore—not even in the place I came from."

"I know something about that myself, after my years in the missions. I'm sure all emigrants feel they're living in the Other…"

A phone rang. I had not realized there was a phone in his office. He had to shift several piles of paper to locate it.

"Hello? Yes? Who? Ah yes, of course I remember you. How are you keeping? Yes? As a matter of fact, he's here beside me. How's that for luck, says you. Yes, yes. I'll put him on to you straight away. Just a moment."

He passed me the phone.

"Dallas? Jayzus. Why are you still there? Catch yourself on, mate."

"Séamus? Where are you? Why are you calling the priest?"

"I wanted to find out if you'd gone. I was sure and certain you'd have done a runner. Listen, Dallas. You have to get out of that place. It's worse than I thought."

"Where are you calling from?"

"I'm having one last pint at Dublin Airport. They've been calling my flight for the past ten minutes. In a quarter-hour I'll be over the Irish Sea, and that's where you should be. I've been feeling bad about your situation. Maybe I feel partially responsible. I made some calls to people I think I can trust, and I heard nothing good. Your man, the Argentine, called in a favor from the local lads. A pair of them are on their way over to you now. Do you hear me? There's no time. You have to get the feck out of there. Now!"

"Is Número Uno coming?"

"Who? No, that fella's legged it out of the place. On his way back to Buenos Aires, he is. No, it's the local lads you need to worry about. Do you hear me? Get out of there."

"I don't know where I'd go. Frankly, I'm tired of worrying about it. I just want it to be over."

"I could drive you somewhere if you need me to," interjected the priest.

"No," I said emphatically. "I'm not letting anyone else get involved. Nobody else is getting hurt or killed because of me. Whatever happens, I'll deal with it on my own."

"Don't be daft," said Séamus. "It's no game."

"Let's go to the Garda station," said the priest. "The guards will protect you."

"Thanks, Father, but no. I told you. No police. I've burned all my bridges."

I heard beeping on the phone.

"Look," said Séamus, "I have no more coins, and I'm about to be cut off. Don't be stupid, Yank. I'm sorry. I'm sorry about everything. I never meant…"

The line went dead.

312

"Look, Father. I have to get back to Tig Bronagh. Lukas came back last night. I have to tell him and Alex they need to leave right away. I don't want them getting caught up in this."

"I'll come with you."

"No. Stay out of it. I'll deal with this in my own way."

He was doubtful.

"It sounds serious. I'm not certain I should stay out of it."

For the priest's sake, I did my best to downplay the danger.

"Look, I know Séamus well enough by now. He gets overexcited. Probably nothing is going to happen. It won't be that big a deal. He's just, you know, like people here say, he's just winding me up. Seriously. Don't give it another thought."

"I hope you're right. I'll say a few prayers, just to be safe."

"Sounds good, Father. In a couple of days, we can meet for a drink and have a laugh about it."

With a heavy heart, I hiked up to the cottage. I hated to see Alex and Lukas go, but there was no other way.

The night before, Alex and I had gone through the better part of a bottle of Jameson. He had poured his heart out to me.

"I don't think I will see Lukas again," he had said sadly. "He will travel the entire world with that woman. It doesn't matter to him this summer was our final time together."

I had nothing but sympathy for him.

"Look, I obviously don't know Lukas all that well, but I definitely know his type. If he's anything like his father, he'll do this to you over and over. He'll take off without a thought and leave you standing there, feeling like a fool. But you know what? Sooner or later, he'll come back. You know why? Because deep in his heart he knows who his best friend is. There's no substitute for the pal who knows you best, who has been with you the whole way. He's never going to forget you, even if he acts like he has."

"You give him too much credit."

"Trust me. You'll see. Anyway, it's just the way things go. Someday you're going to meet a woman…"

I paused. Alex had never actually spoken to me about his romantic life.

"Yes? I'm going to meet a woman?"

"Yeah, you're going to meet… somebody, and then everything will change. That's just the natural way of it. At some point, you meet that one person who makes all other people secondary. That doesn't mean you don't still love your other friends. You'll always have the bond. Always. Even if one of you is dead."

My pep talk depressed him. I needed to do better.

"But Lukas isn't there yet," I continued. "He's a long way from settling down. You two will have a lot of time together before that happens."

*Shut the hell up, Dallas,* I thought. *You sound like you're trying to be his father.*

The awkwardness was broken by a knock on the door. I nearly jumped out of my skin but did my best to appear calm as I opened it.

"I am back!" announced Lukas, giving me a hug.

"Perfect timing," I said. "We were just talking about you."

Alex did his best to look cross, but he grinned in spite of himself when he got his hug.

"What are you doing here, Lukas? I thought we were going to meet in Paris."

He shrugged.

"Annika was bossy. I was tired of doing everything her way. She was especially unpleasant to be around after the customs agents in Iceland took away her knife. I didn't know if you would be in Paris already. I took a chance on coming back here. I wanted to see my *Onkel* Dallas again—if only briefly. You know, we are way behind our schedule. It's mostly my fault, I know, but we should go to France soon."

"I have been having a great time here," said Alex with a smile. "I have a lot to tell you. My quest was a success thanks to *Tío* Dallas."

"'*Tío* Dallas' is it now? Are you stealing my uncle, Alejandro?"

It had been good to see their reunion, and the two of them had a great time, spending most of the night catching up with each other.

As I neared the cottage on my trek back from the priest's, I regretted the remaining time would have to be short. I found them already organizing their backpacks in preparation for their departure.

"Looks like you're about ready to go," I said. "When were you thinking of leaving?"

"Perhaps early in the morning?" said Lukas.

"Are you thumbing?"

"Yes," said Alex.

"Tell you what. If you can be ready in the next few minutes, we might walk down to the village. I bet I can convince Father McGinley to drive you out to the main road. You should easily get to Galway by tonight."

"Are you trying to get rid of us, *Onkel*?" smiled Lukas.

"Not at all. I'm just conscious of how much time has passed. Your summer will be gone."

As we walked to the village, Alex asked me quietly, "Does this have anything to do with what you and Séamus talked about at the funeral? Are you in trouble?"

"No," I lied. "It's nothing like that."

We said our goodbyes at the priest's house. I gave Lukas a Chilean-style *abrazo fuerte*. The older I got, the harder the partings got.

"Have a great time, Lukas. Look after Alex. You're lucky to have him. A friendship like yours is rare. Believe me, I know."

Alex squeezed me extra hard when the two of us hugged. I never ceased to be amazed at the warmth that emanated from him. I would miss him.

"I envy you and all the adventures that lie ahead. These are the best times of your lives. Make the most of them."

"Are you certain you will be all right?" asked Alex with concern.

"Yeah, yeah, sure. Like they say here, I'll be grand."

"I have something for you."

"Keep it, Alex. I don't need anything."

He grabbed my hand and pressed into it a string of prayer beads and a small cross with a lightly engraved likeness of Christ in His agony.

"My crucifix and rosary. I have carried them as long as I can remember. They are my parting gift. As I am no longer a Catholic, I do not need them now. Perhaps they will give you some protection."

I was moved, and words did not come readily.

"*Gracias,* Alex. I appreciate it, but tell me something."

"Yes?"

"If you're not a Catholic anymore, why do you think they'll protect me?"

He reflected a moment.

"That is the insidious thing about Catholicism. You never completely escape."

As they threw their backpacks into the Escort, Father McGinley asked, "Do you hunt, Dallas?"

"Not for years, Father."

"I called earlier to Eamon Geraghty. He's not been well, poor man. He was a great one for shooting hares, but I think that's all past him now. I asked him for the loan of his gun. I told you might have a hare problem up your way. He said you could keep it a while."

"Father, I don't think…"

"Just have it in the house. You never know."

"Well, okay, if it makes you happy. I haven't done any rabbit hunting since I was a kid. My friend Lonnie and I used to go out in the scrubland and shoot at jackrabbits."

"Good man. Now, I'll carry these two lads a ways down the road. It's not at all a bad evening for a drive. I might bring them as far as Maam Cross, you know, just for the spin."

"Thanks, Father. I appreciate it. I appreciate everything."

"I'll see you soon. Don't forget, you owe me a drink."

"Count on it, Padre."

Watching the car disappear, I was overcome with loneliness. I glanced at the rifle in my hand and shook my head. I released the

316

magazine and unloaded the rounds. They would be safer in my pocket. With my luck, I might trip walking up the hill and shoot myself.

I leaned the gun against a wall in a corner of the kitchen and left the rounds in the small room Bernie Conneely referred to as "the back kitchen." Then I went straight for the bottle Alex and I had started the previous night. I tuned the radio to *Raidió na Gaeltachta,* the Irish language station. In the evening, they played classical music. At that moment, it was Beethoven. The music's somber passion suited my frame of mind. I toasted Ludwig van with the first of several sips.

How odd it was now to be alone. I had spent months of isolation in that dwelling, but it only required a week or two of having company to make the return to solitude feel strange. I had become especially accustomed to Alex's presence. I chuckled at his bizarre and fanciful notion he might be Lonnie's reincarnation. I truly did wish Lonnie could communicate with me from beyond the grave.

I took the crucifix from my pocket and put the chain around my neck.

*I know it won't be any good against the Provos,* I laughed blackly, *but at least I'm prepared for vampires.*

I fingered the prayer beads.

*I'll have to get the padre to show me how to pray the Rosary. He'll love that.*

The bottle was soon dangerously low. Did Séamus have his facts right? Was there actually some sort of bounty on my head? Was this the day it would be collected? Was this my last night on earth?

*If it is, I should have splurged on a second bottle of whiskey—a more expensive one.*

My mind wandered back to a night thirteen years earlier. I had gone on a walk on the Golden Gate Bridge. Had I honestly considered throwing myself off? It hardly seemed possible. I hadn't been serious, had I? To think of all the experiences I would have missed. All the places I would have never seen. All the people I would have never known. Never marrying the woman I loved. What future experiences would I miss if my life ended this night?

With the final movement of the Eroica Symphony, a dramatic atmosphere filled the cottage. I had never bothered to turn on a light, so I now sat in half-darkness. I heard a noise outside. It sounded like a vehicle braking and displacing gravel. I turned off the radio. The rumble of an idling engine—a large one by the sound of it—grew louder, then stopped altogether. A vehicle door slammed.

*Is Father McGinley back from his drive? Did he come up to check on me despite my telling him to stay out of it?*

The priest had never attempted driving his car up the path to the cottage. No one had. It wasn't suitable for most cars. He and every other visitor had always come on foot. Of course, it wasn't the priest. That had not been the sound of a Ford Escort.

The whiskey and music had numbed my mind to the point I was barely aware of my chest's pounding. I was now an oddly passive participant in what might be the biggest crisis of my sorry life. Whatever was about to happen, I could do nothing about it— except wait and accept. Were forty years long enough for a life? It was a lot more than Lonnie got. Why did I deserve to have a longer life than him? After all the blunders I had made. After all the people I had let down. After the terrible mistake I made in Belfast.

*Fuck that! I want to live.*

I had to see Valérie again. I was still married to her. I would always be married to her. I wanted us to be together. I didn't want my marriage to be another in a long list of failures.

*I can't die. I still have to find Antonio.*

Whoever was pounding on the door clearly wanted to break it off the hinges.

I stumbled to my feet and all but fell over. Standing too quickly had made me dizzy. In the gloom, keeping my balance was difficult. I almost tripped over my clumsy feet getting to the rifle in the corner. I knocked two metal pots off the kitchen counter. Their clattering went on forever. Gun in hand, I staggered to the back kitchen. When I reached for the rounds, they rolled off the counter and onto the floor. Letting the rifle fall, I got down on my hands and knees. Too dark to see, I searched frantically with my hands until my fingers grasped one and then the other. With all the skill of a drunken blind man, I groped around until they finally slipped into the chamber.

I pulled myself up unsteadily and made my way to the door. Along the way, I knocked a lamp from a table. Tiny shards of glass from the shattered bulb slid across the tile floor.

The pounding had not ceased. How long would it take them to beat down the door?

I steadied the rifle in my hand and ensured my finger rested on the trigger. Would I ask them to identify themselves? No, my best hope lay in whatever element of surprise I could manage.

With my free hand, I fumbled with the door's lock for a good half-minute. So much for the element of surprise.

I yanked the door open and pointed the rifle at the lone figure before me. He was tall and wore an unusually heavy coat for the time of year. He eyed my weapon, calmly reached for the barrel, and pointed it away from his face.

"Careful, Green. You could hurt somebody with that."

I blinked over and over, trying to make out the face, but that was only for confirmation. The voice had already told me who he was.

"Joe? What the hell are you doing here?"

"Doing you the biggest favor anybody ever did for you in your entire miserable life. Are you going to invite me in?"

"Yeah, sure, I guess. Come in."

He sniffed, presumably at the smell of my breath.

"What are we drinking?"

"Jameson. There's not much left."

"That's all right. I won't be here long."

"Am I in some kind of trouble?"

He rolled his eyes and whistled quietly.

"Sit down, Green. I can pour my own drink."

I collapsed into my chair and fought the urge to be sick. He took a glass from the cupboard and poured the last of the Jameson into it.

"*Salud,*" he said, taking a sip.

He pulled over a chair for himself and faced me.

"After the way you talked to me in Belfast, I should have let you deal with your own mess. Of course, if I'd done that, you'd be dead now. I do have a conscience, Green, despite what you might think."

"I wondered if you got out in time, Joe. I figured you had, but you were in the same situation we were. The evacuation missed us. We didn't know about the bomb."

"Yeah, wasn't the best time and place to meet, as it turned out."

"Is my life in danger, Joe?"

"Not anymore, and you're welcome."

"What happened?"

"I did something I promised myself I'd never do. Something I'm not supposed to do. I called in a favor in a neutral country that had absolutely nothing to do with my country's national security."

"What's that mean?"

"Two thugs were on their way over here. They were going to bury you in a bog, but thanks to an 'anonymous' tip, they got picked up by the Garda Síochána. They'll do some prison time in the Republic."

"How? Why?"

"You don't need to worry about your Argentine friend either. What did you call him? Número Uno? He got picked up at Belfast City Airport by the Royal Ulster Constabulary. Another 'anonymous' tip. Turns out Spain had a warrant out for him ever since that business in Algeciras."

"I don't understand. How did you know? How did this happen?"

"How do you think? I was there, remember? The night you told me... what were your exact words? Oh yeah, to go fuck myself. The night they obliterated the forensic lab. The Brits have intelligence sources in some of the republican groups. Eventually, word filtered to us that you were on a list. I was tempted to leave it alone, but like I say, I do have a conscience. Besides, you were a big help to us. I figured we owed you. There's something I don't understand though."

"What's that?"

"Why the hell did you come here? Why didn't you get the hell out of Ireland? Why didn't you go back to the States? Why did you just camp out here all this time like a sitting duck?"

"I freaked out. I couldn't deal with it. My friend died, and it was my fault. I couldn't live with myself."

"Oh yeah, I read about your friend in the report. Look, I'm sorry, but you shouldn't beat yourself up about it. It was just one of those things. She was in the wrong place at the wrong time."

I lost it.

"You didn't know her!" I shouted at him. "You don't know anything about her! Petra Mészáros was never in the wrong place! She never did anything at the wrong time! I didn't have a fraction of her talent, and I had none of her integrity. She wasn't just some bystander. She escaped from Communist Hungary when she was just six years old. She was a world-class journalist.

"I knew something was wrong when I ran and she didn't go flying past me. She always outran me. Always. I looked back and saw her lying there. They shot her, Joe. The bastards shot her. She didn't have anything to do with any of it. She was only there as a loyal friend. I was such a coward, I just kept running. I knew something bad was going to happen, and I left her there. Then the whole world exploded. I thought I was dead. I should have been dead. It should have been me instead of her."

I sobbed like a baby, and I didn't care he was seeing it. Joe sat silently and uncomfortably. He drained the rest of his whiskey in a single swallow and stood. He took an envelope from his coat pocket and handed it to me.

"Look, I know this doesn't make up for any of it, but consider this your retirement bonus."

I took the envelope and looked inside to see a wad of hundred-dollar bills. I wished I had the guts to throw it back in his face.

"I guess this is it, Green. Have a good life. Oh, there is one other thing."

"Yeah?"

"Do you have the photos from that night in Belfast? It's old news now, but there might be something useful in them."

Without a word, I stood and went to the bedroom. I took the roll of film from the drawer and brought it to him.

"You'll have to make your own prints. I never bothered developing it. Take it. Having it here was like a canker sore in my mouth."

I followed him out to his jeep. He started the engine and leaned out the window.

"What will you do now, Green?"

"I'm heading to California. I need to see my wife."

# 33
# Goodbye

EVERY TIME I went home, it felt increasingly like a foreign country. The readjustment always began with the walk from the plane into the terminal building. The American accents of people around me were simultaneously familiar and strange to my ears. From the immigration queue, I looked up at the large, framed photographic portraits of Bill Clinton and Al Gore. The previous time, it had been George Bush and Dan Quayle.

I collected my bags from the carousel and, after clearing customs, headed toward the exit. The usual crowd milled in the arrivals hall, eagerly scanning faces for the passengers they were meeting. A child's face lit up on spotting a grandparent. Husbands and wives smiled warmly at one another. Men in dark suits held signs displaying handwritten surnames. A sign in the back of the crowd caught my eye. It read *Monsieur Vert.* It blocked the face of the woman holding it. I pushed my way through the throng and took the sign from her.

"You came to the airport?" I said, giving her a hug.

She shrugged.

"I felt like a drive," she said, kissing my cheeks.

She looked completely different, but it was the change in her speech that mesmerized me. I could still hear the French accent, but she now spoke English with relaxed confidence. No longer did she search for words. I could almost believe she was American.

"You drove all the way from Kelseyville? That must be…"

"A hundred and thirty-seven miles. I kept track on the odometer."

Her hair had been chopped short and framed her face stylishly. Instead of her usual pullover sweater, she wore a buttoned blouse and blue jeans. Her skin was no longer soft and pale. She had been getting some sun.

"I only gave you my flight information so you'd know when to expect me. I didn't mean to put you to all this trouble."

"It's no trouble. Are you hungry?"

"No, I ate on the plane. Are you?"

"Nope. Let's go home."

"Thanks for picking me up. To be honest, I wasn't sure how I'd get up to Lake County. It only dawned on me the other day, my California driver's license expired ages ago."

"I renewed mine two months ago."

It was a long walk to the parking garage. She led me to a Chevrolet Caprice wood-paneled station wagon. Her confidence in negotiating her way out of the garage straight onto the 101 Freeway impressed me.

"What are you looking at?"

"You. It's great to see you. Also, I've never seen you drive before. So Logan lets you drive his car?"

"I'm on the insurance and everything. He doesn't drive much anymore. It's his eyes."

"That must be tough for a filmmaker."

"You don't know the half of it. How was your flight?"

"Long. I'm glad to be on the ground again. You know I never liked flying."

We headed north into the city where the freeway turned into Van Ness Avenue. She had mastered the exact speed for matching the rhythm of the green lights.

"Did you guys finish your movie?"

"Which one?"

"How many are there?"

"Still just three, but every time I try to move on to the next one, he wants to start re-cutting the previous one."

"Are you sure he wants to finish? Maybe he just likes being in post-production."

"My friends in Deauville will guarantee us a slot if we get at least one of them finished in time. I suppose it has to be the first one. They need to be seen in order. Wait until I tell you the big news. We've gotten an encouraging initial response from La Quinzaine des Réalisateurs in Cannes!"

It reassured me to hear her say the French words. To hear, even briefly, the Gallic speaking voice I had fallen in love with.

"That's amazing. Congratulations. Logan must be over the moon."

"He's not as excited about the festivals as I am. He only cares about the films being perfect. By the way, a woman has been calling on the telephone for you."

"Calling me? Where? At Logan's house?"

"Yes. Should I be jealous?"

"That doesn't make sense. Nobody I know would have his number—or have any reason to look for me there."

"She shrugged. She said her name was Amy."

"Amy? Really? Are you sure?"

"That's what she said."

"Did she say what it was about?"

"No, but she said it was important. So, is she one of your lovers or perhaps your love child?"

"Very funny. She's the wife of a friend of mine. Did she say anything else?"

"No. Only that you should call her as soon as possible. I told her that her timing was good because you don't live in this country anymore, but that you would be visiting soon."

We crossed the Golden Gate Bridge. By coincidence, we were only minutes from Amy and Justin's exit, but I didn't mention it to Valérie. My initial inclination was to ignore the message, as seeing old friends was not my highest priority. Still, I was curious.

"I'll give her a call tomorrow and see what's up."

It was more than two hours before we arrived at Logan's farmhouse. It had gotten only more ramshackle since my previous visit.

"You must be tired. Do you want to go to bed? Or would you like something to eat?"

"I think I'll just hit the hay. I should probably say hello to Logan, though."

"You can do that in the morning. He's asleep."

An awkward moment had arrived. On my previous visit, I had slept with her, but that had been three years earlier. I waited for her to indicate where I should go to sleep. For a moment, she appeared equally unsure, but then she broke into a smile.

"You haven't divorced me, have you?"

I held up my hand to display the ring. Her smile broadened, and she led me to her bedroom. When I removed my shirt, she put her hand on my chest and examined the crucifix.

"Did you finally convert?"

"No, but I do feel strangely safer wearing it. It got me through a tough jam. Maybe it will get me through this."

"This?"

"Yeah, this."

She removed the chain and cross and laid them on the night table.

"I did not let you into this room to feel safe."

Each of our mouths found the other's. It was as if no time had passed. Our bodies felt different. I wasn't sure if it was because we were older or if we just weren't as used to each other anymore. I missed the perfume she used to wear, but only for a moment. Now it was her skin I was smelling, and that was more of a turn-on. Her touch and her natural fragrance vaporized my jetlag. The old feeling of being exactly where I belonged had not changed. To my relief, the same seemed true for her as well—for a moment.

My mouth was ready to devour all of her, but she stopped me short. Her mood turned uncharacteristically solemn. The sudden change took me aback.

"You bastard," she said measuredly. "You scared me to death. For months I could not get through to you. You never returned my messages. I was convinced you were dead."

"I'm sorry. I was going through some stuff. To be honest, I thought I *was* dead—or at least near enough."

"Are you going to tell me about it?"

"Yes, but not tonight. Talking about it will mean reliving it, and I'd like a little more time before doing that. The only thing you need to know right now is that I have come back to you."

"Okay, tell me when you are ready."

The mischievous smile returned. She picked up the crucifix from the table and played with the chain.

"So who is she?"

"Who's who?"

"Something is different. I think you were with a different woman. Was this hers?"

"No, that was given to me by an eighteen-year-old Argentine guy. Stop smirking."

"But there was someone, wasn't there?"

"There's never been anyone but you."

"Bullshit."

"Wow, you really have become American, haven't you? And what about you? Was there anyone else during all that time?"

The red in her cheeks was unmissable. She was not prone to blushing.

"We're talking about you. Was she nice?"

"I wasn't in love with her, but we were good friends. It doesn't matter. She's dead."

She studied me to see if it was a joke. She turned serious again.

"I'm sorry. You always said your work was not dangerous, but I always thought it could be. That is why I was terrified when you disappeared off the face of the earth. If anything happened to you, I couldn't bear it."

"Most of the time it didn't feel dangerous at all, but it sure could be exciting. Remember the last time I was here and I told you about being in Berlin when the wall fell? It was amazing. I wish you had been there with me instead of…"

She ran her fingers through my hair. How much I had missed that.

"I've been trying to figure out what I want to do now. It's like I'm eighteen again—or twenty-eight again. No matter how old I get, I never seem to have my life together. I don't know if I can go back to photojournalism."

"I think you would miss it. Whatever happened, don't let it change who you are. You know that, wherever you go and whatever you do, you can always come back to me. We always manage to find each other again—in spite of everything. I still think we will grow old together. We're just not old yet."

I kissed her again. The warmth and feel of her was the most comfort I had had in ages.

"Don't forget to call that woman," she said. "She did sound as though it was urgent."

The next morning I called Amy and Justin's number. After several rings, she picked up.

"Hello?"

"Amy?"

"D? Is that you?"

"Yeah. What's up?"

"D, Justin wants to see you."

"Sure, Amy. I only got in last night, but maybe we can set up a time for next week."

"You need to come right away."

"Why? What's the hurry?"

She hesitated.

"He's dying, D."

"What? No, that can't be right. Are you sure?"

As soon as I asked it, I knew it was a dumb question. How could she not be sure about a thing like that? It was my stupid mind that couldn't get around it.

"Sure, Amy. Of course, I'll come. Where is he?"

"Here at home. Come as soon as you can."

I explained the situation to Valérie and Logan. He offered to lend me his car, and I thought about taking a chance and driving down to Marin myself. With my luck, though, I figured I would get caught by the CHP, so I had to accept Valérie's offer to drive me.

As we backtracked the route we had driven the night before, she asked, "Is your friend old?"

"No, he's six years younger than I am."

"Has he been sick?"

"I don't know. We haven't been in touch for, let's see, eleven years now."

"Really? But you must have been very close if he wants to see you on his deathbed."

Valérie dropped me off at the house. I couldn't convince her to go in with me. She said she'd come back in an hour.

Knocking on the door, I flashed back to being in the same spot and doing the same thing on the day of Keith's funeral. Justin had opened the door that day. Now it was Amy. She looked as if she had not slept in a week. She threw her arms around me and sobbed quietly.

"I'm glad you're here, D."

"What's happened, Amy? What's going on?"

"It's cancer. He's been fighting it for about a year."

"But he's only thirty-four."

Quietly, I asked the question I could not get out of my mind since talking to her on the phone.

"It's not AIDS, is it?"

"No, it's a rare cancer. He didn't think it was anything serious and didn't do anything about it. Only after it wouldn't go away did he finally get it checked out. One chance in a million, the doctor said. He made it sound like we'd won the lottery or something. It's been really hard, D."

She closed her eyes, and I put my arm around her.

"He was in the hospital for weeks, but now they've sent him home. A hospice nurse comes in most days for an hour or two, you know, to check his pain meds and see how he's doing. She's been great."

She pointed toward the extra bedroom which, for a while, had been mine.

"He's in there. I'm going to let you go in by yourself if you don't mind. He's probably still asleep. He sleeps most of the time. I need to run a few quick errands. I'll be back in a half-hour or so."

My feet did not move. I could not bear the thought of going into that room.

"He might wake up for you. I should warn you, he doesn't always make a lot of sense. He's on a lot of medication. The past few days, he hasn't talked at all. Thanks for coming, D. It means a lot."

"Please don't thank me, Amy. I feel pretty useless right about now."

"Funny how things work out, huh?"

I knew what she had to be thinking. She was not even forty years old. She had two children, and she was about to become a widow for the second time. Life wasn't fair.

As I heard her car drive away, I continued standing like a statue. I wished something would happen to take me out of the situation. I went into the bedroom.

The bed I had used was gone. Instead, a hospital bed was surrounded by bags full of liquids hanging from poles. An oxygen tank with a facemask sat next to the bed. Bottles and tissue boxes covered a small table. The room smelled like a pharmacy.

Sunk deep into the bed was a creature I did not recognize. He was too small. He was bald and spindly. Every once in a while, the sound of labored breathing could be heard. I sat on the chair next to the bed. It scuffed the floor. The sound caused his eyes to open. Only then did I recognize him as Justin. His eyes were drooped, but the irises were the same deep blue.

He looked through me, as if his gaze focused on something farther away. His head did not move. He knitted his brow. His voice was raspy and weak.

"Dallas. You're here."

"Of course, I'm here."

I fought the nervous impulse to make a joke. I wanted so much to put the two of us at ease. I wanted to make the awful situation normal. I nearly asked how he was doing, but I bit my lip.

"Of course, I'm here."

He closed his eyes. For a moment, I thought he had gone back to sleep.

"If you're hungry, you can eat me."

"What?"

"I can be food for you if you need it."

"Justin, what are you…?"

"You can eat me. Like the soccer team."

He spoke so slowly and deliberately, it was painful to listen.

"It was a rugby team, and no one is going to eat you."

"You were wrong. You're the survivor."

I wanted so badly to tell him he would be okay, but it would have been stupid. We both knew he wouldn't.

"You said it was a competition," he gasped. "So you win. You're the survivor."

"Well, there's nothing wrong with your memory, but I'd like to forget that conversation."

A couple of minutes passed before he spoke again. He opened his eyes. He focused his eyes directly on me.

"You always look the same. You never change."

"Trust me, this body knows how many miles it has on it."

Another pause, and then, "I love you, Dallas."

I didn't know what to say.

"I mean it. I love you. I was never as close to you as I wanted. There wasn't a way."

I brushed my hand carefully over his skeletal arm. I was afraid even the lightest of touches might cause pain. Though my impulse was to turn away, I forced myself to study him. I forced myself to remember all the things about him—the hair, the striking good looks, the vitality, the charisma—that had always made me want to look at him, to be around him, and consequently, made me uneasy around him. All those things were gone. All that remained was him. Just him.

After a while, the words came. I don't know where they came from. In the world I came from, they were not words men said to other men. American English did not have a conveniently ambiguous verb the way Spanish had *querer.* Because of that, some words only got said when someone had one foot in the grave.

"I love you too, Justin. I always have, and I still do. Never more than in this moment."

I half-expected to see some sort of smile, some acknowledgement that he had heard me. He only closed his eyes again. A slight spasm seemed to go through his body, and he winced. The twitch was like some strange, faint echo of physical passion, reminding me of the French term for orgasm—*la petite mort*.

He did not open his eyes or speak again. I sat silently until I heard the front door.

"Thanks for sitting with him," she said. "I know it's not easy. He really wanted to talk to you. It's too bad it didn't work out."

"He did talk to me."

"He did? Well, that's good. I suppose he rambled. He hasn't done that for a while now. Of course, it's not like being able to have a conversation."

"I think we did have a conversation."

"You did? An actual, coherent conversation?"

"Yeah, about as coherent as we've ever had."

Her eyes moistened.

"I haven't had a conversation with him for about a week. It's been days since he even rambled."

She closed her eyes and took a breath.

"The hospice nurse said that sometimes they get one last moment of clarity—just before the end. I think that might have been it, D."

She looked suddenly frail. I stood and put my arms around her. Guilt overcame me to think I might have stolen precious last moments that should have been hers.

"I'm so sorry, Amy."

We watched him together for a while. Then we went to the living room.

"Valérie should be back for me any minute," I said. "I want her to meet you."

"Thanks so much, D. I know it wasn't easy."

"No, I want to thank you. I mean that. You don't know how much this has meant."

"Really?"

"Yeah. You know, I'm only forty years old, but I've already lost more friends than I care to count—some of them really close—but..."

"Yes?"

It had become painfully difficult to speak.

"This is the first time I actually got to say goodbye."

# 34
# Lawrence

"I'M SORRY ABOUT your friend."

"Thanks," I said.

"Are you certain you don't want to go to the funeral? Valérie would have no trouble driving you."

Logan sat in his threadbare armchair, studying me through his Coke-bottle glasses.

"I'd rather not. There'd be a lot of people, including someone I don't want to see again. It's okay. I explained to his wife, and she was fine about me not being there. She said I had been there when it actually mattered."

Logan had aged a lot in the years since I met him in Deauville. He had put on weight and had gone bald on top. To make up for it, he had let the lower portion of his hair grow all the longer.

"Why are you going back so soon? You've only just gotten here."

"I'm starting to feel like I'm hiding out here. Kind of like I was doing in the West of Ireland. The longer I'm here, the more it's obvious that I don't have a reason to be here—except to be with Valérie."

"That's not a bad reason."

"It's not enough. She has her life here. You and she have your work. I'm just a tourist."

"We don't mind having a tourist. You're part of the family. I've been wanting to put something to you for some time. If your photography is anything to go by, I think you could make a hell of a cinematographer. You could take some of the burden off me. Truth is, I'm getting kind of long in the tooth for dealing with some of this equipment."

"Thanks for the offer, but I need to get back to my own work. I need to find someone in Paris who'll take a chance on me after the way I bailed on my employer last year."

Valérie walked into the room.

"So you still insist on going? I was just getting used to you again."

"Yeah, and I want you to go with me."

She looked at Logan, then back at me.

"This is not a good time…"

"Not forever. Just for a while. I'm going to call in a favor."

"A favor?"

"Yeah. Eleven years ago I went through a huge amount of hassle and *paperasserie* so you could get a Green Card and eventually a U.S. passport. Now I want you to do the same for me."

"You want to become a French citizen?"

"Yeah. I'm tired of dealing with the carte de séjour. I want to be naturalized. I want a French passport. It would be a lot handier for getting in and out of places. In a couple of years the Schengen Agreement goes into effect, and a European passport would mean I could live and work almost everywhere on the continent."

"But you don't need me. You've lived in France long enough, you qualify for citizenship even without being married to a French citizen."

"Yeah, but you know how the bureaucrats can be. I want you to go to the interviews with me. To back me up, like I did for you."

She looked at Logan again. He smiled.

"Go," he said. "I'll be fine. Besides, he's got a point. You do owe him."

She put her hand on his shoulder.

"How will you remember to take all your pills without me? You're hopeless on your own."

"It'll be good for me. You've spoiled me so much, you've practically turned me into a child."

In the end, she spent three weeks with me in Paris. She fretted about Logan the entire time. A day could not go by without at least one phone call to him.

I found an apartment near Rue de l'Estrapade in the Fifth Arrondissement.

"It's so small," she said. "Why did you ever want to leave California? There you could have a house with a nice garden."

"I left California for you," I reminded her.

I put one of the keys in her hand.

"Here take this. This place is also your home."

"If leaving California was about me, then you can go back now."

"I like it here. Being a foreigner suits me. Dallas of the foreigners, someone called me. *Dallas na nGall. Dallas aux étrangers.*"

"If you like being a foreigner, why are you becoming French?"

"I'm not becoming French. I'll never be French—even if I wanted to. I'm just getting a French passport."

"Funny. I like America because anyone can be an American—even me. Will you go back to the same work you were doing before?"

"Yeah, I've found another outfit that's willing to take me on. Same job, just different people signing the paycheck."

"Will you be traveling all the time—like before?"

"Yeah. That's the whole point of the job."

"Where will you go first?"

I had avoided talking to her about this. Now, however, we were relaxing over dinner in a small, neighborhood restaurant with a nice bottle of Margaux, and the words started flowing.

"I've signed up to go to the Balkans. The last conversation I had with Petra was about the war there. That was her next assignment. She said it was the biggest story of the decade. The Bosnian capital has been under siege for more than a year, and there's no end in sight. That's where I'm going."

"Because she intended to go?"

"Because somebody needs to tell the story, and Petra isn't around to do it."

"I don't like it. Since Yugoslavia fell apart, the news from that region has been horrifying. I have already spent months thinking you were dead. I don't want to go through that again."

"You thought I was dead because I was hiding. I'm not going to hide anymore. I've had two painful reminders in the past year that none of us gets out alive. I can't stop living for fear of dying."

"You sound like a character in one of those American movies. You weren't so macho before. I liked you better before you became... world-weary."

"I can't get over how good your English is. I can only hope someday I will speak your language as good as you speak mine. Finish your coffee and let's go home. If you're calling me macho, then I think it's going to be a good night."

All too soon, the three weeks were over. I saw her off at the airport, and once again I was alone. I had a couple of weeks to kill, waiting for paperwork to be completed on my naturalization and my new employment. I filled the time as best I could, going on long walks, seeing some movies, and spending time on something I had not done a lot before—reading books.

One afternoon, I happened to be sitting in a café in the Latin Quarter, reading *Le Monde*. Nearby a man in a tweed coat sat, reading *The Guardian*. He wore glasses, and his gray beard and moustache were tightly trimmed. He took a cigarette from a pack, then fruitlessly searched his pocket for matches.

"*Pardon,*" he said to me, "*avez-vous du feu?*"

As it happened, I could give him a light. Since Valérie had gone, I had started smoking again. He offered me one of his Gitanes, and I took it. I then lit the two cigarettes.

"*Merci beaucoup.*"

He was obviously American, but he had taken me for French.

"Are you here on vacation?" I asked him.

My question in English with an American accent caught him off guard, but he quickly recovered.

"I'm here on sabbatical. I'm a guest lecturer at the Sorbonne. And you?" he asked.

"I live here."

"Where are you from?"

"California originally. And you?"

"The same. Los Angeles."

He extended his hand.

"I'm Lawrence."

"Dallas."

"Funny thing. I was trying to escape from California, to immerse myself in a different country, but I've been here long enough that it's actually good to meet a fellow countryman, a fellow Californian."

"Yeah, I know a bit about escaping myself, but this city has come to feel like home. As much as a home as I'm ever liable to have again."

"Yes, that's true, isn't it? Once you've spent much time living abroad, you're never truly at home anywhere, are you? Not in another country and not in your own country."

"Yeah, I think that's what I've been feeling. It's like that French drinking song I once learned, about a guy who gets married in another country. *Pour n'être plus qu'un étranger.* To never again be anything but a foreigner."

"Tell me, Dallas. I've had virtually no social life since I've been here. For personal reasons, I just haven't been up to it. I'm thinking now that I should start going out. Do you know the André Gide Bar in Le Marais? I've heard it's a good place."

Because of the years I lived in San Francisco, I knew what he was asking me, what he was trying to find out.

"No," I said. "I don't know it. I don't have any reason to go to Le Marais."

The look on his face told me the answer to his question had been received and understood—or had it? He followed with another question.

"Listen, I know we've only just met, but you're an interesting fellow, and I'm enjoying talking to you. I happen to have a rather pricy bottle of Armagnac sitting on a shelf back in my apartment, and I'd relish a pretext to open it. May I invite you?"

"I'm enjoying talking to you too, Lawrence, but I don't think going home with you would be a good idea."

"I know what you're thinking, but please believe me, this is not a proposition. It's a sincere invitation from one expat Californian to another."

I hesitated. Experience and common sense told me this could turn out badly. Something about him, though, assured me he had no ulterior motive.

"Sure, why not?" I said. "But just to be clear, I'm married."

"Lucky you," he laughed.

On the walk to his apartment, he said, "I would have liked to be married. I was with a man for many years. He died a few months ago. That's why I needed to get away, to have a sense of starting over."

"I'm sorry. I've recently lost two people who were important to me."

We climbed the stairs to his apartment. It was slightly larger than mine but by no means huge. He told me to take a seat and make myself at home. He put a Miles Davis LP on the turntable. True to his word, he produced an impressive bottle of Armagnac. Having retrieved a knife from a drawer to cut the seal, he opened the bottle and poured two small glasses.

"*À votre santé,*" he toasted.

"*On se peut tutoyer, n'est-ce pas?*" I said. "*À ta santé.*"

He drew my attention to his desk and the several photos in freestanding picture frames on top of it.

"This is John. This is my favorite of him. I took it myself. I'm quite proud of it. Do you do any photography yourself?"

"Sometimes."

"This, of course, is of the two of us. That was shortly before his diagnosis. We look so happy. Little did we know."

I glanced over the other photos. My eyes settled on one in particular, and in an instant the air pressure in the room seemed to drop. I gasped audibly, then spoke a single word.

"Antonio."

He turned and stared at me with a look of utter shock.

"How do you…?"

My eyes were locked on the photo. The black-haired youngster with the toothy grin looked about eleven or twelve, but he was definitely the same fourteen-year-old kid who had traveled the length of Mexico with Lonnie and me. There was no doubt. Now I tried to form my own question.

"Where did…?"

In slow motion, the pieces of the puzzle fell into place. Of all the strange coincidences that had occurred in my life, this had to be the oddest. On the night we had camped in a forest in Michoacán, Antonio had told me about Lawrence. A professor at UCLA, he had said. At first he was a client of Antonio's when he was living on the street. Then Lawrence took him in. He lived with Lawrence until there was talk about it at the university.

How unreal to find myself with the very same man, drinking brandy in his Paris apartment. A look of revelation came over his face.

"My God. You're *that* Dallas!"

"You know me?"

"Yes, yes. He's talked about you many times. The two fellows who drove him to central Mexico."

"Wait, you've spoken to him since then?"

"Yes, of course. I've been in touch with him for years."

He motioned toward another of the photos on his desk. In it Lawrence stood with a shorter, darker man. Sporting a neatly trimmed goatee, he was quite handsome. They both smiled broadly, the other man with a distinctively toothy grin.

"That's him?"

"Yes, yes. He lives here in Paris."

"But how did you… how did you find him?"

"He wrote to me. Many years ago at the university. We've corresponded ever since."

"He wrote you?"

"Yes."

"After what you did to him?"

His expression darkened.

"So he told you…"

"You exploited him. You took advantage of him. How could you do that to someone so young?"

Lawrence looked as though he was about to be sick.

"It was a difficult period in my life."

"And that makes child molestation okay?"

"No, no, of course not. I swear to you, that was the only time. I've never touched another child. There was something different about Antonio. It was as if he wasn't a child. He was extremely mature for his age. He had an old soul."

"That just sounds like justifying the unjustifiable to me."

"Yes, you're right, of course. Honestly, Antonio hasn't made it any easier for me."

"Why? What has he done?"

"When he got in touch with me, he punished me and shamed me in the worst way imaginable. He made my guilt more consuming than it had ever been before. He did the single thing that guaranteed my own private hell would become worse."

He paused for a moment, and then said quietly, "He forgave me."

"He forgave you?"

"Yes. For years I had managed to bury the memory. To convince myself it wasn't actually me, that I had somehow not been responsible. Then out of the blue, he wrote to say he forgave me, and the weight of all my guilt came crashing down on me. Only my relationship with John saved me. I was in therapy for years."

How could Antonio have forgiven him? I certainly couldn't, and I wasn't the victim. I hated him—partly out of repulsion and partly out of jealousy. Why had Antonio reached out and contacted him and not me? The question filled me with pain.

"I can give you his number if you like. I know he would love to see you. As I said, he talks about you affectionately."

I hated to be beholden to him for anything, but I let him write it down for me. I slipped the piece of note paper into my pocket.

"I'll be going now."

"You didn't finish your drink."

"I don't want it."

I walked down the street in a daze. I wasn't in the best frame of mind for making such an important phone call, but I had waited twenty-two years for this moment. I would not put it off even an hour longer. I found a telephone booth. A young, bearded guy loitered close by. He eyed me, as I took the phone card out of my wallet. I knew why he was there. He was a phone card collector. He saw that the photo on my card was nothing special, and he went back to puffing on his cigarette.

I inserted the card in the phone's slot and removed the precious piece of paper from my pocket. I punched in the numbers. After several rings, I heard a voice.

"*Allo?*"

I choked. His name was surprisingly hard to say.

"Antonio?"

There was a pause and then, "*Qui est-ce?*"

I swallowed hard.

"Antonio, it's Dallas Green."

Another pause.

"Dallas? Is it really you?"

"Yes, Antonio. It's really me."

"Where are you?"

"I'm here. I'm in Paris. I've actually been living in Paris for most of the past eleven years. I'm in the Fifth Arrondissement."

"Really? You've been here all that time?"

"Yeah. Quite a coincidence, huh?"

"You have to come see me. I live in the *Septième Arrondissement.*"

"I'd like that. Hell, I'd love it. You know, I've been trying to find you for something like twenty years. Ever since the *golpe* in Chile, I was so worried about you. You can't believe how much I wanted to see you again."

I covered the receiver so he would not hear me sob.

"Yes, me too. I've thought about you often over the years. It's so good to hear from you. Please come at once. I'm at home. Come right now."

# 35
# Resurrection

"HOW COME YOU were able to write to Lawrence but not to me?"

I had intended to ask the question casually, as if it was a small matter of curiosity and not a big deal. Instead, my voice cracked, and my eyes threatened to well up. Suddenly, I was ten years old again.

Antonio had not noticed, as he surveyed his surprisingly well-stocked liquor cabinet. He turned his head and looked at me distractedly.

"It was easy to write to Lawrence. I knew he would still be at UCLA. He had tenure. I didn't have your address."

I was still not accustomed to the deepness of his voice. It had a rough richness, doubtlessly owed in large part to the brown cigarettes he seemed to smoke constantly. He spoke English like an American but with inflections of Spanish and French.

"Yes, you did. You sent me a postcard from Cerro Santa Lucía."

"I did? That's right. I remember, but then I lost your address. Things were crazy for quite a while. I didn't have much time for writing letters in those days. Later on, I did think about writing you, but as I said, I didn't have an address. I had no idea where you might be living."

It bothered me that he wasn't as upset as I was about the years with no communication. He showed me a fine-looking bottle of eighteen-year-old single-malt whiskey.

"Do you still like to drink scotch?"

"That's it? You couldn't think of a way to get in touch? After all, I came from a pretty small town. You could have written to just about any address there and it would have gotten to me."

He looked at me quizzically.

"I guess I didn't really worry about it."

"You didn't worry about it?"

"I knew we would see each other again."

"How? How could you know we would see each other again—especially if you weren't trying to find me?"

He shrugged.

"I just knew. And I was right, wasn't I? Here we are. I believe everything happens eventually if you have patience. That philosophy has certainly been borne out in my experience."

"So you were happy to just wait and let the universe decide if we would see each other again?"

He lifted his glass with a smile and waited for me to raise mine.

"*À nos retrouvailles,*" he said.

"*A nosotros,*" I said, "*por finalmente encontrarnos de nuevo.*"

He laughed. We sipped. I was relieved to have been able to put a sentence together in Spanish. Since living in France, my Spanish words kept wanting to come out as French ones.

"You know, you have the accent of a *chileno,*" he said.

"Say, this is good stuff. I suppose pisco was out of the question."

"You know pisco? It is difficult to get here, *huevón.* You know, Dallas, you've barely changed after all these years. I would have recognized you anywhere."

"I don't think I would have known you if I had met you on the street. You were so young when I knew you. I can't believe you're that same kid."

Antonio wasn't much taller than he was when he was fourteen, but his build was stockier. His face was rougher, although his eyes and the smile were the same. His clothes looked expensive. He smelled of cologne and cigarettes.

344

"So you're a photojournalist," he said. "I shouldn't be surprised. You definitely took to that camera you stole from Michael."

"Michael died, you know. About twelve years ago."

"Yes, I worried about him when I heard of so many people dying of AIDS. And Lonnie? What has become of him?"

"Dead too. About three years after you knew him. Antonio, can I ask you something?"

"Of course."

"This is going to be a pretty weird question and not an easy one to ask. It's just that, because of what you went through as a kid, did you get any kind of, I don't know, vibe off Lonnie?"

"I don't understand."

"It's just that a while back I remembered some things, and they make me wonder if something happened to Lonnie when we were fourteen. Something bad. It's a thought that's bothered me a lot, and I just thought because of your experience you might have had some sensitivity to it."

He shrugged.

"I didn't sense anything like that, but when you think about it, I didn't spend that much time with the two of you. To me you were just two guys who got to live in houses, who got to go to school, and who had a car to drive. Your lives were nothing like mine."

"Yeah, I see your point. Like I said, it's just something I haven't been able to get out of my head, but I need to accept I'm never going to get a definitive answer."

"Remember what I told you. The world has a way of making things happen if you can just be patient."

"All the patience in the world won't do any good if there isn't anybody left alive to answer the question. Somehow I don't think Lonnie is going to suddenly come back from the dead to be interviewed by me."

We sipped our scotch for a good minute or so before I broke the silence.

"Tell me about your life. What do you do?"

345

"I am quite busy these days. I work on the Palais du Cinéma project at the Palais de Tokyo. I have worked in cinemas for years—ever since getting a projectionist job in Buenos Aires."

"Believe it or not, I met your former boss. I was that close to catching up to you in B.A."

I admired the surroundings. The large room was richly decorated with floor-length curtains and art on the walls. It was the grandest home I had ever visited in Paris.

"Cinema work must pay pretty well," I said.

"Do you like my apartment?"

"Yeah. It's a heck of a lot nicer than where I live."

He winked conspiratorially.

"I don't pay the rent."

"You don't?"

He laughed.

"When you first met me, I was a kept boy. After all these years, I'm still a kept boy."

"What do you mean?"

"Let's just say I am very close to someone well-placed in the Mitterrand government. Actually, his previous government since he lost the Assemblée Nationale in the March elections, but so far I haven't been kicked out. Thank God for bureaucratic inefficiency."

"Wait, let me get this straight. You mean to tell me you get to live here because you are some minister's lover?"

"I didn't say minister, did I?"

"Man, I was so worried about you all those years, and here I find you living it up in the lap of luxury. You've always known how to land on your feet, amigo. So who is it? Is he anyone I've heard of?"

"He? Why do you assume it's a man? Wait, never mind. I know why. It's because of where I was when you first met me."

"It's just that most of the people high up in government seem to be men."

"Not entirely. You will recall there was a woman prime minister last year."

"Yeah, but she didn't last long. Wait, was it her? Is she the one?"

"No, definitely not her. There's no point in asking. Her name will never pass my lips. She's a married woman, and I am a discreet gentleman."

"Wait, so if you're working on the Palais du Cinéma project, you might know my wife. She used to work at the Cinémathèque Française. Valérie Destandau."

He reflected a moment.

"Yes, I've heard the name, but she would have left well before I was involved. So you married a French woman?"

"Yeah, and there's a funny story about that. When I first knew her, I somehow convinced myself that you might be her lover."

"*¿Qué diablos?*"

"Instead, it turned out to be my friend Ángel. There were just so many coincidences. He was the same age as you. He was from Santiago. She called him Michel. Say, what name do you go by these days?"

"Michel-Antoine Vega-Perez. It's my attempt to reconcile my divergent identities."

"Say, Ángel is coming to France on a vacation with his family in a couple of weeks. You have to meet him. It would be so weird to see the two of you together."

"Yes, that could be interesting."

"A couple of weeks after that, I'll be leaving France for a while."

"Where are you going?"

"Sarajevo."

"Really? Is that safe? Things sound really bad in that region."

"It's a story that needs to be told. The world needs to see the images, to know what is going on."

"You'll be careful, won't you?"

"Don't worry about me. Only the good die young. Besides, the siege has been going on for more than a year. It could well be over by the time I can get there."

Two weeks later, I had my reunion with Ángel. To my disappointment, Antonio did not meet him. His obligations to his mysterious lover required him to spend that time in Brussels.

While Antonio had virtually become a Frenchman, Ángel had more or less completed his conversion to being a North American.

"Mike's been looking forward to this so much," said Janet, keeping a watchful eye on her kids.

They ran around the open spaces of the Bois de Boulogne like miniature madmen. I laughed at Janet's name for her husband.

"Mike?"

"That's what all our friends in Arlington call me," he said, a bit sheepishly.

Ángel could not have looked more different from Antonio. How had I ever confused them? "Mike" had picked up a bit of weight. His body had softened from office work and fatherhood. His English, which had always been excellent, was now indistinguishable from a native speaker's.

"So it all worked out for you," he said. "You found your French woman and your missing friend. Persistence pays off."

"Yeah, I guess it does. Still, nothing turned out quite the way I had expected. By the way, Valérie says hello."

The look on his face warned me to keep my voice down when mentioning that name. He glanced at his wife, who was still occupied with the kids.

"It's better if her name doesn't come up. I think you understand."

"Sure."

"Although to be honest, I would dearly love to see her feet just one more time."

"Gross, man. Anyway, she's not coming back to Paris until next week. She wants to see me before I take off for Bosnia-Herzegovina."

"You two certainly have a funny kind of marriage. Well, we will be gone by then, so you will have to give her my love for me. Oh, and I have a surprise for you. Guess who else is in Paris."

"Who?"

"Vero!"

"Vero? Here?"

"I told her we were meeting you here, and she said she would come as well."

It was indeed a surprise. At first, I wasn't sure how I felt about it. As I adjusted to the idea, I knew I would of course be happy to see her again. No more than Ángel, though, I was relieved Valérie was not there to meet her.

We had brought sandwiches, made from baguettes, and bottles of wine for lunch in the park. We sat on blankets, enjoying the food and drink, and exchanging an endless stream of stories.

I was halfway through my account of the Berlin Wall's fall when I spotted Vero walking across the grass. She looked no different than she had a decade earlier.

After hugging her brother, sister-in-law, nephew, and nieces, she turned her attention to me.

"*Así que nos encontramos de nuevo, gringo,*" she said with a warm smile, giving me my *abrazo fuerte*.

«Well, you certainly look well and happy,» I said in my rusty Spanish.

«And why wouldn't I be happy? Pinochet has been out of power for three years, there will be new elections in December, and the Concertación is heavily favored to win.»

«So he kept his promise in the end.»

«Promise? What are you talking about?»

«Pinochet always said the dictatorship would not be permanent. He said the military would go back to the barracks once democracy was safe. He had a timetable for it. Now he is gone.»

«Do not give that monster credit for this. If it had been up to him, he would still be in power. He only stepped down because the people demanded it.»

«I wonder...»

«What do you wonder?»

«I wonder if Allende would have stepped down after losing an election."

«Allende would never have lost a truly fair election.»

«So he would have been in power forever?»

«Of course not. He was only one man, but in a just world the Popular Unity would have been.»

She did not see the irony in her words. I smiled at her, envying her passion and her certainty.

«It's good to see you, Vero.»

«Equally. Look, there is someone I want you to meet, Gringo.»

«Who's that?»

«Tomás.»

«Tomás? Who's Tomás?»

«My husband, silly,» she laughed.

«The same husband you had when I knew you in Santiago?» I asked nervously.

«Yes, the very same.»

«Look, Vero, I don't know if that's such a good idea.»

«You have to meet him. He is only in Paris for a few days. Then he has to go again. I have told him all about you.»

«You have? All about me?»

«Yes. He is eager to meet you.»

«Really?»

«Yes, extremely eager.»

«How much did you tell him? Why exactly does he want to meet me?»

«It's easier if you just meet him. Look, Ángel doesn't know he's here, so it's better if you and he meet, just the two of you. There is a bench down the path, the other side of those trees. He will look for you there.»

«Why does this feel like a trap?»

«Don't be afraid,» she laughed. «He has not killed anyone in years.»

«You're not reassuring me.»

«Just go.»

Against my better judgment, I excused myself from the others and went for a walk. I found the bench she had described and took a seat. My anxiety level rose. I took a few deep breaths and surveyed the surrounding area. It was relatively secluded, the perfect place for a professional hit job.

I became aware of someone approaching from my left. I did not turn my head. He sat on the far end of my bench. I could feel his eyes boring into me.

"So it is you."

He spoke in English. His voice was not what I had expected. The accent was all over the map, but at its heart it was the same as mine. It was a voice from home.

"Even with all the details Vero gave me, the way it all lined up, it just seemed too wild a coincidence. Yet here you are. How the hell are you, Dallas? Jesus, you don't look much different after twenty-five years."

My brain was frozen, but my mouth answered him anyway.

"Yeah, I get that a lot. It's definitely not clean living, I can tell you."

I turned to look. He was a bearded, middle-aged man without an ounce of fat on him. What remained of his tangled, dirty-blond hair hung to his shoulders. I had no problem recognizing him, only in believing I wasn't hallucinating. My mouth continued to speak.

"I can't say this is the first conversation I ever had with a ghost, but it's definitely the first one I've had while wide-awake and sober. Well, almost sober."

"You think I'm a ghost?"

"I heard you were dead."

"You did?"

"Yeah, a U.S. government guy in Guatemala told me."

"Really? He actually said I was dead?"

I did my best to recall the exact words.

"What he said was that I could tell your parents they weren't ever going to see you again."

"Well, that was certainly true."

"God, Tommy, I can't fucking believe it. Your parents went to their graves thinking you were dead."

"It was better that way, or at least that's what I tell myself."

"Your disappearance broke their hearts. They were never the same after that."

"I don't need to hear that."

"How the hell did you get out of Guatemala?"

"Man, that was a long time ago. A whole different lifetime. I was working with some villagers in the western highlands. One day without warning the army came in and rounded everyone up. They forced us to dig a huge hole. We knew it would be our grave. My attention settled on one particular soldier because he was so young. He didn't look old enough to shave. Every chance I got, I spoke to him in Spanish. I tried to befriend him, to get him to like me.

"It worked. We were nearly finished with the digging, and when there was a moment the other soldiers weren't paying attention, he motioned for me to slip into the jungle. I took off, hoping it wasn't a trick, that I wasn't about to get shot in the back. Minutes later I heard the guns, and I knew all those people—my friends—were dead. I was a coward for running away, but I didn't let that slow me down. I just kept going. Somehow I made it, thanks to people risking their lives, helping me along the way. Man, I couldn't wait to get out of Guatemala.

"That's when I made my way to Chile. Things were good for a few years. I got involved with the Unidad Popular. We got Allende elected. Things were going well. Then all hell broke loose. The reactionaries did everything they could to destabilize the country. Then came the *golpe,* and I was on the run again. I went to Argentina, then Cuba, then to Nicaragua to help the Sandinistas. I went wherever I could be part of things. I can tell you, these past few years have been a tough time for revolutionaries."

"You know, we went looking for you."

"Who?"

"Lonnie McKay and I. We drove the whole length of Mexico in his '66 Chevy, thinking we were going to bring you home."

"You did? Man, that was a dumbass thing to do."

"Yeah, it definitely was."

"How the hell is Lonnie? Now, he's someone I think about fairly often. I always wondered how he turned out."

352

"You don't know? Lonnie died. He got killed back in '74. He got drafted and went to West Germany. Just before he was supposed to come home, he died in a stupid road accident."

"Man, I'm sorry to hear that. I liked Lonnie. He used to spend a lot of time over at our house."

"Yeah, he did, didn't he? I remember, whenever things got too bad in his own house, he would head off down the street to yours. You and your mother were good to him."

"Yeah, he never had it too easy at home."

"Shit!"

"What?"

"It just hit me. All that time Lonnie spent at your house. Didn't he go over to you a lot during that time when June's marriage to Frank was breaking up?"

"Yeah, he was practically living with us for a while."

"Tell me what happened."

"What do you mean?"

"He was out of school for weeks. I didn't see him during all that time. When he came back, he was strange. It took a long time for things to get back to normal. Do you know what that was about?"

"What do you think it was about?"

"I didn't think about it much at the time. I just wanted Lonnie to come back and for things to be the way they had always been, but lately I've been thinking back and wondering what actually happened."

"Sounds to me like you have it figured out."

"I can't be sure if I'm thinking rationally or if I'm just imagining things."

"You're not imagining things. I don't know if you remember, but when Lonnie was fourteen, he was a good-looking kid. I mean, he was always a rough-and-tumble bruiser, but at the same time, with that long blond hair and no sign of zits, he was downright beautiful. Kind of like one of those young cupbearers to the gods in Greek mythology."

"All I was aware of was that he was a hell of a lot better looking than I ever was. No girl ever looked at me when he was around."

"Yeah, well, Frank was a real creep and a downright weirdo. It was pretty clear to anyone who was paying attention that the only reason he married June was to get close to Lonnie. So, no, you're not imagining things."

"I was so stupid. I had no clue any of that was going on. I mean, he was my best friend my whole life. I should have known. I should have done something. Instead I just lived my own stupid life like nothing was happening."

"That's not true."

"Yeah, it is."

"Lonnie told me once that he would never have gotten through that time without you."

"But I didn't do anything."

"You were his friend. You never gave up on him, no matter how hard he was to be around. He knew he could always count on you, no matter what. A lot of kids never get to have someone like that in their lives."

"He never said anything like that to me."

"He didn't want you to know. He was ashamed. You were someone he could be safe and normal around. You may not have known it, but you were giving him exactly what he needed. You have nothing to regret, Dallas."

"Jesus, Tommy, this is some miracle to see you after all these years and hear all this. It's almost enough to make me believe in…"

"Yeah, I know what you're trying to say. It's enough to make you believe in the corrupting nature of an exploitive capitalist system that produces monsters like Lonnie's stepfather."

"Actually, I was going to say God, but I'll definitely give your view of it some thought as well. Vero said you were here for just a few days. Where are you headed next?"

"I think it's finally time to go back to Guatemala. The civil war never ended, you know. I've been missing in action too long. What about you? What are you doing with your life?"

"I'm a photojournalist. I'm headed to the Balkans in a couple of weeks."

"The Balkans, huh? Now there's a real mess. I wouldn't even know how to begin figuring out who to support in that morass. It's all about competing nationalities, not about the class struggle at all."

"Does it ever wear you down, Tommy? You know, the constant struggle, the setbacks, seeing bad things happen? Losing friends? Knowing it's only a matter of time until your number is up? Doesn't it eat at your soul sometimes?"

"Yeah, man, it does, but you know what? You just have to find a moment."

"A moment?"

"Yeah. You just have to find one good, fine moment in your life and latch onto it. You have to find a way to make that moment last forever and to just keep living in that moment. It's the only way."

"So in addition to being a freedom fighter, you're also a poet."

We stood and hugged.

"Take care of yourself, Dallas. It's been good seeing you."

"Same to you, Tommy. I can't tell you what this has meant to me."

For the rest of the day I was in a stupor. In the evening, after I had said my goodbyes to the others, I headed back to my apartment. I did not relish the idea of being alone, but when I opened my door, something was different. The air was warmer than usual. I smelled perfume.

I went to the bed and found a woman lying on her back, an arm draped lazily over her eyes.

"I am jet-lagged. I hate long-haul flights."

"The prodigal wife."

"*Je ne suis pas prodigue moi.*"

"You weren't supposed to come until next week."

"I came earlier."

"Obviously. If I had known, I would have met you at the airport."

"It was a surprise."

"That's for sure. You're wearing perfume again. I missed it before."

She stumbled to her feet. Her half-open eyes were a soft red. I noticed wrinkles around them that had not been there before. Streaks of gray were woven into her disheveled hair.

She had never been more beautiful. I loved the way she smelled.

"I remembered why I used to always wear perfume here. I shower and bathe more in America."

"I'm glad you're here."

"I don't want you to go to Sarajevo. I can't bear the thought of you being someplace dangerous."

"Everyplace is dangerous."

"Don't be a smartass."

I couldn't stop staring at her. It annoyed her.

"Stop looking at me. I am old. Like Cunégonde."

I had found the moment. This was the moment I would hold on to.

I studied every facet of her face, her skin, her mouth, her eyes, her hair. I summoned all my will to burn them into my memory forever. I forced time to stand still. I willed that moment to become the only moment that ever existed. All previous moments were erased. There would be no future moments.

She looked at me with concern.

"*Ça va? Tu as l'air vachement bizarre.*"

I drew her close. She smiled nervously.

"*Oui?*"

I stared deep into her eyes, plumbing the depths of her soul.

"*Embrasse-moi, Valérie. Ce moment-ci doit durer éternellement.*"

She stared back at me. She understood.

"Kiss me. Like it's the last and only time."

# About the Author

Scott R. Larson is the author of five novels as well as several blogs, including one of the internet's longest-running movie review web sites, *ScottsMovies.com,* which has been logging online film commentary since 1995. In addition to three books recounting the fictional adventures of his protagonist, Dallas Green, he also writes in the fantasy genre. Like Dallas, he is a native of California's San Joaquin Valley, though he disavows any other similarities. He has also lived in France and in Chile and many years in and around Seattle, Washington. For some time now, he has called Ireland's province of Connacht home.